Sarah Harvey lives in Northampton and has had short stories published in *Just Seventeen* and *Cosmopolitan*'s short story collection *Girls Just Want To Have Fun*. Her first novel, *Misbehaving*, is also available from Headline.

Also by Sarah Harvey

Misbehaving

Fly-Fishing

Sarah Harvey

HEADLINE

First published in 2000
by HEADLINE BOOK PUBLISHING

10 9 8 7 6 5 4

ISBN 0 7472 6177 6

Typeset by
Letterpart Limited, Reigate, Surrey

Printed and bound in Great Britain by
Mackays of Chatham plc, Chatham, Kent

HEADLINE BOOK PUBLISHING
A division of the Hodder Headline Group
338 Euston Road
London NW1 3BH
www.headline.co.uk
www.hodderheadline.com

To Terry, always.

Chapter One

If men and women were made to be together, then why are we so bloody incompatible? Sure the body parts slot together quite pleasantly, but as for emotions . . . it's like mixing chemicals in the school lab. Two little anonymous phials of liquid, quite innocuous when separate, but put them together and – BANG! Nuclear fall out of the highest level.

But, as always, the human race is so damn' insistent that the things that are bad for us are the things we can't live without. Along with chocolate, alcohol, money, clothes, cars, careers and other status symbols, sex and the opposite sex comes pretty high on the list of 'I want it and I want it NOW!' regardless of the damage it can do to the fine and delicate complexity that is the 'being' part of human being.

Hence the in-built urge to find our soul mate, that mythical creature who will suddenly make our incomplete lives so fulfilled. And if the concept of commitment is so outdated, then why do so many people still feel the urge to find 'The One'? Not only to find that One, but to meet it, mate it, marry it

1

(okay, so the last two shouldn't necessarily be in that order, but hey, it's the twenty-first century), and then spend a happy decline in a pair of incontinence knickers made for two.

I can still remember opening the pale blue air-mail envelope – number seventy-nine if I recall correctly – that announced my best friend was getting married. Nix had been writing to me once a week since I'd left England nearly two years previously, numbering each envelope in her neat hand so that I'd know what order to open them in when they finally caught up with me after chasing me and my backpack throughout Thailand and Australia.

'Dear Belle – guess what? I'm getting married!'

Those three fateful words. Big, bold and scrawled across almost an entire side of a sheet of A4.

They carried such a weight of dreams and expectations, practically floated across the ocean to me on a wave of pure excitement. Nicky could have saved her stamps and flown them to me on an air kiss, an ecstatic exhalation of breath.

Shame it turned out to be a bright bubble of short-lived bliss, prematurely popped by a pompous little prick.

Kula Shaker throbbing in my ears.

Kevin Costner dancing across my eyeballs, temporarily sans wolves and even more delightfully almost sans clothes, his tanned toned bottom covered by little more than a flap of leather which fortunately doesn't appear to be that wind-resistant.

Large vodka and Coke in right hand.

Latest Jilly Cooper and an extremely large bar of Cadbury's finest on the little white plastic tray in front of me.

Extremely tasty guy in chair across aisle to right, eyeing up my long brown legs with extremely flattering regularity.

Who said long-distance flights were hell? This could almost be my idea of complete heaven. I've got all of the things I adore: music, movies, men, booze, books and chocolate, all together, at once, in the same place.

I give a happy sigh and, breaking another four squares off my bar of Dairy Milk, cram them greedily into my mouth.

The only thing lacking is a lovely squashy sofa to curl up on instead of the regulation, not enough leg room, recline on to the poor sod behind you, aeroplane seat; a nice squishy duvet to snuggle under, and my best mate Nicky to share the moment.

But who's complaining? Certainly not me.

Gorgeous Nix, my bestest buddy in the whole wide world, pal for nearly fifteen years, partner in rather a lot of juvenile crimes and one of the few people I had a problem leaving behind when I sodded off to the other side of the world, is now waiting however many feet below me. It's weird, I haven't seen her for nearly two years, and now I'm going to see her again in exactly . . . I look at my watch . . . twenty minutes, give or take customs and baggage claiming. And I certainly have no complaints about my current mode

3

of transport; after some of the places I've stayed in recently, this plane is the Hilton.

Not that I'd get in the Hilton dressed in frayed cut-off denims bleached almost white by the sun, totally wrecked Reeboks, and a faded handkerchief of material masquerading as a halter neck top.

I'm surprised they even let me on the plane from the look of disdain the stewardess threw me when I reached the top of the boarding steps. But what do you expect after twenty months staggering round Thailand, New Zealand and Australia with a back pack filled with only the barest of bare essentials?

I can't look that bad, though. He across the aisle of the sexy profile, and the even sexier legs, is casting his eyes sideways yet again.

It's a mutual leg appreciation society.

I cast another surreptitious glance back.

He's far more brazen than me. He's waiting and, catching my eye, winks heavily. His face looks even better from the front than it did from the side. Masculine, sun-tanned, with a light smattering of five o'clock shadow that suits him in a sexy, macho kind of way, rather than pretentious, posing pop star fashion.

I wonder what his name is?

I think he'd have a strong name to go with the strong face, something short but sassy like Sam – no, too bisexual. Rex? No, sounds like a dog. Adam? Yeah, Adam suits him, very earthy. Adam, the first man. Well, he wouldn't quite be that as far as I'm concerned . . . although I did manage to travel round

4

the East without getting into any close encounters of the torrid kind with members of the opposite sex. I'm not really into one-night stands, and when you're travelling, a long-term relationship isn't exactly a viable thing. Not that I really want a long-term relationship either . . .

It's nice to flirt, though.

I turn down the volume on my head set and look back over to Sexy Knees, ready to immerse myself in a fun flirty game of eyeball ping pong.

Unfortunately somebody has stepped into my spot, casting her very svelte shadow and own form of acid rain over my parade, and is brazenly batting her eyelashes at him as we speak. I'm peeved to see the stunning and immaculate air hostess who gave me the evil eye when I boarded, looking like a refugee from Bondi Beach, smile coquettishly at *my* handsome stranger as she leans in far more closely than she actually needs to, to pour him a glass of champagne. I bet she didn't glance in disgust at his faded shorts as he got on the plane. She probably drooled over his strong muscular legs like I did when I first saw him.

Now if this were a movie, she'd be pouring me the champagne, sent over by him with his compliments, undying devotion, and home telephone number. Instead, he's gazing back into her cobalt blue eyes, and smiling idiotically like all of his brain cells have just fallen down comatosed in a total lovesick swoon, with their little brain cell hands on their little brain cell hearts.

I am a forgotten moment, a fifty-second fantasy, a past flirt.

And they say women are fickle!

Nicky and I decided long ago that man's best friend is the dog because they relate so well on an emotional level. Basically the dog lives his life the way a man would like to. Eating, sleeping, farting loudly without shame and often without reprimand, and best of all shagging indiscriminately and not feeling obliged to wear a condom, stay the night, or call you after.

Sod having to go through the pain-in-the-arse ritual of taking you out to dinner, wining, dining, romancing and pretending to be genuinely interested in your intellect before they can get to the goodies. I'm sure if a man could get away with wandering over, sticking his nose in your crotch, then humping your leg without permission instead, he would.

Nicky and I have our own man scale. It's a bit like a slide rule, with most men we meet slipping well off the bottom, like the scaly serpents in a game of snakes and ladders. My fickle neighbour has just slid from 'potential sexy love object' to 'usual waste of space' level, which means he's still pretty high up there. The levels sink as low as a man will go. It's a bottomless pit.

Don't get me wrong, I do like men – rather a lot actually. I just don't like what they sometimes become when (a) they've had a lot to drink and are out with mates, or (b) they think they've got you completely ensnared by their charm, wit and general good looks, and therefore any further effort on their

6

part to keep you happy is a waste of energy that could be far better expended lifting pint glasses and chatting up other women in order to convince themselves that they've still got *it*.

Having said all of this, my best mate Nicky, a usually sane, sensible and totally sorted woman, has decided to risk the ultimate. Throw herself off the emotional precipice of life. Sell herself into emotional and sock-washing slavery for the promise of a joint bank account and regular sex.

She's getting married.

I repeat this to myself mentally, just to see if it will sink in a bit more.

Nicky's getting married.

Nope, I'm afraid it still doesn't register properly. You see, we vowed we'd never do it, but in just over four weeks' time, she's going to don the sacrificial meringue and let herself be given by one man to another.

However, Nicky's so carried away with the whole thing, that I've been swept along myself in the ever building tidal wave that is my best friend's wedding. I mean, horror of horrors, I've actually let her talk me into donning a lesser peach ensemble and wafting churchwards after her. I've even cut short my trip to go back to London and join in the fun. The only reason I'm leaving behind sunny laidback Aussie, the final leg of my grand tour – a final leg I haven't had much chance to stretch considering I've only been there for just under a month – is to help Nix in the final run up to the big day in my official role of Old

Maid of Honour; well, that and the fact that I'd practically run out of money.

It was a case of cashing in my plane ticket to stay on, then working until I could afford another ticket back – if ever – or coming home and slipping into something silk and sail-like to be Nicky's chief bridesmaid. Strong friendship and sad finances weighed heavy, and so I said goodbye to sun, sloth and sensational scenery, and jumped on to the next London-bound flight.

The pilot announces the beginning of our descent and as the plane tilts I look past the two snoozing passengers beside me and see the lights of London stretched out below. I feel a surge of excitement rush through my body. Helloooo, baby. Civilisation, come to Mama! Welcome back to the good old hedonistic, totally over-self-indulgent reality of the modern world, where chocolate is dispensed in convenient little machines, and public toilets are a bit more upmarket than a fly-infested hole in the ground.

No matter how amazing some of the places I've been to were, London is still home, still a nerve-tinglingly exciting metropolis, made even more welcoming by the fact that I know I haven't got to spend half the night lugging my backpack round the streets whilst I look for somewhere to stay that's within my budget (ten Australian dollars, a pen knife, and a packet of Chinese bubble gum), and that if I suddenly find that I'm desperate for a Mars Bar, a pizza, or a packet of Tampax, salvation is only minutes away.

The first thing that hits me when I stagger off the plane, legs like jelly after being in the same position for over twenty-four hours, is how inadequate my beach clothes are for a rather inclement English spring.

Drizzle. I'd forgotten what it was like. It's a bit different from the sweating streets of Bangkok where a quick downpour was the equivalent of taking a shower in a hot waterfall. Somehow I manage to get through passport control without being asked to bend and brace, claim my rucksack and sad old tattered duffel bag from the luggage carousel, then fighting my way past the other passengers wheeling trolleys piled with luggage, race out into the arrivals lounge, searching the sea of expectant waiting faces for a familiar one.

I always feel really self-conscious wheeling out of customs and into the arrivals lounge, everybody standing there watching you, taxi drivers waving name cards, excited families waiting for home-coming relatives. Is this what it's like being a football player emerging from the tunnel out on to the pitch? All eyes on you, expectant and hopeful.

My sexy knee'd neighbour from the plane wheels past me, his loose-wheeled airport trolley piled high with expensive leather luggage, a black canvas laptop case, and duty free bags overflowing with booze, fags and perfume. The next minute he's knocked flying as a stunning blonde in an even more simplistically stunning Amanda Wakeley suit, with legs up to her tarantula eyelashes, launches herself into his arms.

'Tristan, darling, I've missed you *so* much.'

Tristan? Well, I was way out on the name front. Then again my judgement was pretty warped in all areas as far as he was concerned, fickle flirty man.

'Did you miss me?' she pleads, long eyelashes fluttering like a moth against a window.

'You were on my mind every moment I was gone,' he purrs back.

Liar! Tristan takes a rapid snake descent to 'low down dirty rat bag' level on my man rating scale, just one rung above 'pond scum from the Planet Dirt', and two rungs above the current lowest of the low 'stinking spawn of evil incarnate'.

It's funny, most of the men I met abroad got the same two ratings, the 'only has enough brain cells to appreciate sport, soft drugs, and hard liquor' level, or 'would shag a sheep as long as it lit his cigarette afterwards'. I think I must have been socialising in the wrong circles. I stand and stare straight through Nicky for about sixty seconds before the fact that she's jumping up and down and shouting my name at the top of her voice, finally makes its way through to my jet-lagged brain.

'Annabelle! Belle! You're here . . . you're finally here! Oh my god, you look fabulous! Oh my god, I can't believe it's actually you!' she shrieks, rushing forward and throwing her arms around me.

I breathe in the familiar smell of Nicky – coconut shampoo, Fairy washing powder, and the faint smell of Trésor put on the night before – before she releases me from her embrace and, holding me at arm's length, looks me up and down, her eyes shining with excitement and pleasure.

'Look at you! You're so skinny and so brown. And, my god, your hair's grown at least a foot. You look amazing, totally amazing . . .'

I gaze back at what I think is Nicky, mouth set in what is more of a shocked false grin than a genuine smile. I really wish I could say the same, but I can't without lying, and you don't lie to your best friend, now do you?

'So do you.' I force the grin into something I hope looks a little more natural. Okay, so it's a little porkie, so as not to hurt her feelings, surely this doesn't count? I mean, she does look great to me, I've missed her so much, but . . .

Nicky grimaces.

'Rubbish,' she replied, smiling weakly, 'I look dreadful and we both know it.'

Nix has always been incredibly pretty without realising it. Her eyes are the sort of brown-green of a conference pear, she has a little pointed chin and a sweet little pointed nose, which she hates because she says it makes her look like a pixie but which everyone who meets her proclaims is totally adorable.

Now her dark golden-blonde hair, usually styled into a sleek bob, looks like it's been subjected to a bad home cut, sticking out in different directions, as dry as a camel that's been eight days without so much as a sniff of an oasis.

She has a large red spot on her chin. You know, the kind that's so huge you can almost see it throbbing, like an aeroplane warning light, through the six layers of Max Factor super concealer she's shoved over the top.

She must also have put on over a stone since I last saw her.

'Comfort eating,' she explains, laughing dryly, catching me gazing in amazement at the extra curves her once slender body is now sporting.

'It's funny, isn't it? You eat like a pig, you end up looking like one. By rights I should really look like a chocolate biscuit . . .' She shrugs and laughs weakly. 'Anyway we can't stand here gassing, you must be totally knackered. Let's get you home – well, my place anyway, which if it's all right with you is going to be home for a while. Unless of course you want to go back to your mother's, which you don't, seeing as how you haven't spoken to her in five months, and then you can fill me in on everything that's been happening. I want to hear every single gory story and minute manic detail . . .' She pauses and hugs me again, her eyes suddenly very sad. 'Oh, Belle, it's so good to see you again! You don't realise how much I've missed you.'

'I've missed you too, babe,' I reply, giving her new wobbly bits another amazed squeeze.

Comfort eating? Why should Nicky be comfort eating? Pre-wedding nerves perhaps? She picks up my duffel bag, and clutching on to my arm with a dog-like grip, tows me out of the terminal and towards a nearby car park, chattering away inanely, holding on to me as though she never wants to let go, yet still strangely distant.

I know we haven't seen each other for nearly two years, but it's not that. Nicky and I have kept constantly in touch throughout – letters, telephone calls, enough post cards to start a minor collection.

There's definitely something wrong here.

On the second level of the multi-storey car park, we come to a halt next to a gleamingly posey British Racing Green MG.

'Is this yours?' I ask incredulously, 'What happened to Arnold?'

Arnold is, or should that be was, Nicky's first love. A beaten up old Austin Allegro that used to be more temperamental than a Hollywood A-list actress, but like Emily and Bagpuss, Nicky loved him.

'He's been imprisoned in one of the lock ups near the flat for the past eighteen months,' she explains. 'I couldn't bear to part with him completely, but he didn't quite fit with the new image. Then again, neither do I any more, do I?'

There's that pathetic little forced laugh again.

I'm starting to get worried now.

This isn't the Nicky I know and love. The infectiously happy, sunny, funny girl who's been Nicola Louise Chase for the past twenty-five years.

And she hasn't mentioned the wedding once either, which following our communications over the last few months, which have been *full* of the impending nuptials, is extremely odd.

Nicky pushes the locking device on her key ring, the car's indicators beep twice and the door locks automatically open. She helps me put my tattered bags into the boot, all the time not quite able to meet my eye, and then we both get into the car.

I decide to take a calculated risk.

'Don't tell me, we're going straight to the dress-makers so you can fit me up in something peach and frightfully frou-frou?' I ask as she fires the engine into life.

I realise I've struck with the first arrow as Nicky's face crumples like a Coke can being run over by the wheel of a car.

'Nicky, what's the matter?'

'Nothing . . . oh, everything!' She finally gives in to the tears and collapses in a sodden heap against the leather steering wheel. 'Everything . . . everything's the matter. It's all gone completely and hopelessly wrong, Belle.'

She leans back in her seat again, groping behind her for her handbag. I carefully reach past her and turn the keys in the ignition so that the car engine cuts and dies.

Pulling a handkerchief out of the bag, Nicky wipes frantically at the tears now streaming from her eyes. It's obviously had several outings today already; the white linen is already stained with dark brown mascara and the odd streak of lipstick.

'Oh, Belle, I don't know what to do. I haven't been able to talk to anybody about it. I mean, I tried to talk to my mother, but she just thought I was totally mad even to think it. And I wanted to talk to you, but you were so far away, and I didn't want to worry you in case it was nothing . . .'

She reaches out and clutches my hand. Her own is cold, the nails ragged and bitten. I squeeze it hard.

'What's going on, Nix?' I ask gently.

Nicky stops snivelling into her hankie and looks up at me, her huge eyes wet and sorrowful. 'Richard . . .' she coughs '. . . he's seeing someone else.'

Richard. The husband to be. Mr Perfect according to Nicky's letters, Mr Too Good to be true.

'He's what? Are you sure?'

'Yes . . . No . . . Oh, I don't know. I'm not sure about anything any more.'

She turns to me again, tears and mascara pouring down her cheeks.

'Well, something must have happened to make you think it. Has he said anything? Changed in any way?'

She blows her nose loudly on the already sodden handkerchief, and nods.

'He's suddenly started being very evasive. You know – breaking dates, going out without explanation, going for a drink with "friends" but always managing not to state who, working late at the office, but not answering his phone if I call. I don't know – maybe it's me jumping the gun, but he's never been like this before. I don't know what to do, Belle. Maybe I'm over-reacting. You know, pre-wedding jitters. I mean, I really hope that's all it is. That's what my mother put it down to . . .'

'Don't worry, Nix,' I reply, hugging her again. 'Your mother's probably right. Apparently on top of moving house and divorce, getting married is actually one of the most major causes of stress. Oh, and death as well.

15

Somebody else's obviously, because it's too late to get
stressed out about your own after the fact, isn't it?
Although of course in this case, death could help
relieve stress. I mean, I'd be more than happy to *murder
Richard* for you if you think that would help . . .'

I'm rewarded with a glimmer of a smile.

'. . . but whatever it is, babe, we'll sort it out, I
promise you. One way or another, we'll sort it out.'

Nicky reaches over and wraps me in a sodden hug.

'Thanks, Belle. I knew you'd make things seem
better. You can't believe how bloody glad I am you're
back.'

I squeeze her affectionately, protective instincts
rearing like a mummy marmoset spotting prowling
predators. *She* may be pleased I'm back, but I can tell
you something: if Richard *is* leading her up the
garden path into the tangled briars of treachery,
instead of up the aisle wreathed in sweet-smelling
bowers of happiness, then he'll wish I'd stayed more
than a continent away. You see, if I find out that he *is*
doing the dirty on someone who could quite possibly
be one of the sweetest, nicest people inside the M25,
then I won't just murder him – I will murder him
slowly, brutally, and extremely painfully.

Chapter Two

Nicky takes me back to the flat in Limehouse that has been her home for the past two months. It's part of a huge old Docklands warehouse that has been converted to form three floors of split-level, original-pillared, huge-windowed, stone-walled luxury, in an area that's only just far enough on the wrong side of fashionable still to be vaguely affordable.

Nicky's flat is on the second floor, accessed by a steep flight of stone stairs or a pretty swish new lift which we pile into, my shoes and rucksack depositing little piles of sand on the polished floor.

Despite being upset, Nicky still manages to open the front door to her apartment with a small flourish of justifiable pride.

The new image includes not only a sports car, but an apartment to die for. I step through the door into a sort of reception area with another door off to the right leading into a cloakroom. Three steps then go down into the main part of the space, a huge split-level sitting room with wooden floors and brick walls.

The far wall is made up almost entirely of glass and leads out on to what is not quite a roof garden, but certainly much better than a mere balcony, with a few glossy-looking plants in fat terracotta pots, a wooden slatted table and chairs, a matching sun lounger, and even a barbecue against the right-hand wall.

In fact there seems to be more furniture outside than inside, although the few things she has in the sitting room are very tasteful.

Nicky's always been the sort of person to buy quality rather than quantity. If we were both sent shopping with one hundred pounds, she'd come back with one pair of trousers that would fit like a dream and last her for years, whereas I'd come back with bags full of trash that would last about two washes before bagging, fraying, or fading to the consistency of an old dishcloth.

In the centre of the room is a huge Turkish rug I recognise as having been purloined from her parents' dining room, upon which sit two squishy cream sofas set at right angles to each other, with a curvaceous Conran coffee table centred between them.

There's an extensive shelving unit against the right-hand wall, between the far wall and the door that leads into the kitchen. One of those hi-tech, high-fashion things, made of beech wood and shaped perspex, that houses a select assortment of objets d'art, an expensive stereo, and a small television set.

It's the sort of apartment you see nestled between the covers of *Hello!* as the London residence of some up and coming young starlet. The whole place just screams Expensive. Thank goodness I didn't bring back that didgeridoo. Apart from the problem of lugging it back halfway across the world, it really wouldn't have gone with the ambience; although, whilst the ethnic fertility carving I settled on will fit in far better with the decor, it hardly seems appropriate at the moment.

Then again, perhaps I shouldn't think so negatively.

Like she said, Nicky may just be having a bout of pre-wedding nerves, perhaps a panic attack brought on by her own fear that maybe, just maybe, she's not doing the right thing. Richard seeing someone else would really give her the only excuse she could possibly find for pulling out herself at this late hour. What's it called? Projection, I think, that's it. Projection of one's own fears on to someone else.

Maybe Nicky's like me, not quite ready to take on the outward symbols of adulthood: masochistic matrimony, motherhood, and massive mortgages. And, believe me, this place must have one *massive* mortgage.

'Nix, I know you're doing pretty well, but how on earth can you afford a place like this?' I ask, looking around incredulously.

'I can't,' she admits. 'I'm afraid I had to have a lot of help and a rather large mortgage. The down payment was a sort of enormous wedding present from Mum and Dad. I think they were just so amazingly pleased to be rid of me – well, let's just say amazed – that they were quite easy to talk round. Besides, they're both madly in love with Richard. He's the son they always wanted but never had.'

'What about Toby?' I ask, referring to Nicky's pain of a younger brother.

'Exactly. Richard's the son they always wanted but never had. You know, obedient instead of belligerent, showers regularly, works for a living . . .'

'So Toby's still a total reprobate then?'

'No, that's far too polite. He's still a complete arsehole.'

A small corridor runs to the kitchen. Three doors lead off it. Nicky leads me along, opening the first door on the right.

'This is your room,' she announces, putting my duffel bag on the bed.

There's no window, but above the king-size bed is a huge skylight.

Nicky follows my gaze. 'Sorry you haven't got a view, but you can lie and look at the stars.' She smiles. 'I thought it might help assuage the wander lust. With no scenery, just the night sky above you, you could be absolutely anywhere in the world. Your bathroom's through there.' She gestures to what I thought was a wardrobe door.

'You mean, I get my own bathroom?'

'Sure.' She manages a grin. 'You do remember how to use a bathroom, don't you?'

'Well, I got so used to peeing in holes in the floor, or behind bushes, you'll probably get up in the morning and find me squatting behind a pot plant on the balcony,' I joke, opening the door and peering into what is probably the most immaculate bathroom

I've seen in over eighteen months. It's not a huge room, but it's been cleverly split into two, with the bath hidden behind a dividing wall, a shower cubicle set against the side nearest the door, and a loo and wash hand basin squeezed into the remaining space. It's all pure white with chrome fittings, and it's the first loo I've been in recently where I haven't had to hold my breath while I take a leak for fear of inhaling a stench far worse than the clean tangy smell of lemon Jif.

'What, no bidet?' I mock, gazing round in awe. 'This place is amazing. It's some wedding present! I thought when you married you got things like towels and Teas Maids and five identical toasters . . .'

At least I would. My mother would give me money. She always gives me money – birthdays, Christmas, you name it. No card, just a small brown envelope with a cheque inside. Normally decent in size, but no way near enough to buy a flat. And as for my wandering star of a father . . . a postcard if I'm lucky from somewhere wildly exotic, that would arrive at least two weeks afterwards and owe postage.

'If you don't get married, do you have to give it back?' Why is my humour always so subtle and well timed? I take my foot out of my mouth and follow Nicky back through to the sitting room, where a bottle of wine and two glasses are waiting on the coffee table.

'If I don't get married, I'm not sending anything back.'

'That's a good idea. Keep it all, sort of like a consolation prize. Ditch the man, keep the gifts.'

'Well, why should I have an empty flat as well as an empty life?' Nicky slumps down on the sofa, her bottom lip trembling like a terrified border collie's. 'And I don't care if I have to work every hour that God sends, I'm going to keep this place on with or without Richard.'

'It probably won't come to that, babe.'

I sit down next to her and pat her hand like a nanny trying to comfort a child.

'I'm sure everything's going to be just fine. It's got to be,' I joke gently, 'because no way am I going to stay with my mother, not even if she'd have me.'

'We might both end up on her doorstep begging for a room for the night.' Nicky laughs dryly.

'Now *that* really would be a last resort. I'd rather rough it.'

'Oh, yeah?' Nicky raises her eyebrows. 'I know you've done some slumming in your time, but I can just see the two of us living in an empty gift box under the Embankment.'

'At least it would be a posh box,' I joke.

In one corner of the room lies a heap of already opened presents. Harrods, Harvey Nicks, Conran, Selfridge's . . . the respective rellies have really gone to town.

'Aren't you supposed to open the presents *after* the wedding?'

Nicky shrugs and manages a small smile.

'You know me.'

She was always the sort of child who hunts desperately to find their presents before Christmas Day despite the fact that they'll have no surprises whatsoever on the actual morning. If you buried them in the back garden she'd still manage to unearth them, like a pig rooting for truffles.

'Besides,' Nicky continues, 'it means I can get my thank you notes done beforehand and just relax and enjoy the honeymoon.'

Her face is suddenly stricken.

'That's if there *is* a honeymoon.'

'Well, if Richard doesn't go, can I come?' Whoops, there I go again, another size five deck shoe stuffed between my sunburnt lips.

Fortunately Nicky actually laughs.

'I would have thought you'd had enough of a holiday already!'

'You sound like my mother. That wasn't a holiday, it was a *life experience*,' I mock.

There's a collection of framed photographs on the shelving unit. Several of Nicky and me at various stages of our lives: graduation, parties, a pony trekking holiday in Wales when we were about twelve. There's one of her younger brother Toby in a green rugby shirt, swaying towards the camera with mud in his curly brown hair, a lairy grin on his face and a pint glass in his right hand; another of her parents looking very formal, posed next to the huge carved stone fireplace in the drawing room of their house in Kent, and taking pride of place on a central shelf is a beech wood-framed photograph of a handsome blond man relaxing in a wooden slatted sun lounger, next to a shimmering pale blue swimming pool.

He hasn't taken off his Raybans for the photograph so I can't see what his eyes are like, but his jawbone is square and finely chiselled, and his mouth is curled into what I perceive to be a rather arrogant smile.

'Is that him?'

Nicky nods.

'Yep. That's Richard.'

'He's very good-looking.'

'Isn't he just?' she agrees with just a trace of bitterness evident in her voice.

'If you like that sort of thing,' I add slowly.

'I knew you'd say that.' Nicky's face breaks into a feeble smile. 'He's too perfect for you, isn't he? Hasn't got that element of rough and ready you usually go for.'

'Makes me sound like I normally go for cement dust-covered brickies with fewer brain cells than there are Smarties in a fun size pack!'

'Don't worry, I know you're a little more discerning than that . . . just.'

'Cheers, Nick. When was it taken then?'

'About ten months ago, early last summer, a couple of months after we first met. We were at a house party in Henley . . .'

'Oh, I say, we are going up in the world, aren't we? No, sorry, I forgot, you're already up. House parties in Henley are just a sideways move for you, aren't they? Whereas for me they're about as far distant as an invite to a private party at Buck Palace.'

'Idiot!' she replies fondly.

Hauling my travel-weary butt off the sofa, I go over

and take the photograph from the shelf and look more closely at it.

I'm probably biased from the state I've just discovered my best friend in, but I don't think I like the look of him very much.

He looks arrogant and far too self-confident.

All I'd seen before was a blurred snap shot that had been bent so many times by so many different postmen it was hard to make out anything other than the fact that it was Nicky in a big hat, at some garden party or other, holding hands with a man with blond hair and large crease through the middle of his face.

I think I prefer him with a crease through his face. He looks far less smug. As if on cue, the telephone rings.

Nicky dives on the receiver like a hungry bird being thrown a piece of bread.

'Hello?'

Her voice softens and lowers.

'Oh – hi, you.'

I assume from the seductive tone and the way her shoulders instantly unknot a little that the caller is Richard.

Sixty seconds into the call, however, Nicky's voice changes back from soft and seductive to broken and upset, full-throated with the threat of further tears, and the muscles in her shoulders return to fully knotted pretzel.

'Oh, right . . . do you absolutely have to? . . . Okay, if it's as important as you say . . .'

There's a pause for a moment whilst she tries to recover her composure.

'I love you,' she says softly, but even I can hear the soft whirring tone that indicates Richard has already hung up.

She looks over at me, eyes heavy and sad, and shakes her head despondently.

'He was supposed to be coming round tonight but he's just cancelled on me.' She sighs heavily and shakes her head again as though trying to dislodge the heavy wave of gloom that's visibly descended. 'That's the second time this week. He said he's got to take some clients out to dinner . . . last-minute thing, you know the score, terribly sorry, Nicola,' she mimics, the words catching against the swell of disappointment that's building in the back of her mouth. That 'I've just swallowed a hard-boiled sweet and it's got stuck' kind of feeling that hits when you're fighting back eyeball-and-heart-soaking misery.

She buries her face in her hands, unable to stop the big salty tears spilling through her fingers. 'This is driving me totally crazy. I just need to know, Belle. No matter how bad the truth is, it can't be worse than this.'

'Well, we'll just have to find out the truth then, won't we?' I state firmly, sitting down next to her and pouring her a large glass of chilled wine.

'What do you mean?' Nicky looks up at me between splayed fingers.

'Does Richard know what I look like?'

'Well, he's seen photographs but I doubt if he'd recognise you from those,' she replies, a bemused expression replacing the sad one.

'That's one good thing. Have you got any warm clothes I can borrow?'

'Sure, but . . .'

'Nothing good, just something a bit more cosy than the three pairs of shorts and two bikinis that are currently my sole material possessions.'

I pour a mouthful of wine down her throat for medicinal purposes, then hauling Nicky off the sofa, usher her in the direction of her bedroom, where, after a bit of a hunt through the designer suits, we manage to find a skinny rib T-shirt, a chunky sweater and a pair of jeans.

'You may as well have these, I grew out of them fourteen pounds ago. I've moved on to fatty rib T-shirts now,' she jokes weakly. 'Perhaps I should take a trip abroad?' Nicky looks a little green as I slip effortlessly into one of her long discarded size ten pairs of jeans.

'Yeah, it's amazing what poverty and near starvation do for your figure.'

Her tear-filled eyes widen.

'Was it that bad?'

'Bad? It was incredible.'

'So why come back?'

'Why do you think, you daft old bat?' I reply, hugging her. 'Right, now I need the keys to your car.'

I laugh at Nicky's instantly horrified expression.

'Not your new one, silly. *I* wouldn't trust me in it, let alone expect you to! I meant Arnold, is he still in legal working order?'

'Just. I think he's got about two months' tax and two hundred miles left in him.'

'Well, I need the keys to Arnold, and directions to Richard's place.'

'But why?' she repeats, her pale face still puzzled. 'Belle, what are you up to?'

'Well, if you really want to know the truth,' I reply, pulling on my dusty Cats, and a borrowed Goretex of Nicky's, and heading towards the door before the lure of that lovely double bed in the guest room becomes too much for me, 'then I'm going to make damn' sure I find it out for you.'

This time only two days ago I was on a beach, basking cat-like and contented in the sunshine, azure-blue waves crashing on the shoreline, good book in right hand, cold beer in left hand, a plethora of assorted wet-suited, muscular male bodies bounding around in the surf nearby, bare pectorals glistening with sea-spray.

Heaven on earth.

And I gave it all up to come back to this?

A night spent sitting outside a house in Chelsea, cooped up in a rusting Austin Allegro with no sound system, a broken seat spring up my bum, sipping from a thermos of rapidly cooling black coffee to stave off the jet lag whilst the rain drums a metallic tattoo on the roof and leaks in through the windows to soak the already rotting, stinking carpets. Great. And all for what?

To watch my best mate's fiancé arrive home very late, but very much alone.

So much for my detective work so far.

I've been sitting here for five hours and all I get to see is 'Richard the impeccable' pay the cab driver and sprint indoors with his briefcase over his head to shield his perfect hair from the driving rain.

I reach inside my bag and, pulling out Nicky's mobile phone, key in her home number.

'Hello?' mumbles a sleepy voice.

'The cuckoo has landed.'

'You what?'

'I said, the bloody cuckoo has landed!'

'Who is this?'

Oh, shit. Wrong number. I rapidly kill the call, and suppressing some pretty inappropriate laughter, redial.

'Hello?'

This voice sounds more familiar.

'Nicky? Is that you?'

'Of course it's me!' she whispers urgently. 'What's happening?'

'The potential bastard's back.'

'And?'

'Well he was alone. No two-timing-totty hanging off his arm or hiding out in his underpants.'

'And?' she repeats, the tone of her voice indicating that the desire to know is having a good old-fashioned fist fight with the hide-your-head-in-the-sand-like-an-ostrich option.

'And nothing. He arrived back in a taxi about twenty seconds ago, paid the driver, and ran in the house. Can I come back now?'

'Perhaps you should wait and see if she turns up there?'

'Nicky! It's two o'clock in the morning, I've had about two hours' sleep in the past twenty-four hours, and besides, we don't know if there *is* actually a She, do we? I could sit outside his house until he goes to work in the morning and I might see nothing more incongruous than the milkman delivering a pint of gold top and some full-fat yoghurt instead of semi-skimmed and fruit juice.'

'But, Belle!' she wails. 'Like you said, it's two o'clock. Where the hell's he been until now?'

'I don't know, Nix, and short of mugging the taxi driver, I don't know how I can find out. Look, there's nothing more I can do tonight. This car's so damp my whole body's taken on the texture of an old prune. Put the kettle on, I'll be home in twenty minutes.'

'But if you stay there, you might catch him at it.'

'Nicky, trust me, if I stay here, the only thing I'm going to catch is pneumonia.'

I stagger through the security door of Nicky's apartment building and, legs buckling under me, crawl slit-eyed into the lift. She's already waiting by the time it smoothly swishes its way up to the second floor. She's hanging on to the door frame and watching out for me, face pale with sick anticipation, hair greasy at the roots and scraped back into a pony tail, nails bitten to a ragged edge, just like her nerves.

'Belle! Thank god you're back!' She ushers me inside. 'Tell me everything . . . what did you see?'

'Only what I told you – he came home just before I

phoned you, and he was definitely alone.'

'What was he wearing?'

'Clothes,' I mutter wearily, kicking off my boots without bothering to unlace them.

'What sort of clothes?' she wails.

'Er . . . work clothes, I think. Trousers . . . obviously . . . a suit of some sort? I don't know, Nick. I'm sorry, it was pretty dark.'

'Well, if it was dark you might have missed something important.'

'Trust me, I may not have been able to see exactly who tailored his suit, but I could easily make out the fact that he was on his own. Oh, and he was still carrying a briefcase, so unless he'd been dancing round it in some disco, I'd say it was very possible tonight's business dinner was a real one.'

Heading into the room, I pull off my borrowed gloves and rub my blue hands to try and reintroduce some circulation.

Following, Nicky looks at my ice pop fingers, and her already stricken face clouds with guilt.

'You're freezing!'

'Tell me something I don't know.'

She takes my cold hands between her own warm ones, and begins to rub absentmindedly.

'Sorry, Belle.' The apology's abstracted, her mind obviously elsewhere and working overtime. 'Maybe dinner went on for longer than expected,' she says, lips setting in an 'I'm determined to be sensible about this' fashion.

'Maybe.'

'Or perhaps he called in to see his parents afterwards, to discuss the wedding or something.'

'That's possible.' I nod encouragingly. 'There's probably a perfectly logical explanation for his being so late.'

'I can't stand it, Belle!' Nix wails, letting go of my hands and slumping down on the closest sofa, head in hands. 'I'm turning into Paranoia Woman. Pull on a pair of underpants over my jeans with a big P on the front and that's me. I don't just check his shirt collars for lipstick and perfume – do you know what else I do? Do you know what I've been reduced to?'

I don't, but I have a feeling she's going to tell me.

'I sniff his underpants,' she confides, crossing her eyes behind her fingers in acute embarrassment.

I smile very slowly, hoping that it manages to look like a wry, sympathetic smile instead of a preliminary to a fit of hysterical laughter.

'Well . . . that's not so bad. Some people are into that sort of thing, you mustn't feel totally weird. I mean, it's better than having a fetish about drinking your evening cocoa from his cricket box or something.'

'No!' she howls. 'I don't mean for pleasure . . . I mean for evidence.'

'What sort of evidence?'

'Well, you know . . .' She frowns.

'I do?'

'Don't be obtuse, Belle, of course you know what I mean. You know . . . the scent of a woman, that sort of thing.'

'Really?'

'Really,' she admits sadly. 'I go round to his house when I know he's out, let myself in and rifle through his underwear.'

I'm fighting very hard to suppress the smile which is steadily blossoming into a pretty cheesy grin.

'It's not funny,' Nicky mutters sulkily, 'it's totally sad. And what's worse he even caught me at it once.'

'He didn't!'

'He bloody did.' She goes crimson at the memory. 'He caught me pant-handed, face down in the linen basket, pair of boxers in one hand, pair of Ys in the other, and my nose buried in his best pair of Calvin's.'

Picking up a goldfish bowl-size wine glass from the coffee table, she takes a huge gulp of Frascati and shakes her head.

'What did you do?'

'Apart from having an instant heart attack when he opened the door? Told him I thought it would be a nice surprise if I did his laundry, as he'd obviously been so busy at work recently.'

'The underpants fairy,' I giggle. 'Go to work with tacky trollies, then come home and find some little nymph has whisked in and washed them for you. Er . . . did he ask why you were doing a pre-wash with your tongue, snorting the skidmarks so to speak?'

'Belle!' Nix cringes heavily.

'Well, did you find any?'

'Find any what?'

'Evidence. You know: long blonde hairs, the lingering smell of scampi fries?'

'Annabelle!' Nicky pulls a shocked face at me. 'I honestly don't know if spending over twenty months roughing it was any good for you.'

'Now you sound like my mother,' I sigh. 'So, if you didn't find anything incriminating in the pant department, what makes you think he's seeing someone else anyway?'

'Oh, I don't know.' She frowns. 'Apart from the cancelled dates, I've just got this terrible feeling something's wrong.'

'So it's fact-based then,' I reply sarcastically.

'No, more gut-based. I've seen what the guys at work are like when they're playing around: all the lies and pretending to be working late when they're actually entertaining one of the secretaries from floor three to an evening of unbridled passion in the stationery cupboard.'

'Sex, lies and sticky tape, a story of lust in the filing cabinet?' I joke.

Nicky laughs weakly.

'Please don't make fun of me, Belle. I know I'm acting like I'm a few supermodels short of a fashion show at the moment, but I really need to know the truth, because even if it is all in my imagination, I'm going to ruin the relationship anyway by being so bloody paranoid about it all.'

She buries her face in her hands again, but I can still see the tears trickling over her fingers.

'I feel like I'm going crazy, Belle,' she sobs. 'You've *got* to help me.'

Nicky has always been the bright one, the focused

one, always knowing where she's at and where she's going.

I've been the dreamer, with the lounge-in-the-sunshine mentality, always following my heart instead of my head.

Now here she is, green eyes brimming with sadness, underlined by bruised purple shadows, slumped upon the sofa in her beautiful flat, surrounded by the material evidence of her overwhelming success, and completely and totally knocked for six by a member of the opposite sex.

Looking up again, she reaches for the wine bottle on the coffee table, a different one from the bottle that was there when I left the flat, and tips it glass-ward.

She is rewarded with a mere trickle.

'Whoops! Empty.' She forces a false smile and, getting up rather unsteadily, heads in the direction of the tray of spirit bottles on one of the unit shelves.

'Just have to hit the hard stuff.'

This can't be vibrant, confident, totally in control Nicola Chase – pale, drawn, on the verge of tears, and heading for the brandy at three o'clock in the morning.

For the first time in our lives she needs me to be the strong one, to take control. Taking her by the shoulders, I steer her away from the drinks tray and back on to one of the sofas.

The wedding is just over four weeks away.

You can do a lot in four weeks.

I perch on the edge of the coffee table opposite, and taking Nicky's shaking hands, make her look at me.

'Look, Nix, I'm your best friend, okay? You've always looked out for me, now it's my turn to look out for you. I may not have discovered anything tonight, but trust me, if something *is* going on I'm going to find out for you. For the next twenty-one days I'm going to eat sleep and breathe Richard Ackerman. Whatever it takes, if I have to bloody follow him everywhere he goes – although I may draw a line at following him into the gents – I'll find out the truth for you, I promise.'

'Oh, Belle.' She looks up at me, huge eyes hopeful. 'You'd do that for me?'

I nod determinedly.

'I could be the new James Bond,' I joke. 'In drag.'

'Well, I can't be Blofeld,' Nicky sniffs, managing a smile, 'I'm allergic to cats.'

I shake my head. 'He's the baddy anyway. Richard has to be the baddy.'

'I thought the baddy was called Oddjob?'

'He was the small one.'

'Well, that's definitely Richard then.' Nicky sniggers into a man-size tissue.

'Okay, so Richard can be a mixture of the two.'

'What – BlowJob?' she shrieks. 'Well, that would certainly be appropriate.'

'Yeah, and you can be Miss Funny Fanny,' I giggle.

'Thanks a lot, Belle!'

Nicky stops laughing through her tears, and squeezes my hands hard.

'No, I mean that. Thanks, Belle.'

'Anything for you, babe.' I tell her. 'Besides, I'm

quite looking forward to becoming Richard's own personal Cato, his second shadow, sliding in and out of doorways, tailing him wherever he goes. I suppose it could be kind of exciting really . . .'

Blimey, Richard's a boring bastard!

He eats lunch at the same restaurant every day except Wednesdays, when for some inexplicable reason he never reappears from the building until it's time to go home. Apart from the first night that I watched outside his rented Victorian terrace, he always leaves work at seven o'clock on the dot, and arrives home by taxi forty minutes later, depending on the traffic, of course.

He wears a different suit every day of the week, but after almost two weeks of Richard-watching I realise he wears the same suit on the same day, like he's got a Monday suit, a Tuesday suit and so on, and for some reason Friday is always Armani day.

Richard in the flesh is very good-looking if definitely not my type. But then again, Nicky and I have never gone for the same type of guy, which is lucky I guess.

He's actually a bit of a change from Nicky's usual type as well. When we were at university, she had a thing about skinny young bohemian types with long hair and loose morals. She liked to take them home at weekends to frighten her very conservative parents. They must think Richard's completely wonderful. He's got a great job, with a brilliant future beckoning, and looks completely squeaky clean – floppy blond hair all clean and shiny, designer glasses, designer suits, strong jaw. That type. Definitely not my type. He looks like John Boy Walton interbred with Clark Kent.

Does he have a hidden alter ego too? Does he whisk into phone boxes, Mr Nice Guy in pure white Calvins, then zoom out in dirty old man mac, underpants and sock braces, clutching a handful of 'Call Me for Hot Fun' cards?

And, more to the point, to go with the hidden alter ego, does he have a hidden lover secreted away somewhere?

The fact that he only sees Nicky a couple of times a week at most would indicate that he's got a pretty busy life in other respects, but what takes up the rest of his time apart from work? He seems to be far too boring for it to be anything of major interest.

I don't know why I thought Richard-watching would be exciting. It was more fun hiking the last thirty miles from Kelang to Singapore in the pouring rain after the excuse for a bus I was on broke down when its forty-year-old lawn mower engine finally revved its last.

In the past twelve days I've sat in Nicky's old banger and read all of the monthly glossies currently out, from *Cosmo* to the naffest cheapest soap and scandal rag mag. I've run up Nicky's mobile phone bill by phoning all of the magazine call-in competitions and phoning her for regular Richard updates, which usually consist either of 'has just arrived for work' or 'has just left to go home'.

I've played noughts and crosses on the steamed-up windscreen, solitaire eye spy, hunt the new facial wrinkles (alarmingly high number found, I'm afraid) in the rear-view mirror, and reacquainted myself with all the chocolate bars you can only get in Europe, which was a wonderful way to spend . . . well, I'm not going to tell you how indecently short a period it took me to work my way through those.

I've got a permanent bruise on my right cheek from that blasted spring, and the rest of my arse is getting soft from being sat on so long.

I'm so bored I even sit and watch a spider spin an intricate web between the rear-view mirror and the windscreen, its long legs waving around like a conductor leading an orchestra in an intricate, delicate piece of music.

It takes nearly two hours for the spider to finish weaving her delicate threads – and then the rear-view mirror drops off.

Could this be an analogy for life? I wonder. Probably, but I think I'd get too depressed if I made it into one.

So far, from my lengthy (yawn) observations, I've worked out that the guy from the building next door to Richard's, which is home to a firm of chartered surveyors, is having an affair with his secretary; the pretty young Italian-looking girl who works behind the counter of the local brasserie two doors down has got two boyfriends on the go at the same time; and the senior partner of Richard's firm has a wife, an ex-wife and two mistresses slotted into his organised,

Viagra-fuelled life. But so far Richard seems to do nothing but work, sleep, and carry out the same monotonous routines that make up his boring little world.

We managed to avoid my actually having to meet him by saying that I've changed my dates of departure and am coming back in another couple of weeks' time, which suits me just fine as it means I can put off getting in touch with my mother (The Wicked Witch of the Wharf) for another couple of weeks at least.

It hasn't been too difficult to avoid him as he's only been round to Nicky's twice in the last two weeks, at which point I made myself scarce at her request. I think this is more down to her concern that I'd murder Richard at first sight rather than the fact that he might recognise me as the mad woman who's been permanently parked outside his office in a rotting car.

At 6.15 on the Friday night of the second week, I'm sitting in my usual spot outside Richard's office, Arnold the Allegro quietly flaking rust around me, flicking half-heartedly through an old issue of *Company*, wishing I was back on Bondi Beach, drinking ice cold bottled beer, and bottom watching.

I'm waiting for the minor excitement at 7 p.m. of following Richard home, then sitting outside his house until his bedroom light goes off, when I suddenly have an unexpected flash of activity.

Richard leaves early.

He walks out of the black gloss front door of Sherman, Davis & Ackerman, Solicitors, cashmere coat thrown casually over his right arm, and hails a passing taxi. I should have known something exciting might happen today when he appeared this morning, not in his usual Friday Armani but a brand new navy blue Hugo Boss.

Navy blue on Richard. How avant-garde for the original man in a grey suit!

'Follow that cab!' I chortle to myself as he gets in the back and directs the driver. Ooh, my first car chase!

Now that we've got some action, I could actually start to enjoy this. This is what secret agents should be doing, isn't it? Car chases and all that.

I mean, I never envisioned that the chase would take place between a black cab and a knackered old Austin Allegro. By rights, I should be in something sleek, sporty and distinctly James Bond, with buttons for torpedoes and smoke screens and ejector seats. The only buttons I've got to press in Arnold are the windscreen wipers and the indicators, and neither of those work properly! I shall probably be the only secret agent to be pulled over mid-chase by the police for driving an un-roadworthy vehicle.

Another problem with Arnold is that he gets from nought to sixty in about fifteen – fifteen minutes, that is, not seconds. By the time I've got up enough revs to move from first gear into second, Richard's cab has cut niftily across some amber lights and left me behind.

Shit! I can't believe I've lost him. The first time in two bloody weeks that he's broken the monotony of his usual routine, and I have to go and bloody lose him. I bang my hands on Arnold's dashboard in frustration, and the engine responds by cutting out completely.

When I finally manage to wake Arnold from his coma and get on my way again, I decide the only course of action is to go to Richard's house and wait . . . and wait . . . and wait. At 11.30, a taxi pulls up outside his three-storey Victorian terrace, the throbbing tick of the diesel engine waking me from my semi-frozen stupor.

I slide my collar up around my face, slip further down into my seat, and watch. I can see two figures in the back of the cab. One of them leans forward to pay, and Richard's chiselled profile is briefly illuminated by the cabbie's light. They both get out of the cab and my heart sinks to my cold blue toes.

He's with a woman.

She looks a picture of respectability in a perfectly cut pin-stripe Jil Sander suit and elegant Office courts. She's carrying a slimline leather attaché case in one hand, and a larger briefcase in the other. Her face is neatly attractive, very symmetrical, and her dark shoulder-length hair is swept back into a sleek chignon held at the back by a silver clip that glints in the lamplight.

They don't speak as Richard leads the way up the steps to the front door, inserts a key and ushers her through.

I feel kind of disappointed. I've sat here every night for two weeks, and seen nothing. I was three and a half hours off informing my best mate that if she marries Richard she'll come to no worse fate than death from monotony, and now he has to go and prove me wrong by doing something that could be classed as illicit.

Although that is dependent on the circumstances.

I mean, I don't want to go screaming 'Slimeball' to Nicky when they could just be going in the house to get a pot of coffee and go through some paperwork. Although at this time of night, this seems as likely as me deciding that my mother's my guiding light and inspiration.

There's only one thing for it. I'm going to have to go and find out for myself exactly what they're up to.

I've got Nicky's key to Richard's place in my jeans pocket, but I can hardly let myself in the front door, can I?

Clambering damply out of Arnold, I hesitate for a moment and then sprint to the end of the road, my worn flat-soled deck shoes slipping on the wet tarmac, turn the corner and head down the narrow dirt track that runs along the back of the houses, past garages and garden gates, shadows looming eerily in the darkness, my own panting breath echoing loudly in my ears.

Counting the houses I come to what I calculate is Richard's, and then find that I am faced with a well-bolted gate.

Fortunately the adrenaline's kicking in with a vengeance now. Turning round, I pace backwards a few steps, then sprint for the gate like Linford Christie on a mission.

I hurl myself at it from about two feet away and manage to get the upper half of my body wedged over the top of the gate, with the hard edge digging firmly into my stomach. I hang there for a few moments like a sock slung at a linen basket and not quite making it, before I manage to hoist one arse cheek a bit further over, and using my bottom for ballast, rely on gravity to pull me over the other side. I slump, panting, in the shadows for a few moments, convinced that the sound of splintering, protesting wood will have alerted someone to my illegal presence, but there's no movement from the house, no twitching of curtains, no security lights flashing over me like search lights at a prison break.

Skulking along the edge of the garden towards the house, lurking in the shadows that fall across the wall that runs between Richard's house and his neighbour's to the right, I decide that I feel like a cat burglar – a very incompetent cat burglar.

This feeling is obviously shared by the Yorkshire Terrier in the garden next door, although his opinion of my competence seems to be far higher than my own. In fact, the way the little bugger's reacting to me, anybody would think I'd just escaped from Broadmoor and was wandering through Chelsea with a meat cleaver, a manic grin, and a demonic desire to kill and mutilate.

It's currently bouncing along the other side of the stone wall like it's on a pogo stick and its own little four-pawed mission to save the residents of Langham Terrace from the mad woman who just catapulted over the garden gate like a sack of flung potatoes. It's like someone's throwing the little dog up in the air, catching it when it falls then propelling it upward again, and every time it appears over the top of the wall it barks at me.

Bounce, YIP. Bounce, YIP. Bounce, YIP.

I hiss at it to shut up, which just increases its fervour.

I think this is the point where most enterprising agents pull a drugged pork chop out of their pocket, but all I've got in mine is half a packet of fruit pastilles and a screwed up tissue.

I'd offer it a fruit pastille but the next one's a black one so I stuff it in my own mouth instead, stick my tongue out at the little barking git, and attempt to 'case the joint'. The light's on in Richard's sitting room, which I know from Nicky's description runs the entire length of the first floor of the house.

I cast my eyes around the garden in the hope of finding something to stand on that will raise me the extra five feet I need to be able to peer into the window.

Nothing. Richard's garden is as neat and regimented as Richard himself, with wall to wall grass, neatly clipped, broken only by a path that runs from a small patio area to the rear garden gate.

There's nothing else for it, I'm going to have to attempt a quick shin up the drain pipe. I was always first to the top of the ropes in gym class, so this shouldn't be too difficult. I hope. Okay, cue the theme to *Mission: Impossible*, get my mental crampons on and start climbing.

Unfortunately, whilst my ascent is actually relatively easy, it is also added anathema to old dogged over the garden wall.

Deciding that I am definitely a loony burglar on the loose, the dog scrabbles at the dividing wall until it gets a paw in a loose bit of cement, and manages to haul its scrawny little arse over the top and into Richard's garden.

It stands below me, skinny hackles raised, mouth bared in a snarl that reveals a row of needle teeth, then bouncing on an air bag of misplaced venom and tiny terrier heroics, manages to get enough height to attach that snarling mouth to my ankle. The mouth, even when fully opened, is only the size of an old ten-pence piece; the level of pain, however, is definitely not commensurate. More like fifty pounds worth, actually. Sod that, write a cheque for a thousand pounds and it should just about cover it!

Ow!!!!

Suppressing a scream, I waggle my leg ineffectually in a vain attempt to dislodge the dog. It's like trying to shake off a snake with lock jaw.

This is ridiculous. I've got a key, and here I am attempting to shin up a damp drain pipe with a bloody bastard of a terrier with a Dobermann complex hanging off my ankle like a piranha with lock jaw. At least the little git's stopped yapping. I just wish the reason for this wasn't because it's got its mouth full of the tender flesh of my tibia. It's still managing a pretty throaty growl.

If I can just climb a bit higher I'll be able to stick my foot in the rain butt and drown the bastard – sod this being kind to animals lark. It's a case of survival, his or mine. I mean, if I went and picked the little shit up, shoved it in my gob and started to chew with relish, some outraged old granny would soon come and clobber me with a rolled up copy of the RSPCA monthly review.

I reach the top of the water butt and hesitate. I can feel its teeth still stuck like a row of pins in my ankle. Dog – man's best friend. Sod it, I'll send a tenner to Battersea Dogs' home tomorrow.

I take a deep breath as though *I'm* just about to plunge underwater, and stick my foot in the dark murky depths of the rain butt. Terrier the Terrible gets ten out of ten for tenacity. He holds on for another eight seconds at least before finally releasing me, then snorkels to the surface to swim frantically round and round like one of those wind-up bath toys, far more intent on getting toothily reattached to me than actually getting his butt out of the butt.

After all that, I don't know whether to be relieved or disappointed when, on finally reaching the sitting-room window, my jeans and left ankle ripped by razor sharp canines, my knuckles scuffed, flaking drain-pipe paint in my hair and prickling my eyes, I see Richard and female companion respectably seated side by side on a rather funky lime green sofa, poring over paperwork spread out on the coffee table.

It takes me a few moments to work out what's wrong with this cosy little scene of diligent industry.

It's not the fact that Richard the Grey would have such hip taste in furniture. It's not the pair of wine glasses sitting together on the coffee table next to the paperwork. It's not the half-empty bottle of Pouilly Fumé standing next to them. It's not even the soft music on the CD or the fact that they are sitting pretty close together on aforementioned funky lime green sofa. It's the fact that beneath that coffee table, balanced delicately on top of those smart Office courts, sits a pair of lilac silk and lace La Perla knickers. Keeping her ankles warm so to speak.

Unless her elastic has died a death and she hasn't noticed yet, I'd say there was something pretty illicit going on here, especially as Richard's left hand is ferreting around somewhere underneath the table too.

The next thing I know, he drops the Mont Blanc clutched tightly in his right hand, she kicks off her shoes, losing the La Perlas at the same time, and they turn and envelop each other in a passionate embrace, ripping at each other's clothes like possessed animals.

It is at this point, where I'm staring through the window in open-mouthed outrage, that Terrier the Terrible heaves himself out of the water butt, teeters unsteadily on the narrow wooden rim for a few seconds, then launches himself like a pistol out of a bullet at my backside, whereupon, contact achieved, he sinks his fangs into the flesh of my gluteus maximus and hangs there like a desperately determined sucking leech. I let out a huge yell of surprise and pain, lose my grip on the drain pipe and fall earthwards.

As my head cracks against the solid ground with a loud thud, the window of Richard's sitting room is thrown open, and through a haze of pretty silver stars I see two open-mouthed, semi-naked people peering down at me through the gloom, before my view is obliterated by the appearance, nose to nose, of one scary, hairy, irate, snarling, halitosis-breathed, vindictive son-of-an-absolute-bitch.

The last thing I notice before the sound of wailing police sirens fills my ears is that Terrier the Terrible has a little pink bow tied neatly on top of its head. A bit like coming face to face with Arnie the Terminator only to realise he's wearing lipstick, blusher and false eyelashes.

Thank God Nicky's a solicitor. It's going to take some fast talking to get me out of this one.

The police are just about ready to frog march me off for attempted burglary when she appears hopefully to back up what sounded like a bloody dubious explanation for being caught in Richard's garden at midnight, dressed like Cato from *The Pink Panther*.

Unfortunately, instead of explaining that I'm not actually responsible for a series of recent local break ins, she flies past me and the two laughing policemen to attack Richard with a rolled up copy of *Vanity Fair* she'd grabbed off the passenger seat.

Great. I'm going to get done for breaking and entering – although the only breaking I've done is personal. My head, my pride, and my knackered knicker elastic, which pinged (along with several of my vertebrae) into knicker heaven the minute I hit the ground – and Nicky's going to get hauled up for ABH.

There is, however, something very satisfying about watching her bash Richard over the head with a well-known magazine.

In the end, after she's been prised away from a cowering Richard, I've been warned for cheering her on like a bloodthirsty granny at a bare knuckle fist fight, and we've both been threatened with handcuffs, it's Richard who manages to persuade them it's purely a domestic, and we're both finally released with a verbal caution to go home and behave in future.

The policemen feel it's wise, for Richard's safety rather than ours, to escort us both back to Nicky's flat.

I then just about manage to persuade them not to book me for daring to drive a wreck in a residential area, before spending another hour persuading Nicky not to go back round to Richard's to continue her assault on his person – this time focused on a certain part of his anatomy that she blames just a tad more than the rest of him – with the carving I bought her from Australia, in the hope that it would have the opposite effect on his fertility to the one originally anticipated.

Nix and I spend the weekend locked away in her flat with a large bottle of blue label vodka, and a double economy pack of Kleenex.

She spends all day Saturday alternating between tears, disbelief, anger, more tears, vodka, silence, screaming, more vodka, resigned lucidity, hopeless desolation, and more vodka, before finally passing out on the sofa in a heap of used tissues. I manage to wake her up enough to steer her semi-comatose towards her bedroom, where she falls face down on the duvet and promptly passes out again.

Oh, sweet oblivion, the only respite for a wounded heart.

Sunday morning, I struggle back to life at about ten. I wasn't matching Nicky drink for drink, but my head's still telling me I had far too much alcohol last night, and should now redress the balance by swallowing at least two buckets of water.

I shrug on my gown and go in search of Nicky.

Amazingly she's up.

She's in the kitchen, slumped on a stool against the breakfast bar, still in the same dressing gown she's been wearing all weekend, the last inch of vodka that was left in the bottle now in her glass and half-drunk, and she's lighting a Marlboro with shaking hands.

'Since when did you start smoking?' I flick the switch on the kettle and go and lean on the bar opposite her.

'About . . . er . . . *two* minutes ago.' Nicky shrugs, inhaling hesitantly and instantly bursting into a fit of unhealthy coughing. 'My father must have left these here last time he came up.'

'Er . . . can I ask *why* you started smoking?'

'Supposed to be good for the nerves?' she offers distractedly, rubbing her other hand across her red-dened eyes, 'Something to do with my hands being occupied so I can't get them round that bastard's throat . . .'

'I think it would probably be healthier to strangle Richard. Do you want some toast to go with that vodka?'

Nicky shakes her head, groans at the effort, and downs another slug of Smirnoff's finest.

'Could I at least persuade you to add a bit of Coke?' I ask sarcastically.

'It's hair of the dog.' She stares at me defiantly for a moment, then her face crumples, 'That should be hair *for* the dog. Oh, Belle, I'm not surprised he doesn't want me – I never knew why he wanted me in the first place. I mean, look at the state of me. Fat, sad, pathetic woman . . .'

Her eyes, which are already two red swollen slits, fill up again, tears rolling down her cheeks in a fresh stream of heartache.

'I don't know why someone like him ever chose to go out with someone like me in the first place,' she repeats, 'let alone want to marry me . . . but then again, it turns out he didn't really want to marry me after all, did he? He probably wanted to be found out. It was the easiest way to get out of it, wasn't it?' She pauses for a moment, face contorted with a fresh burst of emotional pain.

'Was she very beautiful?' she whispers, half wanting and half dreading the answer.

'No,' I lie emphatically, thankful that she of the loose La Perlas had the sense to scarper at the first sound of sirens and sniff of scandal. 'Besides, beauty's more than skin deep, you know. You're sweet, kind, thoughtful, bright, tenacious, wonderful . . .'

'You'll be telling me next he wasn't good enough for me,' Nicky interrupts. 'That I'll find someone better, someone who really deserves me.'

'Well, it's true, but I'll try and avoid the platitudes, if you want.'

'You may as well be the first to get them in,' sighs Nix, gingerly attempting another puff of her cigarette, then scrubbing the back of her hand across her pale face to wipe away a fresh stream of tears. 'Just wait until it gets out . . .' Her eyes cross in horror at the thought. 'I need another drink.' She picks up the vodka bottle, then puts it back down again, 'No, I don't, I just need Richard . . .'

'I know what you need. It's not Richard, and it's not this either.' I confiscate her vodka before she can pick up the glass again.

'But you bought it,' Nix wails, as I empty the remains down the sink.

'Sure, but not for breakfast.'

I flick the switch on the kettle and get two mugs out of the cupboard, hastily swapping the one I just picked up with *Richard* emblazoned on it for something a little less controversial.

'Okay, let's make a golden rule,' I tell her as the quarter-full kettle comes swiftly to the boil. 'Life dumps on you, okay? Some dumps are little annoying splatters on the shoulder of your favourite jacket. Others are great big smelly wet cow pats smack bang on target right on top of your head.'

'This definitely classes as a dump of the cow pat variety,' Nicky snivels, looking despondently at the cup of tea I hand her, obviously wishing it was laced with something a little stronger than skimmed milk and two sugars.

'I know, babe, but let's agree that we're not going to rinse off the shit with vodka for breakfast, okay?'

'You needn't worry,' she sighs, 'I'm not going to turn into a lush, Belle.'

'Well, just in case, why don't we agree that we have one glorious evening of self-indulgent grief where you can drink as much as you want, and then move on? What do you say?'

'Was my glorious evening last night?'

'Uh-huh.' I nod.

'Well, I'd have appreciated some advance warning. If I'd have known it was my one and only chance I could have gone through another box of Kleenex and a bottle of brandy while I was at it.'

'Is that a glimmer of a smile I see?'

'No.' Nicky's bottom lip starts to wobble again, heralding the arrival of more tears.

'Oh, Belle, I just feel so . . . so . . . useless . . . so frustrated. I mean, would you believe he hasn't even phoned or come round or tried to contact me at all?'

'Well, that's pure cowardice . . . what's he going to say to you?'

'Sorry would be nice for starters,' Nicky snaps.

'Is that word in his vocabulary, do you think?'

The ringing of the door bell echoes against the high ceiling of the sitting room, making us both jump.

Nicky and I look at each other. Neither of us moves. It rings again, longer and more persistent.

'If that's the total bastard then I don't want to see him,' Nicky cries perversely, snatching up a box of tissues and a half-eaten bag of Maltesers from the fruit bowl on the table, and heading for her bedroom almost at a run.

It's not the total bastard, however.

When I gingerly open the front door, ready to slam it straight shut again, instead of the expected total bastard is a total babe.

Tousled golden-brown hair, beginning to curl as it grows a fraction too long all over, slightly dissipated blue eyes, shadowed purple underneath through a constant lack of sleep, the angelic beauty diminished only by a broken nose from rugby playing. He looks like a cherub who's fallen along the wayside, several times, and usually in a drunken stupor.

'Jamie!' I shriek, hurling myself at this new arrival with the enthusiasm of an Olympic diver, heart set on gold, throwing themselves off the high-dive board.

Apart from Nix, my step-brother Jamie is one of my most favourite people in the whole world. He's the son of my mother's fourth husband. She managed to stay with him for, oh, at least five years, and so for a period of time we were brought up together. When that marriage fell apart, Jamie and I somehow managed to hang together. Stability in a mad world of wedding freak parents. It's weird, I'm actually closer to him than I am to my half-brother Adrian, who is strictly speaking my own flesh and blood. Then again, Jamie and I are the same age and have a lot in common – including completely dysfunctional families – whereas Adrian is ten years older than me, and is, in my opinion, a complete and utter nerd.

Blood is definitely not thicker than water, but Adrian is thicker than Jamie, who although on the surface appears to be delightfully scatty, is actually in his fourth year of GP training.

I'm instantly enveloped in a massive bear hug, which is followed by the usual cacophony of noisy greetings.

'You're brown!'

'You've grown.'

'You've lost weight!'

'You've put it on!'

'Did you miss me?'

'No.'

'You should have called more, you old bag.'

'You should have written more!'

When we finally stop squeezing the life out of each other, and hurling affectionate insults, Jamie asks after Nicky.

'How's the patient?'

As she predicted, the jungle drums have obviously been beating loud and in overtime.

'You've heard already?'

He nods.

'In the same conversation that alerted me to the fact you'd finally come home. Why didn't you call me, Belly?'

'Sorry, babe, but I think you can work out the answer to that one. I've been a bit busy.'

Jamie grimaces sympathetically.

'So how's she doing?'

'Needs morphine.'

'Thought that might be the case.' He pulls a paper-wrapped bottle from the folds of his jacket.

'Reinforcements,' he says, handing me yet another bottle of vodka.

I quickly hide it in a large Moorcroft vase which stands sentinel by the door, like a time-served alcoholic with a stash.

'That bad?' Jamie asks.

'Let's just say she's had more than enough already,' I tell him, ushering him in and closing the door behind him.

'Poor old thing,' he murmurs, shaking his head. 'To be honest with you, Belly, I wasn't that surprised. I met him a couple of times and he seemed like an arrogant prat. Where is she?'

'Hiding out in her room. Thought you might be the arrogant prat.'

'Shall I go through or is she coming out?'

'Neither. She doesn't really want to see anybody at the moment.'

'But I might be able to help,' he replies, looking hurt.

'Not really. You know what it's like. We're at the "all men are bastards" stage.'

'That can't include me, surely?' Jamie asks in disbelief.

'Well, if you think you can cope with the questions.'

'Questions?'

'You're a bloke, Jamie. The enemy. If you're ready for a mind probe on why men behave the way they do, then by all means go in and speak to Nix. But she'll expect you, as a member of the same subspecies, to be able to explain exactly why Richard did what he did.'

'Oh, I see.' Jamie bites his bottom lip. 'Well, how about me being an honorary girl instead? I don't mind joining in on the "all men are the same" bitch fest. You could lend me a dress. And, hell, I'll even wear girl's underwear if it helps.'

'You're supposed to be here to help Nicky, not get your rocks off,' I chastise him. 'Look, why don't we have a drink, and wait and see if she emerges on her own? You never know,' I joke wearily, 'if we open a bottle of wine, she might smell the alcohol and come running.'

'Drowning her sorrows?'

'Holding them under till they stop kicking.'

'Oh, by the way, that reminds me,' Jamie follows me through to the kitchen as I hunt for a cold bottle of white, 'your mother wants to see you.'

Those two dreaded words, 'your mother'.

'She can't do,' I reply in horror, stopping mid-hunt, corkscrew in one hand, expression of fear on face. 'She doesn't know I'm back yet.'

'She does now.' He doesn't even have the grace to look guilty.

I can't understand those girls who insist their mother is their best friend. My mother is my worst nightmare. Oh, enemy mine. I blame all of my insecurities, hang ups, and general behavioural problems on my mother. I had planned to leave her blissfully ignorant of the fact that I was now back in the same country as her for as long as feasibly possible.

'You didn't tell her I was back . . . Jamie, how could you? I never put you down as a snitch.'

'She'd have found out sooner or later, and the later it was the more grief she'd have given you. I did you a favour, Belle. Call her and get it over with.'

'Do I have to?'

'Doctor's orders.' He puts an arm around my shoulder. 'Don't worry, what's the worst thing she can do? You're hardly a kid any more, she can't ground you or stop your pocket money.'

'No, but she can cut out my heart and offer me up as a sacrifice to commercialism and conformity.'

'Sure, but that's a damn' sight better than confiscating your weekly chocolate ration.'

Nicky finally emerges from her bedroom the following day, only to scuttle straight back in there when her mother Kate appears on the doorstep, wafting Arpège and angst.

I offered to take over the wedding deconstruction – informing guests, cancelling the caterers, sending back gifts, castrating Richard without anaesthetic, but Kate began to attack this task on Monday morning as if her very life depended on it. She was expending as much energy on cancelling the wedding as she had on organising it. I think she needed something to do, a purpose, to stop herself from having complete hysterics about the whole thing. Nicky's father had to be practically locked in his study to stop him raiding the gun cabinet and heading up from Kent to Chelsea with the dogs baying in the back of the Range Rover, to exact a swift and bloody revenge involving Richard's backside and a rather large amount of buck shot.

Initial outrage subsided, the next instinct was to get an industrial-size carpet sweeper and brush the whole thing under the Axminster.

Nicky's parents are of the stiff upper lip variety.

There are some things one simply doesn't discuss, especially if the neighbours get wind of them.

Nicky's mother was on a mission to get rid of all physical evidence that there was ever actually going to be a wedding in the first place, and then everybody could get on with their lives as though nothing had happened, with hopefully as few friends and relatives as possible remembering or referring to 'this unfortunate incident' beyond twelve months tops.

Despite previous protestations the wedding gifts had to go back, the dress was packed in mothballs, and the ridiculously virginal underwear was spirited out of Nicky's wardrobe before she could spot it and weep another reservoir full of tears. The only thing a weak and wet-faced Nicky put her foot down about was the wedding cake, insisting that the level of comfort eating she intended to embark on needed something spectacular as a starter. It was hard, but somehow I managed to stop her from overdosing on mixed fruit and marzipan, and bearing in mind that love is said to be very close to hate, and that hate is far easier to endure when upset than unrequited or disappointed love, set about helping Nicky get over her broken heart in the usual time-honoured ways.

1) Revenge

The Balcony Scene – Not Quite Romeo and Juliet

'I'm really glad you're back, Belle, I couldn't have handled this without you.'

After five days, she's weak, she's battered, she's bruised, but she's better. Only a fraction. But from being as squashed as a road-splattered rodent, there's a little spark of fighting spirit struggling through Nicky's gloom.

I give her a hug, and coming over all motherly, do up a few more buttons on her little grey Morgan cardigan.

'That's what mates are for, babe . . . any room left on that grill?'

Beside us, the barbecue is sending a shimmer of grey smoke above our heads into the dark pink canopy of the evening sky.

Nicky nods. 'You could probably chuck on something small.'

I gaze at the assorted goodies on the wooden table.

'How about a kipper?' I ask her, just managing to suppress a giggle.

'Excellent choice.'

I throw it on and we both watch in satisfaction as it's quickly enveloped in the rising heat from the red hot charcoal, edges curling like a tongue preparing to lick an ice cream.

'Would you like another glass of wine?'

'That would be lovely, darling, thank you.'

I pick up the rapidly emptying bottle of Shiraz, and fill Nicky's glass to the brim.

'Cheers.' She smiles, knocking the edge of her glass against mine. 'You know, it was a wonderful idea of yours to christen the barbecue, babe. Do you think this sole is done yet?'

Nicky holds up a pair of tongs between which what was once a patent leather brogue smolders blackly, filling the air with the deliciously disgusting aroma of burnt leather.

'Mmmmm.' I inspect it closely. 'Perhaps a few more minutes on the other side, but I think those are about ready.'

Nicky prods at a couple of pairs of what were once white Calvin Kleins, blackening nicely next to the pure silk tie I've just added to the funeral pyre of Richard's clothes.

'Lovely,' she agrees. 'You're right. Nice and crispy. Just the way I like 'em!'

'There's only one thing missing.'

'Richard's balls!' we yell in unison.

2) Revival

The fact that I only let Nicky have one evening drinking her poor shell-shocked brain cells into glorious oblivion has not quite been forgiven, and despite previous protestations to the contrary, Jamie's bottle of Blue Label Russian best has managed to find its way out of the vase and into a pair of glasses.

After several shots each, I decide the best way to help Nicky climb back on that Bucking Bronco called manhood is by taking her out for a good old-fashioned girlies' night out. She has decided that she's through with men. I take this announcement with a pinch of salt, as I do the insistence that the only real choice she has left is to become either a nun or a lesbian.

I tell her that she would suit neither wimple nor crew cut and drag her into town in order to remind her that men still have a place in her life, be it simply to flirt outrageously with her in an overcrowded club and boost her poor battered ego.

I think it would have made her feel just a little bit better if Richard had grovelled for forgiveness and begged her to have him back, but she hasn't seen sight nor sound of him since she chargrilled the expensive designer clothes he'd left at her flat on the balcony barbecue, then posted their remains back to him in thirty-five separate A4 envelopes.

Nicky and I have decided that men fall into two distinct categories:

(1) nice but nerdy;
(2) lying cheating arseholes who are somehow far more sexually attractive.

What we really want is somebody who has the best parts of each category. Somebody dynamic, arrogant and exciting, but also considerate, intelligent and attentive in just the right measure as to be wonderful instead of smarmy.

If such a mythical creature exists.

Nicky thinks we have more chance of inventing calorie-and-fat-free chocolate than we do of finding a man with such qualities.

Not that she cares any more.

Third bar of the evening, heading for last orders, and we've moved on from red wine to B52s then, taking our life into our hands, order a couple of rounds of Tequila Slammers just to round things off – or perhaps finish us off would be more appropriate.

We're both drunk.

Well, I of the asbestos stomach developed over two years of concentrated foreign boozing am merely drunk, whereas Nicky's at that stage of alcoholic insulation where nothing matters any more, where the world is viewed through a haze of artificial anaesthesia.

'You know, it wasn't the infidelity,' she slurs, finishing her drink and without really being aware of her actions, picking up mine and downing that too. 'I mean, everyone's entitled to change their minds about someone, to fall out of love – if he was ever in love, that is – no, it was the insincerity. If I wasn't really what he wanted then why take everything so humiliatingly far?'

'Everybody finds their arsehole.' I put my arm around her shoulders and we both sway dangerously on our bar stools. 'Just count yourself lucky that you managed to ditch yours before you got stuck with him for life.'

'Well, there are plenty more to choose from in here.' Nicky encompasses the entire male population of the bar with a wide swing of her arm, sprinkling those around us with a liberal dose of tequila from the glass she's still clutching. 'Is there a limit on the number of arseholes in a girl's love life? Do I just get the one, or have I got to wade knee-deep through shit heads until I find a real man?'

'Well, you know what they say, you have to kiss a lot of frogs . . .'

'. . . before you find your prince,' Nicky finishes for me. 'Maybe I should snog a frog or two. You've got to snog a frog or two, girls . . .' she bursts into song. 'You've got to snog a frog or twoooo . . . Hey, Belle, I'm Fagin it again!'

'Did that a lot with Richard, did you?'

'Yes,' Nicky replies, looking solemnly at me, then the drunken grin slides back on to her face. 'Yes . . . Oh, yes . . . OOOOH, YES!'

'Oh, no, she's doing a Meg!' I cry, hiding my face in a pool of spilt beer on top of the bar.

Nicky's fake passion attracts the attention of a group of guys sitting next to us at the bar, who, almost as drunk as us, have been playing a noisy game of Bi-Spy, which basically involves proclaiming that every girl who turns down their beer-soaked advances has to be a lesbian not to want to instantaneously rip off her clothes and indulge in a spot of spontaneous lust.

The guy on the bar stool nearest to us, who I must admit is kind of cute in a rather rumpled just-fell-out-of-bed-and-where-the-hell's-my-hairbrush kind of way, turns to look at Nicky faking nooky in openmouthed admiration.

'Blimey, you're gorgeous!' he exclaims, eyes crossing as he gazes in drunken awe at her impressive cleavage.

'Kiss my arse,' she slurs.

Instead of turning away insulted like most of the guys who've been on the end of this particular barb all evening, this one bursts into peals of delighted laughter.

'I've got a better idea – you kiss mine!' He slides off his stool and, turning, swiftly undoes the button fly of his Gap moleskins and pulls them down to his knees, to reveal a rather bitable backside.

I turn to look at Nicky, shocked and laughing, unsure of her reaction, but to my amazement she's actually smiling.

'I like a man with a bit of cheek,' she says, and taking a pen from her hand bag, writes her phone number on his left buttock.

I wake up on Monday morning still with the raging hangover I spent all day Sunday nursing, the first one

I've had since my last night in Australia when I said
goodbye to my newfound Antipodean friends in
somewhat spectacular style.

Nicky's somehow managed to drag herself out of
bed and head back to work for the first time since that
fateful Friday just over a week ago, a note pinned to
the fridge with a Klimt magnet stating simply:
'Aaaaaaaaaaaaaahhhh!'

Nicky and I may have spent the best part of two years
apart but we've fallen comfortably and easily back
into the synchronised friendship we've shared since
we were skinny, giggling eleven year olds. We're not
quite so skinny any more, and the laughter's not as
plenteous, which considering recent circumstances is
understandable, but the bond is still as unbreakable,
and we still seem to share that strange almost sixth
sense that used to have us so fine tuned we would
often finish each other's sentences.

We've both changed in the past two years, grown
up, absorbed a few more of life's experiences into our
personalities, but although she's putting on a brave
face to the world, I still know her well enough to feel
the true emotions hiding painfully underneath the
bravado.

For the rest of the week I struggle with nail-biting
concern about how Nicky will cope with what should
have been her wedding day, only to find when the
actual day dawns like Friday the thirteenth inviting
trouble and a day spent hiding in bed with the curtains
drawn, that she's actually got a date for the evening.

The guy from the wine bar did as he threatened after she'd endorsed his flesh with her phone number, and didn't wash for long enough to transfer it from his backside to his phone book with the aid of a small hand mirror.

I'm really surprised she accepted. I thought she'd spend the day sobbing into her duvet and had even stocked up on our emergency supply of Kleenex, vodka and chocolate. I don't know who's the more nervous about tonight's dinner with he of the pert bottom, me or her.

At least it's taking her mind off the fact that by now she would have been Mrs Richard Ackerman, and heading out on to the floor to lead the first dance as a married woman, me shimmying next to her like a huge peach jelly on a plate.

'It's like preparing the vestal virgin for the ritual sacrifice,' I joke, as she scrubs, shaves, teases, tweezes, scents and paints, and then rampages through her wardrobe on a desperate hunt for a suitable outfit.

'How do you feel?'

Nicky stops hunting for a second, and thinks.

'Numb,' she says eventually. 'Weird. I really thought I'd never have to do this again, you know, get all tarted up to go on a first date. Especially not today.' Her voice breaks momentarily before she takes a deep breath, exhales and carries on. 'Help me, Belle. What am I supposed to do? What do I say to the guy?'

'Er . . . talk to him, find out a bit more about him, flirt a little – you know, the usual stuff.'

'That's the thing, what is the *usual* stuff? I think I've forgotten the art of flirting.' She pulls a face and discards the rather floral floaty blouse she'd just pulled on over her little black dress to hide the bulgy bits.

'Don't worry, it's just like riding a bike.'

She pulls a face at me instead of her outfit.

'That's not really the best analogy to use in the circumstances, Belle!' She grimaces. 'Seeing as that was what Richard was doing last weekend!' Changing her mind she pulls the floral offering on again over her rather sexy, but rather tight little black dress.

'How does this look?' She pouts into the mirror, turning from side to side, smoothing her hands repeatedly over her hips as though the palm action will erase the months of Mars Bar-munching.

'Honestly?'

'Honestly,' she replies firmly.

'Like a confused Laura Ashley. That dress is a bit too sub dom to go with that blouse.'

'Why am I doing this, Belle?' Nicky cries, ripping off the blouse, hurling it on the rapidly growing heap of rejected clothes in the corner, and hunting frantically through the remnants of her wardrobe for something else.

'You don't have to go, babe.'

'That's the thing.' She pauses in mid-rummage, and turns back to face me. 'I really think I do.'

'You don't have to prove anything to anyone, Nicky.'

'Only to myself. I need to prove to myself that there

is life after Richard. That he wasn't the only man on this planet.'

'Trust me, he wasn't.' I grimace. 'Especially as Richard doesn't really classify as a *man*, now does he?'

'Worm,' states Nicky.

I shake my head.

'Insult to worms.'

'Dirt bag.'

'Far too kind.'

'Well-meaning but misunderstood . . .'

'Ooh, severe sarcasm. Now I know you're feeling better.'

'How about "the last stubborn piece of dog turd stuck in the tread of the heel of the knackered old foot-odoured boot of humanity"?' she offers.

'Now that's a category we haven't used before.' I nod approvingly.

I'm like an anxious parent pacing the carpet until she gets home. I manage to shovel a whole tub of Chunky Monkey down my throat through sheer anxiety, and then work my way through a double saver pack of Jaffa Cakes. This only serves to make me feel sick and fat as well as worried.

We've finally added a category at the very bottom of the man scale, lower even than the previous worst 'stinking spawn of evil incarnate', entitled simply but quite succinctly 'a Richard'.

Nicky finally makes it home just after midnight.

I hear the tell-tale scraping sound of someone trying to connect key with lock and failing dismally, and taking pity, go and open the door for her.

'Belle, babe!' Nicky, one hand clutching the door frame, swings inward in time with the door.

'How did it go?'

'I am a highly desirable woman,' she warbles, practically falling down the steps into the sitting room.

'Oh, that's nice.' I laugh nervously.

Nicky is drunk.

I thought she was drunk on Saturday night. I was wrong.

By comparison, that was merely a demi-drunk, as opposed to the full-blown, fall over, mega-drunk that is Nicky now.

She staggers over and slumps down on the sofa, grinning broadly.

'I am a *highly* desirable woman,' she repeats, stressing the 'highly' and giggling like a maniac. 'Shame he wasn't a highly desirable man.' She picks up my nearly empty wine glass and drains the last sediment-filled dregs, her dry lips staining dark Burgundy red.

'Still had a nice arse, though. Nice arse, shame about the personality.'

'Well, as long as you had a good time, that's all that matters.' Blimey, I sound like Nicky's mother, but I'm just relieved that she made it home in one piece, both physically and it would appear emotionally, despite the fact that if she started crying again now, I think the tears would be fifteen percent proof.

'I s'pose you're right,' Nicky slurs, taking off her heels and rubbing at her toes. 'D'ya think I should have shagged him, though?'

'Why, did you want to?'

'Well, not really, but he paid for dinner.'

'Would you have expected him to shag you if you'd paid for dinner?' I drawl sarcastically, raising an eyebrow at her.

'Oh, absolutely,' Nicky jokes, getting the point straight away, despite the fact that she must have killed off at least half of her brain cells through the amount of alcohol she's obviously consumed. 'Especially if he'd had two bottles of Champagne, smoked salmon to start, lobster for main, pudding and coffee.'

'Pig!'

She grins happily at me, like a fat cat who's just stuffed a whole stolen turkey in five minutes flat and now just wants to lie in the sun, purr, and appreciate its satisfactorily full stomach.

'You know, I've decided to handle men the way I handle food,' she announced.

'What's that? Stuff it in your gob, then swallow quick before you taste?'

'Nah!' She giggles nasally. 'As much as I want, as often as I want.'

'Variety is the spice, and all that?'

'You've got it. And once they've gone past their use by date . . .'

'Bin them?' I offer.

'Bin them!' she repeats emphatically. 'Man. A disposable commodity. Should have a sell by date stamped on their bits, or better still a mileometer, so you can see how many times they've been round the block! A shagometer, clocks up another number every

72

time they introduce their todger to a new woman, so you can tell exactly how many and, more importantly, when. But then again, the devious bastards would probably work out some way of clocking themselves, knocking a few hundred girls off the register. "Honestly, luv, I'm practically a virgin . . ." ' she mocks.

Despite the fact that her full to bursting stomach is visibly straining over the top of the striped velvet boot legs she finally ended up wearing, she looks hopefully into my empty Jaffa Cake packet.

'Huh! All gone! Should have kept the bloody cake.'

'Cake?'

'Bloody wedding cake. Could do with a nice big slice right now.' She smacks her lips at the thought.

'But I thought you did keep it?'

The giggle bursting out of Nicky's throat turns into a rather large belch instead.

'Well, you know I asked you to get me some more stamps?' she slurs, pupils crossing drunkenly.

'Oh, Nicky,' I gasp in admiring horror. 'Tell me you didn't!'

'Should have got there this morning.' Nix nods slowly, eyes beginning to droop as she struggles against her body's overwhelming urge to give in to the alcohol and pass out in spectacular fashion. 'First class to Chelsea. Twenty-two . . .' she yawns cavernously '. . . padded . . . envelopes.'

I peer blearily at my alarm clock. In the dim light I can just make out that it's nearly four in the morning.

The sky above me is changing, like somebody's poured water into dark grey paint, diluting and sending it lighter, heralding the arrival of dawn. My mind, still half asleep, searches vaguely for a brief second for whatever it was that woke me up from a lovely dream about a never-ending supply of fat-free chocolate, but my ears which are more awake than the rest of me hear nothing. It's only as I free fall helplessly back into a deep sleep that I catch the quiet sound of sobbing from the next room.

Chapter Three

Have you ever woken up one morning and realised that you have absolutely nothing to do? Not
the usual Sunday morning, there's nothing on TV, it's
raining outside, you've read everything you possess
twice and your brain feels like it's been watching the
washing machine go round for the past two hours
kind of feeling; but the 'you have absolutely nothing
to do for the rest of your life' sort.

It's a killer, I can tell you.

This happens to me on the Monday after what was
supposed to be Nicky's wedding day, almost one
month since my plane hit the well-used tarmac at
Heathrow. The slam of the flat's front door as Nicky
leaves for work wakes me from a strange dream
about drain pipes and Yorkshire Terriers wearing pink
lipstick and La Perla knickers.

I stagger out of bed, make a pot of tea, burn myself
some toast, tune in to breakfast TV for a mind-
numbing couple of hours, finally get dressed, and
then wonder why I bothered.

Richard watching may have been mind-numbing

(and bottom-numbing) at times, but at least when I was doing that I had a purpose.

There were loads of things I thought I'd do when I got back to England.

Visit old friends, old haunts, show off my tan.

I certainly planned to leave a family reunion for as long as possible, but Jamie's now dropped me in it.

My mother and I have a somewhat strained relationship.

My mother's Wonder Woman, whereas I take after my father – Wander Woman. Ambling along wherever life happens to take me, since I haven't quite decided for myself yet where I want to go.

That's one of the things I've always admired about Nicky; she's been so focused, so positive about what she wants to do with her life. She's wanted to be a solicitor since she was thirteen, a time when I had gone past prima ballerina, through to vet, and was just moving on to movie/pop star. She was dreaming of chambers and courts of law whilst I was prancing round in front of the mirror miming to *Top of the Pops* with my hairbrush, or acting out scenes from *Grange Hill* with Jamie's Action Man taking the role of Tucker Jenkins.

It somehow seems okay not having a sense of purpose in Thailand and Australia. The beach, the blue skies, the air of living life leisurely, the general desire to have fun and live a little, made it seem okay to work only when I really needed the money.

You'd think that in a city as vibrant and alive as London I'd feel okay just to sit back and listen to the buzz, but maybe it's the fact that everyone else seems to have something to do, somewhere to go, places to be, people to see, that makes me feel so stagnant.

At least stalking Richard gave me something to do, I felt like I was earning my keep. I zap the remote at the hyperactive blonde TV presenter perched on a squishy sofa, toothy thin-lipped grin seemingly fixed with Araldite, and send her plummeting into celluloid oblivion.

It's no good. I'm finally going to have to do the thing I've been desperately avoiding all my life.

I'm going to have to get a job.

Jobs.

Sod's law, irony, call it what you will, but now that I've finally decided I want one of the bloody things, I'm damned if I can get one. It's like going shopping for clothes. When you've actually got some cash in the bank, you can't find a thing. When you're so overdrawn the cashpoint bursts into peals of sarcastic laughter when you insert your card, you find loads of gorgeous little outfits you've just got to have.

So far I've been to every agency in town. I've filled out more application forms than a serial computer dater. I've grovelled, pleaded, lied through my teeth, changed my degree from a scrape through second to a fully fledged first, and still can't find some mug willing to employ me.

I have no experience. Sure I've got a degree, but my total work experience amounts to about five broken months of bar work. I can't even type. Experience of life apparently doesn't count.

Wish I had something other than Richard and Judy to take my mind off of my current lack of job offers. No, lack isn't a strong enough word, it's a trade deficit. Nix and I sit poring over the classifieds after dinner.

'What about telesales?' she suggests.

' "Good evening, moddam, can I interest you in a year's subscription to *Pig Farmers' Weekly?*" No, thanks. I suppose I could always try for another bar job.'

'Bar work!' Nicky screeches like I've just announced I'm thinking of heading down to Soho and auditioning for a bump and grind spot in a sleazy strip joint.

'It's better than bloody telesales, and I have experience,' I mumble through a mouthful of tea-dunked cookie.

'You also have a degree in business management,' Nix states snootily.

She traces her pen down the page, and then suddenly breaking into a broad grin, circles an advert several times before turning the paper round to face me.

'Which at the moment is about as much use as Viagra to a eunuch,' I mutter, helping myself to another double choc and nut.

'Okay, how about this then?' She looks triumphantly at me, tapping her pen above the red circle she's scored around a box ad. 'Bar Manager required. Sounds just the job for you. You've got a management degree, you've got bar experience, you've got enough nous to bullshit your way round the rest of it.'

'I suppose it's a possibility,' I reply, scanning the ad.

'Go on, phone them,' she encourages. 'You've got nothing to lose.'

'Only my dignity,' I reply. 'And I think I lost the last of that in a little bar in the Khao San Road about eight months and eight hundred litres of alcohol ago.'

I tug at the hem of the skirt of my borrowed suit.

Nix is a good two inches shorter than me, and what was a perfectly respectable mini on her is threatening to be a bit of a high-thigh-revealing nightmare on me.

I've been tugging at the hem all the way here, walking with my legs buckled at the knee in an attempt to coax a bit more coverage in the thigh area. I've been wolf whistled by two sets of builders, a taxi driver, two twelve year olds on mountain bikes – which did absolutely nothing for my ego, I can tell you – and a group of shaven-headed Chelsea supporters in a suspensionally challenged XR3i who went round the block three times just to get another look at the woman in the amazing self-raising skirt. This is definitely not the knock 'em dead but totally businesslike image I was hoping to project. I think I'd stand more of a chance if I was going for the bump and grind strip job in Soho.

Al Fresco's is a totally too trendy wine bar just off Sloane Street. It's midday. The place is crowded with businessmen and women on long, laughing, loud, liquid lunches. The atmosphere is cosmopolitan, the raucous unintelligible babble of numerous different languages bouncing off the shocking lilac-painted walls, as workers from the nearby foreign embassies exchange world trauma for the delights of Pouilly Fuissé and Gravadlax.

The mouth-watering smells of hot bread and garlic hang heavy on the air, reminding my stomach I was too nervous to have breakfast. It immediately decides that a complaint should be registered about this fact and starts to grumble like a back bench heckler at question time.

Nigel Palmer is wearing a pin-striped three-piece suit more fitting for a City banker than the owner of a bar-cum-restaurant. His shoulder-length dark hair is slicked back with a heavy coating of wet look styling gel, which I thought became extinct in the eighties, and his heavy thick-lipped face is coated with a slightly uneven layer of fake tan.

He lounges by the bar, wide backside half on and half off a dark oak bar stool, mobile phone in one hand clamped against his ear, large glass of Scotch clutched firmly in the other. His starched white shirt cuffs are held together by cufflinks in the shape of old tap faucets; heavy gold bracelets circle both wrists like twenty-four carat handcuffs.

I'm guided to him by one of the waiters whose white waist-tied apron is fraying as fast as his patience, several besuited businessmen at a nearby table arrogantly summoning him with imperious clicking of fat fingers.

Nigel Palmer makes me wait for ten minutes until

he's finished his phone conversation before even bothering to acknowledge me. His voice is loud and self-important as he drones on to someone called 'Piers, you old bastard' about a shipment of foreign beer.

I stand awkwardly nearby, shifting uncomfortably in the incredible shrinking skirt, hopping from foot to foot like a nervous school girl waiting outside the tyrannical and terrifying headmistress's office, until Nigel Palmer finally jabs at the End button on his Ericsson and deigns to notice me.

Well, he sort of notices me. What he actually notices first is my legs.

'Er . . . Annabelle Lewis,' I stutter, my nerves made worse by his eyeball-burning inspection of my 10 deniers. 'We've got a twelve-thirty appointment . . . about the Manager's job.'

When he shakes my hand, his own is warm and clammy. When he says hello, he addresses my cleavage rather than my face. He also, rather disconcertingly, slides the hand that just took mine inside his shirt and thoughtfully scratches his own left nipple whilst running his eyes slowly up and down my body like a hand-held scanner being drawn over an intricate document.

Despite serious misgivings about the sanity of my actions, I follow him through to a quieter table at the back of the bar. He sits down, and indicates for me to do the same.

'So you've been abroad for two years?' is his first comment.

'Nearly that, yes,' I reply, trying not to fidget nervously.

'Nice tan.'

He glances quickly through the CV Nicky fabricated for me on her PC, looks at my legs, looks back at my CV, looks at my cleavage, looks back at my CV again, and then finally looks at my face.

'I was really looking for someone with more experience.'

Here we go again. Thanks for nothing, slimeball. I reach for my bag and start to stand up.

'Right, well, thanks for your time.'

'But I'm sure we could probably come to some arrangement . . .'

I put my bag down again.

'You mean, you could provide training for the areas you don't think I have enough experience in?' I prompt as he once again falls silent, and his gaze returns to the hem of my skirt.

'Something along those lines.' He smiles, but he's still not looking at me.

'Yeesss?' I encourage.

'You're a very attractive girl, Annabelle,' he says, once again addressing the shadow produced by the padding in my Marks & Sparks plunge bra.

I'm not sure I like the sound of this.

'People like a pretty face around the place. You'd be good for business, and anything that is good for business is good for me.'

Well, I'd rather get a job on the strength of my qualifications than the depth of my cleavage, but what the hell? Beggars can't be choosers. Let the boobs get me in the door and then I can impress him with my business acumen.

I suppose it's not very PC, but who cares about that when you're homeless, penniless, and the only clothes you possess in the new fashion capital of Europe are sun-dyed seventies rejects which may have been fine for a beer with a bonzer sunburnt Bruce in Burke Town, but don't exactly go down like a glass of ice cold Soave in a wine bar in deepest Knightsbridge? I'm sick of having to pretend I don't live within spitting distance of Harvey Nicks, which is a distant pot of gleaming gold at the end of a not very constant rainbow, of kidding myself that Selfridge's is a purely white goods retailer, and the Ghost sale a mere spectre haunting my couture-free imagination. Nigel Palmer may be a leering, over-sexed little slimeball, but at the moment he's my passport to paradise in the form of charge cards, cuisine, culture, couture, and all the other essentials to enjoyable London living.

Besides, I'm used to handling leering over-sexed little slimeballs, aren't I?

I take a deep breath, beg the Pankhursts for forgiveness, and force myself to smile brightly at someone I'd much rather be spitting on.

'So you'd consider taking me on?'

He smiles back, the toothy leer reminding me of an alligator I had far too close an encounter with when sightseeing fever took me on a misguided tour up the Great Divide.

'Yes, I'd consider taking you on,' he echoes, an unhealthy emphasis on the last three words. 'I think we could work well together, Annabelle. You know, you be good to me and I'll be good to you.'

I suddenly have a strong yearning to be back with the alligators, a Great Divide between me and nauseating Nigel.

'I beg your pardon?'

'You know – you scratch mine, I scratch yours,' he continues, waggling his eyebrows at me.

I don't like it when men waggle their eyebrows at me. I have this theory that a man's eyebrows are somehow connected to his groin area, a little annexe, a subsidiary branch or outcrop of his pubic hair, and when the eyebrows waggle at a woman, the groin is usually raring to join in.

I also really don't like the thought of scratching Nigel's. In fact, the thought of what affliction Nigel might be suffering in this area to require a jolly good scratching is simply too much for me.

I can cope with innuendo. I have a pretty good line in good-natured, good-humoured put downs that usually work quite nicely, thank you, but I have a feeling that Nigel would need to be put down with an elephant gun to be in the slightest bit deterred. I suddenly decide I don't want to spend my summer stuck behind a twenty by five foot bar with slimy Nigel attempting to get his grubby hands on my optics; that purchasing power in the top shops isn't worth humouring such a total slug.

Putting my chair into reverse, I scrape the four legs

backwards across the polished floorboards like finger-nails running down a blackboard, so that Nigel's hand which was reaching out to squeeze my knee falls into thin air and throws him off balance.

'Thanks for the thought,' I shoot at him, grabbing my bag and heading for the exit, 'but I'd rather get a job as official bottom scratcher to a pile-ridden, man-hating, red-arsed baboon than get paid to scratch *anything* of yours!'

On the way back to Nicky's, Arnold takes umbrage that I'm working out my bad mood on his clutch, and decides to shame me completely by conking out at the head of a long queue of traffic waiting to go over some lights.

I sit there like a total idiot for the longest five minutes of my life, until a passing bunch of joggers in training for the London Marathon take pity on me and practically lift us out of the way.

The minute we're off the main road and in a side street, Arnold decides to start up again. I don't even try turning the ignition, he just fires into life of his own accord and stays running long enough for me to do an eight-point turn and head back out into the early-evening traffic. As soon as we're back in the rush-hour queue, Arnold's engine gives out a throaty, gurgling sort of noise like demonic laughter and promptly dies a death again.

I take my strangulating shoes off in the lift and stretch my poor pinched feet. So much for dressing to kill.

The only thing that's been knocked dead are my little toes, which are currently so numb I think I may have lost them on the tube home. I have visions of them sitting side by side with artificial legs, the odd coffin, and plastic-packed hospital specimens, in the lost and found office.

Nix is in the living room, drinking coffee with the girl from the flat across the corridor. They both look up as I crash my way grumpily through the front door.

'How did it go?'

Nicky doesn't need an answer, my face and obvious attitude say it all. I hurl my shoes on the sofa and slump heavily down next to them.

'That good, eh?' She pointedly removes them before offering me a cup of coffee. 'Never mind, we may just have a solution to your . . . er . . . employment problem. You know Lucy from number eight, don't you?'

The beautiful oriental girl smiles at me.

For the short period of time I've been here, I've got to know Lucy well enough to smile hello at her every time we see each other, and to envy her couture wardrobe, her eighteen pairs of Manolo Blahnik shoes – and, yes, I have counted each pair with jealous precision – her long shimmering curtain of jet black hair, huge slanted brown eyes, razor-sharp cheek bones and full soft pink lips. In fact, her total effortless gorgeousness.

'Well, Lucy's got a proposition for you,' Nicky tells me, not quite meeting my eye.

If it's anything like the one slimy Nigel made me today, I don't want to know. Then again, Lucy's much better looking and far more wholesome than Nigel. Not that I'm into women in that way – although the men I've come across recently could certainly give a girl an excuse.

Lucy looks up and smiles at me.

'Nicola was telling me what you did for her, Annabelle.'

'You know, regarding Richard,' Nix clarifies, coughing as she inhales a recently lit Marlboro Light.

Richard has by now become a dirty word, to be pronounced with the same vocal inflection as 'bastard'.

'Well, that's what friends are for,' I reply, shrugging lamely, accepting an elegant little espresso cup from Nix and wishing it was a large vodka.

There's a pause for a moment whilst Nicky refills Lucy's cup. She sips at her coffee, then looks up at me over the porcelain rim.

'Do you know my husband, Gordon?'

'Well, not really,' I reply, surprised at the question. 'I've seen him around on the odd occasion, but we've never spoken.'

'That's good,' says Nicky to Lucy.

She nods her agreement.

'Why's that good?'

'Because I want a divorce.'

Er . . . what do I say? I'm sorry? Congratulations? What's it got to do with me never having seen him close up? Does she want a divorce because at close range he's a total gargoyle?

I fail to come up with the correct verbal response and merely smile in what I hope is a sympathetic manner.

Lucy continues slowly, her voice full of self-deprecation.

'Gordon and I have been married for nearly eighteen months. It was a bit of a whirlwind romance. You know what they say: Marry in haste, repent at leisure. The problem is he was so bloody charming when we first met, and like a fool I was really taken in by him.' She takes a deep breath. 'Basically, the charm isn't an exclusive. He's been constantly unfaithful to me from the moment we got back from our honeymoon . . .'

'This is where you come in,' Nicky explains.

Lucy nods.

'I want a divorce, but I don't think Gordon will give me one.'

'But how on earth can I help you with that?'

'Gordon's the managing director of my father's electronics company. That's how we met. I need to get hard evidence that he's cheating on me. He'd be so petrified that my father would find out, I know he'd agree then to a quick and very quiet divorce.'

'We thought perhaps you could catch Gordon out, like you caught Richard.' Nicky smiles nervously at me. 'What do you think, Belle?'

What do I think? I think they're mad. It's no picnic, errant boyfriend watching. It's full of scary hazards like drain pipes and wayward hormones.

Once was quite enough, thank you.

'I really don't . . .'

'I'd be happy to pay you for your time,' Lucy cuts in before I have the chance to finish my refusal.

'You would?' I ask her in surprise.

'Of course. I don't expect you to work for nothing.'

I slide a sideways glance at Nicky who's looking at me hopefully.

'Nix, could I have a quick word – alone?'

'It's okay.' Lucy darts a glance at Nicky. 'I'll go, give you a chance to think about it. Let me know what you decide. You know where to find me,' she laughs.

I wait until Lucy has closed the front door behind her then turn to Nicky, who's munching on a choco-late biscuit and not quite daring to meet my eye.

'What are you trying to do to me, Nicky?'

'I don't know.' She shrugs. 'You need the money, Lucy needs help, I felt sorry for her . . . I've been there, haven't I? Gordon's been acting like a total shit and she really doesn't deserve it.'

'But she's gorgeous! What man would have the gall to cheat on her?'

'Gordon, apparently.'

I shake my head in disbelief. What hope do I stand of ever retaining faithful love if somebody as stunning as Lucy can't keep someone as stunningly ordinary as Gordon the Gargoyle happily monogamous? I mean, I know there's more to a relationship than looks, but Lucy's got it all anyway. She's bright, funny, beautiful, sexy, solvent . . . what more does Gordon want? Maybe it's the supposed thrill of illicit sex, the adrena-line rush, the cheeky little high you sometimes get when you know you're being naughty.

'Well, supposing I did decide to help,' I say cautiously, 'what can I do anyway?'

Nicky brightens, sensing weakness.

'Follow him like you followed Richard,' she says enthusiastically. 'See where he goes, what he does, who he does it with.'

'Yeah, but how far do I actually have to go?'

'Like Luce said, she just needs some hard evidence.'

'What, like a photograph of his erect willy?'

Nicky giggles.

'I said hard, not semi-flaccid.'

'Well, I do need to get myself a job, don't I . . . and I suppose it's better than a nine to five. As you know, I've never been a nine-to-five girl.'

'Will you do it for her, Belle?'

The prospect of yet more nights freezing my nipples off in Arnold the Allegro isn't desperately appealing, but then again it's far more tempting than fighting off the advances of Knightsbridge Nigel while attempting to sell over-priced drinks to over-paid arseholes.

'I don't know . . .'

Nicky pushes an envelope toward me.

'What's that?' I eye the stuffed manila suspiciously.

'Cash.'

'Cash?'

'Yep.' She grins. 'I know you haven't seen any for a while, but you can't have forgotten what it looks like already.'

'I may have forgotten what it looks like, but I

could never forget the distinctive scent of money!' I joke, picking up the envelope and pretending to breathe in the aroma like it's fresh coffee and warm croissants.

'Go on, count it,' Nix urges.

I tentatively pull the wad of twenty-pound notes out of the envelope, and quickly flick through, mentally adding as I go.

'Five hundred pounds!'

'That's for the first week. And Lucy said she'd pay all of your expenses too.'

'She did?'

Nix nods.

'And what exactly classifies as expenses? All the chocolate I can eat, a hot water bottle and some waterproofs?

'Oh, you know, if you have to sit in a bar all night, I suppose she'll pay for your drinks, travel expenses, stuff like that.'

'Travel?' In that case sod the waterproofs. 'Well, if it covers travel, the first thing I'm going to do is hire another car!'

'You can't want to get rid of Arnold, surely?'

'No, I don't want to get rid of Arnold, I want to KILL Arnold. I want to take him to a breaker's yard and personally put him in the car crusher, twist and grind that metal, squash him till his springs groan for mercy.'

I catch sight of the horrified yet fascinated expression on Nicky's face, and stop spouting forth about the terrible death I've planned for Arnold.

'Sorry, babes.' I grin sheepishly. 'I know he was your first love and all that . . .'

'No.' Nicky shakes her head and breaks into one of the broad, laughing, old Nix grins that I haven't seen for nearly two years. 'I was just thinking that's exactly what I'd like to do to Richard.'

Gordon is forty-two, with grey hair brushed back at the temples into two neat wings. He has a battered face, lined and tanned, and if denied access to Nicky Clarke and taken out of the Gucci shoes, Armani suit, Pierre Cardin glasses and Patek Philippe watch, would probably look like a weather-beaten Cornish fisherman. He is a wide boy made good, who managed to ride the recession by always being in the right place at the right time, then struck twenty-two carat gold by marrying the boss's daughter.

My remit is simple. I'm to do the same with him as I did with Richard, only this time I won't be climbing up or falling off any more drain pipes – I hope.

I'm on slightly safer territory – well, almost slightly safer, as for the second time in one week I'm going to Al Fresco's, domain of nauseating Nigel and current location of Gordon, who's out on the town with some cronies.

My orders are to hang out in a nearby corner, watch and learn.

If he steps out of line – you know, tonguey snogs, groping in dark corners – I'm to make sure I get it on film, whip out the old Instamatic, snap him in action, then hopefully leg it before I'm spotted.

Simple, really. You must get tons of mad women leaping round busy bars with a camera. Nobody's going to suspect a thing. As if! I suppose I could always pretend I'm a thick paparazzo who's got him confused with a celeb, but seeing as the only celluloid personality he even vaguely resembles is Keith Floyd, this might be a hard one to swallow.

What makes things even worse is that there's nothing suitable in my meagre wardrobe for a night out in a trendy bar. And as Nicky's two sizes bigger than me, I've had to borrow something from Lucy. Normally I'd kill to get my hands on just one thing from her copious collection of couture, but the main problem is I don't get to choose, and *her* idea of inconspicuous is something pink, short and shimmery that's very designer, but also very revealing.

Another small problem, emphasis on the small, is that Lucy's also provided the underwear. (Brand new, of course. I'm afraid I'm not into the dubious pleasures of fitting my bits into other people's knicks.) My practical and comfy *proper* knickers, whilst great for making sure your buns don't chafe when trekking eighteen miles a day, don't exactly sit well under a dress that fits like clingfilm. My VPL was *so* visible you could see it from space along with the Great Wall of China.

My concern that Gordon might recognise the outfit as being one belonging to his wife is quickly quashed by a quick trip over the landing to Lucy's flat for something skimpy in the smalls department.

It'd be like Casanova remembering the face, name

and inside leg measurement of every one of his conquests. I was impressed by Nix's cupboards but Lucy doesn't have a walk in wardrobe, she has what could almost be a separate apartment for her clothes. Harvey Nicks en-suite.

Brand new clothes still in their bags and tags, acres of delicious designer. I've never really had the urge to amass possessions, but find myself turning a rather noticeable shade of pistachio. If this is what a good career can do for a girl, maybe my idea of carefree non-materialism is a little outdated, and I should stop feeling guilty at misting up the windows of Harvey Nicks with my drool.

'I've died and gone to fashion heaven,' sighs Nix, gazing in covetous awe at the rails and rails of wonderful clothes surrounding us.

To be in Lucy's dressing room is the fashion lover's equivalent of being a chocoholic let loose in Cadbury World with a mission to 'Destroy all Evidence'.

I've soon replaced my three-year-old M & S specials with something almost non-existent, appropriately from Agent Provocateur, which have the consistency of a piece of dental floss and are about as comfortable to wear as a strong brace on wayward teeth.

What with the dress, the undies, and the party slap Lucy paints on my face, the whole effect is kind of a pornographic Christmas Barbie.

I draw the line when Nicky advances toward my head holding glitter spray. I still look like the fairy off the top of the Christmas tree, though.

An hour later and I'm walking into Al Fresco's, my face as pink as my dress with embarrassment.

I feel a bit better when I see that the place is filled with trendy young clubbers wearing outfits that would give my granny an instant heart attack, but I'm still one of the most outrageous.

This dress makes you look like you're completely naked except for some well-placed pink chiffon and body glitter.

Walking into this bar for my interview was bad enough. Walking into this bar, on my own, dressed like an Essex girl on a Saturday night beano, is a living nightmare. I push my way through the throng to the long wooden bar and park myself on a stool I have to fight for, only to find that the moment I sit down, the garrotte masquerading as a pair of knickers instantly tightens its vice-like grip on my bits.

Very sexy dress. Not so sexy furrowing furtively up the back of it to retrieve my underwear.

I can't work out whether the attractive young barman is laughing or leering as he ignores several other longer waiting punters to serve me.

I don't feel like I can order lager in this dress so I ask for a gin sling and end up with a neat little frosted glass which some joker's seen fit to chuck a cherry in.

It doesn't take me long to spot Gordon. He's at a corner table with three friends being loud, lewd, rude and obnoxious, just as Lucy described him.

They've obviously chosen this particular table because they're perfectly sited to gawp at anybody who comes through the door in a short skirt, which is an incredibly frequent occurrence. They should really be sitting there holding score cards. It's like a beauty pageant where none of the girls is actually aware that they're in a competition.

The guy closest to the door, who appears to be totally rolling drunk, is accosting any girl who dares to wander too close with the same scintillating interest-grabbing line: 'Hi, I'm Evan, let me take you to paradise.'

Seems more like hell to me.

Six foot of lean, leering, unleashed testosterone.

Don't get me wrong, testosterone has a very important and valued place in my life, but it's not a pretty sight when seeping in copious untamed quantities from a drunk, dishevelled, bottom dweller the wrong side of forty.

I quite like older men. But, call me fussy if you will, I quite like my older men to be *attractive* older men.

The focus of my investigation is leaning back on his pine and chrome bar stool, designer glasses perched on the end of his nose, through which he is peering with the evaluating scrutiny of an expert on the *Antiques Roadshow* at every girl who passes.

Unfortunately it's not long before he spots me as well.

In this dress, everyone's spotted nearly *all* of me.

The guy on the stool next to me is leaning in so close, any further and he'll fall face first down my cleavage and I'll have to fish around and pull him out like a lost false eyelash. I slide my eyes sideways and

Gordon's gazing at my legs. I give him another couple of minutes and when I look back the roving eyeballs have slid up towards my cleavage.

A few more minutes and when I look back he's staring straight at me. I quickly look away.

Unfortunately when I dare to risk looking back again, he's still looking my way and our gazes lock for a brief moment.

He smiles.

Oh, dear.

He's spotted me staring over at him and is taking it completely the wrong way.

He thinks I'm trying to make eye contact.

He *thinks* I fancy him.

I look away quickly.

Two minutes later I sneak another glance sideways, and am rewarded with a flirtatious smile which reveals a row of very white, very capped teeth.

Oh, shit!

He definitely thinks I'm interested.

Now what the hell do I do? How on earth am I supposed to watch the guy when I daren't look round in case he's looking at me!

It's this bloody dress. I'm supposed to be inconspicuous and my bloody mates send me out dressed to thrill.

I stare rigidly in the opposite direction, not daring to look over again in case he's still staring, teeth bared, crotch raring, but my tactical retreat is too late.

I watch, cringing, in the mirror behind the optics as Gordon says something to his companions, nods in my direction, and with much noisy encouragement threads through the crowd, running his hand through his hair, even scratching his two front teeth with a hasty thumb nail, until he's standing behind me.

'What's a gorgeous girl like you doing all on her own, then?'

Very original.

I turn slowly to face him, tilting my head to one side, forcing a small smile.

'Er . . . I'm waiting for a friend.' Also highly unoriginal, but the only thing I can think of at the moment.

'Perhaps I should stand guard until your friend gets here. This place is full of wolves who prey on sweet young things like you.' He leers at me, winking heavily.

'Oh, and you're not one of the pack then?'

He laughs – a deep, husky, put on laugh that makes him sound like Tom Jones with emphysema.

'I'm the leader.'

Add a 'b' to that and he's more on target, according to Lucy.

'Why don't you let me buy you another drink whilst you're waiting?'

This really is not going to plan. No matter how vague the plan was in the first instance.

'Thanks, but like I said, my friend should be here any moment.'

'Well, if your friend is as lovely as you, then I think I should stay right where I am.'

'My friend's a he, not a she.'

'Then I'm glad he's not here yet.'

Gordon slides on to the stool next to me, which has finally been vacated by the over-friendly drunk who was trying to dive down the front of my dress.

'Let me buy you a drink,' he wheedles again. 'I promise I'll behave.'

He steals the cherry from my third gin and, putting it in his mouth, sucks and rotates it in what is supposed to be a suggestive manner, but is actually pretty revolting.

'You're nearly empty.'

'Like your promises?' I raise an eyebrow at him.

'Well, you can at least tell me your name.'

I can?!

'Come on, sweetheart, what's in a name?'

That's a good question. Only the ability to put out a trace.

'I'll go first, shall I?' he mocks. 'Hi, my name's Gordon.' He cocks his head to one side. 'There, it wasn't that difficult, now was it?' He's trying to be cute. It's not working. He's about as cute as Chucky running amok with a meat cleaver.

'Er . . . Annab—' I just manage to stop myself blurting out my real name. It's definitely not a good idea to give him that, and we never decided on an alias due to the simple fact that we had absolutely no idea I'd be needing one!

'Er . . . I mean Annaliese. My name's Annaliese.'

Fortunately Gordon's already had more than a few and doesn't notice the slip. I feel one of his large hands slide over my arse.

'Well, how would you like to join my friends and me for a drink, Annaliese?'

Blimey, he's persistent!

At the moment what I'd like to do is stab Gordon's roving hand with the cocktail stick he just sucked my cherry off, but a more overwhelming urge is to get the hell out of here and fast. The question is, how?

'Sure, Gordy, that would be lovely . . . but, er . . .' I look frantically around me and spot a rather drunken Nigel staggering through the door. 'My friend seems to have shown at last.'

I shrug apologetically, and reach down to pick up my bag which is sitting at the side of my stool like a little silver mushroom sprouting from the floor.

Gordon's face falls.

'But we were just getting to know each other . . .'

I shrug apologetically and, sliding off my stool, make to move past him. He hasn't given up yet, though. He fishes in the inside pocket of his suit jacket. Catching my arm, he presses a business card on me.

'My number – call me.'

He takes my hand and, placing the small square of card in my palm, curls my fingers around it.

'We could go out for dinner sometime maybe.'

'Maybe,' I reply slowly.

'Promise you'll call?'

I smile up at him in what I hope is a coquettish rather than a terrified fashion.

'Maybe,' I repeat, starting to pull away.

'No, not maybe, say yes.' He winks at me.

'I've got to go. My . . . er . . . boyfriend is a very jealous man,' I stammer, elbowing my way rudely through the heaving throng of people around us in an effort to get away.

When I'm a semi-safe distance away, I look back. He's still watching, glasses slipping down his nose as he stares at my retreating arse.

'Shit!'

I'm not going to get away with walking out of here alone, he'll be after me in a flash. Drawing level with Nigel, who's obviously been out sampling the delights of the other local hostelries before returning to hold slimy court in his own, I grab hold of his arm and spin him back round in the direction of the door.

'Hi, babe,' I shout loudly, 'I've been waiting for you for ages, where on earth have you been?'

Nigel looks at me in vague if somewhat startled recognition.

'I know you, don't I?'

'Never mind, darling, we'd better hurry, the reservation was for ten.'

Thinking it's his lucky night, an incredulous grin spreading over his drunken rubberised *Spitting Image* features, Nigel lets me tow him outside and into a conveniently waiting black cab.

He's not so happy when, having driven a hundred yards up the road, I ask the surprised taxi driver to stop and unceremoniously boot him back out again, before collapsing back against the sticky plastic seat and exhaling the breath I've been holding for the past fifteen minutes.

Well, that certainly wasn't how it was supposed to happen. Sure I was supposed to catch Gordon hitting on someone, but it wasn't supposed to be me!

How am I going to explain this one to Luce? She'll be so pissed off that I blew my cover on the first night.

Lucy and Nicky are curled up side by side on the sofa, stuffing tortilla chips and watching Antoine of *Eurotrash* fame dancing round set dressed up as part of a giant salad sandwich, with a celery-stick thin model as the meagre filling.

The minute I stagger through the door, attempting rather indelicately once again to remove the G of my string from the deepest recesses of my butt cheeks, Nicky grabs the remote and cuts the sound, and they both turn to me, faces expectant and eager.

'You're back early.'

'How did it go?'

'You mean apart from feeling like a piece of Gorgonzola having a close encounter with a wire cheese cutter? Where did you get these knickers, Luce? An S & M shop? Slice and Mutilate! Look, I'll just slip into something less painful, okay, then I'll tell you all about it.'

I head for my room finally and thankfully to remove the clingfilm dress, and the knickers that bite, and shrug on the lovely, saggy, baggy, ratty, tatty, comfortable dressing gown Nick bequeathed me when I first arrived back in England, homeless and clothesless.

I'd love a shower to remove the trail of Gordon drool that's drying on my shoulder, but I don't think the girls could cope with the wait.

I head back through into the sitting room, thinking longingly of my lovely clean chrome and white-tiled shower, and join the girls. They make room for me between them on the sofa. Nicky hands me a glass of wine.

Lucy, eyes bright with anticipation, contains herself long enough to offer me the tortilla bag.

They both look at me expectantly whilst I'm allowed one swig of alcohol, then one bite on a slightly chewy cheese Dorito.

'Well?' they chorus.

I take a deep breath.

'Well,' I start, 'they were all in Al Fresco's like you said they would be.'

'Them?'

'Yeah, there were three of them: Gordon; another one whose name I didn't catch – he had a sort of dark blond crew cut, grey eyes, a small scar above his lip . . .'

Lucy shakes her head.

'Doesn't ring any bells.'

'Well, anyway, there was him, Gordon, and Evan somebody or other . . . total prat.'

Lucy nods in recognition.

'Evan Landers, he's head of Marketing.'

'Well, he wasn't doing a very good job of marketing himself.'

'Behaving atrociously as usual.' It's a rhetorical question, but I still nod.

SARAH HARVEY

'So,' she asks eagerly, 'did Gordon do *his* usual and target some poor unsuspecting female, flashing his diamond-encrusted Rolex in her face in the hope that she might be dazzled enough to drop her knickers?'

'Well, as a matter of fact, yes, he did.'

Lucy breaks into a broad grin.

'Great! And did it work? Did you get any incriminating pictures?'

'Well, that was the tricky part . . .'

The grin disappears.

'Why? What was the problem? Did you lose him?'

Did I lose him? I wish!

I take a deep breath.

'Not quite, no. You see . . . well, the thing is . . .' I look from Lucy's concerned face to the floor, which isn't so expressive, and force the words out. 'The girl he was waggling his wristwatch at . . . well . . . it was me. It wasn't my fault, he must have seen me looking over and thought . . . well, you know. Because I kept looking he must have thought that I was interested.'

I look up nervously and am surprised to see that Lucy's grin has returned with a vengeance.

'But that's great!' She beams.

'Is it?' I ask in surprise.

'Of course it is. It means we've got him just where we want him. How did you leave it? Did you arrange to meet again?'

'He gave me his mobile phone number, but I think I've lost it.'

'Well, that's not a problem, is it? Call him.'

'What, now?'

'There's no time like the present.'

Nicky hands Lucy the portable phone set, and she taps in Gordon's mobile number.

'This is the first time I've arranged a date for my own husband,' she giggles.

I wish I was finding this so amusing.

'Ooh, quick, it's ringing!' She literally throws me the hand set just as Gordon answers. The background noise tells me he's still in a bar somewhere. I can hear music and laughter and drunken Evan singing some bawdy rugby song.

'Yo! Gordon McClure!' he shouts above the din.

Yo? Good grief!

'Hello, Gordon. Er . . . it's Annabuh . . . I mean, Annaliese.'

Nicky raises her eyebrows at me and sniggers, mouthing scornfully, 'AnnaLIESE!'

I throw a 'For heaven's sake, shut up,' glance in her direction.

'Yes, *that* Annaliese.'

'Yes, I was thinking of you too . . . Uh-huh, yeah, I knew I wouldn't be able to resist calling you either, you're just soooo irresistible.' I pull a face at the girls. The ego of the man wouldn't permit him to question why a girl he met for a nano second in a crowded bar would actually fall so hard for his drunken advances she'd call him up the very same evening.

'Look, I was thinking about your invitation . . . well, yes, I'd love to, that's why I called . . . What's that? Saturday?' I look over at Lucy and Nicky who nod enthusiastically. 'Yeah, sure, Saturday would be great . . . Sorry, this is a bad line, did you say you want to pick me up at eight?'

Their heads immediately stop nodding and shake vigorously instead. Lucy mimes having her throat cut. I can hardly ask Gordon to pick me up from here, the address might seem a little familiar.

'No, there's no need really, I'll meet you there . . . yes, that's fine, Vigaro's in Little Venice. Yes, I know it . . . Eight o'clock . . . Yes, I'm really looking forward to it too. See you then. *Ciao*.'

'*Ciao!*' mocks Nicky, as I rather viciously press the Off button, and chuck the hand set back at her.

'He said it first,' I moan, and turn to Lucy. 'Okay, the dirty deed's done, now what?'

She pushes a curtain of blue-black hair out of her eyes.

'It's simple really. I'll "go away" for the weekend, leaving him free to do exactly as he pleases, which means he'll probably bring you back to the flat . . .'

'What if he doesn't? What if he takes me to some sleazy hotel somewhere miles from anywhere, with no escape and no one to hear me scream?' I fantasise dramatically.

Lucy raises her dark brown eyes to the ceiling.

'You'll just have to engineer it so that he does, won't you? Get him talking about golf then you ask to see his trophies, he'd love that . . .'

'Come up and see my golfing trophies? A little more original than etchings, I suppose.'

'You know, I once heard an awful story about a woman and a golfing trophy . . .' starts Nicky.

'I don't think I want to hear it.' I wince, taking a huge gulp of Frascati.

'Okay, forget the golf,' Lucy cuts in impatiently, 'but it's simple. You let him chat you up, then accept his offer to come back to the apartment with him.'

'If you're sure he'll offer?'

'Trust me,' she smiles dryly, 'he'll offer.'

'Okay, so he offers, then what do I do when I get him home? Whip out my camera and insist I'm into kinky pictures? No, thank you! I don't fancy doing a David Bailey on your naked husband. Besides, for them to be incriminating, I think I'd need to be in a few of the shots as well, actually *doing* something, and believe it or not I've got my limits, and Gordon's way *way* beyond them. No offence, Luce.'

'Don't worry. None taken. Believe it or not, getting naked with Gordon isn't high on my list of recreational activities either.'

'No,' Nicky interrupts, 'if you do it right, you don't have to take off so much as a trace of lipstick.'

She seems to have it all worked out.

'All you've got to do is lure him into the bedroom with a sexy, come-hither smile, and encourage him to remove several key items of clothing and drape himself across the duvet. At which point Lucy, who's waiting here, comes across and catches you in a compromising position.'

'How compromising?' I ask apprehensively.

'Well . . . er . . . enough,' Nicky replies, not very helpfully.

'And how compromising is enough?'

'Well . . . pretty compromising.' She twists an earring and pretends to study the back of her hand.

'You mean, I've got to actually . . .'

'Dear god, no!' Nix shrieks, finally deigning to look at me.

'Well, thank goodness for that.'

'I mean, you should be in bed with him,' she continues, looking shifty again. Lucy nods her agreement at this point.

'But you don't actually have to . . . you know.'

'. . . shag him?' I finish for her.

'Yeah, you don't have to shag him.' Nix smiles, helping herself to more wine and then topping up my and Lucy's glasses.

'Well, how very magnanimous of you,' I reply sarcastically. 'Honestly, Nicky, next thing I know you'll be floating round the apartment in blacked out sunglasses, psychedelic flares and a floppy hat, calling me your bitch and talking rates with customers.'

Lucy chokes on the mouthful of white wine she was attempting to swallow as laughter bubbles up in her throat instead.

'Don't worry, Belle, there's a big difference between seduce and shag.'

'Yeah,' Nicky joins in the laughter, 'you can keep your underwear on.'

'You bet I'll keep my underwear on! And you can bet I'll be wearing iron ankle-length knickers, a steel full body bra, and an unopenable, unbreakable chastity belt too!'

'Don't worry, I'll be waiting to burst in before anything can happen.' Lucy grins at me.

'Oh, yeah? And what are you going to do then, listen at the door? Your timing's got to be spot on or I'm in big trouble.'

Nicky shakes her head.

'Far more simple than that, my friend.' She grins, pulling out a box from under the table.

'You want me to have his baby!' I shriek, looking at the huge Mothercare sign on the side. 'I mean, I know you wanted concrete evidence, but isn't that pushing things a bit?'

Nix raises her eyes to heaven.

'Don't get your knickers in a twist!' she mocks me. 'They're baby listeners. We put one in Lucy's bedroom, and the other one in here. Then as soon as you say the word, Lucy's through that door.'

'And what exactly is "The Word"?' I ask.

'How about, "Do it to me, Big Boy—"?' suggests Nicky, biting her bottom lip to fight the giggles.

'Or "Take me now, my Luscious Love God!",' breathes Lucy, not even bothering to hide her laughter.

I take a swig of slightly warm Frascati, in an attempt to suppress the giggle that's threatening to burst from my own mouth.

'It's not funny,' I protest weakly.

'I know.' Lucy grins kind of sadly, offering more wine all round. 'But if you don't laugh . . .'

'You cry!' Nicky and I chorus together.

Nicky's going out again.

I know I wanted her to get on the horse, but I didn't expect her to saddle up quite so frequently.

I think this is the third man this week.

She calls it therapy; I call it ridiculous.

Talk about rebound! She's the rubber ball in a vigorous game of squash, falling in and out of lust as regularly as you or I floss our teeth. She's mooning over the window cleaner this time. It's just like the Diet Coke ads; every time he swings past like Tarzan on his little platform, she's there draped seductively across the sofa in something skimpy and supposedly alluring. She actively encourages the sea gulls to come and dump all over the windows so that she can call him out time and again. She'll be hanging out of the window smearing sardines on the glass next.

It's not even as if he's that wonderful. Sure he has muscles, and a great tan from showing off said muscles at every opportunity, but he's far more in love with himself than any woman could ever be.

He looks like the hero off the front of a Mills & Boon special, with his rippling torso and long tousled blond hair; a Dream Boy stripper taken straight from the stage and suspended outside the living-room window for Nicky's own private viewing.

Personally I think he's about as attractive as any other long-haired pretentious poseur, but at least it's taking her mind off Richard.

She's in her room now, showered, made up, best undies on, trying on every single dress in her wardrobe.

'You know, I swear it's getting bigger.' Nix eyes her bum in despair. 'Oh, that this too, too solid flesh would melt,' she giggles, prodding at a bulgy bit. 'The thing is, I tell myself that that bar of chocolate or packet of crisps is just going to make it bigger but my taste buds absolutely refuse to listen to sense.'

'Oh, come on, Nix, it isn't that big.'

Her eyes widen incredulously.

'It's huge!' she moans. 'If it gets any bigger the meteorological department'll slap a warning on it, 'cause every time I bend over there's an eclipse.'

'Well, it doesn't seem to have affected your pulling power in any way. You've got a man for every day of the week.'

'Apart from Sunday,' she laughs, 'my designated day of rest!'

'Joking apart, babe, don't you think it might be an idea to ease up a little?'

'Why? There are plenty more fish in the sea, and I'm just doing a spot of trout tickling.'

'Yeah, sure, but you're supposed to throw in the occasional rod, not trawl for shoals with the biggest net you can get your hands on.'

'Says who? You're always refusing to conform to the accepted norm, Belle.'

'Sure, but this isn't *your* norm, Nicky.'

'Wasn't, Belle,' she corrects me. 'It *wasn't* my norm. But things change, don't they, and there's absolutely nothing wrong with playing the field for a bit. Perhaps if I'd done that to start off with, I wouldn't have rushed head first into such a disaster. I need to be able to understand men better, Belle, and what better way than to spend more time with members of that species? Besides, I'm having fun,' she adds, not entirely convincingly.

'You needn't worry about me, I'm just enjoying going out and meeting new people. It doesn't matter if the guy's not the man of my dreams. One dinner doesn't constitute a promise to love and cherish till death us do part.'

'So long as you don't get hurt.'

'You have to be in love to get hurt, Belle, and I'm certainly not in love with anyone. Besides,' she turns and smiles wryly at me, 'if I meet somebody I really like, I can always get you to check him out for me first!'

Saturday night arrives with somewhat unwelcome haste.

Lucy, who's been camped out on the sofa since Friday night, on her supposed weekend away, and Nicky, who's enjoying the whole drama far more than I am – enough even to turn down a second date with the window cleaner so that she can help me get ready – set to work on turning me into the kind of glamour puss that could lure Gordon out of his underpants and into the divorce courts.

They've got their work cut out.

In the past few days my body's gone through a bit of a culture shock. I'm not exactly as slim as I was when I first hit the tarmac at Heathrow. In Australia, I was tanned, toned and healthy. Since I came back to

England, I've put on a few wobbly pounds in all the wrong places – thighs, bum, tum – my hair's rather straw-like, and seemingly overnight my tan's turned a pale jaundiced yellow and my nails have split and crumbled to dust. Not only this, but my skin is so dry I need to take a long soak in a whole bath of moisturiser before the parched earth look will disappear.

How on earth am I supposed to look seductive and gorgeous when my whole body has turned into a complete eco-disaster area?

The first two weeks that I was back in the country I sat on my arse in Arnold, stuffing my face all day long to try and keep out the cold. After that I had to join Nicky in her comfort eating, you know, show some solidarity to my best mate in her hour of sorrow, and the effects have suddenly caught up with me. The fat fairy has jumped out of the fridge and yelled 'BOO!' with a vengeance.

I'm not saying I'm fat, two years of lean living can't be killed off completely in just over a month, but I think I really need to give up chocolate now.

Unfortunately to give up chocolate is like giving up breathing. I can only hold my breath for so long. I go three days without so much as a sniff of choccie, carried only by the sense of power I get at controlling my own cravings. But then, on the fourth day, I'm like a ravenous wolf on the prowl, liable to steal Smarties from a toddler if not watched very closely.

I can't turn on the TV for fear of being sucked into those seductive adverts with melted chocolate running in delicious dark brown rivers across the screen.

However, with the aid of a bucket of tinted moisturiser, a whole sack full of Elizabeth Arden, a mega-strength hot oil treatment, and a few well-chosen words of encouragement, they manage to pour me into one of Nicky's pre-fat skimpy little DKNY dresses, a shimmering, almost neon white practically see-through shift, and a pair of gorgeous strappy ankle-threatening Jimmy Choo shoes. My bot's feeling hot in some outrageously pervy knickers from Agent Provocateur, a rather appropriate gift for luck from Nix. My sun-lightened brown shoulder-length hair has been cruelly twisted away from my face and now sits in a pinned, feathered heap on top of my head that's so tight I feel like I've had a face lift.

'What do you think?' Nix asks Lucy.

She walks around me as though she's a judge assessing the form of a top dog at Cruft's.

'I look like a complete bimbo,' I grumble.

'Just Gordon's type then.' Lucy nods her approval. 'Oh, one last thing.' She reaches into her handbag and, pulling out an atomiser, mists me with perfume.

'His favourite,' she explains.

'It's disgusting,' I moan, holding my breath as the sickly sweet floral scent assaults my nostrils.

'I know,' Lucy shrugs apologetically, 'but it seems to do things for him.'

I don't particularly want to 'do things' for Gordon. In fact, I don't particularly want to 'do' this evening at all. Misgivings have slid around my chest and throat like a boa constrictor, stifling me with nerves. Either that or this bloody dress is too tight.

★ ★ ★

Nicky drops me off just round the corner from the exclusive Italian restaurant where I'm due to meet Gordon. I'm twenty minutes late and he is already seated at the table waiting for me. He has sunk several large glasses of wine judging by the near-empty state of the bottle of Merlot on the table, and is chatting up the waitress who has come over to take his order for another bottle.

I feel disgustingly self-conscious as I totter through the restaurant on my high heels. I want to tell everybody who looks up in astonishment as I pass that this isn't the sort of outfit I'd normally be seen dead in. Perhaps I could kick the guy crooning jazz off his piano stool and make a public announcement over the microphone.

'Ahem – excuse me, ladies and gentlemen, but I'd just like you to know that I am actually a normal human being and I *don't* think I look good in this dress, honestly. Thank you.'

It has the desired effect on Gordon, however. The waitress is dropped from his radar with insulting alacrity as he spots me weaving my way precariously through the tables of other diners on my three-inch heels.

I can't look as dreadful as I thought. Well, not to Gordon anyway. His tongue practically lolls out of his mouth, like a red carpet being unrolled for royalty. If he were a cartoon character little pound signs would light up in his eyes. He obviously thinks he's hit the jackpot tonight.

I'm a walking white surrender flag.

A drool-inducing Barbie Doll.

Gordon's fantasy woman for the evening.

Help, Mummy!

'Annaliese . . .' the last syllable rolls off Gordon's tongue like syrup dripping down the hot edge of a waffle '. . . you look absoLUTEly stunning!' He practically jumps out of his seat and, taking my hand, presses it to his lips.

I've always quite rated this gesture, if done properly. It can be intimate, tender and very seductive. Or it can be totally and utterly tacky, like the showy, wet-lipped, lechy sucker Gordon plants on the back of my mitt.

Especially as, in doing so, I notice that on his own left hand the deep mahogany tan ends underneath the recently removed wedding band.

He then insists on helping me into my seat, and gawping down my cleavage as he pushes my chair in for me.

'I'm so glad you called. But then, I knew you would.'

Arrogant git!

I have a hard-to-suppress longing to pop Gordon's little self-inflated bubble with a few well-chosen home truths about how attractive I really find him – we're talking week-old rubbish in hot weather here – and how low he actually falls on the man scale. 'Pond scum from the Planet Dirt' level.

Showing off, he calls the waitress over with an imperious click of his fingers then orders for both of us, without even asking for my opinion. For all he knows I could be a vegetarian or wheat intolerant or something. Gordon intolerant springs to mind – I'm finding *him* pretty hard to stomach.

Arrogant git intolerant.

'I think we should have a bottle of Champagne, don't you, Annaliese?'

Does it matter what I think?

I remember that I'm supposed to be flirting with the guy, and swap the scowl on my face for a simpering smile.

'That would be lovely.' I manage an air-head giggle and am rewarded with a scathing look from the waitress. Oh, this is soooo humiliating.

Luce and Nix warned me to keep off the alcohol and maintain a clear head, but it's hard when he keeps topping up my glass after every tiny sip.

I think he's trying to get me drunk.

If only he knew I was already a dead cert for getting back to his flat, he wouldn't have to try so hard.

When the starter arrives, he insists on pulling the legs and shells off my *crevettes* and then feeding them to me, which in anybody else's book could be construed as seductive but in my circumstances makes me want to puke. I think he actually expects me to take his buttery fingers in my mouth and suck them clean. Yeuk! Instead I take the food very gingerly, like a fussy Persian pussy, choosing only the tastiest morsels from her plate with dainty mouth movements, making sure my lips don't touch his flesh each time.

When the steaks that he ordered are set sizzling on the table, I almost expect him to lean over and cut mine up for me into little baby pieces.

He orders another bottle of Merlot to go with the steak, and pours the majority of it into my glass. Fortunately he hasn't noticed that I've been surreptitiously tipping the contents of my glass into the massive pot plant next to my chair every ten minutes or so.

I wish I was drunk. It would make this evening with Gordon the Moron far easier to endure. As well as endeavouring to force enough alcohol down me to kill off my 'No' brain cells, he keeps asking me to pass the salt because every time I reach forward the already low front of my dress descends a couple of centimetres to show the soft swell of the top of my boobs.

I can't even kick his brain back up into his head from where it's settled in his groin with a well-aimed wallop, either verbal or physical. Instead I have to sit there and smile sweetly at him as if I'm enjoying his pathetic advances and leering glances. Throwing him hot 'I want you badly' glances, instead of 'Piss off, you pathetic old fart' looks, which is how I really feel.

Dirty old git! I hope all that excess salt blocks his arteries!

When he asks for one pudding with two spoons, I know I'm in trouble.

I insist that I'm no longer hungry and sit back and sip nervously at my Russian coffee whilst he demolishes an ice cream with much spoon sucking and long lingering looks, his eyebrows waving up and down at me like an excited relative heading off on a cruise.

When the bill comes he pulls a roll of notes from his pocket and showily peels off what appear to be an extortionately high number of twenties. Well, that's one good thing about Gordon's display of pure machismo, he doesn't expect us to go Dutch, which is good because it looks like the cost of that meal would have been enough to keep me and Nix in Maltesers and cheap red for a month.

Totally unaware that your place or mine is literally the same, he eagerly bundles me unprotesting into a waiting cab. He's beaming like a Cheshire cat, obviously still in a state of disbelief at quite how easy this particular conquest looks like being.

There's a dodgy moment in the taxi where Gordon lunges for my lips, but I manage to move my head before he makes contact, so he ends up nibbling on my borrowed earring instead.

Rather confusingly for him, I suddenly make a rapid swing from hot to trot to coy and virginal, shuffling my bottom along the plastic seat as far away from him as I can, and just about manage to fight him off until we get back to the flat in Limehouse.

'Well, here we are, home sweet home.'

Not knowing that I was in this place only days earlier raiding Lucy's wardrobe, he reaches over me and casually pushes open the wide heavy front door of their apartment.

He obviously expects me to be impressed.

I am but I've seen it before.

Lucy's flat is twice the size of Nicky's and filled with wonderful exotica collected by Lucy in her jet-setting days of being a Hong Kong financier before she settled in London with Gordon the Groper.

I slide swiftly under his outstretched arm, just managing to dodge the puckered lips, and undulate across the thick sand-coloured carpet, swaying my hips from side to side like Marilyn at her finest.

'Beautiful place,' I murmur, running my hand seductively over the smooth stone curves of a replica Tang horse.

'Not as beautiful as you,' Gordon growls throatily, prowling across the carpet towards me.

Somebody pass me a sick bag!

'Would you like a coffee, or perhaps something a little stronger?'

He's close behind me, his warm whisky-sodden breath fanning against the back of my bare neck, his large hands roaming over the curves of my hips.

I effect a rapid escape by walking over to the sliding glass doors that lead on to the balcony and pretending to admire the view.

There is absolutely no way that I'm going to go through the 'let's pretend to drink coffee whilst we have a pre-shag groping session on the sofa' section.

Gordon chooses this moment to slip a little seduction music on to the CD.

Oh, shit! What the hell am I doing here? I think to myself as Neil Diamond croons over the speakers. And to think I actually believed this would be preferable to fighting off slimy Nigel. At least I wouldn't have had to pretend to fancy him, I could just have whacked him where it hurts with a beer bottle if he got too fresh!

I think there's only one way to do this without actually having to stick my lips on Gordon's, or worse still having Gordon stick his lips on me. Uck!

I turn to face him and smile in what I hope is a bold, come-hither kind of fashion.

'I take it that one's the bedroom?' I purr, and head off in the direction of the door that, unbeknownst to Gordon, I already know damn' well leads to the master bedroom.

He must think I'm the fastest drawer dropper in the West End. He hasn't even kissed me yet, and here I am already heading for his duvet.

I wonder if I can get away with leaping into bed fully clothed? The question is, how to get Gordon naked and vulnerable without removing a stitch myself.

I solve the problem by getting to the bedroom well ahead of him.

By the time he's come panting through the doorway, I'm already reclining on the bed Mae West-style and purring up at him, 'Strip for me, Big Boy,' in a voice that has shades of Mariella Frostrup with severe tonsillitis.

Fortunately he only hesitates for a moment before this big incredulous grin spreads over his craggy face, and he begins to divest himself of his clothes with indecent haste.

'No, over there, where I can see you.' I direct him

to the other end of the room, as far away from the bed as I can get him.

'And do it slooowly,' I rasp, hoping that he thinks it's lust not panic that's dictating this last. 'I want to watch you.'

Fortunately I've obviously picked on a favourite fantasy. Gordon immediately slows down and starts to do a Full Monty to the music. By the look on his face he's loving every moment, gyrating his hips, taking off his shirt to reveal an extremely hairy chest, then twirling it round his head before he throws it on a chair in the corner.

I don't know where to look when he starts on his trousers. The belt goes first, pulled out of the waist band with a whip-like crack and then flung in the general direction of the shirt.

He eases his trousers over his angular hips, swaying to the beat as they slide ever lower until he kicks them free from his feet and stands gloatingly before me in nothing but a pair of pale blue Y-fronts.

'No!' I shriek as he goes to whip those off too.

He stops and looks at me in concern, obviously expecting another breathtakingly quick volte face from uptight virgin to full on seductress.

'I like them,' I breathe, thinking not so much on my feet as on my back. 'They're very sexy.'

Gordon looks at me in disbelief.

'I have this thing about Y-fronts,' I try again, 'they really turn me on, especially pale blue ones.'

Pale blue Y-fronts topping a pair of skinny white hairy legs. Luvverly!

This ad libbing stuff is even harder knowing that Nicky and Lucy are eavesdropping on every word I say, probably stuffing the sofa cushions in their mouths to suppress the laughter.

I think it's time to call in the back up.

'Gordon, I want you now,' I yell at him, projecting my voice in the direction of the bedside cabinet where Lucy hid the second baby monitor.

He looks at me in amazement, the grin returning to his face faster than diners at an 'all you can eat' heading back to the salad bar.

Unfortunately, as well as alerting Lucy, this also spurs Gordon on.

'Oh, Gordon, I want you now,' I repeat our distress call, in a stiff, flat monotone as he's threatening to remove his underpants.

Ignoring the bull about his off-putting undies being the best aphrodisiac since oysters, Champagne and Spanish fly, he rips them off to reveal a raging monster of a hard-on which then flies towards me like an Exocet missile heading for a pre-determined target.

'Oh, Gordon, I want you now!' I shout.

It may have seemed hilarious at the time, after a good old bitch and two bottles of rather potent Australian Shiraz between the three of us, but now it's highly inappropriate to shout 'Come and get me, Big Boy' when I'm trying desperately to think of a way of fending him off without being done for GBH.

Gibbering and Bellowing Help.

Just as Gordon leaps on to the bed, and on to me, and just as I'm about to sod waiting for Lucy and take the matter of my honour, or rather dishonour, into my own hands – or rather, out of my cleavage – the bedroom door bursts open to reveal Lucy waving a Kodak Instamatic.

Well, she wanted compromising evidence.

How much more compromising could she get, with Gordon's mammoth hard-on resting heavily against my diaphragm and both hands wrestling with the buttons on my dress.

Lucy's performance is far more worthy of a BAFTA than my low-budget porn acting. She starts laying into Gordon heavily and very verbally in a stream of Chinese. Although I can't speak a word of the language it's obvious to anybody that what she is saying is bluer than a block of loo cleaner.

As instructed I take this as a cue to grab my bag and run, pausing only briefly as I realise that I've left my shoes behind, only to remember that they were Lucy's anyway. Thank goodness I've only got to sprint across the corridor. The way I'm running you'd think I'd got a whole horde of mass murderers chasing after me with raised sharpened axes.

Reaching Nicky's and safety, I slam the front door behind me and lean against it, panting in cross-eyed panic like the petrified black cat chased by an incorrigible love sick Pepe Le Pew.

Nicky is collapsed on the sofa, tears streaming down her red-cheeked face as she tries to control a fit of hysterical giggles.

The baby listener is still on.

Apart from the sound of my own heart thumping like a bass drum, my phone pervert's heavy breathing, and Nicky's fit of red-faced, gasping-for-breath laughter, I can hear the ear-piercing sound of a full domestic going on across the corridor as Lucy threatens to acquaint the Tang horse I admired earlier with the shrivelled and under-utilised contents of Gordon's skull.

Despite her calm and almost clinical manipulation of her husband's weaknesses, there's real raw anger in her voice.

When Lucy slams out of her flat and sneaks into ours five violent minutes later, I'm almost ready to be lambasted as well, but as soon as the door is shut safely behind her, she leans against it and bursts into sobs of hysterical laughter, the stern face falling away like a discarded mask at a costume party.

'Oh, god, that was SO good! You should have seen his face.' She dances over to me and, catching my hands, swings me round the room in a brief polka before letting go and falling backwards on to the sofa, still giggling like a maniac.

'You should have *seen* his face!' she repeats. 'That just made up for everything he's put me through, everything . . . he was almost wetting himself.'

'So was I!' I shriek. 'God knows how I got through that without being eaten alive.'

'Well, the ad libs were pretty entertaining from our end,' Lucy laughs. 'Strip for me, Gordon . . . and do it *slowly*,' she rasps mockingly.

'Oh, I just *love* pale blue Y-fronts,' breathes Nicky, joining in.

'You wouldn't have found it so bloody funny if you were there,' I snap indignantly.

'I wish we could have seen it. It was like listening to the Goon Show on the radio. I really wish we'd video-taped it now,' Lucy sniggers.

'Oh, Gordon, I want you now!' Nicky howls with laughter. 'Perhaps Belle could do a re-run, then we could send it in to *You've Been Framed*!'

'Never again!' I shriek. 'NEVER again! I should get danger money. Anyway what took you so long to come through, Luce? If I thought you two were stalling deliberately . . .'

'Well, it was better than *The Archers*,' Lucy nods, biting her bottom lip to stop herself from laughing.

'Oh, Gordon, I want you now!' they shriek in unison, then fall about shushing each other in case the object of their mockery stops cowering under the coffee table, hears familiar voices and decides to investigate.

I'm trying to look affronted, but it's not working.

My outraged face crumples as I collapse on to the sofa with them, joining in the laughter with almost as much gusto.

Lucy grabs her abandoned wine glass from the table and raises it in mock salute.

'Good riddance to bad husbands.'

'Farewell to faithless fiancés!' Nicky joins in the toast.

'Yeah, and a speedy sayonara to cheek-cutting

killer knickers!' I add feelingly, knocking back my glass in one go. 'Can you hold fire on the celebrating, girls? I'm just going to slip out of this into something . . . er . . . more comfortable.' I slide back into my Mariella Frostrup-with-a-throat-infection voice. 'You know, I've been desperate to get out of my knickers all evening . . .'

Chapter Four

The horrors of last night are thankfully receding in the light of a new day. Every time I close my eyes I still see visions of a semi-naked Gordon gyrating in front of me like a reject from the Dream Boys. Well, more of a nightmare boy than a dream boy really. But what puts things into perspective is the fact that I have a far more dangerous mission today, something that would have even James Bond quaking in his tailored tux.

I'm meeting my mother.

Since Jamie took it upon himself to rat on me and tell her I was back in the country, I thought I'd better muster as much courage as I could and call her.

We're having lunch.

She's picking me up at twelve. High noon. Baguettes at twenty paces.

Nicky's as happy about this fact as I am.

'You mean, you told her where I live!' she shrieks, immediately shooting into the kitchen to hide behind the contents of the fridge. I don't know why she thinks a cold Kit-Kat will protect her, but she's

SARAH HARVEY

shovelling it down her throat like my mother's poison and it's the only antidote.

Nix has always been petrified of my mother. In fact, come to think of it, I find her pretty scary sometimes as well.

Especially at the moment.

She's not happy with me.

She's never happy with me, so I shouldn't be surprised, but I think the fact that I got back five weeks ago and have only just got in touch might have increased the 'not happy' factor somewhat.

At five to twelve I'm standing outside the foyer of Nicky's building, shaking in my borrowed Chanel boots, and it's not because the wind's whistling ice cold and intrusive up one of Nicky's skirts either.

I think I've sent Mother a total of about three postcards, one Christmas card, two *very* belated birthday cards, and one letter since I went. Yet another failure of daughterly duty!

I'm in for nearly two years worth of nagging in one go. A trade deficit of nagging, a food mountain of nagging, which will no doubt turn into a slow painful avalanche of nagging until I'm buried up to my neck in it.

When she was my age she had her second husband, her first child, and a fledgling business balanced lightly under the ball of her right thumb.

She's always been so bloody capable. Maybe that's why I always feel inadequate. Everything I do is compared to her achievements, and considering I haven't really achieved anything so far, I'm not doing very well in the comparison stakes. I may have travelled, often solo, halfway across Asia and Australia and survived intact, but according to my mother that wasn't an achievement, it was an extended holiday. My mother believes in a new breed of Superwoman, one who can excel at work, whilst raising a family, being a socialite, and doing all her own interior design to boot.

I can't even paint my nails whilst watching TV. Somehow I always manage to spread more varnish on my cuticles than anywhere else.

And as far as a career's concerned, I haven't got a clue. I've no particular calling, no fire, no burning desire to be anything . . . except happy.

Which I'm definitely not at this precise moment in time.

She pulls up bang on twelve o'clock, tyres screeching as she gets in far too close to the kerb, nearly running over the toes of the black leather boots I've borrowed from Nicky.

I see her profile before I see her face: hair cut into a short sleek bob, straight nose, thin lips painted a sharp vermilion.

Isn't it strange that no matter how old they are, your parents always look the same? It's like no time has passed at all. In fact, I've regressed. I'm twelve and being picked up outside the school gates the time I was suspended for putting clingfilm over the toilet bowl in the head mistress's private loo.

She gets out of the car and looks at me appraisingly. I can tell she doesn't know whether to smile, greet and hug, or threaten to put me over her knee and spank me.

I save her the choice by forcing a grin, bellowing 'Hello!' in what I hope is a 'Gosh, I'm *so* pleased to see you' fashion, pecking her on each cheek, then darting round to the passenger side of the car and getting in.

She gets back in next to me and, putting her keys in the ignition, turns to me as she fires the engine into lion-roaring life.

'Well, it really is you. I almost had to do a double check, just to make sure.'

The sarcasm hasn't changed either.

'I thought you were going to the Far East. Instead you must have stepped off the plane and straight into oblivion.'

'Bangkok actually, but you're close.'

Humour. A self-defence mechanism that really isn't appropriate when used with my mother as she has absolutely no concept of this particular human faculty.

She shoots me a black look and shoves the car rather violently into gear, pulling out into oncoming traffic with heart-stopping confidence that everyone will just move out of her way, despite the fact that she's the one violating traffic laws.

My mother drives a brand new Mercedes SL.

She has a new one every year, viewing it rather like a fashion accessory, a handbag or a lipstick or something. The colour has to be 'in' or it's out of her life.

Unfortunately, although her taste is the latest YSL, D&G and the famous double CCs, her driving style isn't as current. She belongs to an era when a little man in a tall hat would walk in front of your car waving a red flag, driving everywhere at about fifteen miles an hour regardless of traffic or speed restrictions.

'The problem with having a sporty car is that every numbskull wants to race you,' she moans as, having pushed her way out over to the other side of the road, she then continues along it at arthritic snail's pace, a stream of cars very sensibly taking the opportunity of a lull in traffic coming the other way to shoot past her.

'I'm very disappointed in you, Annabelle,' is her next comment. 'You know, I really hoped that going abroad would help you grow up, but it's obviously done nothing of the sort. I can't believe you've been back in the country over a month and haven't even bothered to contact me. Do you know what it's been like for me, worrying about you . . . I don't know what on earth possessed you to take off in the first place. I mean, it's not as if you can look after yourself, you've always been completely irresponsible . . .'

I lean over and turn the heating up to full. I'd forgotten what it's like to get goose flesh. I've forgotten a lot of things in the past two years. One being the reason I went to Australia in the first place. Mother's quite happy to remind me, though. According to her it was to escape responsibility, evade the necessity to grow up and decide what I wanted to do with my life.

What's wrong with not knowing what I want to do? With not following the accepted route through life that most people seem to fall so easily on to?

It's like being processed. Everybody is expected to follow the same path. Born, school, work, wedding, kids, mid-life crisis, retire, die. It we watched ourselves from far away I'm sure we'd look like a little hive of worker ants, running round in seemingly useless patterns.

Apparently when I was born my grandfather, in his own inimitable way, looked into my cot and pronounced that this child would either be a genius or an idiot. Well, I know I'm definitely no genius, so where does that leave me?

I'll tell you where it leaves me. It leaves me twenty-five, homeless, careerless, and completely directionless. I think I believed that I'd go abroad and by the time I came back I'd know what it was I wanted to do with my life. Like I'd suddenly find myself, my purpose, perhaps in some amazing and magical foreign place; maybe voices in the desert, like Jim Morrison.

Perhaps I'm just a late developer. That's probably it. I didn't need a bra until I was fourteen, I lost my last baby tooth when I was fifteen, had my first French kiss at seventeen, lost my virginity at . . . well, let's just say I was very near the end of my teens. Who was it that said youth is wasted on the young? I'm petrified that by the time I've decided what I'd really like to do with my life, it'll be too late.

Although I suppose I could set a trend and be the first OAP jump jockey, or the first grey-haired granny to grace the catwalks at London Fashion Week. Knowing my luck, I'll waste my life away until I end up an octogenarian tea tout, leaning weakly against my trolley like a cup-and-saucer-covered zimmer frame, curlers in my hair, fag between my thin pinched lips, dripping ash into the Earl Grey. Hilda Ogden with an attitude.

If the worst came to the absolute worst I could always take up my mother's open-ended offer of employment.

She wants me to go and work for her.

She repeats this offer several times throughout the car journey to the restaurant, but I fortunately manage to avoid giving a response each time by saying something inane that I know will irritate her. It's the only way to avoid a subject with my mother: get her on to another one that pisses her off even more.

I don't know exactly what she does for a living. When people ask, she always says that she's in media. I know she earns a lot of money, goes to a lot of parties, and quite often pops up on the odd sofa on breakfast TV, giving her usually ridiculous opinion on current affairs. To be honest with you, she's quite happy to tell me what she does. The problem is, she's such a bore about it, I tend to switch off after the first three syllables have been uttered and never end up knowing.

My half-brother Adrian already works for my mother, under the grand if rather vague title of Director of Artistic Consultation. This means he gets to drive a Saab convertible, turn up for work at about ten in the morning, take a long lunch with his very attractive secretary, and leave the office at about four.

Could be my ideal job if there really was one, but the thought of having to spend every day with my mother and Adrian is just too much to bear.

My mother thinks the sun shines out of my brother's arse. Well, I suppose there's plenty of room up there because all the crap comes out of his mouth.

Pompous – a word specifically invented for Adrian.

Arsehole – a word specifically invented for most men, but fitted to perfection by Adrian.

Boorish. Insensitive. Plonker . . . I could go on forever.

So could my mother. The monotonous moan I've blanked from my mind for the past ten minutes is still going on when my consciousness resurfaces into reality, like a deep sea diver coming up for air.

'I can't believe you'd go away for that length of time and only contact me once in a blue moon. What am I supposed to think? For all I knew you could have been banged up in some foreign brothel, tied up in an opium den, sold into the slave trade . . .'

'All secret sex fantasies of mine which unfortunately never actually happened,' I quip.

'It's no joking matter,' she snaps. 'I certainly don't think it's very funny. There are some strange men inhabiting this world . . .'

'I know, I think I met most of them whilst I was away.'

'You know I don't like men very much, Annabelle.' She glances in her rear-view mirror, not to assess the traffic but to check the amount of lipstick that's managed to survive the constant lip movement.

Of course you don't like men, Mother, that's why you've had four husbands and then worked your way through about eighteen boyfriends since I left for distant shores. Since my mother divorced Jamie's father, her fourth husband, she has been engaged about five times, but never actually remarried. She keeps a spare robe hanging on the back of her bathroom door for 'gentlemen friends'. This robe is a bit of a standing joke, having housed more bodies than the local morgue.

'Of course, the mistake I make is treating them like they're adults,' she continues.

Lucky them. I still get treated like I'm nine.

She shifts gear viciously then honks at a taxi driver she's just cut up, as though her bad driving is his fault.

'All men are basically little boys at heart,' she continues, warming to her theme, 'searching for a replacement mummy.'

'You mean, they want someone who'll embarrass them in front of their friends?'

'Don't be cheeky, Annabelle, it doesn't suit you. You know, I really think you should come and stay with me. Nicky's a nice enough girl, but she was never a very good influence on you.'

Poor Nix, I wondered when it would be her turn. Despite her usual total innocence, every youthful misdemeanour of mine was blamed on her. It's nothing personal, my mother just couldn't bear the thought of having a child who wasn't perfect. If I failed an exam it was because Nicky distracted me; if I bunked off school it was her idea; if I got caught choking on a forbidden cigarette in the basement, Nicky got the fag out of the packet, lit it, and forced it into my protesting mouth.

In fact, nothing could be further from the truth. It's actually Nicky's down-to-earth attitude that's got me through the past twenty-five years. It was Nicky who swotted me into and dragged me through my uni course. She was the one who got me up, dressed and Alka-seltzered in time for my finals; who made sure we didn't starve on our mega-meagre student grants by thinking up six different variations of seasonal vegetable and baked bean casserole. It was Nicky who picked me up from Heathrow – although admittedly my mother probably would have done if she'd known I was flying back – and it was Nicky who, without being asked to, and without question, gave me a home now that I'm back in the country.

I don't know why my mother thinks living with her would actually be better for me. If she didn't nag me to death, I'd probably starve. Whenever I've been grocery shopping with her, all she ever seems to buy is a large bottle of gin, a bottle of tonic, and a cauliflower.

Mother moans about Nicky for the next half a mile until we reach Chelsea, where she abandons her car on double yellows in the Kings Road.

I've learnt to keep my mouth shut until she runs out of steam. Unfortunately it appears that today my mother has more steam than a constantly boiling kettle.

Once seated in a restaurant that's a bit too posh for a couple of filled baguettes and a bottle of Frascati, she continues the man theme.

'When you find a good one, you really should hang on to them. Trust me, I know what I'm talking about.'

This coming from the woman who never hangs on to a man for more than five minutes.

'You're not getting any younger, Annabelle.'

'I'm only just twenty-five, I'd hardly call that ancient!'

'In my day and age you were classified an old maid if you were still single at twenty-five.'

Yeah, and men still clubbed you over the head and dragged you back to their cave for a furtive fumble under your bear skin.

I know what she's building up to, I'm going to get the Simon lecture again.

Simon – the respectable ex. The man I had a brief, misguided, and now unmentionable fling with before I went away. The man who, for some unfathomable reason, my mother thinks is the epitome of male perfection.

Male perfection. Now there's an oxymoron for you.

This is another reason I went to Australia – to escape him!

I met him in the year after Nicky and I had moved down to London together where she was forging her way in her first job and I was bar tending in order to scrape together enough money for a pair of hiking boots, a backpack, and a return ticket to Bangkok. We were initially introduced by Nicky, a fact I only recently managed to forgive her for.

I think my mother fell in love with the man far more than I ever did. For some reason, the minute she met him she decided he was the one for me, and wasted an incredible amount of energy trying to marry us off.

'I honestly don't know why you gave up Simon . . .'

There it is, the dreaded S word.

I normally like being proven right, but the fact that I knew this was coming doesn't make up for the fact that I'm facing another ear bashing on the absolute absurdity of letting go of such a wonderful male specimen!

I don't know about how I could give him up – I honestly don't know why I ever went out with Simon in the first place.

He is eight years older than me.

When I first met him, he seemed so mature and responsible. I think the thing that I liked most about him was his confidence. He had a good job, nice apartment, expensive car, was well educated, and had what I thought was a grown-up attitude to life.

Everything I thought I should have and didn't.

I soon realised, though, that Simon was just a kid masquerading as a grown up. A big brat.

Spoilt, arrogant, demanding and incredibly immature.

'Such a charming young man,' my mother's still rattling on about Mr not-so-bloody-wonderful, 'I do think that you should get in touch now that you're back in the country.'

'I doubt very much he'd actually want me to,' I reply, smiling at the waiter who's just handed me a menu.

'Oh, I'm sure you're wrong,' she flashes her expensively capped teeth at me, 'he's still very fond of you.'

'He is? How would you know?'

'Oh, we've bumped into each other quite a few times in the past couple of years. He always asks after you . . . not that I've ever had much news to pass on, but at least he's made the effort . . .'

A double barb, that one, I'd forgotten how good she is at this.

'I do believe I've seen him in this restaurant on the odd occasion actually,' she continues.

I should have seen it coming: the posh restaurant, the table for four, the big build up . . . but I didn't think even my mother would be that conniving or that bloody obvious. Not so soon into lunch anyway.

But suddenly, as if on cue, a familiar figure is weaving its way towards us through the tables, and I'm attempting to slide under the table cloth to join the glass of wine I just dropped in shock.

He's put on weight. He was always big, quite muscular, sort of rugby player build, but the stomach has grown into what could definitely be described as a belly. And whilst the stomach has expanded, the hair has receded. The cropped blond curls are steadily creeping back at the temples to form a veritable widow's peak on his forehead. The pale blue eyes are underlined with a fine spider's web of new wrinkles.

It's been nearly two years since I last saw him, but it could be ten judged by his appearance. When I first started seeing him, he was thirty-one and I was into the idea of the older partner: confident, reassuring, established, a man not a boy.

Now he's creeping steadily towards middle age, he doesn't look handsomely mature, he looks old.

And now I'm older myself, I realise that instead of confident and reassuring, I should have read controlling and arrogant.

He gives off this impression of being the ultimate businessman when in reality he's still this big over-grown schoolboy who the minute he's left alone in the office is whipping out his willy and slapping it on the photocopier.

The fact that he would have to press the Enlarge button several times to get a decent shot has nothing to do with why I went off him, honest.

I don't know about my thespian tendencies, Mother's going for her own gong. She's out of her seat and moving into gush mode in seconds.

'Oh, my goodness, look who it is! It's Simon. Talk about the sexy little devil, we were just discussing you, weren't we, Annabelle darling? Were your ears burning, and here you are, in the too delicious flesh! Fancy bumping into you – what a lovely surprise!'

About as much of a surprise as a twigged rigged birthday party.

His acting is worse than my mother's.

Simon: 'Ahem (clears throat and looks nervous), I've just popped in for a spot of lunch.' (Said as though read from O-level English set piece in class in front of your sniggering mates and an over-enthusiastic teacher.)

Mother: 'Well, why don't you join us?' (Dawn French playing Baby Jane)

Simon: (completely wooden, now reading from shirt cuff) 'Oh, no, I couldn't possibly impose.'

Mother: (gesturing grandly) 'It's not an imposition, it would be our pleasure, do sit down.'

Simon: 'Well, if you're sure?' (all polite deference)

Mother: 'We'd love you to join us, wouldn't we, Annabelle darling?'

I'd rather have lunch with a swarm of angry bees and only one small honeycomb between the lot of us.

'Oh, I don't know, it would be really impolite to drag Simon away from his friends. He can't be lunching on his own, Mother.'

Gotcha!

They obviously hadn't thought of a plausible excuse as to why Simon would suddenly appear on his own in the very restaurant we're eating in.

Not good research.

My mother's slacking.

She's usually so thorough, but then again she didn't really have much time to throw this lunch together. I only called her last night. She must have been straight on the phone to you-know-who to organise an 'accidental' meeting.

Why expend so much effort?

She's obviously on a mission, time is ticking away and the daughter still isn't running according to schedule.

She's missed out on two years of manipulation, and wants to get me a man, a home and a career all in one lunch time.

The scary thing is, knowing my mother, she'd do it. With my cooperation. But who says I'm going to bloody cooperate? She's the one who thinks Simon's so wonderful, not me.

According to her, he's perfect son-in-law material. So focused and businesslike, able to hold a conversation about corporate affairs, world politics or the arts in three different languages.

Well, able to hold a conversation with my mother in all of the above anyway. I can swear quite profusely in French, and that's about it really, and what I know about corporate affairs would fit on the back of a postage stamp.

It's a lost cause. Even if I actually fancied the guy, which I don't, we're completely incompatible. I'd want to go out, get drunk and party till I dropped, and he'd be sitting in a corner with his coat on, ready to go home at ten o'clock.

He was the get home from work, cycle five miles, come back home, eat a healthy meal and go to bed at a reasonable hour so you could go to the gym before work next morning kind of guy.

I'm the, if I get back at all, crash out on the sofa with a pizza and a bottle of alcohol watching trash TV until the early hours, then stagger off to work with a raging hangover and five minutes to spare, kind of girl.

It took me five months to realise that Simon and I were the worst matched couple since Jekyll and Hyde.

I'm sure nearly everybody has that one relationship they look back on and think 'How could I?' or 'What on earth possessed me?'

Well, he's mine.

I mean, don't get me wrong, he's not a complete gargoyle or anything, he's just so . . . so . . . not me is, I think, the best and fairest way to describe it. He's like that dress you buy on impulse on a sale, no return basis, then really regret the fact that you wasted your money on it. It could look totally wonderful on somebody else, but is destined to spend its life span hidden at the back of your wardrobe because it makes you look like a badly stuffed bolster.

Despite an awkward moment, where a plausible excuse was hunted for agitatedly, like a lost coat at a house party, the 'Ill Fitting Impulse Buy' is now seated opposite me, tucking into a huge plate of rather garlicky lasagne.

Mother excuses herself and disappears toward the ladies, leaving Simon and me alone. There's an awkward silence while I pick out the prawns in my salad and refuse to look up. Very gauche, I agree, but I don't know what to say to him. 'Hi, Simon, you're looking very fat and old these days. Still as pompous as you used to be'?

I sneak a look sideways, when he's calling the waiter for more wine; scour the features, the body, trying to remember exactly what it was that could have attracted me to him in the first place.

Nothing.

Not the slightest thing.

It's scary really.

Was I so different then? Was I so lacking in judgement? Was I just desperate? No, I suppose that's not very fair, on Simon or myself for that matter.

I'm sure he's *someone's* Mr Wonderful. Despite the fact that he's my Mr How Could I?

He finds his voice first.

'You look well, Annabelle.'

'Thanks,' I reply, averting my face from a heavy blast of garlic breath.

'In fact, you look more than well. You look great.'

'Thanks.'

'It's really great to see you again.'

'Thanks.'

'Have you been back in the country long?'

'No.' Give myself a quick round of applause for new word.

'So, how was the Far East?' He shovels another fork laden with food into his wide mouth.

'Very warm.' Ooh, two words, almost a sentence. Annabelle Lewis, last of the red hot conversationalists.

Fortunately Simon can talk for England. He loves the sound of his own voice as much as I love a large bar of Dairy Milk.

'You know, I find it such a fascinating culture . . .' he begins. 'The Asian people are so disciplined, and so focused, yet their history is fiercely and passionately romantic . . .' And he's off.

A conversation with him is a bit like watching TV. Just press the right button to switch him on, then sit back and let him do all the talking. This used to infuriate me. I mean, it's hard for somebody as . . . er . . . *vocal* as me to sit back and shut up while somebody else gets all the time on the soapbox, but it's quite good at the moment because it means I don't have to struggle to find scintillating conversation. Not that I could actually come up with conversation Simon would find scintillating. We have about as much in common as a bag of peanuts and a soap scourer.

It doesn't help that my mother keeps disappearing to the loo every five minutes. She's either suddenly developed a severe bladder problem or she's very unsubtly leaving us on our own for her own perverted reasons.

The first time I've seen my mother in two years, and she's acting like Cilla spotting a potential hat-wearing opportunity.

When she finally returns to the table after what must be her fifth trip, during which pee break I spoke, oh, at least two syllables, and Simon's managed a monologue about the house white, worthy to be spoken of in the same light as the Ancient Mariner, I decide it's my turn to hide amidst the wash basins.

'Erm, I've just got to . . . you know . . . take a trip to the lav,' I announce as she slides back into her seat and smiles benevolently at us both, chirruping, 'Well, isn't this nice?' for the fourteenth time.

'Back in a mo'.'

Make that several mos. I need a break before the pulse that's pounding in my left temple finally explodes.

Mother's exerting more pressure than a whole ocean full of water on a small submarine. I'm determined not to crumple under the weight, though. I redo my make up, then thinking Simon might feel the freshly tarted look is in his honour, wipe it all back off again.

How long can I hide out in the loo without them thinking I'm constipated?

Who cares! So what if Simon thinks I've spent the past fifteen minutes breaking wind. You never know, it might help to put him off me, which would be wonderful. I can't believe after all this time, and after the way I sodded off without a backward glance, he's still even the slightest bit interested in me.

I'm certainly not interested in him.

And I'm certainly not interested in my mother's quick fix solution to my single status. I'm quite happy as I am, thank you. I have absolutely no desire to get shackled to another human being by a piece of paper and broken promises.

I thought being unable to commit was a male problem.

Maybe it's just circumstances, or maybe the only things I've ever had the opportunity to commit to put me off completely.

Like Simon.

When he finally seizes the moment during Mother's sixth trip to the loo to ask me to meet him for lunch the next day 'to catch up and get reacquainted', I politely decline, citing a previous engagement, but I'm not to escape so easily. By the time lunch has ended, Mother's invited us both to join a party attending the opera the following Friday, to spend two days at her house in Cornwall the first weekend in July, to lunch the same time next week, and to some launch party for a new peak-time TV show she's been involved in somehow.

I solemnly note all of the dates in the diary she just so happens to be able to give me as it's spare, sincere in my thanks for this gift only because I'll be able to make sure I'm out of the country, washing my hair, or in bed with a migraine or a hot lover on each occasion.

'Well, wasn't that a wonderful surprise, bumping into Simon like that?' Mother chirps happily, as lunch finally and thankfully ended, we drive back toward Nicky's place. It was neither wonderful nor a surprise but I think it's wise to keep quiet at the moment.

'So where's Simon taking you for lunch tomorrow?'

'He's not.'

'But I thought . . .' She just manages to stop herself, not actually having been present when he asked, and therefore theoretically not in a position to 'have thought' at all.

I know what she thought. She thought she'd got it all set up and sewn up. Or should that be, she thought she'd got *me* well and truly stitched up? Well, if there's one thing I have learnt in the past two years of travel, it's how to say no to a man and mean it.

'So now that you've finally deigned to come home, what exactly are you going to do with yourself?' she sniffs, moving on to a safer nagging subject.

'Oh, I don't know, I thought I might sign on and doss around, do a few drugs, go to raves, that sort of thing.'

My mother needs a humour implant, a bit like a skin graft or a blood transfusion. Rather than laughing at what is obviously a joke, she goes bright purple with outrage, tapping her perfectly manicured red nails against the steering wheel in agitation.

'All the money I wasted on your education! I don't know why I bothered. I always knew you'd never make anything of yourself,' she spits angrily.

'I know, you should have just sent me to the colonies to start off with. That way at least you'd have saved me the airfare. But then again, they stopped doing that to problem children nearly forty years ago, didn't they?'

Okay, maybe I'm being a bit childish, but so what if I'm not ready to play adults yet? Who said there was a time limit? The official coming of age may be eighteen and I'm well past that, but who cares? Who am I hurting? Why do I feel like I have to conform to other people's (Mother's) ideas of the correct procedure for life? Well, actually, strike that, I don't, not really, but other people (Mother) feel I should.

She's sitting next to me, lips pursed in a thin angry line.

A momentary urge to appease and make amends, a hangover from a childhood of walking on eggshells, is suddenly swamped by outrage that she's angry with me once again for not giving in and doing what she wants, rather than what I want. I can't believe that I'm in my mid-twenties, and my mother's still trying to run my life like she used to when I was in my mid-teens.

Why can't she just be happy that I'm home, alive and well, and let it rest at that?

We travel the rest of the way in silence, both refusing to cave in and break the frosty atmosphere by speaking first.

I finally give in when we reach Nicky's place.

'I'll call you,' I mutter, reaching across and pecking her on one stiff cheek.

'Oh, you do know how to use a telephone then?' she bites back. 'Only the number of times you *didn't* manage to call me in the past two years made me think you hadn't quite mastered that particular life skill.'

Refusing to rise, I get out of the car, and then changing my mind go back and tap on her window.

Still glaring, she unwinds it with a whirr of electrics.

'You know, you should be pleased with me, really,' I tell her. 'You see, after everything, I didn't let you down.'

'Well, I don't know how you worked that one out,' she sniffs.

'Because,' I smile sweetly, 'you always expected me

151

to be a disappointment to you, and that's exactly what I am.'

Annabelle Lewis' Uneventful Love Life to Date

Age 13:   Unrequited crush on Simon Le Bon. Much poster snogging, and dancing round sitting room to *Top of the Pops*.

Age 15:   Unrequited crush on Jamie's best friend Callum, resulting in first bitter taste of severe sexual invisibility to a member of the opposite sex, extreme embarrassment, and the teasing torment of an insensitive, testerone-filled teenager, who found my crush on him a constant source of amusement.

Age 18:   Reality bites with one-sided fling with older man on the rebound, resulting in soggy tissue syndrome – used then flushed.

Age 19–21: University – one long game of musical men. Fun, flirting, and furtive fumbling, but no further until reunited with Callum at graduation ball, whom I then proceed to hump and dump in revenge for two years of teenage torture.

Age 22:   Simon – say no more.

Age 23–24: Fun, flirting, friends and a big fat feeble zero for anything further.

Okay, so I'm not doing particularly well for myself so far in the sweep-me-off-my-feet romance stakes, but to be honest, who cares? I'm still not totally convinced I want to be swept off my feet. The term itself implies a total lack of control, and when you give up control, that's when you end up getting hurt. Look at Nicky.

And besides, what honestly are the odds on meeting somebody in your late-teens, early-twenties, who's going to be compatible enough to spend the rest of your life with when you change so much over these years?

It's like saying, I'm going to keep the same hair style for the rest of my life just because it happens to suit me at the moment. I mean, just imagine it. Anybody who was in their twenties in the seventies would still be walking round with Farrah Flicks, and as for the eighties . . . well, let's just say Madonna would have a lot to answer for!

My mother trying to fit me up with Simon is like she's still trying to force me into Laura Ashley when all I really want is to get my kicks with Karan, or maybe have a fling with Farhi, or go mad with Moschino.

I suppose what I'm trying to say is, I don't know what I do want, but I do know what I don't want, and that's going to have to be good enough for now, for my mother, and for me.

Nix is in the kitchen scraping a wooden spoon rather viciously around a mixing bowl and watching

Junior Masterchef on the portable TV.

'It comes to something when a twelve year old can knock up a perfect soufflé in half an hour, and I can't even make a Yorkshire pudding batter,' she moans.

'Let me take over. According to my mother I'm still a child, so perhaps I can do a better job.'

I take over with the bowl and spoon and proceed to give the creamy mixture a harder time than Nicky was. This is why it's called batter, you bash it to death whenever you're in a bad mood.

'Had a good time with Zsa Zsa then?' Nicky asks sarcastically, as I splatter batter all over the work top.

'Oh, absolutely wonderful,' I mutter, my mouth set in a grim line. 'According to my mother, at this stage in my life I should be married to a mogul, with two point five children, the social life of Tamara Beckwith, and a career to rival Richard Branson's. And the fact that I'm not means I'm a complete disaster as a human being.'

Nicky pours me a large glass from the litre bottle of wine she's been steadily drinking down to the sediment, and then sits at the dining table and starts to pop peas from their pods alternately into her mouth and a bowl.

'Lunch went well then?'

'Don't ask.'

'As bad as that.'

'Worse. She'd only set it up so that Simon accidentally on purpose bumped into us in the restaurant.'

'Simon . . .? You don't mean Simon Rafferty, do you?'

'Yep. The one and only big boorish blockhead. I nearly died of shock. I kept wanting to pinch myself to make sure I wasn't asleep and having a horrible dream. She's so unsubtle. I think it's all part of her devious ongoing scheme to turn me into a respectable, normal human being. Well, her idea of what that entails anyway, although why this seems to include Simon Rafferty is totally beyond me. I don't know why she's so determined he's the one for me.'

'But he's so eligible, my dear.' Nix does a pretty passable impression of my mother. 'He has a steady, respectable job, his own house in a nice area, good family, no skeletons, no diseases, an early release pension plan, he even irons his underpants . . .'

'Well, why didn't you say so? Book the caterers, I'll marry him tomorrow,' I snap grumpily.

'Does this mean you're in a bad mood then?'

'How can you tell?'

'Well, the fact that you've just murdered the Yorkshire pudding mix instead of a little light assault and batter-y is a bit of a giveaway.' She grins. 'I was kind of hoping you'd be in a good mood.' She leans over and tops up my glass.

I've only taken a couple of swigs.

If I didn't know better I'd think she was trying to loosen me up.

'Why, what have you done?' I ask, suddenly suspicious.

'Done?' Nicky purses her lips, eyes determinedly focused on the pea pod she's holding. 'Well, I've been thinking about your career.'

'Don't you mean, my lack of career? My complete and utter absence of career? My non-existent, never to be discovered career?'

Nicky grimaces, leans over the table and refills my wine glass to the very top again.

'Well, I might just have a solution for that,' she says when she sits back down at the table.

The fact that she still doesn't look at me when she says this is slightly disconcerting.

'Oh, yeah, you've heard that there are some counter staff vacancies at the local McDonald's then, have you?' I laugh half-heartedly.

'Er . . . not quite.'

'Nicky, what have you done?' I repeat, worried now.

'Who says I've done anything?' she replies cagily.

'Your face says you have. It's written all over you. I could always tell when you were up to something, even when we were little. You're normally so bloody angelic, the minute you do anything you even think might be just slightly out of order, you positively reek of guilt.'

'Well, okay, maybe I've had an idea . . .'

'An idea about what?' I prompt as she pauses again.

'Well, an idea about what you could do as a job. You did such a good job for me, you see, and there are so many other women out there going through the same thing. Lucy was more than happy to pay you for your time, and pay you well. If I could find you someone else to do it for, would you do it again?'

'What are you saying, Nicky?'

'I'm saying that you could do for other women what you did for me and Lucy . . . you know, follow cheating men, catch them out. So what do you think?' she asks, twisting an empty pea pod nervously.

'What do I think?' I stare at her incredulously. 'I think you've gone mad. My mother's just finished telling me what a bad influence you are on me. Maybe this time she's right!'

Nicky shrugs. 'Sure, I know it sounds totally loopy but I don't think it's actually as mad as it sounds.'

'You don't?' I ask her incredulously.

'Did you think it was mad to stop me from marrying a cheat and a liar?'

'Well, nooo . . . of course I didn't.'

'Think about it, Annabelle. You get a last-minute phone call cancelling a date. The excuse might sound plausible, but wouldn't it be wonderful if there were some way of actually knowing for sure if he's telling the truth?'

'What about trust Nicky?'

'Sure, in an ideal world, but as we both know,' her eyes cloud momentarily and a tiny sigh flutters out of her, 'this world is far from ideal. What if you're worried that your other half may succumb to temptation?'

'What? Have one Sarah Lee gâteau too many?'

'No.' Nicky laughs. 'He might go out with the lads, have a few drinks, meet an attractive girl, be offered it on a plate, and think, "Oh, what the hell? She'll never find out." Wouldn't you rather know if the guy you're risking your heart on is the right one, or *a* right one?'

'And how do you propose we differentiate?'

'We send *you* out to chat them up. You know, proposition them, see if they respond . . .'

'Well, they'll all remain totally faithful then, won't they? What makes you think men with the potential to be errant are going to find me so bloody irresistible?'

'You're a really attractive girl, Belle. Gordon went for you, didn't he? Okay, so maybe he's not a prime example, but like I said, if it's offered on a plate . . .'

'. . . then a slime bag wouldn't refuse?' I finish for her.

'Exactly. Or you could just do what you did with Richard. Follow them and find out what they get up to when they don't know they're being watched.'

'And you really think anybody would want to hire someone to do that?'

'I don't think, babe, I know.' Nicky breaks into a somewhat nervous grin. 'Lucy called round earlier.'

'Well, that's not an unusual occurrence, how is she this morning?'

'Great, but that wasn't what she wanted. There's this friend of hers, you see. She's having a few man problems and they thought you might be able to help . . . She'd be happy to pay for your time, like Lucy did.'

'Really?'

Nicky nods vigorously. 'Lucy said she's really keen on the idea. Not only that but there are a few more of her friends who've said they might be interested in using you as a sort of . . . what's the word . . . agent provocateur for seemingly untrustworthy boyfriends.'

'Well, this could certainly make a girl cynical.'

'I already am cynical, Richard saw to that.' Nix draws on a cigarette and manages to inhale and exhale a little smoke without choking.

'So what do you think?' she asks.

Do I really want to go through all of that again? I'm sure the Gordon escapade has already knocked a few years off my life. But what's the alternative?

I could attempt to get a normal job. Let's see now, what are my qualifications? I've got a degree, but that seems to be about as much use as an expired credit card. Besides, I've tried that and failed dismally so far.

'Isn't it a bit unethical?' I ask, as Nicky refills my wine glass once again.

'Why? It's just like quality testing a product or something. If you're going to invest a hell of a lot in something, you want to make sure that what you're getting is pretty good, don't you? I mean, if you're going to buy yourself a second hand car, for example, and face it, most men come with a good few miles on the clock, you want to make sure it's going to be totally reliable. You know, not slipping out of gear all the time with a totally loose clutch.'

'So, you're really saying what I'd be doing, *if* I agree to do it, is a bit like an MOT test for men?'

'Something like that, yeah. Basically you'd be a kind of mechanic, an emission tester, but for relationships instead of cars.'

'Well, I suppose I could meet this girl to discuss it . . .' I muse.

'Oh, good, I'm glad you said that,' Nicky squeezes my free hand, 'because she's coming round on Saturday morning.'

'You've already arranged it!'

'Yep.' She grins triumphantly at me.

'What made you so sure I'd do it?'

'Adventure, intrigue, exposing the bad apples?'

'Right up my street.'

'You're not a nine-to-five girl, Belle, and you hate it when other people tell you what to do.'

'You do all the time!'

'Yeah, but I've only got your best interests at heart. Besides, I'm so subtly charming about it . . .' she laughs, mobbing herself up.

I suppose it will be good work experience. I mean, look at what I've learnt so far, helping Nix and Lucy. How to flirt with men I find about as attractive as dried, dirt-encrusted chewing gum that was spat out by a tramp with halitosis, breaking and entering, lying through my teeth . . . All good grounding for a top management position in the City.

On Friday night Nicky forsakes an evening of rampant serial dating to spend a girlie night in, in front of the TV. I think this is partly because she's worn out from going out so much, and partly to make sure I don't do a runner before tomorrow morning's 'appointment'.

I've lost the toss and am just about to head off on a popcorn, chocolate, alcohol and take away run, whilst Nicky snuggles down on the sofa, when her mobile bursts into life with a micro-chip rendition of *Mission: Impossible*.

She rolls her eyes at me.

'I really wish you'd stop changing the tune all the time. I was in an important meeting the other day and it started ringing "The Stripper"!'

The smile falls from her face, however, when she reads the number on caller display. I only ever see her looking like that for one reason.

'Is it Richard?'

She nods, visibly ashen.

'Are you going to answer it?'

'I don't know if I want to.'

'Why not? I thought you were feeling stronger now?'

'I am, but it's eight o'clock on a Friday night, and I'm sitting at home in my dressing gown and fluffy slippers with a mug of cocoa with marshmallows in it.'

'Well, there's decadence for you,' I joke.

'I want him to think that life goes on without him, that I'm going to wild parties every night, and getting chatted up by gorgeous sexy men.'

'You normally are.'

'Yeah, but he doesn't know that, does he? He has to call the one time I decide to have a night off.'

'You make it sound like a job.'

'Call it a vocation,' she laughs bitterly.

'Well,' I grin at her, 'I might not be able to provide the gorgeous sexy men, but I think I can do something about the wild party bit.'

Whilst Nicky reluctantly takes the call, I head for the stereo and crank up Pete Tong to ear-splitting level. Then, getting as close to the receiver as possible, make Bird's Eye pea-popping noises with my finger in my mouth to stimulate champagne corks flying, bang Nicky's best crystal together in mock toasts, whilst jumping up and down on the squeakiest floor board and pealing with laughter every twenty seconds.

If the fake party noises haven't fooled him, the fact that Nicky's dissolving into fits of uncontrollable laughter at the sight of me has certainly disconcerted him.

I never thought she'd end a phone call with Richard wearing a smile, but it's amazing what your best friend making a total prat of herself can do to lighten even the most dismal situation.

'He wants to come round and collect some of his CDs,' she says, pressing the End button on the phone.

'You mean, we didn't barbecue everything? Tell him you'll have to consult your social diary.'

'Yeah, to make sure I'm out. I don't want to be here, Belle. I don't want to see him.'

'Well, I don't want to see him either ! Put them in a box and post it to him, preferably in lots of tiny pieces.'

I follow Nicky over to the side unit and watch as she begins to take Richard's CDs off the shelf.

'Blimey, it'd be a pleasure to pound some of these. Richard's got pretty suspect taste, hasn't he? Barry White, Lionel Ritchie . . . oh, don't tell me that's a Barry Manilow CD!'

'It's his seduction music.' Nicky sighs heavily. 'Probably found some other poor unsuspecting female to go through his briefs with him.'

'Well, at least you're not sniffing them any more.'

She laughs weakly.

'Just go out and get the pizza, Belle. I think I'm going to need some serious junk food, and *lots* of it.'

Half an hour later I return to Nicky's flat, bearing two large pizzas, a bucket of Ben & Jerry's, a slab of chocolate, and two bottles of Azure Bay.

As the lift door opens I can hear voices and raucous laughter coming from inside. Sounds like there's a bit of a party going on.

The TV's on, the stereo's blaring, voices are on full volume . . . in fact the music and laughter is so loud that the two people who make up this impromptu, if rather small, party don't hear me let myself into the flat.

Nicky is nose to nose on one of the squishy sofas with Jamie.

He's a miracle worker. She's thrown off the miserable face that was threatening earlier and is grinning like a maniac, a broad, beaming, toothy Nicky grin that usually only comes out at night after several glasses of something alcoholic.

He's lounging next to her in ripped jeans and a T-shirt that says 'Trainee Gynaecologist', hands waving madly like he's talking in sign language, as he relates whatever anecdote it is that's making Nicky laugh uproariously for the first time in aeons.

He greets me and the pizza with equal enthusiasm.

'Great, my favourite sis and my favourite food!' he cries, swooping down and relieving me of the warm greasy pizza boxes.

'Trust you to turn up at the slightest whiff of hot Mozzarella,' I joke. 'I'll just stick the ice cream in the fridge so it doesn't melt *too* much. Leave me at least *one* slice, okay?'

I head through into the kitchen, but pull up short as a vile smell assaults my nostrils. Thank god I stopped; two more short steps, and my feet would have made contact with something squidgy and extremely disgusting.

Gagging, I head back into the sitting room.

'There's a heap of stinking crap in the middle of the kitchen floor!'

'Oh,' Nicky replies with complete unconcern, 'that must be Elvis.'

'I know a lot of people have claimed to see Elvis in some pretty strange places, but you're the first ever to have claimed he was reincarnated as a heap of stinking crap in the middle of their kitchen floor.'

'No!' Nicky giggles. 'The heap of stinking stuff is a by-product of Elvis. The actual Elvis himself is asleep in my bedroom.'

Now I know she's cracking up.

'Okay, so Elvis is in your apartment. He crapped on the floorboards, then crashed out on your duvet?'

'Basically, yes.' Nix helps herself to another biscuit. 'But it'll be all right once I've got him house trained.'

Is that why Jamie's here, as a forerunner to the men in white coats?

I look at him and raise my eyebrows in a 'Help, she's gone round the bend' kind of fashion, but he merely starts to laugh as well.

They've *both* gone mad, either that or they've been drinking, but there aren't any incriminating bottles on the table, only the rapidly emptying biscuit tin, and two coffee mugs.

'I'll go and get him. He might not appreciate being woken up. I think he wore himself out trying to eat Jamie's feet, but you've got to see him, he's just *so* adorable!'

Nicky disappears into her bedroom then comes back out again, soppy smile on face, something small, fat and furry wriggling in her arms.

'Jamie gave him to me. Isn't he gorgeous?'

'What is it?'

'What do you mean, what is it? It's a dog, silly, isn't that obvious?'

It looks more like a baby seal with a quiff, a strange tuft of hair sticking up in the air then flopping over one huge chocolate brown eye. Hence the name, I suppose. It's chocolate brown all over. Chocolate-coloured fur, chocolate-coloured eyes. Good colour at least. Of indeterminate parentage. Huge wet nose. Floppy ears.

'Where on earth did you get that?'

'Bodger had a liaison with the pedigree Labrador next door.' Jamie reaches out and scratches the sleepy puppy on its nose.

Bodger is Jamie's father's mad mongrel, who's a

sort of Staffordshire crossed with heaven knows what. It's a bit like some mad local yokel getting off with Princess Anne.

And now we're supposed to live with the result.

'Son of Bodger . . .' I sigh. 'I hope you realise what you're letting yourself in for, Nicky?'

'Well, he's already found the fridge, peed on all the pot plants, and claimed my duvet.' Nicky sighs, but she's still smiling. 'And now I suppose I'd better start poop duty. I don't suppose he came with a free pair of rubber gloves, did he?'

The minute she's gone into the kitchen to tackle the terrible turd, I turn accusingly to Jamie.

'Why on earth did you have to give Nicky a dog?'

He scratches the side of his nose thoughtfully, a habit I think he's picked up from Med school, to make himself look more intellectual, as though he's considering his answer before he speaks.

'Well, I was worried about her, she's acting really out of character. Running around with lots of different men . . . that's not Nicky.'

'And you thought a dog would help?'

'She needs something to help her through, she's not coping as well as she makes out.'

'Couldn't you have just written out a prescription for some happy pills, something she can take for a few months till she feels better? Not have to live with and look out for, for the next fifteen years.'

'I can't believe you said that, Belle.'

'You know I didn't mean it about the pills, but a dog of all things, honestly.'

'She needs something to love.'

'She's got her friends.'

'Oh, yeah, and you're going to be there whenever she just needs a cuddle.'

'I'll try, yeah.'

'It's not the same, Belle.'

'Well, I'm not going to sit on her lap and lick her face whenever she's upset and crying her eyes out. But then again, I don't crap on the kitchen floor or eat the furniture either. I know you meant well, J, but she's got enough to cope with. Don't you realise how time-consuming dogs are?'

'Exactly. She'll hopefully spend too much time caring for him even to think about what that arsehole did to her. Trust me, Belly, it'll do her more good than harm.'

'Why is that whenever you ask me to trust you, my gut always tells me not to?'

Jamie ignores my comment and helps himself to another biscuit.

'She needs affection,' he mumbles through a mouthful of crumbs, 'and I think it's better she gets it in the form of Elvis than from a series of self-destructive, one-night stand-ins, where all she's trying to prove is that men still find her attractive.'

'I thought you were a GP, not a psychologist.'

'Well, tell me I'm wrong?'

'I can't.' I sit down next to him, and pinch the last piece of biscuit before he shoves it in his mouth. 'You're right, as usual. Although I don't know that a dog was the best prescription you could give her.'

'Well, if it doesn't work out, I'll take him back home to Dad's to terrorise step-mother number three, okay?'

'Fair enough. How is the old dragon?'

'Still breathing fire and eating virgins for breakfast.'

'Oh, she's mellowed then.'

At 10.30 the telephone rings again. Nicky and I stop fighting over the last spoonful of Cherry Garcia, and look at each other.

'You answer it.' Nicky pulls a face.

'No, it might be Simon.'

'Yeah, but it's more likely to be Richard again.'

'This is ridiculous! We're girls. We're supposed to hang over the telephone, not hide from it.'

'Well, why don't you answer it?' Nicky suggests. 'And if it's Simon, pretend to be me.'

'Well, why can't you do that in reverse?'

'Because Simon hasn't seen you for two years and it's a damn' sight less likely that he'd realise it was really you pretending to be me, whereas Richard would know for a fact that it was me pretending to be you.'

There's logic behind this one somewhere. It's *way* behind, but it's there. In the end we remember that we are living in the age of modern technology, and let the answer machine do the dirty work.

It's Lucy.

'Hi, Nix! Hi, Belle! It's Luce. Look, I'm at work. I've been called in for some Euro crisis that won't wait until Monday, and it looks like I'll be here for the duration which means Amanda's going to have to come and see you on her own tomorrow. I know I promised to be with her, smooth the way so to speak, but don't worry, babes, you'll love her, she's a riot. Speak to you soon! Byeee!'

A riot, eh? Great. Why do I have a feeling this means I should bring my own CS gas, water hose and unbreakable plastic shield?

Chapter Five

He leans in closer, eyes gazing into mine, full of tender yet burningly passionate emotion. He doesn't speak, gently running a caressing hand against my cheek, drawing my face toward his, lips parting softly as we move together full of ill-concealed longing. He's so close I can feel his warm breath gently fanning my face . . . it smells of Pedigree Chum. Hang on a mo! The sexily gorgeous Ben Affleck wouldn't have breath like stale rabbit and liver . . .

'Belle!'

He wouldn't shriek my name in a high-pitched girly voice either.

'Annabelle!'

It'd be low, seductive and sexy, a whispered verbal caress, like a warm steady finger trailing slowly and teasingly down your spine.

'Belle! Wake up!'

Ben disappears back into dream world, to be replaced by the horrible reality of Nicky bouncing up and down on the end of the bed, and Elvis balanced on my chest, whiskers gently tickling my chin, breathing hot dog breath into my face.

No! It's not fair. The first snog I've had in ages and it's gone. Yeah, I know it was only a dream, but even that's better than nothing!

'Nicky, I love you to bits, but bugger off, okay?' I grumble, attempting to wrestle the duvet from under Elvis's heavy little body and over my face. Perhaps if I go back to sleep quickly enough, Ben will still be waiting for me, lips puckered.

Elvis thinks I'm playing and, grabbing the duvet between his teeth, starts a tug of war.

'Sorry, babe, but you've got to get up. You've got your first customer coming round in half an hour.'

'I have?'

'Yep, Lucy's friend, so you'd better get up, get showered and get dressed.'

I finally manage to dislodge Elvis, and pulling the duvet up to my chin, stare grumpily back at my friend.

'So what is it this time? Faithless husband? Boyfriend who's got his own harem?'

'I'm not sure. Lucy said her friend would explain when she got here.'

'And who exactly is this mystery friend then?'

'Amanda Hartley-Davies,' Nicky replies. 'She sounds rather posh, so you'd better make yourself presentable.'

'Well, if you'd like to remove your dog,' I tell her, pointing at Elvis who's belly crawled back on to my part of the bed and is now snoring heavily across my legs, 'I'll get up and put my posh frock on.'

★　★　★

Amanda Hartley-Davies arrives twenty-five minutes late and doesn't apologise, which pisses me off because I could have stayed asleep long enough to have had that longed for lip lock with bonkable Ben after all.

When Nicky answers the door, Amanda double-barrelled-surname chucks her coat at her with the attitude of someone who's used to servants and strides into the centre of the room, looking about herself, assessing the flat and us with narrowed distrustful eyes, whilst I huddle in an early-morning grump on the sofa and gaze distrustfully back at her.

She has wild blonde hair, once expensively streaked but now neglected and going dark at the roots, a real sink plunger of a mouth, that would be remarkably sexy if it wasn't set in such a miserable expression, and navy blue eyes that are currently zig-zagged with a grid map of little red lines and shadowed purple-grey underneath, with great dark circles of kohl drawn shakily around their circumference.

She appears to come from the Nicky Foundation of misery eaters anonymous, her copious bosom straining out of a button-through Donna Karan top that is at least two sizes too small, the lower half of her body encased in ripped jeans, flesh pressing through the tears like partially cooked sausages splitting their skins.

She's wearing expensive brown cobra skin boots to match her expensive brown cobra skin handbag, and has the jittery air of someone living on a diet of nerves, tears and chewed fingernails.

We stand around looking awkwardly at each other for a moment until Nicky, still clutching the coat like a nervous housemaid, gestures for her to sit down. Amanda scrutinises the sofas, obviously decides that they're just about designer enough to merit the honour of accepting her incredibly plump backside, and sits.

'So,' says Nicky, as I simply continue to stare at this personification of attitude in wonder, 'Lucy said that you wanted some help? What can we do for you?'

Amanda looks at me carefully for a moment before answering.

'Basically Lucy told me what you did for her with regard to her soon-to-be-ex-husband, and suggested you may be able to help me out too. I need you to follow someone for me . . . God, that sounds ridiculous, doesn't it?' she rolls her eyes, and sighs heavily.

'Yes?' Nicky encourages.

'His name's Eddie . . . Eddie Farrar.'

She pulls an envelope out of her bag and places the photographs it contains on Nicky's coffee table.

'He owns a couple of clubs – one in Soho, Black Betty's. I don't know if you know it?'

Nicky nods. 'Been there a couple of times, but it hasn't been open that long, has it?'

'Well, it was Knight's before. Eddie bought it about six months ago. It's closed at the moment whilst he completely revamps the place, but it's due to reopen in a couple of weeks.'

I pull towards me a five by ten of a man leaning against a bar. Visions of a Peter Stringfellow lookalike are banished by the reality of several photographs of a rather attractive man.

He doesn't know his picture's being taken and is laughing uproariously, head thrown back, mouth stretched into a broad, kind of creased grin, to reveal strong white teeth, perfect except for the right eye tooth which is rather crooked in a strangely endearing way. He looks to be in his early-to mid-thirties, has short brown hair, a strong masculine face, and bright red eyes thanks to the camera flash.

In fact, he's really extremely attractive.

I can see Nicky's thinking the same thing. She's got that little sparkle in her eye that appears every few days or so when she spots yet another conquest in the making, and her lips are vacuuming into that kissy pout that always appears at the same time. Imagine someone who simply adores chocolate, spotting the most sticky, moist, fudgy piece of chocolate cake they've ever seen in their life, and that's the sort of face you'd get.

'Do you mind if I smoke?' Without waiting for an answer, Amanda pulls a packet of Marlboros from her bag and lights up, inhaling deeply as though it's cigarette smoke and not oxygen that her lungs depend on for life.

'How long have you been seeing each other?' I ask her.

'Well, it's not quite that straightforward. We're not. I mean, we did . . .' She draws to a halt and pulls on her cigarette again, brushing a lock of dry blonde hair out of her eyes.

'We saw each other for a while last year, nearly two months, then he . . .' She fiddles with her lighter. 'Then it ended.'

She offers no explanations as to why. I am therefore left to assume from her omission and her expression that it was his decision and not hers.

'So what do you want me to do?'

'I want to know if he's seeing someone else. That is what you do, isn't it?'

Yeah, but only if you were actually in a relationship recently. I can hardly say this to her face, though. I try and think of a more polite way of putting it.

'Is it really worth wasting your money? I mean, if it's already over . . .'

'I think so,' she replies coldly, looking straight at me.

Well, that's telling me.

I pick up another picture.

'Can I keep a couple of these?'

She nods, and takes another huge gulp of smoke. 'I've got copies.'

Yeah, I bet, in triplicate no doubt. Probably wallpapered her bedroom with them Andy Warhol-style.

My internal warning bell's starting to ring a rather loud wake up call.

Nicky was very good at persuading me to have a go at this mad scheme of hers, but this doesn't seem quite right. Do we have a touch of the old Bunny Boiler here? The manic ex who refuses to let go? Maybe I should introduce her to Simon.

Nicky, ever the diplomat, senses my unease, and switches on to hostess mode.

'Can I get you a drink?'

She stands up and starts to head towards the kitchen.

'Oh, yes, please.' Amanda rakes her blonde haystack out of her eyes again. 'A large G & T would be lovely. In fact, sod the T. Just fix me a large G.'

It's ten o'clock in the morning.

Nicky crosses her eyes at me, but nonetheless switches direction and heads for the drinks tray instead of the kettle.

'Look, er ... Amanda,' I start hesitantly as she sinks her nose into the large gin Nicky's just poured her, 'I really don't know if this is such a good idea.'

'But Lucy said that you'd agreed to do this for me?'

'I agreed to *talk* to you about it, and see if I could help, but I'm not so sure that I can. When I followed Gordon for Lucy and Richard for Nicky it was to find out if they were seeing someone else *as well as* them. What good will it do tailing somebody you split up with over six months ago?'

She looks angry for a moment, taking another huge gulp of gin, then in an unexpected volte face, her face crumples painfully.

'Well, I was ... I mean, I was hoping that maybe there was a chance we could get back together, but if I know he's seeing other people then it sort of stops me from hanging on indefinitely, doesn't it?'

She shrugs. 'Maybe it's a stupid idea but I just need to know. We were so happy, you see, I still can't quite believe it's over. I mean, one minute it's wedding bells. The next minute it's goodbye.' With difficulty she pulls a tissue from the pocket of her tighter than tight jeans and mops at her eyes which are suddenly brimming with tears.

'I'm sorry.' She visibly pulls herself together, blows her nose rather violently, and then shoves the disgusting tissue back in her pocket. 'Isn't it odd how it's sometimes so much easier to pour out your heart to strangers?'

The tender-hearted Nicky is instantly at her side, offering clean tissues and more gin, both of which are gratefully received in large quantities.

'I'm sorry.' Amanda trumpets into another man-size. 'God, this is so embarrassing. It's just, I really thought he was the one . . .'

They gaze over at me, both of them pleading with puppy eyes.

'So, do you think you'll be able to do it?' Amanda sniffs.

I have to be careful what I say in response to this.

'Trust me, I'm a pro' could be slightly misconstrued, and I hate to think what the consequences of a resounding 'No' would be.

'Of course we can,' Nicky replies, squeezing her shoulder. 'We just need you to give us as much information as you can, then Belle will get straight out there for you, don't you worry.'

As soon as Mad Manda's been ushered out of the door, I turn to Nicky and shake my head.

'I really don't know if I want to do this, Nick.'

'Someone's offering to pay her to tail a really tasty guy, and the girl says she's not interested!' Nicky jokes, rolling her eyes.

'It's not the guy, it's the potential client. She worries me.'

'I admit she seems a bit flaky.'

'A bit? That's like calling Glenn Close mildly obsessive. One minute it's wedding bells . . . Honestly! How long did she say they were seeing each other for – the odd date over six weeks? And when it peters out, dies of natural causes, she's goes completely to pieces like she's just split with a long-term lover?'

'How long does it take to fall in love?' Nicky shrugs. 'Sometimes it just swoops down and hits you, with absolutely no regard for expected time-scales.'

'I suppose, but it obviously wasn't a mutual avalanche.'

'Well, there's no harm in checking it out, is there? All you've got to do is find out if he's seeing someone else.'

'Yeah, and if he is, then what? She chucks herself off Tower Bridge, or worse still chucks him off instead, or even worse chucks us off. You know, the shoot the messenger mentality.'

'I'm sure nothing as drastic as that's going to happen. She was just a bit upset, Annabelle. She's obviously still madly in love with the guy. I mean, she must be or she wouldn't have come to us in the first place . . . please, Belle, I know what it's like.'

'That's not fair, Nix, that's emotional blackmail.'

'But she needs our help.'

Nicky the eternal bleeding heart gazes at me with bigger, cuter, puppy dog eyes than Elvis, who is currently framed in the kitchen doorway having a very vocal teeth and paw wrestling match with a pair of her old knickers.

'I don't know, Nicky . . .'

'At least give it a go. Give her say a couple of weeks and see how it works out. What possible harm could it do?'

Amanda is back the next morning antisocially early. In fact, she's so early I once more have to be dragged out from under the current love of my life – my duvet – complaining bitterly to Nicky about the sanctity of Sunday morning lie ins, and the audacity of those who dare to break that sanctity.

She's waiting for me, sitting on the sofa drinking black coffee, her curvy bits squeezed into something designer and far too tight, and chain smoking, a haze of cigarette smoke hanging around her head like her own personal cloud of doom.

She looks me up and down as I slop out of the bedroom in faded shorts, an old grey T-shirt and flip-flops, and collapse on the other sofa. It's the sort of look reserved for a bag lady attempting to assess the hallowed portals of Harvey Nicks. She obviously doesn't approve of my taste in fashion, which I must admit is more Red Cross than Red or Dead at the moment.

The poor little let down, love-sick, abandoned

puppy of yesterday has been kicked into touch. Amanda's in bossy school mistress mode today.

'Right. I've had a few ideas about what I want you to do. I think we should start by drawing up a timetable . . .'

'A timetable?'

Timetables. Hated from school years and unreliable bus routes.

'Yes, I think it's best that we stick to a schedule.'

Schedule. It gets worse.

'I thought I'd just got to follow him?' I interrupt.

'You have, but it's not quite as straightforward as that.'

'Why not?' I ask, thinking longingly of hot coffee and a large bowl of Cornflakes as my stomach erupts in a Vesuvius-type rumble.

She can't answer this one straight away, finally saying, 'He's a very busy man,' as though this explains it.

'And I think there should be set times that you report back to me . . .' she adds quickly, my obvious antagonism making her instantly defiant and defensive.

Did I say school mistress? Strike that and replace with Sergeant Major or Parole Officer.

I'd just about managed to quash my misgivings about the advisability of actually going through with this. Now they've resurfaced like a body in a lake in a Morse episode, all bloated, black and distended.

I can just see it now. I'm going to be stuck in Arnold the 'Orrible twenty-four hours a day, getting wrinkled and cellulitic, at the end of a constantly ringing telephone with no reprieve.

As I am learning that Amanda has what one could describe (if being polite) as a forceful personality, I either squash this one now or I'm in trouble.

My problem is I can sometimes find it a little bit hard to say no to people. Not to lairy men of course, I'm good at telling them where to go, but to requests and favours. I suppose it's some kind of perverse hangover from my childhood, believing that it's my duty to make others happy, to please and appease, in order to be loved or liked. It's mad, isn't it? Despite the fact that I'm not that keen on Amanda myself, I still want her to like me. The urge to be universally loved by all! Causes some major problems, I can tell you. Especially when it comes to doing things you don't want to do. The daft thing is you sometimes get more respect for standing your ground. Would Amanda respect me more if I said no? I don't think so.

I'm not quite sure what she does respect. Money, position and power probably – of which I have none except perhaps a little bit of power. Which I think I should wield now, for my own sake.

'Well,' I say as forcefully as possible, 'that's not how *I* want to do it. Give me two weeks to check him out and I'll report back to you at the end of that time.'

'But . . .'

'There's no point in its being any shorter. If he's as busy as you say he is, then he could spend an entire week working, and the day that I stop following him is the day he decides to take a break and go out on a date.'

Never having been able to wait for anything myself, I soften a little at the sight of her stricken expression. 'I'll call you in between to let you know how it's going. You know, liaise,' I offer.

Whilst I'm in a no messing mood, I veto her idea of somehow bugging his telephone, or placing a miniature camera in his house, a ban that is thankfully backed by an indignant Nicky, who agrees with me that this would be crossing the very fine line between investigation and intrusion.

Having said no to most of Amanda's ideas, I'm then sort of negotiated into a corner I'd really rather not be backed into. She's not quite recreating the vomit scene from *The Exorcist*, but I have a feeling that if I refuse her one more time, the steam coming out of her ears may turn into bolts of lightning aimed directly at me. Therefore, my first mission, should I choose to accept it, is to go to Eddie Farrar's house and hunt for evidence of other women. Not that I really have a choice left about whether I do it or not.

She hands over a key to his house that she somehow managed to procure and hang on to, and a note book containing the following details:

- His car make, model, and registration number (Porsche – posh)
- The name and address of his club in Soho, and the new place he's just bought down in Docklands, called Lazy Daisy's.

- His date of birth, middle name (which incidentally is Alexander), and his inside leg measurement (joke, but I wouldn't have been surprised)
- The name and address of his parents
- His bank details, including account number, type and branch
- His home phone number, his work mobile phone number, and his personal mobile phone number

I don't know what Amanda needs me for, she could go on *Mastermind* with her comprehensive knowledge of the life and times of Eddie Farrar. Surely such a minor fact as 'Is he seeing somebody else?' is something that's well within her own power to find out.

Eddie Farrar lives in a Victorian villa in Hampstead.

For the first time since I got back from Australia it stops raining. The sun even manages to struggle through the wispy grey cloud as I urge Arnold, more through force of will than power of engine, through the lunchtime traffic.

I park a couple of streets away, and as nonchalantly as possible make my way to his house and let myself in.

Does it class as breaking and entering when you actually have a key?

If it doesn't then it should because that feels like exactly what I'm doing. The door swings shut behind me, making me jump as the noise of the latch dropping echoes through the hallway.

Splinters of coloured light fall through the stained

glass panel in the door behind me, lighting on the deep polished wood of the floor boards, the beautifully carved balustrades and the absolutely disgusting red flock wallpaper. What a mixture, the elegant beauty of an original Victorian hallway tangled with seventies bad taste of the highest degree!

Who lives in a house like this?

To be said in your best Loyd Grossman impersonation voice.

I have this theory that if you want to get a feel for someone's personality, then you sod the decor and take a sneaky peek in their fridge.

I head down the hall to the door at the end and what I assume will be the kitchen. I'm wrong. It's a cupboard. A cleaning cupboard, housing one of those plastic boxes with a handle in the middle that's home to an amazing assortment of cleaning fluids, polishes, and dusters that are actually more pristine than my underwear. Taking pride of place, though, is a state-of-the-art hoover, sleek, shining, with more attachments than the most expensive vibrator in an Ann Summers catalogue. A Ferrari among hoovers, which would get more envious looks at red traffic lights than my car, which isn't difficult really considering you don't get many envious looks in a clapped out old Austin Allegro.

I try the next door and find myself in a rather tasty kitchen.

It takes me a while to locate the fridge. It's one of those kitchens where every appliance is hidden from view behind limed cupboard doors.

When I do finally locate a rather high tech Zannussi, I realise that it probably wasn't a good move. I could easily go from illegal entry to actual theft.

It's a bit like the fridge in Nicky's kitchen without the chocolate or any actual bits of food.

Mainly a repository for alcohol, instead of a cool place to store food. Wine, bottled beer, more wine, two bottles of Champagne, and a carton of grapefruit juice are the only contents.

I'd kill for a drink.

Oh, treacherous tastebuds!

It's definitely not the time or place to help myself to a cold one and kick back with my feet up, no matter how hard my mouth and stomach are trying to convince me. I tear myself reluctantly away from the chilled bottles of Sol that are calling temptingly to me and head back into the hallway.

This is definitely a man's house, if only for the fact that there isn't even a single sniff of chocolate in the place.

A door to my right takes me through into the drawing room. Originally two, it's been knocked through to make one immensely long room stretching from the front to the back of the entire house.

A pair of French doors with stained glass to match that in the front door lead out on to a patio area. Beyond that, down three steps, lies a long stretch of lawn cut into neat stripes, but with wildly overgrown borders packed with damp flowering lilac and old roses that look in desperate need of a bit of dead heading.

The room has little in the way of furniture. A sofa, a wide-screen TV, and an expensive state-of-the-art Bang and Olufsen stereo.

I like his taste in music; he's got all of the CDs I've ever wanted to buy but couldn't afford. Then again, his sound system must have cost more than the house. His taste in music seems to be pretty varied, from Meatloaf to Massive Attack, the Kinks to Kula Shaker, and even an old collection of Elvis LPs.

I used to love all the old Elvis films. I'd sit glued to the screen as a teenager, watching yet another set of re-runs.

Reminding myself that I'm not actually here to get to know Eddie, just to find out if he is with any other women, I move on, heading up the wide sweep of stairs to the first floor.

Ooh, luvverly. The bathroom is home to a whole parade of pale purple water nymphs floating ethereally across the tiles. White suite with huge corner bath, gold taps in the shape of fish spewing water from their mouths, and pale purple water nymphs. Delightful combination.

There are no tell-tale signs in the bathroom, no long hairs in the plug hole, no stray cosmetics lurking on the shelves or in the medicine cabinet, which is pretty empty except for a packet of soluble aspirin, a half-used bottle of cough mixture, a new packet of razor blades and some aftershave.

What did I expect – something as obvious as his and hers towels?

He wears Aqua Di Gio, which I've always rather

liked. I unscrew the lid and dab a couple of drops on my pulse points. Then, realising that what I'm doing is really tantamount to stealing, hastily screw the lid back on and shove the bottle guiltily back into the cabinet.

It's a remarkably clean house for a man. I know it's an unfair generalisation to say that men are usually pigs when it comes to domesticity. I'm sure there are certain males out there who are well aware of how to steer a vacuum cleaner, kick start a can of Mr Sheen and fire up an iron, but since when have you ever seen a solo male with a clean overflow on their bathroom sink? Yes, they may slop a Vim-covered cloth around the bowl on the odd occasion, but would they ever think to take that Vim-covered cloth and twiddle it in the little hole at the back? Come to think of it, would I?

Perhaps he's a neat freak. An uptight, tank top-wearing, duster-clutching, rubber-glove-passionate neat freak.

Perhaps that's why he gave Amanda the elbow so quickly. She strikes me as the sort of girl who'd be hanging her soggy knickers out to dry in his bathroom before you could say, 'Fancy coming in for a coffee?'

I head out of the bathroom in search of his bedroom which should hopefully give me a few more clues.

The room to the front of the house that I thought would be the master bedroom is actually totally empty.

A large room to the back, overlooking the garden rather than the street, is the only bedroom with any furniture in it. Therefore, this is obviously Eddie's bedroom. Either that or he sleeps on the floor and rents out part of the house to a schizophrenic upper-class brothel keeper.

The room has a mirrored ceiling, foot-deep cream shag-pile carpet and a mirrored ceiling.

How naff can you get? In contrast, however, the walls are painted a beautifully deep red, the linen is heavy, cream, clean and fresh, and the bed is a wonderfully intricate wrought-iron affair, the sort of thing that I'd choose if (a) I could afford a bed, and (b) I could afford a place to put it in.

This house is just a complete contradiction, some really tasteful things amidst hideous decor. Perhaps it goes with the contradictory personality that Amanda complained of so bitterly. The loves me, loves me not unpredictability of Eddie Farrar.

The bedroom is the same as the rest of the house: no photographs, no clothes, no girlie knickers nestled next to the underpants in his top drawer, no little designer numbers hanging in his wardrobe. But then again, that could be an indication of his own tastes rather than the taste of a possible girlfriend.

The bed's unmade, and there's one dent in the pillow where a head has lain solo the night before.

I pull open the top drawer of a chest of drawers and come face to face with about twenty pairs of neatly balled black socks, a heap of white handkerchiefs, and numerous pairs of assorted coloured pants.

I keep getting this manic urge to giggle which I suppose is highly inappropriate. It's a weird feeling. I'm in somebody else's home, going through their personal things. What is it that burglary victims say? They feel violated? I can understand why. The thought of somebody trawling through my bedroom without me having a chance to have a clear out first is really awful. Especially with *my* undies. Well, the few faded and greying objects in my top drawer that *used* to be underwear, several years and several continents ago. I mean, I haven't quite got to safety pin stage but they're not far off. You know the sort of thing: elastic hanging on to its stretch by the skin of its rubber teeth, lopsided bras that only have the underwire still intact in one cup. The sort of stuff that would cause you to die of total embarrassment if it ever got a more public airing, but is still considered wearable enough to be slung on most mornings for lack of more pleasing alternatives – or, in other words, when you haven't had a chance to wash the three pairs that are still the colour they were born. You know, the ones that are normally kept for those days when you have a hot date or a doctor's appointment. I realise I should probably chuck out my old faithfuls and invest in something that doesn't look like a recycled dishcloth, but just because they got tie dyed with a stray blue sock in the wash one day doesn't mean they're not still a pair of perfectly wearable knickers.

It's not as if I'm going to go out and get run over by a bus or anything. Anyway the last thing you're going to worry about if you're half flattened by a number

15 is whether you've got your whitest Marks &
Sparks on. Well, your tibia's broken, your kidneys are
squashed and your lungs are flatter than a pancake
on Shrove Tuesday, but that doesn't matter because
your underwear's completely pristine!

Eddie Farrar wouldn't have a problem, though.
There's not a hole or sad saggy bit of material in sight.
Neither is there anything in his underwear drawer, or
indeed entire bedroom, that would indicate the presence of a woman in his life.

The only thing I can really determine is that Eddie
Farrar is a neat freak who has flock wallpaper in his
hall and mirrors on his bedroom ceiling.

With this evidence alone, I can probably convince
Amanda she's better off without him. Then again,
she's probably already acquainted with the hygiene of
his bathroom, the state of his undies, and the view
from his duvet, and she's still panting for more. He
must have some redeeming qualities. Either that, or
she actually *is* a complete and utter raving lunatic as I
suspected.

A Ralph Lauren shirt is thrown over the Queen
Anne chair in the corner. I pick it up and inspect the
collar for traces of lipstick, then hold the white linen
against my face, breathing in deeply in search of any
lingering scents.

The shirt smells of faded aftershave and a pretty
heady smell of clean warm male skin. God, he smells
good.

I take another deep breath, amazed and somewhat ashamed at how pleasurable I'm finding it

sniffing a man's abandoned shirt, when I'm pulled rather viciously out of nostril heaven by a noise from downstairs.

It's the sound of a key in the front door lock.

You know the phrase 'Time stood still'? I stop breathing, blinking, thinking. I swear my heart stops beating for a moment. You see, the reason for the immaculate plug hole, is that he has a cleaner.

I slide behind the bedroom door and listen as she pulls open the door to the cupboard in the hallway and wheels out the hoover. I can hear its little wheels squeaking across the floorboards as she heads for the living room, and then the sound of her footsteps as she goes back to the cupboard and pulls out the box full of cleaning materials.

What the hell am I going to do?

Any minute now she could come up those stairs and find me standing in a puddle of my own making, with my heart in my tatty trainers and no reasonable excuse for what the hell it is I'm doing in this man's house. What am I going to do? I suppose I could always do a speed strip, hurl myself into his bed, and pretend I'm a leftover from last night.

Fortunately I'm saved by the Ferrari of hoovers.

Singing 'If you wanna be my lover,' in a quavering falsetto, she plugs in and begins to attack the rug in the sitting room. I take advantage of the din to slide open the sash window in the bedroom and haul my arse out of there.

What was it I said about drain pipes? 'Never again' springs to mind. Yet here I am, second floor this time, hanging off yet another one.

I manage to make it to the ground without the aid of gravity this time, and sprint away from the house like a greyhound out of the traps.

Who needs adrenaline sports? You want to get a blood rush, get caught rifling through someone's house. My heart's making up for the fact that it stopped completely a few moments ago and is now beating in double time, double volume, like the bass on some totally grooving garage track.

I reach the safety of the end of the garden and lean back against the cool lichen-covered stone of the garden wall, hidden in the long shadows of the afternoon and the wild foliage of some shaggy plant that's scaling the wall with boa constrictor-like tenacity, and exhale all of the breath I've been holding for the past few minutes.

Boy, that was close.

I've never been so scared in my life, not even when Gordon whipped off his underpants and catapulted himself across the bedroom towards me, dick a foot in front of him like a fearsome flying French stick.

I'm trembling like a chastised whippet, my legs feel like jelly, and my skin is prickling with damp heat, despite the fact that I feel ice cold.

I start to wipe the perspiration from my forehead, then realise with a start that what I'm actually using to mop my fevered furrowed brow, clutched between claw-like fingers, frozen with fear, is a pair of pale green underpants.

What sort of man wears this sort of underwear?

They're not Y-fronts, they're not baggy boxers, they're not horrid little men's mini-briefs either. You know, the disgusting little shiny pouch-type things some sad gits insist on sporting; they're just basic cotton pants, kind of soft to the touch, and smelling somewhat pleasantly of washing powder.

Perhaps I should put them on my bedroom wall like a trophy, tack them on to a plaque and hang them above my bed.

I end up hanging them over the metal corner pole of my wrought-iron bed frame at a rather jaunty angle, like a pirate displaying the flag of a stolen ship.

I kind of like the image of myself as a pirate, a bit of a Robin Hood for women's emotions. It's far better than the thought of myself as someone who's just violated another person's privacy in the name of sisters doing it for themselves.

No, I am not a sleazy snoop.

I am a freedom fighter.

A furtive faithfulness facilitator for forward-thinking females.

A piratical pale green pant plunderer.

I spend the next two weeks following Eddie Farrar like a spare shadow. I think poor old Arnold adds at least another couple of thousand miles to an engine that's already gone round the clock once with extreme reluctance, and is now threatening to die a spectacular death if I force it to attempt to follow Eddie's madly speeding Porsche on yet another circuit of the M25. To be honest, although I start off following Eddie, I usually end up losing him, but I've worked out now that if he accelerates away from me he can usually be found in one of three places: Black Betty's, Lazy Daisy's, or if it's an ungodly hour of the morning when even Dracula is thinking about winging it back to his coffin, at home in bed, alone.

He hasn't got time for a relationship. The man's a workaholic. The fact that his job entails hanging out in bars a lot must make it easier to put in the hours that he does, but he still spends more time working than Nicky does eating and dating.

I reluctantly decide that it's time to pass on this information to Amanda, and put in the phone call she's been waiting for and I've been dreading, asking her to come round for the final verdict.

Mad Manda, as Jamie has now christened her, flies in on her broomstick at a speed to rival Concorde.

She has obviously been busy since last we met.

She's had her roots done, and her split ends chopped, and now has snaking blonde curls falling over her shoulders.

She's also been working out since I last saw her, having squeezed a slightly smaller bum into a pair of tight leather trousers that along with a matching jacket make her look a little sub dom and slightly more scary than usual.

She's still chain smoking, puffing away like a coked up steam train, her navy blue eyes screwed up against the smoke, and casting covetous sideways glances at

Nicky, who's currently munching her way through a whole tube of Pringles dipped in Philadelphia cheese.

Fortunately, or unfortunately, whichever way you look at it, she has things of far more interest than tastebud heaven in a tube, and wiping the drool off her double chin fixes me with aforementioned blue eyes whilst I give her a run down of the past two weeks.

'Well!' she demands, fixing me with a stare.

'Nothing,' I reply bluntly.

'You mean, he's not . . .'

'No sign of any other women whatsoever in the past couple of weeks. Well, I mean there are a lot of girls at the club . . .'

The blue eyes narrow.

'He obviously talks to a lot of people, a lot of people talk to him . . .'

She looks like a cobra about to strike.

'But nobody close. I mean, there's no sign of anybody on the girlfriend front. Not so far anyway. He's been home alone every night. I've been following him round like a pet poodle for the past two weeks and all he seems to do is work. I usually follow him into the club between eight and nine in the morning, and he hardly ever gets home before two the next, and he's been alone every time. He must be knackered. I bloody am.'

I laugh weakly, but Amanda doesn't join in, although she's actually verging on a smile. I even manage to smile back myself at the thought of my final cheque – emphasis on the final as in no more working for Miss Mad.

Amanda pulls out a wad of money from the Gucci wallet in her Gucci handbag and laboriously counts out the amount we agreed as a fee, but instead of handing it to me, holds it a few feet away, like a child waving a carrot in front of a pissed off beach donkey in the hope that it'll suddenly develop more enthusiasm for a quick canter than Red Rum entering the final furlong of the Grand National.

'Before we call it a day,' the smile is suddenly saccharine sweet and scary, 'there's just one more thing I want you to do.'

An early night and a long lie in.

Bliss!

I lie in bed, snuggled under the duvet, watching cartoons on Nicky's old portable, until my stomach starts begging me for a huge bowl of Cornflakes, some toast and Marmite, and maybe a nice bar of chocolate to round it all off, with the excuse that after all the running around I've been doing lately, I need the sugar to replace lost energy. Stumbling out of bed, I pull on my robe and stagger sleepily out to the kitchen with the intention of gathering supplies and returning to the comforting bosom of my beloved duvet.

Nicky's at the counter, back to me, metal clattering melodically against china as she spoons coffee into mugs.

At least, I think it's Nicky.

I winch my eyes open another couple of millimetres and take a closer look.

It's Nicky's dressing gown but it's definitely not Nicky wearing it, not unless she's gone in for an overnight sex change to include broad shoulders, thick hairy legs, and a crew cut.

The kettle boils to a steamy crescendo.

The *thing* in Nicky's night wear slops hot water into the mugs with one hand whilst scratching its arse with the other, then clutching both mugs in one big hand, shuffles out of the kitchen, registering me with bloodshot eyes and a gruff 'Morning', floating into my face on a blast of sour whisky breath.

I watch it slouch into Nicky's bedroom in disbelieving distaste.

Elvis, whose nose is also decidedly out of joint, looks disdainfully after the retreating figure and chooses to bunk in with me instead, the two of us sitting morosely side by side under my duvet, grumbling and fighting over the last slice of toast while Nicky's bed springs start their own squeaking impression of a speeding metronome as she and the latest take-away bonk boil to a rather steamy crescendo of their own.

I've decided that Elvis is kind of cute, it's nice to have someone other than Nicky and Jamie who's always ecstatically pleased to see me.

At least he's cute until he decides to eat my only decent pair of shoes, refuses to go to sleep unless it's on my only hole-free jumper, and insists on sharing every piece of food I attempt to eat.

And as he grows – daily and rapidly – eat, sleep,

cuddle, crap, moves on to eat, sleep, cuddle, crap, steal and vandalise.

The dog's a hooligan. And what's worse is that Jamie was wrong. Sure Nicky's late nights and numerous dates start to slow, the phone isn't constantly jammed with male admirers offering invites, and the queue at the door finishes at the elevator instead of in the foyer, but she's still gone out with more men in the past few weeks than Zsa Zsa Gabor and Elizabeth Taylor on a roll.

Okay, so I'm exaggerating her conquests a little. But only a little. She hasn't quite got to the spare robe stage like my mother, but recently I have found quite a few strange men wandering round the kitchen dressed in Nicky's robe and clutching coffee mugs.

One wonders where a woman would find so many eligible men. Well, that's just the thing. They're not actually *all* what I'd class as eligible. It's amazing how many men you can actually have in your life when you totally lower your standards. I'm not being condescending here, I'm being honest. Everybody will admit to having a 'type'. Typically that 'type' is the specimen of maledom that you feel fits within your parameters of need or desire. For example, my list reads:

(1) Sense of humour (that's compatible with my own)
(2) Enough brain cells to hold a more than decent conversation
(3) Financially independent (this has to work both ways)

(4) Not too tall (for some reason I really don't find
     tall men attractive)
(5) Broad chest and strong arms (excuse me, I'm
     starting to drool)
(6) Truthful, but naughty
(7) Attentive, yet independent
(8) Should conform to my definition of attractive
     (beauty is very much in the eye of the beholder)
(9) Bum you can bounce a pound coin off
(10) Mentally, physically and emotionally faithful.

Not asking for much, am I?

Typically, each man won't conform to all the standards on your list (number ten is nigh on impossible). Lose one or two, and they still stand a chance.

At the moment Nicky seems to have scrapped her list entirely and settled on one single requirement. Is it male? Yes, I'll date it.

Although Jamie's plan hasn't quite worked as hoped, there is a plus side. With the sudden appearance of Elvis in Nicky's life, potential dates now have to fulfil a new requirement.

Does Elvis like them?

As he is one of those non-discriminating dogs who bloody loves absolutely everybody on this entire planet, from mass murderers to traffic wardens, this isn't a hard test to pass. Fortunately, however, I soon realise that this also has to work in reverse.

Do the potential dates like Elvis?

So far he has managed to fart loudly and repeatedly on one young hopeful, throw up over the suede shoes of another, crap in the car of a third, eat the fourth's season ticket to Arsenal, and pee discreetly yet profusely all over the Armani'd trouser leg of the last potential suitor.

Wait till he's old enough to start humping legs and the dross'll be dissed in no time.

Chapter Six

Amanda's got tickets for the grand re-opening of Black Betty's, the first in the line of Eddie the Entrepreneur's clubs to be completed ready to be relaunched and hopefully welcomed back with open rave-waving arms on to the hectic London club scene.

Amanda's logic has told her that if he's seeing somebody then, this being the occasion that it is, he's bound to invite this 'her', if she exists, to the opening party. Therefore I am to be dispatched once again, on a watch, listen and learn, photograph, and if necessary 'kill the interloper' mission.

For the second time in far too short a period, I'm poured kicking and screaming into Lucy's 'let's go out looking like we're naked' dress, which she very magnanimously donated to my poor deprived wardrobe. I also have a choice of wearing the same cheese cutter underwear, or letting my butt swing naked in the wind. I go for the second option. I'd rather suffer a slight draft than have my poor old privates suffer the return of the killer knickers.

Jamie's roped in as my escort for the evening, but

having lurked self-consciously in the doorway of the art gallery opposite the club where we agreed to meet for over half an hour, there's still no sign of him.

Bloody Jamie! I'm going to have to do it on my own again. It's a good job I'm not shy and retiring. Then again, if I were shy and retiring I'd be stuck in some back office in a tower block, shredding confidential paperwork for a living, instead of chasing round London after a gorgeous guy on behalf of someone with more trust fund than sense.

Looking far more confident than I feel, I stride over to the opposite side of the road, and the double front doors of Black Betty's, which are flanked by two of the hugest bouncers I've ever seen in my life.

The queue's longer than one outside the only loo at a raging house party, but I'm damned if I'm going to stand outside in nothing but skin, chiffon and body glitter for a moment longer. I head straight past the shivering crowd toward the door, waving Amanda's doctored invite, and to my relief and surprise get shown straight through by the huge bouncer, who obviously appreciates the fact that I'm now so cold my nipples are like two ramrod-stiff sentries saluting a friendly greeting in my skimpy dress.

There's a kicking party going on inside Black Betty's. Despite the fact that it's ticket only, the place is packed to the gills, voices and laughter barely heard above the pulsating throbbing beat of Greece 2000 – Three Drives.

Betty's is basically one huge, high, blacked out room packed with bodies, lit only by strobing lights flickering in time to the music across a heaving dancing crowd, dry ice weaving through their legs like sea mist. There must be at least three hundred people in here. How the hell am I going to find Eddie Farrar, a man I've only ever seen in photographs or from a distance through a fogged up windscreen, amongst this lot? I could spend the entire evening following him round and round like the second hand chasing the first on a clock and never quite catching up.

Nicky would love it here, though. If she hadn't been out on yet another date I could have dragged her down with me instead of my missing step-brother. There are enough men in here to fill her date diary for the next twelve months.

And they all seem to be single and desperate.

On my first full circuit of the room, despite not having any luck in the Eddie department, I end up with eight propositions, five free drinks, and a small string of the more persistent admirers tailing me like baby ducks scuttling after mummy.

I feel like Benny Hill in the closing scenes of a Saturday night special, with a troop of men in a straggling line chasing me full circuit round the night-club, the usual mating cry of 'Can I buy you a drink?' echoing in my ears at regular intervals.

Lucy's sparkly pink designer offering is doing its stuff again. It's amazing what a tight dress and a plunging suntanned cleavage can do for a girl, especially in a dark room full of drunk men.

I come to a halt by the DJ's station, which I'm sure I've passed more than once, and try and get my bearings.

A manic DJ with headphones like huge black ear muffs rammed over his dreadlocks is behind the mixer desk, sliding knobs, rotating records, and dancing harder to the music than any of the crowd. I wonder if he takes requests like 'Could you tell me where the hell to find this man?'

I could whip a picture of Eddie out of my bag and wave it at my little following like an undercover cop, but I think that's a bit obvious.

The DJ moves down a gear from hard-core rave and throws on a club version of 'Staying Alive'.

The cries of 'Do you want a drink?' have now changed to 'Do you want to dance?' I can either stand like a lemon in the corner, clutching the drink that the last hopeful thrust at me and looking lost, or I can appease my itching feet and get out on that dance floor and boogy. Lose myself in the gloriously friendly anonymity of disco. Join an instant club of people prepared to look like total prats in the name of fun!

Hell, they always say that once you stop looking for something you usually find it, and it's ages since I let my hair down and enjoyed myself – even if it is to some upbeat Bee Gees.

I lead my little posse of poseurs out into a wild and wacky hand-waving, finger-thrusting version of seventies flary disco at its worst.

Side slide, back shuffle, side slide, back shuffle.

John Travolta eat your heart out.

Give me a black shirt, white suit and sideburns, and stick me on celluloid! I even start shouting WOO! every time I thrust a finger skyward, until the feeling of eyes burning into me with startling directness produces a rare feeling of self-consciousness.

I know a few people are watching me – and probably having a bloody good laugh – but this is a vaguely familiar face.

It takes me a few moments to place it, however, but when I do I think I blush for probably the first time in my entire life.

Eddie Farrar in the flesh.

Instantly recognisable and sitting only about twenty feet away.

He's watching me, a slightly amused smile on his face.

I feel myself colour up the same raspberry as my lipstick.

Great. I decide to act like a prat and enjoy it and get caught pointy finger-handed doing it by the one man I'm supposed to be invisible to.

I do a few funky shuffles and manage to manoeuvre behind my group of elbow-flapping gleeful drunks and hide until the club music comes back on, when I forget that I'm supposed to be hiding and slide delightedly into some Moby.

I love to dance. I love the total free-fall freedom of losing your mind and body in music. Like throwing yourself off the edge of a cliff and being caught by the wind. Completely swept away on the beat, natural adrenaline pumping through your body. Totally oblivious to everybody around me.

And, hell, it's great for your thighs. Sod aerobics, just hit a nightclub twice a week, have a ball and tone up your wobbly bits at the same time. Who needs a gym? I always sweat off about four pounds every time I go clubbing. Okay, so some of it's probably down to dehydration, but I can dream until I've had my first cup of tea in the morning, can't I?

Besides I can probably manage to bump off some of the unwanted male attention with my wildly thrusting hips. BOOM to the left and the creepy guy with ginger hair who thrust the first Bud bottle on me on my Eddie-hunting circuit round the club is propelled into the cleavage of another clubber. BOOM to the right, and the balding totally pissed prat who insisted I make his day by accepting a large G & T is set on course straight into the gents urinals.

Okay, so I'm fantasising.

Bumping myself back into reality, I take another sneaky sideways look at Amanda's ultimate fantasy.

About five ten, broad-shouldered, short brown hair shot through very lightly with a sprinkling of pepper and salt grey, which makes his roguish face look slightly more distinguished than I'm sure it normally would. I'd say he's in his mid-thirties. His photographs didn't do him justice. Sure they capture the look, but they don't capture the air.

Self-made. Self-confident.

He's in a group, but slightly set apart by something more than geography. There are about fourteen people in his party. They all look very businesslike as though they've come here straight from work, mainly men in suits, drinking heavily, laughing loudly, leering lots, as drunk men out in packs are wont to do.

He's sitting slightly apart from the main group, talking with an Italian-looking guy, whose suit is as beautifully cut as his cheekbones, and a girl.

The girl's extremely pretty: long tumbling brown hair, as glossy as a freshly shelled horse chestnut, full Chanel-stained lips, and the sort of fresh creamy complexion that doesn't need foundation. Slim, toned, taut and elegant in a neat cream on the knee skirt, a pale blue cashmere twin set, and the most covetable pair of suede kitten heel mules, that hold just the right balance between work and wow. Completely different from Amanda who's about as understated as a Vivienne Westwood bustier.

The Italian guy on the other side of her is really rather gorgeous on closer inspection. Lucky girl. She's a gorgeous guy sandwich, and from the smile on her face she's enjoying every moment of it.

Could this be the dreaded 'her'? The previously faceless woman that has Amanda spitting with indignant raging jealousy at the merest hint of the tiniest whiff of just her essence?

I cast another surreptitious glance back in Eddie Farrar's direction, and find myself once again in direct eye contact.

He smiles at me.

Not a cheesy, come on smile, but the sort of half-friendly grin you throw at people you think you know from somewhere, but whose name totally escapes you. I can either pretend I haven't noticed him and slide back behind my posse, or smile back.

I can't help myself. I smile back.

You know when you do something that feels right at the time, then as soon as it's done, you know it was the wrong choice?

Well, that smile was the wrong choice.

Totally wrong choice.

He leans in, says something to the Italian, then gets up and heads across the dance floor.

He's coming over! What the hell do I do now? It's too late to grab my bag and dive for the exit. I could pretend that I don't understand English, but knowing my luck, I'd jabber something incoherent in my useless schoolgirl French, and he'd be totally fluent. I am so CRAP at this job!

Totally foxed, I rapid reverse off the dance floor and push my way through into the anonymous midst of the crowd milling three deep at the bar.

I think I've lost him.

Using mild yet subtle elbow violence, I manage to capture a lone bar stool, and catch the eye of the lean muscular black bar man covering my area.

'Bud, please.'

'Make that two.'

I obviously didn't make as clean a getaway as I first thought. I feel the soft warmth of a cashmere-covered thigh sliding up against mine as Eddie Farrar squeezes in next to me at the bar.

'Hi.'

He's smiling at me again.

He's got a really sexy smile.

This isn't fair.

His mouth sort of curves up more at one corner than

210

it does at the other, eyes are creased, tired, yet friendly and bright. Intelligent. Measuring and assessing.

The bar man puts two cold bottles on the wooden counter in front of us.

'Put those on my tab, thanks, Andy.'

I grab the retreating bar man's arm and thrust my crumpled twenty into his hand.

'No, put those on my tab, thanks, Andy.'

The bar man grins broadly at me, perfect white teeth almost luminescent in the strange strobing smoky light.

'Sure, lady, anything you say.'

Well, that was really clever, Belle. Be rude to the guy, why don't you?

Great start. Not that there should have been a start at all. I should be watching the guy, not socialising with him.

Well, I've tried hiding and that didn't work.

I draw myself up, mentally and physically, and turn to meet his gaze. He doesn't look at all peeved that I just snubbed his offer to buy my drink. In fact, his smile's broadened.

He takes his bottle of Bud from the counter, and raises it to me.

'Well, you're the first person to buy *me* a drink all night. Cheers.'

'You must've been sitting with the wrong crowd – I've had more offers than an undiscovered Renoir on auction at Sotheby's. Then again, you're not wearing a dress that has less material than a child's self-assembly kite, are you?'

SARAH HARVEY

He coughs up a little of the Bud he just tried to swallow.

'No, I'm not, am I?'

At least he looks amused instead of bemused.

Annabelle Lewis, Life Skill Number 1: Ability to say totally stupid things at totally inappropriate moments.

He breaks the awkward pause that follows, whilst I assess whether or not my brain actually has more gears than Arnold, by introducing himself.

'Eddie Farrar.' He holds out a hand, which I tentatively take. 'We know each other don't we?'

Well, I know him. All *about* him anyway, from Amanda's Encyclopaedia of Eddie, but how does he think he knows me? I suppose this could be something to do with the fact that I've been following him round for the past two weeks. I'm obviously not as subtle as I thought I was.

What do I say? Yes, I'm the one you see in your rear-view mirror every waking moment?

'I don't think so.'

'It's just you look so familiar, and then I saw you looking over and I thought perhaps . . .'

'I'm sorry, I didn't mean to stare, it's just that you look sort of familiar too.'

Quick thinking, Annabelle. Bit corny, but definitely not bad under pressure.

'So we might just know each other after all?' he asks.

I shake my head.

'I don't think so, you probably just remind me of someone.'

212

'I do? Who's that then?'

My next lover.

Oh, shit, did I really just think that?

Thank god I didn't say it! Apart from the fact it would have been one of the naffest chat up lines of the century, I can't believe I actually just thought that.

Well, yes, I can believe I just thought that, actually.

I'm sorry but you'd have to be blind, drunk or stupid not to realise how bloody attractive this man is.

No wonder Amanda's planning a seduction campaign with the calculating precision of a high-ranking SAS officer.

He's still waiting for a reply.

I stop myself staring inanely at him like he's a big bar of chocolate and I'm hungry, and smile in what I hope is an enigmatic fashion. Hey, it worked for the Mona Lisa and she wasn't exactly an oil painting, now was she? Pardon the pun. Take away the smile, give her a pair of wing-edged glasses, and she'd be a dead ringer for Nana Mouskouri.

'Oh, just someone I used to go to university with,' I lie smoothly.

'Friend or lover?'

'Neither.'

'Oh?' he questions.

'Someone I used to watch from a distance and dream about.' I grin, pretending to flatter him.

'Liar,' he replies, but he's still smiling. 'Are you here on your own?'

'Well, I was waiting for a friend,' I say, using my old standby which this time is actually the truth. I pretend to glance at my watch, and pull a face, 'but I think I've been stood up.'

'Well, in that case . . .'

He pauses, obviously waiting for me to introduce myself.

'Annabelle . . . Annabelle Lewis.'

'Annabelle.' He smiles slowly. 'Well, in that case, Annabelle, will you promise not to be insulted if I try and buy you another drink?'

I'm just about to reply no thanks, an automatic response programmed into my brain, by years of fobbing off undesirables in pubs, bars and clubs, when I actually think about who it is that's offering.

The thing is, now that I've been officially spotted, I'm hardly going to be able to follow him around all over the place any more, am I?

My only option is to befriend the man.

It would be so much easier just to ask the guy about his love life than to follow him around town and hang from his window ledges by my breaking nails.

'Oh, I think the Pankhursts might just forgive me, but what about your friends?' I indicate the Italian and the pretty brunette.

'I'm sure they won't mind losing the gooseberry for a while.' He slides down on to the stool next to me.

Gooseberry? Well, that strikes the brunette from my list, Amanda *will* be pleased.

'Well, in that case, I'd love another one of these, thanks.'

He orders us two more Buds, then turns back to me.

'So what do you do, Annabelle Lewis?'

Why is this always one of the first things that people ask you?

I suppose it's so they can fit you into a neat little category in their head. It's inevitable really, but is it fair to be labelled by your job? I mean, on the surface I may be a beach bum, but deep down I could have the heart of a brain surgeon – NOT.

'Oh, nothing at the moment. I've just come back from a long stint abroad and I've only just started job hunting . . .' It's only a small lie.

'Yeah, I had noticed the tan,' he replies.

I check surreptitiously, but he's still looking at my face and not my cleavage, which earns him instant up points on the man scale.

'Been anywhere interesting?'

'Bangkok, Hong Kong, the Philippines, New Guinea, a quick trip to Fiji, and then a brief spell in Australia.'

'Not far then?' he quips.

'Nah. But a bit better than a quick trip to Bognor.'

'And what sort of thing are you looking for?'

'Job? Haven't got a clue, really. I wasn't planning to come back to Britain quite so soon, and to be honest so far the job hunting's not going very well. Everybody seems to want experience and all I've ever done is the odd student and traveller's standby. You know the sort of thing – fill ins, bar work, waitressing when pushed.'

'Really?' He pauses for a moment. 'You know, I might be able to help you out there. I know of a place that's just going through a major expansion and, well, if you fancy a bit more bar work, just to tide you over, they're looking for more staff.'

He takes a card out of the back pocket of his trousers, scribbles an address on it with a Waterman he pulls from the inside pocket of his suit jacket, and hands it to me. 'Take this down and ask to speak to Ben, the manager. Tell him I recommended you.'

'But how can you recommend me when you don't know me? For all you know I could be an escaped lunatic or something.'

'Well, from the way you were dancing earlier . . .' The smile quirks back into life again. 'No, seriously, I'm usually a pretty good judge of character – I *think* my mother would approve of you. Besides if you're no good you'll get sacked,' he says bluntly, 'it's as simple as that. Go and have a word with Ben, see what you think . . . if you want to, of course, it's up to you.'

'Thanks. I might just do that.'

I'm asserting my independence and buying us another drink as a thank you when I spot a familiar face pushing its way through the throng, eyes searching from left to right as he combs the crowd looking for me.

Clothes rumpled, hair looking like it hasn't been combed for a week, eyes tired and shadowed, but still as gorgeously adorable as ever.

'Jamie!'

I call out to him and he staggers over to me in relief. Practically falling round my neck, he's so pleased to see me.

'Belly, babe. I'm *so* sorry, I overslept. I'm rostered on A & E and I only got off a thirteen-hour shift at midday. I woke up an hour ago, and I've just spent half an hour fighting my way round this place trying to find you. Jeez it's crowded in here, talk about meat market . . .'

He squeezes on to my stool and, helping himself to my drink, finishes it in one, with the casual easy intimacy developed between us over the years.

'I'm abso-bloody-lutely knackered,' he wails, dropping his head on to my shoulder and pretending to fall asleep, until opening one eye, he notices Eddie looking at him narrowly.

He looks from me to Eddie, and grins.

'My timing's obviously worse than I thought.'

'Don't worry, babe,' I assure him, 'as usual your timing's impeccable.'

'It is?' He looks confused.

'Yeah, you're just in time to give me a lift home.'

I use my bum to lever him off the stool, and hold out my right hand to Eddie.

'Look, it was really nice to meet you.'

'You're going already?' He looks kind of disappointed.

'Yeah, got to, I'm afraid. Early start tomorrow and he's,' indicating Jamie, 'already dead on his feet. Thanks for this, though.' I wave the card at him before posting it down my cleavage and dragging a protesting Jamie out of the hot club into the cool of the night air.

'Whaddya do that for, Belle? I'm gasping for a beer.

217

And you were well in there. I wouldn't have thought you'd want to leave so soon, seeing as that's the first time you've pulled anything other than a muscle for god knows how long.'

'Don't be daft, I hadn't pulled, that was Eddie Farrar.'

'What, *the* Eddie. Mad Manda's Eddie?' He grins in disbelief.

'Uh-huh.' I nod.

'Well, she's gonna be even madder after this 'cause he was panting for you.'

'Have you been administering drugs to yourself instead of the patients again, James?' I sigh, hailing a passing taxi driver, who chooses to ignore me completely.

'I'm telling you, you'd pulled, girl.'

'. . . 'cause it's not good for you, you know. One day you'll swallow something strange and hormonal and end up wearing frocks and nicking my make up . . .'

'Look, Belle, I'm a bloke, I can tell when another of my species is gazing lustfully, okay?'

'You're hallucinating.'

'So why was he with you then?'

'He thought he knew me, and came over to chat.'

He bangs the palm of his hand against his forehead.

'He thought he knew you? Come on, Belle! Even you know that's the oldest line in the book!'

'Yeah, maybe from total sad perverts like you, but I don't think someone like Eddie Farrar needs to use tired old chat up lines.'

'And the feeling's mutual!' he shrieks gleefully.
' "Someone like Eddie Farrar",' he mocks me. 'You
like him too! Admit it.'

'Get lost.'

'You're telling me you didn't fancy him in the
slightest?'

'Nope.'

'Not one small flicker of lust?'

'Nope.'

'Not even just a little flicker?' he persists.

I hesitate for too long to get away with a lie.

'Okay, so he's attractive,' I admit.

'Attractive?'

'*Very* attractive. But it's just a job.'

'What sort of job?' he teases, dancing about in front
of me. 'Hand job? Blow job? Take me home and take
me now job?'

'You know, sometimes I wish I didn't love you, so
that I could KILL you. Slowly and painfully.'

'Hold on to that thought, Annabelle.' Jamie throws
himself into the path of the next taxi, which stops just
short of his navel. ''Cause a slow and painful death is
what you're gonna get if you ever admit to Amanda
just how attractive you think Eddie Farrar is. But
then again,' he pulls a fish face at me, 'I suppose you
have to admit it to yourself first, darling, don't you?'

Nix is curled up on the sofa in full make up and her
dressing gown, having arrived home half an hour
before us. She's nibbling sultanas and watching a late
repeat of *Reeves & Mortimer*. Elvis, who was asleep and

snoring on her feet, wakes up and thunders across the room to greet Jamie like a long-lost lover.

'Hi, babe, have fun?' Nicky jokes, knowing full well how reluctant I was to go to the opening party in the first instance.

'Yes, thank you.' I smile, kicking off my shoes.

'You did?'

'As a matter of fact I had a very pleasant evening. I spent most of my time chatting to a very nice man.'

'A very, very nice man,' mocks Jamie, who's currently being love attacked by a desperately pleased to see him Elvis.

'And I don't mean that git who was late as usual,' I spit over my shoulder at Jamie, who's been taunting me about my so-called 'lust at first sight' all the way home in the taxi and is starting to get on my 34Bs.

'Well, Amanda won't be very pleased with you.' Nicky shakes her head. 'You were supposed to be watching Eddie Farrar.'

'You're right,' Jamie taunts, picking Elvis up so that the fat pup can cover his face in doggy kisses, 'Amanda won't be very pleased with her. She *was* watching Eddie Farrar, closely actually. He was the very nice man in question.'

'Really?' Nicky's attention is instantly focused away from the TV and on to me. 'You actually spoke to him?'

'Uh-huh,' I nod, pinching a handful of sultanas.

'And he was nice?'

I wait until Jamie's plonked Elvis back on to Nicky and headed into the kitchen to raid the fridge for beer before answering.

'Lovely. Not at all like I expected.'

She makes room for me on the sofa, Elvis grumbling as she shifts him on to her lap and scratches absentmindedly at the soft fur on the top of his head.

'Go on, tell all!' she demands as I flop down next to her.

'Not much to tell, really. We just chatted for a while . . .'

'And?'

'And he was on his own at the party, no gorgeous girlfriend in tow.'

'Well, that's good . . . anything else?'

I smile smugly at her.

'And!' Nicky repeats, almost shouting with frustration.

'And he offered me a job.'

'He did what?'

'You heard me.'

'What kind of job? Personal assistant? Personal masseuse?' she jokes, picking up one of the five by tens of Eddie Farrar that Amanda left with me, which have lived on the coffee table for the past couple of weeks so that Nicky and I can have a quick drool whenever we feel like it. 'Personally I'd go for the second option. Wouldn't mind giving him a quick rub down with a limp lettuce . . . or my limp libido for that matter.'

'Bar work, at Daisy's.'

'Daisy's?'

'Lazy Daisy's. According to Amanda's *Guinness Book of Eddie*, it's a club he's just taken over somewhere down

221

in Docklands. I've got the address in my cleavage.'

'Which is, of course, where you keep all of your addresses.' Nicky crosses her eyes at me. 'So what are you going to do?'

'Er . . . take the address out of my cleavage?'

'I meant about the job!'

'I don't know, I was going to ask you that.'

'Well, I suppose you'd better speak to Amanda and see what she thinks.'

'Seeing as how my life is no longer my own,' I sigh melodramatically, falling back on to the cushions, hand on forehead. 'Why should I ask Amanda? Hopefully, after tonight, she'll no longer be in a position even to hint at what I should be doing with my time.'

Nicky shoves a glass of wine into one of my hands, and the portable phone in the other. I roll my eyes at her.

'Give me one good reason why I should call her now? It's gone eleven-thirty.'

'She'll be waiting to hear from you about how tonight went. You know what she's like. She'll have finished dining out on her fingernails and be trying to stuff her toes in her mouth.'

'Nope, not a good enough reason.'

'She pays your wages.'

I shake my head.

Nicky sighs.

'Okay, we've just had the last quarter's phone bill in and over two-thirds of it are long-distance to friends in the Southern Hemisphere, and seeing as how the only friend I had in the Southern Hemisphere is now back in this one, using my telephone . . .'

'Well, that's good enough for me. What number's Amanda on at the moment, 'cause if it isn't local I'm reversing the charges?' I look pointedly at Jamie as I pick up the receiver to dial. 'I thought you'd got an appointment with your duvet?'

'No way, I want to meet Mad Manda.' He digs his bum further into the sofa cushion, refusing to budge.

'Well, I'm not sure Mad Manda would want to meet you.'

'Oh, please let me stay. My life's so boring, just one long endless round of medical emergencies and real-life crises,' he mocks. 'You never know, I may be able to help, offer you my professional opinion. After all,' he drops his voice to do a bad impression of Isaac Hayes, 'I am Dr *Lurve* . . .'

'How about Dr No?'

'Pleeeease?' He wobbles his bottom lip at me, the way he used to when we were ten and he'd pigged all of his Saturday morning sweets in five minutes flat, and therefore felt it was only right he should help me finish mine.

'Oh, okay.' I cave in as usual. 'You can stay on condition you offer absolutely no opinion, professional or otherwise, on anything at all, especially not Eddie Farrar.'

'Eddie who?' Jamie jokes. 'Oh, yes. *Eddie*. Ready for you, Eddie. The guy who was offering to polish your tonsils with his tongue in the club tonight.'

'You what!' shrieks Nicky.

'Take no notice,' I tell her. 'He's been sniffing pure oxygen again.'

I'm now absolutely convinced Amanda has a broomstick. I put the phone down, the next thing I know she's ringing the doorbell.

It takes her ten minutes to get from her parents' town house in Highgate to Nicky's, which really could only be done as the Old Crow flies.

She's lost more weight.

The only thing she still hasn't managed to do is grow her ragged nails, which if anything are bitten down even further than before. Nicky was right, she's obviously been waiting by the telephone all evening.

'Well, what happened?' she cries, thundering down the steps towards me, ignoring Nicky who'd opened the door for her. 'Did you see him? Was he with anybody?'

She's too keen for information even to take any notice of Jamie, who's still slumped on the sofa clutching a can of Foster's, heavy eyelids sliding shut like elevator doors but determined to stay awake long enough to see the legend that is Amanda Hartley-Davies.

'Well, you'll be glad to hear that he was definitely on his own at the party.'

'Are you sure?'

'Absolutely positive.'

Jamie makes a strange snorting noise into his lager can.

I throw him a filthy look, but Amanda doesn't notice. I don't think she'd notice if I ripped off my clothes and did a naked victory dance on the coffee table.

Her face is shining like she's just had a vigorous work out, and she's gazing into space like a shopping junkie in full Harrods high.

This was the point where I was expecting Amanda to depart from my life, either beaming from ear to ear, sobbing violently, or threatening painful death according to the outcome of my . . . er . . . investigation.

Amanda's beaming, but unfortunately she shows no sign of actually budging. In fact, she flops down on the sofa and, reaching out, helps herself to Nicky's glass of wine, knocking back a large amount in a solitary toast.

'So . . .' I say, hoping to wrap her up and move her out as quickly as possible. 'It looks like you don't need me any more.'

'Er, there's just one more thing, isn't there, Belle?' Nicky interrupts, looking pointedly at me. 'You know, about the offer you had . . .'

Cheers, Nick. I still hadn't decided whether it was a good idea to pass on this particular piece of information. I mean, what's the point? I've done what she wanted and now hopefully my part in her life is well and truly over.

'Yes?' Amanda stops slurping wine and looking rapt, and looks at me instead. It's Nicky's turn for a filthy look.

'I've been offered the chance of a job at Lazy Daisy's,' I tell her reluctantly. No way am I going into the details of how this miracle offer came about. Fortunately Amanda is too preoccupied by the what to wonder about the how.

'That's Eddie's latest place,' she exclaims.

'I know.'

'But that's excellent!'

'It is?'

'Of course it is. It's perfect.'

'*It is?*'

'You've got to take the job!'

'But I don't want the job.'

'Take the job!' She's almost screaming.

'But why? What's the point? We've already established that he's young, free, single and sexy, what more can you get from me carrying on?'

'I'll pay you extra . . .'

It's sod's law, isn't it? There was a time in the none too distant past when I would have been over the moon to have been offered a job, let alone to be paid by someone else just to do it.

'It's not the money, Amanda. It's the point, or rather lack of it. Is it really worth it? I mean, I've been tailing the guy for two weeks and the coast appears to be well and truly clear for a hostile takeover.'

'There's no need to be facetious about it, Annabelle.' She glares at me.

'Okay, but now you know he's definitely available, why do you want me to carry on?'

'Well, now I know there's no major competition, I

can plan my campaign, can't I?'

'You can?'

Campaign? This sounds ominous. I help myself to a glass of Chardonnay, I have a horrible feeling I'm going to need it, and involuntarily edge a bit further down the sofa, and away from Amanda's leather-encased thigh.

'I want him back. I don't know why it ended and I want him back,' she states, talking more to herself than us.

'It ended because he obviously wanted it to,' I blurt.

'Only because he didn't get a chance to know the real me.'

Yeah, and if he had he'd probably never have started seeing her in the first place!

'Okay, so you want him back. Now you know *he's* free, *you're* free to go after him, and my job's done, isn't it? Finished.'

'Finished? Oh, no.' She looks at me incredulously. 'This is just the beginning. I want you to take that job, Annabelle, and find out as much as you can about Eddie Farrar. I need you to find out what he does and doesn't like . . . what sort of woman he finds attractive, who turns his head when they walk into his bar: blonde, brunette, slim, curvaceous, knock 'em dead glam, or *au naturelle*. What sort of personality he clicks with: wild and outgoing, or quiet and reserved . . .'

'Sporty, Posh, Baby or Scary?' says Nicky.

'What?' Amanda looks at her like she's insane.

'A different type to suit all fantasies,' Nix explains. 'You want to know which one is his . . .'

'I suppose so.' Amanda's obviously not convinced by this particular analogy.

'But why?' I ask her.

'*Because I want him.*' She stares at me, challengingly. 'And I don't want to blow it this time. It's too important to me.'

'So you want to find out what his idea of the perfect woman is, and try and turn yourself into that ideal?'

'Exactly.'

Love is not love which alters when it alteration finds.

'I thought you said you wanted him to get to know the real you?'

'It *will* be the real me, just a new improved version,' she states defiantly. 'What's wrong with wanting to get a head start? I don't see a set of rules anywhere that tell me I can't help things along a little. After all, all's fair in love and war.'

'And you want to send me in as the advance party?'

She nods enthusiastically.

'Please, Annabelle,' she pleads. 'Take the job at Lazy Daisy's, it would be so perfect. You'd be able to keep a really close eye on him, *and* you'd be able to let me know when he's going to be in there. Then, when the time's right, I could just sort of bump into him, couldn't I?' Her eyes start to shine at the thought as she goes off into a little fantasy about lounging seductively against a bar, looking totally hot, and him spotting her across a crowded, smoke-filled room and realising that he wants her so much he can't breathe.

She wants to employ me to chase after an ex so that she can mould herself into his ultimate fantasy, and then just happen to appear at all the places he hangs out in, at just the right moment, looking drop dead gorgeous.

How sad can you get?

Or how sensible?

If I'm honest I must admit I've had this little fantasy myself on the odd occasion. The one where you've lost enough weight to fit into that gorgeous little dress you bought when you couldn't really afford it on the promise that you'd give up chocolate, cakes and other junk food, thereby saving enough money to justify paying for it, and shedding the required inches to fit into the thing. The one where your hair is miraculously doing exactly what you wanted it to, rather than its own thing which is usually just sitting morosely on your head like a bored teenager slumped on a sofa. The one where your eyes have lost their lack-of-sleep bags, your make up is immaculate, your shoes match your handbag, and your breath doesn't smell of last night's garlic bread.

I get so fed up with other people trying to tell me what I can and can't do, what's right and what's wrong. Who am I to judge Amanda for wanting to rewrite the rules a little, especially when the rules can be so unfair?

Besides I'm just the hired help, really, aren't I? Emphasis on the hired, as in employed, as in earning enough money to pay my way with regard to rent, food, and other essentials. If I quit what I'm doing now, behind a bar is probably exactly where I'll end up. This way I get paid extra by Amanda, and I get paid by Eddie Farrar ... Although that does seem a little unethical, like *he's* actually paying for the dubious privilege of being watched by me ... not right.

I take a deep breath and exhale slowly.

'Okay, I'll take the job, but you don't have to pay me for the time I spend working at the bar.'

Did I really just say that?

'Really?' Nicky and Amanda both say this at the same time, one incredulous, the other ecstatic.

'You heard me,' I reply reluctantly, slightly unsure how to view this new surge of slightly vague morality, 'and don't ask me to say it again in case I change my mind.'

We eventually manage to turf Amanda out of the flat an hour later.

Not so Jamie, who finally gave in to the lure of Morpheus and is crashed out on the sofa, snoring softly, Elvis stretched out next to him, snoring loudly, both with their mouths wide open, but fortunately only Elvis has his tongue hanging out and is drooling on the cushions.

Nicky and I open another bottle of wine, and kick back on the other sofa, feet on the coffee table.

'He's a real Sleeping Beauty, isn't he?' she whispers.

'Jamie or Elvis?'

Elvis chooses this moment to fart loudly.

'No contest really.' Nicky grins.

'Yeah, has to be Elvis . . . You know, this worries me.'

'Let me guess. Amanda?'

'Yeah. It's a classic case of more money than sense.'

'Well, if that's what she wants to do with her money . . .'

'But I feel like I'm taking advantage of her vulnerability . . . and desperation.'

Nicky pours us both another glass of wine.

'It's no worse than being, say, an estate agent, or a bank manager or something.' She hands me a full glass of Australian Shiraz, which I accept gratefully. 'Besides, you're helping her, this is what she wants, look upon yourself as a therapist.'

Now I know why Nix became a solicitor; she has a knack for saying the right thing at the right time, apart of course from the obvious mistake of answering 'Yes' when Richard popped the question.

'I thought Jamie was supposed to the lurve doctor,' I giggle. 'Oh, well, at least I'm cheaper than an analyst.'

'Only just.' Nix grins. 'You know, I don't think it's such a daft idea. In fact, I think Amanda's sensible really. She's just doing her homework. You revise for exams, don't you?'

'Er, yeah, theoretically.'

'Well, maybe that's not the best example to give *you*, but I think you know what I'm driving at. She's found something she really wants, and she's just decided to give herself that little bit of an edge which might mean she ends up getting it.'

'I suppose so, but I can't helping thinking it's a little unfair on Eddie Farrar.'

'Maybe, but since when are they ever fair to us?'

'I assume by *they* you mean the male of the species?'

'Yep. Don't exactly have a strong code of ethics themselves when it comes to the dating game, now do they? And as Amanda pointed out, they do say that all's fair in love and war. And for that statement to be fair and true it has to work both ways.'

'Sure.' I yawn loudly, suddenly overcome by weariness. 'I just don't think many people expect the ex to send the undercover troops into battle on their behalf.'

Chapter Seven

L azy Daisy's is a huge old Docklands warehouse that was originally converted into a bar and restaurant, and is now undergoing further work to add a club area in the massive cellar.

The ground floor houses the bar, with a pretty good restaurant on a mezzanine floor to the rear of the building, and there's an office area along with the public loos on the first floor.

I've been here a few times in the past few weeks 'Eddie Hunting'.

It's a typical bar: wooden floors, stone walls, smell of beer and polish. A cheerful woman with a mop of glossy chestnut curls is sweeping debris, ash and ripped beer mats from tables into a bucket. She looks up as I walk in and smiles, pushing wayward curls out of a tired face.

'We're closed, darling, thank goodness.'

'Er, hi . . . yeah, I know. I'm looking for Ben – Ben Meredith. I've got an interview.'

She points to a man sitting at a table near the bar, sleeves of his yellow and blue checked Ben Sherman shirt rolled up to his elbows, Levis ripped at the knees through wear rather than design, and scuffed brown leather Caterpillar boots. His dark blond hair is flopping over his face as he chews on a pen and pores over the account books in front of him.

'Don't worry, he won't bite!' She grins as I hesitate. 'Not that I'd complain if he offered me a little nibble.' She has a laugh like a slightly more feminine Sid James.

I make my way over to where Ben Meredith, Manager of Daisy's, is scouring paper heavily with a biro that's refusing to work properly, shoes clattering noisily on the wooden floor.

He looks up, his face creasing into a friendly smile. He has chocolate brown eyes, the same colour as Elvis's but showing a considerably higher degree of intelligence.

'Hi.' I hold out a hand. 'I called earlier . . . about the bar job.'

'Ah, yes.' He leans back in his chair, pushing the front legs away from the ground as he stretches his own legs to their full length. 'You must be Annabelle, I've been expecting you. Take a pew . . .' He shoves the chair next to him towards me with his foot, wobbling precariously as he does so.

'You know, you look familiar.'

I'm going to have to work on my disguises: i.e. get some. I might treat myself to a blonde wig; I've always fancied testing out the theory blondes have more fun without the permanency of peroxide.

'I drink in here sometimes.'

'And you still want to work here?' he jokes.

Ben fetches us both a cup of coffee from the Espresso machine behind the counter, then, eyes crinkling at the corners as he continues to beam like a friendly bear, gives me the low down on Lazy Daisy's.

'As you can see, we're in the middle of a major expansion – well, really we should be nearing completion of said major expansion, but you know what builders are like.'

'Only by reputation, and I don't mean their work qualifications,' I joke, thinking of Nicky who has the odd builder's bum in her knickers.

'Well, when they say a week they mean three. They should have been finished and out of here by now. We've had to put the Grand Opening back to next month which the boss isn't very happy about.'

Ah, yes, the boss. The real reason I'm here instead of a burning ambition to pull pints.

'With the addition of the club downstairs, we'll more than double our capacity. It'll get hellishly busy. At least, I hope it will otherwise I'll be out of a job. If your idea of fun is helping drunk arseholes turn themselves into even drunker arseholes, then you should thoroughly enjoy yourself.' He grins broadly, to reveal very white teeth and a very blue tongue where's he's chewed way too hard on the end of his biro.

'Er . . . your tongue . . . the pen . . .' I tap the end of my own tongue with the tip of my finger.

He tastes the end of his tongue, then sticking it out as far as it will go, bursts into peals of infectious laughter, calling to the woman who's now back behind the bar bottling up.

'Dot, my darling, do us a favour – fill this up for me. I've got the most horrible taste in my mouth.' He pokes his dark blue tongue out at Dot who once again does her Sid James impression and heads for the Espresso machine.

'Do you want another one?'

I shake my head as he completely unselfconsciously begins to blot the end of his tongue on a paper napkin.

I think I like Ben.

He reminds me of Jamie. Not in looks. Jamie has a kind of ethereal, angel who's just staggered away from a punch up, kind of beauty, whereas Ben is ruggedly good-looking, but they seem to have the same warmth and openness.

'So, Annabelle, when can you start?'

I reel back slightly in surprise.

'Just like that? You don't want to ask me any questions? You know, interview me properly.'

He looks at me, slightly confused.

'But you've already been hired, this meeting's just to sort out the details.'

'I have?'

'Yeah. Look,' Ben pushes back his chair and stands up, 'why don't I show you around?'

Downstairs in the massive vaulted cellar is the new club area. It's like a church without the pews or pulpit, and is still inhabited by a small posse of workmen, hammering away, staining woodwork, sound proofing.

And what a peachy posse!

Forget builder's bottom, a great wobbling crescent moon rising from a sad slump of denim. Think, fit, tight and muscular.

Think, yes, please.

Think, wipe the drool off your chin, you sad woman.

When one of them looks up and wolf whistles I feel flattered rather than insulted. Nicky would be in potential date heaven. Ben is still chattering away.

'I've been doing this job for about five years now, working for Eddie for the past year.' He refers to 'Eddie' as if I know him really well. 'Great guy, isn't he? Personally, I figured I spent so much time in a bar anyway, I might as well get paid for it. And I was kind of hoping for my liver's sake that it'd be a bit like working in a sweetie shop – you know, have far too much to start off with, then don't ever touch the stuff again. Unfortunately, I'm still on the far too much stage. The kill or cure tactic hasn't quite worked, I'm afraid, but I haven't died of alcohol poisoning yet, touch wood. I'm more likely to die from frustration if this lot don't get their arses into gear!' He waves a mock-threatening fist at the builders, who jeer back good-naturedly.

'But in the meantime, life upstairs goes on as usual, so if you're ready, willing and able, I'm going to offer to throw you in at the deep end. One of our girls, Abi, has come down with 'flu, so could you do Saturday night? Do you think you can handle it? It's one of the killer shifts, start at six, go through till three . . .'

'I'll be there.'

'Great.' He beams, genuinely pleased. 'Eddie said

you'd suit us down to the ground, and I think he's right. But then, he's got an eye for good girls.'

'Yeah, and he's got an eye for bad ones as well, I shouldn't wonder,' I mutter without thinking.

Amanda's so excited I'm going to be working at Daisy's she displays a rare moment of insane normality and practically dances me round the living room.

What was she actually doing in the living room when I got back from the club? Well, since my encounter with Eddie Farrar last weekend, she's become almost as permanent a fixture in Nicky's apartment as the furniture, or the bottle of wine that's usually open on the coffee table, or even the bar of Cadbury's Nicky 'hides' at the back of the cutlery drawer in the kitchen; although Amanda's not nearly as sweet, or as welcome.

The plan, albeit rather a vague plan, is to get as much information as I can before the official opening of the new Lazy Daisy's cellar club, which, builders willing – and apparently they aren't, very – is in about six weeks' time.

Being an employee, I will of course ensure that Amanda's name gets on the guest list for the launch party, where she will hit Eddie full on with the new, improved, tailor-made for him Amanda.

We already know that Eddie found her physically attractive enough to go out on a few dates with. Therefore all she really needs is to lose another stone, and get a personality transplant.

Easy.

★ ★ ★

Here I am again, back where I belong, pulling pints. Bars and I seem destined to be together, be it behind one, or propped against one with a glass in my hand and a stupid, drunken expression on my face.

Having crawled bug-eyed under my duvet at four in the morning after sitting outside Eddie's house waiting to see if he came home alone from a night out 'networking' with business associates, the last thing I really want to do is slog my guts out in a busy bar until three in the morning, but I'm learning fast that it's very hard to say no to someone like Amanda.

She's obviously used to getting her own way, and has perfected the technique of mind manipulation to a tee, alternating between sobbing and snarling, cheerfulness and churlishness, according to the emotions of those around her.

The daft thing is I can see what she's doing, but I'm still letting her do it!

I must be going soft in my old age.

When I get to Daisy's I find that I've been rostered on with Dot, the chestnut-haired woman I met at my 'interview', and a happy-go-lucky bleached blond gay guy whose real name I think is Simon, but everybody for some inexplicable reason calls Sylvia.

Despite the fact that only the bar and restaurant are open at the moment, Dot assures me that we're in for a busy night.

'This is the quiet part of the evening. You wait till nine, the place'll be totally heaving with people – I hope you're fit!'

'Yeah, fit for nothing,' I joke.

Despite Dot's assurances of a busy night to come, the staff currently outnumber the customers. Apart from myself, Dot and Sylvia, there are three bored waiters, and a rather scary head chef who apparently rules the commis chef, sous chef and kitchen dogs-body with his somewhat tyrannical temper.

Sylvia's boyfriend David is perched at the end of the bar, drinking strawberry daiquiris and talking nineteen to the dozen to anybody who happens to stand too near to his bar stool. Apart from him there are four guys at one of the tables who are apparently such regular regulars they spend more time in the bar than any of the staff. They're getting steadily drunker and louder as the evening progresses. They're also increasing the arsehole factor with every slug of alcohol poured down their shaved, cologne-slapped throats.

They're currently moving through 'men behaving like dickheads' level, heading at a rapid pace towards 'total pain in the arse moron' level.

We leave Sylv, who for some reason they're rather scared of, to deal with their frequent demands for refills, whilst Dot shows me the ropes.

After she's shown me the bottle store, how to work the Space Age till, and reminded me of the technique of changing a beer barrel without breaking my back, a sweat or any fingernails, I decide to make the most of the lull and see what information I can glean about Eddie.

Fortunately for me, whilst I'm still working out the best way to broach my subject subtly, Dot does it for me.

240

'Have you met the boss yet?' she asks, pouring us both half a lager.

'Ben?' I query, feigning ignorance.

'Ben?' she laughs. 'Bless him, he may run the roost but he doesn't call the shots. No, I mean Eddie, Eddie Farrar, the guy who owns Daisy's.'

'What's he like?' I ask as casually as possible, avoiding Dot's initial question.

'He's got nerves of steel. He can make you quake in your boots with just a glance.'

'Really?'

'Really,' she giggles, 'when he's in boss mode, but he's bloody gorgeous too.'

'Personality or physique?'

'Both. He's got a wicked sense of fun, he can be a right laugh, he's ever so broad-minded – ooh, and he's got a lovely broad chest too.' She smacks her lips. 'Half of our customers are women who come in to drool!'

'And you?'

'Me?' She bursts into peals of laughter. 'No, not me! He's not *quite* young enough to be my son,' she fluffs up her curls with the palm of her hand, 'not that age ever bothers me, but I'm afraid that's what he feels like to me.'

'You've known him a long time then?'

'Since he was about, oh . . . so high.' Dot indicates somewhere around waist height. 'Right little bugger he was then – still can be sometimes. Nowhere near as bad as this lot, though!' she says loudly, referring to the regular regulars who have moved over to stand at the bar so we're within easy harassing distance.

'Can we get some service down here or what?' yells the ringleader of the group, an arrogant blond guy in his late-twenties, who looks a bit like one of the Bros Goss, with less hair. 'I don't know, the bloody bar staff in this place ... think they're employed to stand around gossiping whilst the poor old punters die of thirst.'

Dot hands me a white wrap-waist apron.

'That's for wiping the blood off your hands after you've killed that lot,' she stage whispers. 'Trust me, by the end of the night you'll be spiking their drinks with the bleach they use to clean the loos ...'

She grins at me and heads over to serve Blondie, who is leaning against the bar, eyes magnetised by Dot's mega-cleavage as it advances towards him.

'All right, keep your hair on,' she heckles back. 'You can't afford to lose too much more of it at your age.'

'Four pints of best and four whisky chasers, Dot, and make mine a large one, please, darling.' He leers at her.

'I'm a pint puller, not a miracle worker,' Dot retorts, looking pointedly at his crotch.

I give her a hand with their order, figuring there's safety in numbers.

'You've done this before, haven't you, I can tell.' She looks in approval at the pint I've just poured, which fortunately is pretty near perfect.

I nod, and put the last pint glass on the bar.

'Sad, isn't it? I'm twenty-five and the only thing I

can do well is pour a pint of lager. Well, I suppose I'm quite good at drinking it as well as pouring it . . .'

'Don't knock it.' Dot grins. 'The last girl was a total waste of space – the only thing she could pull was the men. Completely stunning, but nothing up top apart from two sacs of silicone and a single brain cell. If you ask me she was a bit off her trolley. Don't know what she was doing working behind a bar, it was obvious Daddy wasn't short of a bob or two. When I asked why she'd taken a job as a lowly bar tart, do you know what she said to me?' She leans back against the counter and draws on her cigarette, eyes narrowing with disgust at the memory. 'Said she wanted to see what it was like in the real world. Condescending cow! Well, the "real world" obviously wasn't up to her expectations, she only lasted two weeks.'

'I'm not surprised. How do you put up with this lot?'

'You think they're bad? The builders are a total pain in the arse. We've got eight different types of coffee and all they want is endless cups of tea,' Dot moans, 'and you're not to give them alcohol, no matter how much they moan, groan, flirt or plead.'

Dot's amazing.

I nearly die of shock when she tells me she's in her early-forties. If asked I'd have placed her at, say, thirty-three, thirty-four, tops.

She swears her youthful looks are due to a diet of younger men.

About five foot four, with shiny chestnut hair in layered curls to her shoulders, pale greeny-brown eyes hidden behind glasses she doesn't really need, she's a total man magnet. It might have something to do with the immense amount of cleavage she normally has on display, but I think it's more to do with her personality which is as warm and welcoming as a real fire blazing in a grate.

She has an hour-glass figure and a queue of willing men that stretches further than the queue to Daisy's on a Saturday night, which believe me is bloody long.

Just as Dot predicted, by eight-thirty, the place is absolutely heaving with people. I've been chatted up more times in one evening than I have in the last two months. I'm the new girl. The others have already heard all of the regular guys' tired old lines, so they figure they might have a little more luck with me. I may be new, but I'm not naïve, and fortunately I can remember how to give a good knock back. It's hard work, though.

I feel like a matador swirling his cape at a constantly charging load of old bull. After just an hour, my smile has turned into a set, gritted-teeth grimace, and I'm quite prepared to brain the next moron who tries something corny in the come on department with me.

'Hiya, sexy, what's a nice girl like you doing in a place like this?'

I turn round, Bud bottle in hand, quite ready to swing it at the offending bonce, only to come face to face with a wickedly grinning Jamie and a slightly dazed-looking Nix.

'Thought we'd come and show a bit of moral support,' Jamie yells over the buzz of the crowd, and the music which was cranked up a few levels when the punters started to arrive in droves.

'Immoral support would be more appropriate,' I sigh, pushing my sweat-damp hair out of my eyes for the fiftieth time. 'You wouldn't believe how many times I've been propositioned tonight.'

'Lucky you.' Nicky grins at me. 'I haven't been propositioned for at least . . .'

'A day?' I cut in. 'I'm sure if you ask Jamie nicely he'll make up your quota for you, won't you, Jamie?'

'Sure.' He grins, turning to Nix and pretending to waggle his eyebrows lasciviously at her. 'Hello, darling, fancy a shag?'

Nicky bursts out laughing.

Jamie shakes his head.

'I don't know, I offer the woman my body and she laughs in my face. Not very good for a man's ego, Nicola.'

'Yeah,' I tell her. 'It's a fragile thing, unless well insulated by alcohol, when it suddenly develops the resilience of asbestos.'

'Well, I'd better have a drink then,' Jamie sniffs in mock upset. ''Cause mine's still smouldering from that burn off.'

I ignore the berks at the end of the bar who are now trying to attract my attention by synchronised mooning, and crack open a couple of bottles of Bud.

'I wanted to bring Elvis,' Nicky says, accepting hers, 'but I'm off on a hot date tonight so I had to leave him with Amanda. They're both sulking madly at being forced to stay at home and miss out on the fun.'

'You think this is fun! You should have brought him, he'd have fitted in really well with the arseholes I've had to put up with tonight. In fact, strike that. Elvis has got *better* manners. At least he takes his snout out of your knickers when you tell him no.'

'Oooh, lots of persistent men.' Nicky grins. 'Just my kind of place!'

I think I'm the only one who notices Jamie frown at this comment.

'I'm afraid there's nothing worth getting excited about, Nix.'

'No sign of the edible Eddie then?'

'Not even a whiff of his aftershave.'

'Amanda will be disappointed. I think she was expecting you to be able to watch his every move from behind the beer pumps, then report back with your version of his ideal woman by the end of the evening.'

'You're joking, aren't you! Even if he was here I wouldn't have had time to breathe near the guy, let alone get him in deep conversation.'

I watch Nix and Jamie head off half an hour later; Nicky grinning at the prospect of her second date with the window cleaner who thinks he's Tarzan, Jamie sulking at the same thought, hinting heavily that she should forget long-haired losers and join him for a Chinese. I'm left to slog my way through the rest of tonight, yearning for my bed with all the longing of Juliet hanging off her balcony hoping for a glimpse of an elusive Romeo, who's sodded romance and gone down the pub to get rat-arsed with his mates.

It doesn't help that the restaurant closes just after midnight, which means I get to watch most of the other staff members head for home, except the kitchen dogsbody, an impoverished university student who clambers damply out of the kitchen sink and starts wearily to stack the glass washing machines instead.

'Poor old thing,' I whisper to Dot, watching him droop over yet another wire tray of steaming glasses.

'Poor old thing, my foot! Eddie pays him well over the odds to stay on after midnight, that's the only reason he does it.'

'Bit altruistic, is he?'

Dot looks blankly at me.

'You know, Eddie. Thinks of others, generous . . .'

'Well, he's not a soft touch. He's had to work bloody hard for what he's got, and doesn't see why others shouldn't too. But he's always fair.'

Add that to my mental Eddie list.

Always fair, and likes people who work hard. Well, that strikes Amanda off immediately, unless you count wafting round Harvey Nicks spending family money as hard work.

I certainly count bar work as hard graft.

On your feet all night, at the beck and call of others – normally drunken and obnoxious others at that. Finally my shift comes to an end. The last punter is surgically detached from his pint glass and coaxed out of the door, the last glass is washed, and my legs are threatening to develop instant varicose veins from pounding up and down the length of the bar more times than Linford Christie in training.

'Right, we're off.' Dot wipes her hands on her apron before taking it off, screwing it up and throwing it at the dirty linen bin. 'Sylv and I are sharing a taxi back to Islington. Do you need a lift, darlin'?'

I shake my head.

'No, thanks. I'm in the other direction completely. Don't worry, I'll make my own way.'

Sylvia sticks his spiky bleach blond head round the door and yells to Dot.

'Cab's here, Dotty, get your lardy arse into gear. It's the miserable one tonight, he always charges extra if we keep him waiting.'

'Well, the cab may be here, darling, but Ben isn't. We've got to wait for him to come and lock up.'

'Oh, pooh!' Sylvia's elfin face falls. 'I want to go home – I'm soooo tired. I stayed up last night to watch a late film with Cary Grant. I knew I shouldn't, but I do love a good Cary Grant.'

'Don't worry,' I offer, wiping my damp hands on a cloth, 'you go, I'll wait for Ben.'

'Are you sure?' Dot asks reluctantly. 'I don't think we should leave you here on your own, not on your first night.'

'Positive, it's not a problem. I promise not to run off with the takings.'

'I'm more worried about somebody running off with you,' Dot jokes. 'Although the arseholes have gone, and Ben *should* be here any minute.'

Dot's as desperate to get home as Sylv. More so considering she did the same shift the previous night as well. I'm so knackered I'm ready to drop, but I figure I may as well take the opportunity to speak to Ben, see if I can find out anything else about the Elusive Eddie.

If Amanda *is* lurking back at the flat hungering for details then I think I'll feel safer if I have some to feed her.

'It's okay, I'll be fine, you go.'

'Well, if you're absolutely sure you'll be okay . . . Thanks, darling. And thanks for tonight, you did great. We'll see you in the week then.' She hesitates at the door. 'Are you sure you'll be all right?'

'Absolutely. Go home.'

Dot pulls the door to behind her on the latch. Pushing my hair out of my eyes, I take off my apron, which is no longer white but stained with beer from the drip trays, empty a missed ashtray, eat three leftover cocktail cherries before washing up the bowl, and pray that Ben and his huge bunch of keys won't be very long. I can feel my eyes sliding shut as I rinse the little glass bowl in the metal sink behind the bar, weighted and heavy with repressed sleep.

'Well, how did your first night go?'

I snap round abruptly, taken by surprise, only to come face to face with the man himself.

Not Ben, but Eddie, who, judging by the fact that he has a massive bunch of keys in one hand, has come to lock up in his place.

'Oh, hi.'

I suddenly feel incredibly gauche and awkward, like I really have no right at all to be here, as if somehow he knows I'm here under false pretences.

'Um, first night, yeah. It's been busy, very busy.'

'Glad to hear it.'

Despite the fact that I've seen him practically every day since, this is the first time I've actually spoken to the man since that night in Black Betty's, just over a week ago now.

He's dressed more casually tonight, in jeans and a polo shirt, and he looks like he's had a hair cut, the soft brown hair at the back of his head cropped closer than before, and at least half an inch shorter on top. It suits him. He also looks as tired as I feel, grey shadows circling each blue eye.

'You look totally shattered.' He echoes my own thoughts.

'Like I said, it's been a busy night, totally hectic.'

I can hardly tell him I'm shattered because I was sitting outside his house in the early hours of the morning, Eddie watching on Amanda's behalf.

'Right, well, you'd better get off then.' He looks at me for a moment. 'That is, unless you fancy a drink before you go?'

I want to go home and collapse under my duvet for the next fortnight but Amanda would never forgive me. Instead of quizzing Ben, I have the main subject right in front of me.

I suppress a yawn.

'Sure, but if I sit down I might not get up again.'

'That's okay, you'll be early for your next shift.'

'Slave driver!'

'I always like to get the most out of my employees.'

'So I've heard,' I joke. 'Flog 'em till they drop, eh?'

Cue instant vision of Eddie with a whip . . . I shake my head violently to dispel the picture. Where the hell did that come from?

'Okay, okay.' He pretends to sigh and surrender. 'Don't want you collapsing on your first night. Go and sit down.'

We swap places. I take a seat at the bar and he heads behind it.

'What can I get you, madam?' he mocks.

'Any good with a cocktail shaker?'

'I could give Tom Cruise a run for his money.'

'Oooh, so could I!' I growl lasciviously.

'I'm sorry, we only sell alcohol not fantasies.'

'Well, in that case, I'll have a Long Slow Screw . . .' I joke. 'No, vodka and Coke would be great, thanks.'

I watch him chuck some ice into a glass, pour me a large vodka and add a dash of Coke from the hand pump, suddenly glad that I'm *not* heading towards home and my duvet.

I take an enthusiastic slurp of a majorly well mixed V & C and stretch out my toes in my Cat boots in pleasure. It's amazing what a slight change in geography can do for a girl. The world is viewed very differently depending on which side of the bar you find yourself.

I've spent the whole evening slogging my guts out serving other people happy juice. Now it's my turn to kick back, relax and hit the good stuff.

Then I remember Amanda sitting on Nicky's sofa waiting for me, fingers crossed, legs crossed, double crossed, and what I'm supposed to be here for. Information not relaxation.

Time to pump the man instead of the beer.

'You look at home behind there,' I tell him, as he pours himself a pint of Foster's.

'I've done my share.'

'Yeah?' I prompt.

'My first job was humping crates in and out of a beer cellar. Besides, I think if you want a business to be successful you need to know how it works, which means being able to muck in on all jobs.'

'Even cleaning the loos?'

'I said muck in, not muck out.' He grins. 'You have to draw the line somewhere, and mine stops short at a bottle of Toilet Duck and a pair of pink rubber gloves.'

'I don't know, some people get their kicks from stranger things,' I joke, grinning into my glass.

'Like bar work?'

'Well, I'm certainly not doing it for the money.' I look at him over the rim of my glass. 'The pay's lousy. I hear the boss is a bit of a miser . . .'

'You don't say?' The smile quirks into life again. 'You know, that's what I'd heard too. Makes his poor put-upon minions slave for a pittance whilst he just sits back and amasses the millions.'

He comes out from behind the bar, and sits beside me on the next bar stool.

'So how did you get into this sort of thing in the first place?' I ask him.

'Followed in my father's footsteps. He was a bar manager.'

'Was he proud of you?'

'God, no!' Eddie shakes his head. 'He wanted me to be a bank manager, something respectable, only two letters and a whole world apart. He did what he did, so that I didn't have to. You can imagine how he felt when I announced I wanted to come and work with him.' He opens a bag of peanuts and offers me first dip. 'I did try, for his sake. I went to college, stuck it for nearly a year . . . but sometimes you just have to be true to yourself. You can only waste so much time trying to please other people. Trying to conform to what they want, what they expect of you.'

'Amen.' I raise my glass in whole-hearted agreement. 'I bet he's proud of you now, though?'

'Sure.' He grins. 'But he'd never admit it. And what about you, Annabelle Lewis? What do you do apart from travel the world? Any dreams, aspirations, or unfulfilled ambitions?'

I cross my eyes.

'The only ambition I have is to *get* some ambition. I'm twenty-five and I still haven't got a clue what I want to do with my life. It's sad, I've never really had any burning desire for anything. Not even a slightly smouldering want.'

'So you don't class travelling round Asia as an achievement?'

'Do you?' I ask him in surprise.

'Yes,' he states simply. 'Don't you?'

'I don't know. I suppose I've always thought of it as

a bit of a cop out. You know, running away from the real world.'

'It depends what you classify as the real world. Believe it or not, I don't think commerce is the only legitimate way of living.'

'This, coming from London's King of Clubs?'

'I hardly think two places can earn me that title.' That sexy smile crinkles into life again. 'You know, I sometimes wish I'd done the same thing when I had the chance. No ties or anything.'

'Well, it's never too late.'

He shakes his head.

'Too many commitments.'

I'm unable to suppress the major league yawn that's fighting its way out of my throat.

He drains his pint.

'Come on, finish your drink and I'll give you a lift home.'

'You don't have to do that,' I reply hurriedly, very much aware that Amanda's probably still lurking, like a vampire thirsting for information instead of blood. 'I'll get a taxi.'

'No, you won't.'

'But we've been drinking.'

'My first one all evening. It's not a problem, Annabelle, honestly. I can't let you leave on your own at this time of night.' He looks at his watch. 'Strike that, it's morning . . . I can't let you go without making sure you get home safely. It wouldn't be right.'

'I'm a big girl now, I can take care of myself.'

'Yeah.' He looks at me consideringly for a moment,

and then smiles. 'I'm sure you can . . . but I'm still taking you home, okay?'

Despite the fact that I'm desperate not to be seen in it, it's actually a relief to be in this car rather than struggling behind in Arnold, trying to keep up as it zooms along in front of me.

As we draw closer to Nicky's flat, I sink lower in the black leather seat of Eddie's Porsche, praying to God that Amanda's not chosen this moment to gaze mournfully out of Nicky's window at the moon which is shining full and bright above us in a navy blue sky.

Would Eddie think I was mad if I just slipped into the foot well, or made him drive slowly past Nicky's building whilst I belly rolled out of the car like an escaped convict?

What do I mean, would he think I was mad? Of course he would! He'd think I'd just spent two years in Broadmoor, and the backpacking story's just a cover!

I'd direct him somewhere nearby, into a side road or something, only I get the feeling he'd sit and wait until he'd seen me safely behind a locked door, so I just sit and shake as Eddie pulls over by Nicky's building.

'Thanks for the lift, and I suppose I should say thanks for the job as well,' I tell him, reaching for the door handle in an attempt at a speedy exit.

'No need.' He shakes his head. 'I'm sure you'll do really well.'

SARAH HARVEY

'I'll see you around then.'

'When's your next shift?' he calls out to me as I go to step out of the car.

'I'm rostered on properly from Tuesday night.'

'Well, I'll probably see you on Tuesday night then.'

I get out of the car and look up toward Nicky's apartment.

Amanda's not looking out of the window. If she was she'd have hurled something at me from a great height. Probably herself. A howling, plummeting elephant of doom aimed directly at my head.

I'm willing him to zoom off in a cloud of wheel spin dust, but like I thought, Eddie sits outside until he sees the door safely shut behind me, and then pulls painfully slowly away. Great. When I want to keep up with him he's harder to catch than the Road Runner on speed. Men! Why do they always do the exact opposite to what you want them to? Are they trained to be perverse from childhood? Is it something they learn in their pram to keep their mothers dancing attendance, or is it in the genes, part of their in-built man map, which includes balls dropping, voices breaking, hormones racing, and the ability to be so frustratingly obtuse without even trying?

Amanda pounces the minute I'm through the front door of Nicky's flat. 'What happened . . . was he there?' she gasps breathlessly.

She's been exercising to one of Nicky's never-used videos, a sad Olivia Newtron-Bomb headband holding back a mass of sweaty blonde hair. It's nearly four in the morning. The woman's obsessed.

I'm not going to tell her he gave me a lift home, she'd probably freak and try to garrotte me with the incredibly high-cut leotard that's currently flossing her butt cheeks.

'He came to lock up.'

'Was he with anybody?' I don't know whether her face is red from an overdose of exercise, or from Eddie-induced anxiety and anticipation.

I shake my head, bending down to undo my Cats.

'Nope.'

'What time did he get to the club?'

'I told you, in time to lock up, which was just after three.'

'So where had he been all evening?'

Cue Gestapo hat, black trench coat, fake German accent, and spotlights.

'I don't know,' I mutter tetchily.

'Did you actually learn *anything*?' She stresses the 'anything', her voice heavy with sarcasm.

'Well, one of the other girls seems to know him pretty well . . . not in the biblical sense,' I add quickly, as Amanda starts to growl. 'She said he's lovely.'

'Well, I know that, don't I?'

'All right, keep your hair band on.'

The sound of a key in the latch heralds the return of Nicky from her 'hot' date. Fortunately she hasn't brought Tarzan home with her. I don't think I could cope with an overdose of testosterone on top of Amanda.

'Helloooo,' she calls, tottering through the door on spiked drink heels. 'You just beat me home, Belly babe. We could have shared the lift if I hadn't been having my tonsils tickled in the back of an old Escort van!' She giggled. 'Which, by the way, was a new life experience I *wouldn't* recommend to my friends. Never snog a man with more hair than you in the back of a van full of chamois leathers – ugh!' She shudders. 'I can still taste hairspray and Windolene . . . not nice. By the way,' she turns to me, 'who was that who dropped you off, hon?'

Oh, shit!

'Er . . . taxi,' I reply hurriedly.

'Taxi? But I saw you get out of a Por—'

'Portuguese taxi driver? Yeah, I know, knew his way round London about as well as I'd know my way round the inside of Elvis's brain. If he's got one, that is. I'm surprised I even made it home at all . . . so, did you have a good time then?'

Fortunately Nicky's pretty pissed.

'Good time? Are you kidding? Jeez!' She whistles through closed teeth. 'I've never met such a poseur in all my life . . . what's that song, the one about finding a restaurant with glass-topped tables so that you can look at yourself all evening?'

Amanda and I both shrug.

'Well, I think you get the gist.' She hiccups, chucking her handbag on the sofa, then parking her bum next to it. 'I'm surprised he didn't carry a handbag himself to hold his brush and hair spray. I swear if he'd flicked his hand through his hair one more time, I'd have trailed his split ends in the candle till they caught.'

Elvis, who had been hiding out from Amanda by sleeping in my dirty laundry basket, wakes at the sound of Nicky laughing, and skitters into the living room joyously to celebrate the return of Mummy and, hopefully, the departure of the mad woman who growls more than he does, and spends half her time in the flat jumping up and down on the complaining floor boards like a fat demented prima ballerina.

Nicky scoops him up for a cuddle, his whole body wagging, he's so pleased to see her.

'How's my baby then? Did you have a nice evening with Aunty Manda?' she coos, much to Amanda's obvious disgust. 'Did you miss mummy? Yes, you did, didn't you . . . How did the rest of your night go, babe? Any joy with Edible Eddie?'

'That's what I was just trying to find out,' snaps Amanda impatiently, obviously not amused by Nicky's choice of nickname.

'Did you see him?' Nicky persists.

'Yes,' Amanda and I both reply at the same time.

'What happened?'

'Not a lot really. He came in to lock up.'

'And then what?' Nicky kisses Elvis's quiffed head as he chews frantically on one of her dangly silver earrings.

'And then he left.' I yawn widely, now desperate just to reach my bed and collapse.

'That's it?' cuts in Amanda, voice tinged with disappointment.

'What were you expecting? Him to sit me down and confide all his secret desires. It was only the second time I've ever met the guy, for goodness' sake!'

I chuck my jacket on the back of the sofa as Amanda glares at me in frustration.

'Well, why on earth didn't you follow him when he left?'

'Because, believe it or not, I can't actually follow him anywhere on foot and I also don't function very well without sleep. Which is what I'm going to get right now. So if you have a home to go to . . .'

'But he could have gone anywhere,' she complains, not budging.

'Well, seeing as he's a human being too, despite your protestations that he's a love god, I would imagine he probably can't function without sleep either, and has therefore gone home to bed.'

'Yes, but whose bed?' she wails.

'Oh, the entire Wimbledon women's basketball team probably,' I joke, as I skirt rapidly out of the room towards my own bed and sanctuary.

'Oh, and apparently he's a really good laugh,' I throw back over my shoulder as she goes bright purple with rage, 'so I'd assume he'd like his ideal woman to have a sense of humour!'

'Annabelle!'

I walk through the door of Daisy's on my second night to a friendly greeting. Dot, Ben, and a pretty red-haired girl I'm introduced to as the previously ill Abigail, who has recovered from her 'flu enough to return to work. They are all seated at one of the tables, sharing a pot of coffee, the two women smoking as they talk across Ben, totally engrossed in the crossword in a copy of the *Sun* one of the builders has abandoned, about a guy called Bloody Jerry.

The bar is empty, as are the restaurant and kitchens which are apparently closed every Tuesday night.

I'm invited to get a cup and take a chair.

'Wasn't sure if you'd come back after Saturday night,' Dot laughs, pouring me a coffee. 'Another night with the punters from hell . . . She was a real trooper, though,' she says to Abigail, then turns back to me. 'Don't worry, darling, it should be a bit quieter tonight. As you can see . . .' she sweeps an arm around the empty bar '. . . Tuesday everybody takes off to get an early night and recover from their excesses, so they can go out and start all over again the following day.'

'We call this the graveyard shift,' agrees Abigail. 'We should get the odd corpse in later. Bloody Jerry'll probably put in an appearance at some point.'

'Who's that then?'

'My boyfriend,' Abigail sighs unenthusiastically. 'But that may only be temporary.'

'Oh, yeah?' I question.

'I'm just waiting for something better to come along.'

'Well, you shouldn't have a very long wait then.' Dot pulls a face at me conspiratorially.

'Either that or I'm waiting for Ben finally to realise that I'm the love of his life and sweep me off my feet,' Abigail jokes, blowing a cloud of cigarette smoke into his downturned face.

Ben looks up from his crossword, eyes screwed up against the fug, and finally notices that I've arrived.

'Hey, Annabelle! Good to see you. Sorry I missed you on Saturday. Had to go home, minor crisis with my plumbing.'

'That's what comes of using the same bunch of cowboys for your flat that you somehow lost enough brain cells to hire for the cellar conversion,' Dot sighs.

'No, that's what comes of sleeping around,' jokes Abigail.

'Sleeping around!' Ben puffs. 'Would that I had the opportunity!'

'Well, I keep offering you my body . . .' Abigail pouts at him.

'Yeah, and I keep telling you it wouldn't suit me.' Ben pats his own rather rotund stomach. 'My big head on your slim frame . . .'

Abigail giggles.

'That's not quite what I was thinking. More like your big head between my slim . . .'

'Abigail!' Ben and Dot shriek in unison.

'You'll be giving poor old Belle the wrong impression of us,' Ben laughs.

'Or the right one.' Abigail grins broadly at me.

I decide I like this girl whose beautifully soft lilting Irish accent belies the brashness of her actual speech.

'It's not you that I really want anyway.' She throws a sideways glance at Ben. 'I'm sorry, darling, whilst my bod belongs to you, my heart belongs to another.'

'Not Bloody Jerry!' Dot moans, topping up our coffee cups.

'Certainly not! The man of my dreams is as far removed from Jerry as the sun from an old, worn out, dust-encrusted light bulb. No, I'm thinking of someone far more delicious than my roving-eyed Romeo.'

'You're not still fantasising about getting your manicured nails into our gorgeous boss, are you?'

'A girl can dream, can't she?'

'Yeah. The only problem is not every girl's dreams are ripe for broadcast on the adult channel.'

Abigail leans back in her chair and grins broadly.

'I'm sorry, Dotty darling, but times have changed. A girl's allowed to have a sex drive nowadays without feeling like she has to say three Hail Marys every time her libido kicks in.'

'The way you talk, anybody would think your generation invented sex,' Dot retaliates. 'You're forgetting, when I was in my teens free love was on its first official outing.'

'Yeah, and you've been a devoted follower ever since!' Abigail teases her good-naturedly. 'You know, I wish Eddie was into free love – I could ask for an orgy as the next company do.'

I think back to Eddie's flock wallpaper and mirrored ceilings, and wonder if perhaps he's a closet child of the seventies too. You could just imagine several pairs of flares being ripped off with wild group abandon, as lava lamps bubble provocatively in the background, in that house. Maybe Abigail's dream isn't so far-fetched. Although I suppose there's a big leap between the decor of the seventies and the sexual ethic of that time. I mean, just because you drive a

Porsche doesn't mean you belong to the owners' club.

'Then again,' Abigail continues enthusiastically, 'if it was an orgy I'd have to share him, and I want that luscious bod all to myself . . .'

'Excuse me, this is one of my best friends you're lusting over,' Ben interjects indignantly.

'Oh, so you're back on the same planet again. Thought we'd lost you to your little mind game,' she says, referring sarcastically to Ben's barely completed crossword. 'If you're going to pretend to be intellectual, Benjamin, the least you could do is fail to finish the *Times* crossword instead of that thing!' She leans over and peers closer. 'And he's not even using the cryptic clues, it's the quick and easy!'

'Isn't that just the way you like your men?' Ben grins back at her.

'Proven by the fact that she's seeing Bloody Jerry . . .' Dot joins in.

'Do you think he'll be in tonight?' Abigail's still on Planet Eddie.

Ben crinkles his nose. 'Doubt it, not on a Tuesday, he'll be down at Betty's . . .'

'That's a shame.' Abigail's face falls a little. 'I wanted to show him off to Belle.'

'I've already met him,' I admit cautiously.

'You have!' she exclaims, like she's just discovered we have a shared hobby or something, 'So tell me,' leaning in conspiratorially, 'what did you think?'

'He seemed nice.'

'Nice? She calls the man nice! That's like calling Michaelangelo's David a sculpture when it's obviously a work of art. He's gorgeous!' Abigail sticks her little finger in a half-used plastic pot of cream and sucks it slowly, head tilted back, eyes distant and dreamy.

'Wonder what Eddie'd look like in nothing but a fig leaf?'

'David hasn't got a fig leaf,' I giggle.

'He hasn't? Even better! Those Italians certainly knew how to do things properly, didn't they? Naked men, ice-cream, and cappuccino.' Abigail fills our coffee cups. 'What more could a girl ask for?'

'A Swiss bank account, a flat in Mayfair and a devoted toy boy,' states Dot emphatically. 'In fact, I think it should be government policy that every woman who hits forty automatically gets a toy boy. Sod getting a pension when you're sixty, get laid when you're forty instead. Life really would "begin" then, wouldn't it? Well, your sex life anyway.'

'Your sex life began well before forty, Dotty darling,' Abigail interrupts her.

'Unless she's talking in numbers instead of years,' Ben teases, deftly ducking a swift cuff from the back of Dot's manicured hand. 'It took her the first forty men to get the hang of it properly.'

'What about you, Belle?' Dot turns the spotlight on me. 'Seeing as we've heard our sad sex stories ten times over, you can tell us about *your* love life.'

'What's one of those then?'

'You're single?' Abigail queries.

'Totally.'

'Don't sound so surprised, Abi.' Ben taps the warm spoon from his coffee on the back of Abigail's wrist, making her jump. 'There are a lot of us about, you know.'

'Yeah, like Eddie.' Dot winks at her.

Further confirmation that Eddie's definitely running solo at the moment. Jot that down in my mental note book.

'Mmm,' Abigail muses thoughtfully, sizing me up. 'You know, I've just had a marvellous idea. You're single, he's single, we could fix you up . . .'

'What about me?' wails Ben. 'Why don't you ever want to fix anyone up with me?'

'Eddie?' I ask, surprised. 'I thought you wanted him for yourself?'

'Not all fantasies translate well into reality.' Abigail shrugs. 'Besides, I have Jerry.'

'*Everybody* has Jerry,' Dot says, the scornful note in her voice softened only slightly by the laughter that accompanies this statement.

'That's only rumour . . . I haven't concrete proof yet, as evidenced by the fact that he's alive and still attached to his dangly bits.'

'Look,' I cut in, 'I don't mean to sound ungrateful, but I don't think I'd really want to be fixed up with Eddie.'

'You wouldn't?' all three ask in surprise.

'I mean, he seems nice . . .'

He seems very nice, but I like life too much.

'There's that word again – nice.' Abigail shakes her head. 'Never mind, give her time, she'll soon fall in love with him herself and be begging for our help as amateur Cupids. We all fall in love with him eventually, you know. To varying degrees, of course, but it's inevitable . . .'

'Please assume that Abigail's talking about the female staff members.' Ben grins, sticking the tip of the spoon he's just assaulted Abigail with in the sugar bowl, and then sucking it.

'Although I think Sylvia may have had a momentary blaze of unrequited passion.'

'Maybe our Annabelle's immune.' Dot taps her ash-laden cigarette into an ashtray, and winks at me again.

Abigail snorts dismissively.

'Nobody's immune to love. It's like 'flu – you get over one severe bout, weak and sniffling into a tissue, vowing never to expose yourself to the germs again, only to end up catching another strain you haven't had before.'

Perhaps that's why Nicky's working her way through so many men, building up an immunity, a modern-day Marie Curie in search of the ultimate cure for the one thing that seems to ail all women: men.

As the evening progresses, Daisy's slowly but surely begins to fill. The others' idea of quiet is the equivalent of a pretty swinging party in my book. Admittedly, it's not the mad, heaving throng that graced us with their party-hearty presence on Saturday night, but it's still pretty busy.

I wait for a quiet moment, claim a loo break, but instead of heading there, slide into the offices on the first floor and rootle through the drawers until I find Eddie's desk diary showing all of his appointments over the next eight months.

Amanda's going to love this. She'll be able to know where he is at practically any moment of any day.

My heart's tap dancing in safety boots upon the bones of my rib cage as I walk over to the photocopier. I'll die if someone comes in and catches me doing this. They've all been so nice to me. I feel like the school cheat preparing to photocopy exam papers when the teachers have taken time out to cram me.

There's a pin board above the photocopier covered in photographs taken in the club. It's obvious this is where Amanda nicked the shots she gave us of Eddie. There's a few more pictures that must be from the same reel, the same group of guys drinking and laughing in Daisy's bar, with Eddie to the right of the shot.

As I look closer, I suddenly see something in the back of one of the photographs that I hadn't noticed before.

I lean in closer. Oh my god, it isn't . . . is it?

It's Amanda. At least I think it is. The navy blue eyes are hers, and so are the bee-stung Beatrice Dalle lips, but she must be at least three sizes smaller.

She's also smiling, something I don't see very often.

Well, at least I can stop wondering about whatever it was that attracted Eddie to someone like Amanda in the first place.

She looks absolutely heart-stoppingly gorgeous, and it's not just the slimmer, fitter figure – it's the broad, beaming, headlights on full grin that's just radiating from her face.

She looks fun, the sort of person I'd be attracted to as a friend.

What's happened to her? The Amanda in the picture looks nothing like the self-centred controlling Miss Bossy I know.

I look back at one of the photographs of Eddie and Ben I haven't seen before, obviously both slightly the worse for wear. You know, the drunken buddies, arms around shoulders type of shot, with Ben practically stopping Eddie from sliding to the floor. For once Eddie is looking straight at the camera, smiling that sexy, cheeky little lop-sided grin of his, mouth curling up at just one side.

This doesn't feel right.

It's all very well checking out if a husband to be is actually worth taking the plunge with, to check on his faithfulness factor, or rather lack of it, before you offer to spend the rest of your life with him. It's just like checking that a potential business partner isn't hiding any dodgy deals before you invest your hard-earned savings.

But this is different.

This feels like cheating, like I'm participating in a con or a scam.

Amanda should want him to want her for herself, not feel she's got to turn into his ideal woman. She wants to offer him something that isn't real. It's like paying for that must-have dress with counterfeit cash, or putting it on your card and ignoring the fact that one day soon you're going to have to pay it back with interest.

I put the diary back where I found it, uncopied.

Nicky is sitting on the sofa in the open-plan sitting room when I get back, the Conran coffee table littered with empty chocolate bar wrappers. A half-eaten tub of Chunky Monkey sits melting gooily next to an open box of Mr Kipling's French Fancies that someone – no guesses as to whom – has eaten all the chocolate and lemon ones out of.

'Why do I always want stuff that's bad for me?' Nicky moans, stuffing handfuls of smokey bacon crisps into her mouth and chewing miserably. 'It's just so unfair. Why can't I be one of those women who lose their man then completely lose their appetite, so I can waste away to a wafer of sensual, sexy slimness?'

'Sorry, babe. For you and me food is just a sex substitute.' I sit down next to her and, nicking a pink French Fancy, bite off the iced dollop of cream on the top, before beginning to nibble the icing off the edges. 'Give me a few more months of enforced celibacy and I'll be an easy size sixteen.'

'Join the club,' Nicky sighs, tugging at the waist band of her fit and flare trousers, which are fitting rather too much in all the wrong places, and not flaring particularly well in others.

'I suppose we could always exercise or something, burn off calories and excess energy at the same time?' I suggest, dipping my remaining piece of sponge in melted Ben & Jerry's.

Nicky tips the last of the crisps straight from the bag into her mouth and looks at me like I've just suggested she redecorate the entire flat in orange paisley flock wallpaper.

'Exercise?' she spits, cracking open a bottle of Bud viciously between the open legs of a bronze statue of a male athlete. 'You sound like Amanda. Sod that! I'm just going to find myself a man who doesn't care if I've got a size eight or a size eighteen bum. Or even eight bums for that matter.'

'*I'm* a bum,' I state morosely, nicking Nix's Bud and necking half the bottle.

'Well, I know that.' She rolls her eyes and heads into the kitchen for further supplies. 'You're a beach bum at heart.'

'Not that sort of bum, I meant it as an insult.'

'Can you insult yourself?' She staggers back into the room, buckling under the weight of four bottles of Bud, a fresh tub of Cherry Garcia and two spoons.

'I am insulting myself by doing what I'm doing. I don't think I want to do this any more – be Amanda's stool pigeon. It doesn't feel right. Snooping around. It feels like we're laying an ambush for the guy.'

'We are.' Nicky struggles to push the cardboard lid off the ice cream tub. 'A lurve ambush. He's going to be hijacked by high passion.'

'And I don't like lying to the people at work,' I continue with my whinge.

'Well, you can hardly tell them the truth, now can you?'

'But they're all so nice, I feel awful!' I wail. 'I

honestly don't know why I agreed to do this sort of thing in the first place.'

'Because you're providing a valuable service to women.'

'Yeah, if you don't want to humiliate yourself, hire me to humiliate myself on your behalf!' I grumble.

'You can't give up now, Annabelle. Amanda needs you . . .'

The minute she's said this, Nicky realises it isn't the best incentive to wave in front of me.

'Okay, so forget Amanda,' she replies to my raised eyebrows, 'and think of the money, the lovely loot, the luscious lolly.'

'Yeah, and the fact that I'm working nearly twenty-four hours a day to earn it!'

'Think of all the things you could buy yourself,' Nicky continues.

'Yeah, if I had any time to go shopping. And even if I could go out and buy lots of clothes, I'd have absolutely nowhere to wear them. I hardly want to be crawling through the undergrowth in a gorgeous little Moschino dress, or cleaning out slop trays in something silky from Donna Karan. I suppose I could always get a 'specially commissioned Vivienne Westwood balaclava, or Calvin Klein combat jeans – or how about asking Miu Miu to run me up a gorgeous little pair of black satin bovver boots with a Johnny loves Rosie back pack to accessorise?'

'You're thinking along the wrong lines,' Nicky giggles. 'You're thinking GI Jane when you should be thinking the Avengers, Emma Peel, Honor Blackman.

She managed to look outrageously glam and still leap off the odd building or fight off three armed oriental attackers without breaking a finger nail. Sod kamikazi khaki, why not go in for the old kinky boots and tight cat suits?'

I could go for that look. There's always been something appealing about the *femme fatale* image, but I think I'd be a bit more conspicuous sidling down an alley in a skin-tight black leather number than I would in my old jeans. And tatty trainers, whilst giving off more of a vagrant than a rampant image, are far better for climbing up drainpipes and shinning over walls than a pair of pointy heel vamp boots. I can just see it now: I'm poised in my favourite position, behind a bush, ready for a quick getaway, only to find that my three-inch spikes have sunk in the mud and I'm stuck like a cat in quick-dry concrete.

The absurdity of this image helps me realise even better the total lunacy of what I'm doing.

'You know, Nicky, joking apart, I really think I should quit and get myself a proper job, in an office or something.'

'Yeah.' She nods sagely. 'I suppose you could be right. After all, the hours you're working are atrocious, you're out in all weathers . . .'

I nod my agreement.

'And if your mother knew what you're doing!' Nicky rolls her eyes heavenward. 'You know, you're right. She'd be *so* pleased if you gave it up and got yourself a proper career. I mean, even though you tried so hard and couldn't find anything, I'm sure you'd be able to get something working in *her* company. I know, you could be her toady, employed to suck up and generally arse lick all day long . . .'

Sneaky but effective. By 8.30 I'm back in my boots and balaclava (metaphorically speaking) and ensconced in a bush outside Eddie Farrar's house in Hampstead (unfortunately literally), with a rogue leaf affectionately tickling my left ear, and a sharp twig digging into my right bum cheek.

Chapter Eight

Eddie Farrar's Ideal Woman

Intelligent
Attractive
Stylish
Informed
Independent
Business-minded
Should enjoy find wines, good food, travel, fast cars.

Stretched out on the rug, pen in mouth, note pad in hand, Elvis chewing my bare toes, I re-read our list and realise that what we've actually drawn up is a list of Eddie's own attributes and interests.

'So you're going to turn yourself into a clone in the hope that he'll find you devastatingly attractive?' I mock Amanda, who's perched on the sofa, rubbing moisturising lotion into her neck and drooling as Nicky tucks into a Big Mac.

'Who do you think he is – Narcissus? Besides, what

happened to opposites attract?'

'Yes, but it's supposed to be better if you have things in common, isn't it?' says Nix, through a mouthful of burger and mayonnaise.

'Blimey, this is confusing,' I sigh, pushing my hair out of my face. 'Can't you just be yourself, then if it doesn't work out, you know it wasn't meant to be because you aren't compatible?'

'I've tried being myself, it didn't work,' Amanda snaps, anger driven by hunger.

'Well, doesn't that tell you something?'

She narrows her eyes contemptuously at me.

'It tells me I should try again, and make sure it works this time.'

She makes it sound like she's re-sitting her driving test or something.

'Don't look at me like that, Annabelle! I won't be changing the essential me . . .' she continues, gazing into the mirror on the table at her own reflection.

The Essential Me . . . great name for a self-help book.

'. . . I'll just be doing a bit of fine tuning.'

'Like for an MOT test,' chips in Nix. 'Just because you make sure the car fits all the test requirements, doesn't mean it isn't still the same chassis.'

'Don't start the MOT analysis again, babe.' I cross my eyes at her. 'That's one of the things that got us here in the first place.'

Even if we do make Amanda into the sort of person we think Eddie would fall in love with, it doesn't mean to say he's actually going to. It's not always the people you think you'll get on with that you do.

Look at me and Amanda.

No, don't look at me and Amanda, we don't really get on.

How about Amanda and Nicky then?

No, Nicky's such a sweetie everybody loves her, even egocentrics like Amanda.

Anyway, what I was trying to say is that you can't make a formula for attraction. You can meet somebody who *should* be totally perfect for you, and decide you'd rather have a home-made lobotomy without anaesthetic than a relationship with them.

There's a certain key element to *Amour* that is totally indefinable.

Perhaps it's lunacy.

Or a virus.

I think Abigail's right. Love should officially be classified as an illness. I mean, look what it can do to you. It can be far more debilitating than the worst kind of disease. It can turn a normally sane, happy person, into a wailing, jellified, manic-depressive, paranoid schizophrenic lunatic.

I should know, I've been that lunatic myself on the odd occasion, although looking back, I don't think I've ever really been in love. Not properly. I mean, I've *thought* that I was in love, but isn't it all about finding someone you want to spend the rest of your life with? The prospect of spending the rest of my life with any of my exes is about as appealing as spending the rest of my life on Death Row.

Call me an old cynic – well, I'd rather be called a young cynic if I'm going to be called a cynic at all –

but it seems to me that this LOVE thing is more hassle than it's worth. My dad's got this theory that as long as the good times outweigh the bad times then something is worth doing, or someone is worth having (or something is worth having, and someone is worth doing, whichever way round is the most relevant at the time).

It seems to me, though, that love is neither worth having nor doing because it ends up inflicting a lot more pain than pleasure. Nicky loved Richard and got hurt. Amanda professes to love Eddie, and appears to hurt constantly. I mean, what's the attraction? Can someone please enlighten me? Why do we do it? Ooh, yes, I think I love you, here's my heart, trample on it. Masochism at its height.

If love is an illness, I think Amanda must be terminal.

I wonder if I could find her a cure in the form of another man? A luscious panacea of bulging bicep and bank account – that should make her happy.

Amanda's Ideal Man

Successful, Wealthy, Powerful, Generous

Maybe we do need to change Amanda after all – into someone who's not quite so shallow.

Refusing to be monopolised by Amanda, who would like me to be watching Eddie Farrar's movements twenty-four hours a day, and as a favour to Nicky, I agree to take on another customer, and spend an afternoon out following the boyfriend of one of the secretaries at Nicky's firm. Thankfully for my ever-increasing disillusionment with the opposite sex, it turns out to be one of the nicer occasions where a formerly attentive and considerate other half, who had suddenly become elusive, secretive and sneaky, turned out to be whisking around madly arranging a surprise thirtieth birthday party. The absolute relief more than made up for the ruined surprise, leaving one happy customer who had just under a week to practise looking pleasantly shocked, and was actually quite pleased that she'd know to redo her make up on her way home from work, before flinging open her sitting-room door to a room full of beaming, streamer-throwing, full party-outfitted friends and relatives.

Returning home, I hear strange noises as the lift arrives at the second floor, music and what sounds like the regular thump-thump-thump of a jack-hammer.

Nicky and Amanda have pushed back the sofas and the coffee table and are synchronised sweating to an exercise video, floor boards groaning as they scissor jump, side slide, waist stretch, and pelvic thrust their way along with Cindy Crawford.

Nicky's in a T-shirt and a pair of saggy, baggy jogging trousers that are older than her. Amanda, of course, is in the very latest matching Marzano, train-ers, socks, cycling shorts, and the sort of leotard that should really chop you in two every time you bend to touch your toes, although I'm sure the Olivia Newton John sweatband which has once more re-emerged to hold Amanda's tumbling blonde hair out of her very red face went out about sixteen years ago.

Elvis has sensibly retired to a safe distance and is watching them from under the temporarily displaced coffee table, chocolate brown head to one side, totally bemused and somewhat fearful expression on his little doggy face.

As part of her mad attempt to lose another stone in only six weeks, Amanda's joined a rather exclusive health club down in the docks. She's even persuaded Nicky, who views exercise in the same light as period pains and unwanted facial hair, to go to the club with her on occasion.

Nicky hasn't yet lost any weight, but she's shed a certain bond dealer pretty quickly, and is now in lust with a Belgian tennis coach called Christian, who apparently has a face like Leonardo and a body like Jean-Claude Van Damme. Whilst this seems to make the other two drool like hot Rottweilers, I get a vision of a pretty little head on top of a massive muscular body. Perhaps I should see this vision for myself. I need a little side tracking to take my mind off work . . .

This must be homework.

Helping myself to a nice cold Kit-Kat from the fridge, I lean against the kitchen door frame and sharing it with Elvis, watching them sweat their way through the last five minutes.

That's one good thing about working in the club at the same time as doing Amanda's dirty work – it's stopping me from making a speedy jump to size sixteen and over! When the bar's full, you're totally run off your feet. When you're not so busy the music's so infectious, you end up boogying away behind the bar.

It also helps that when I'm there I don't have time to eat. I seem to survive on a diet of sucked sliced lemon and cocktail cherries, and the odd plate of leftovers when the restaurant chef's in a good mood. Which is about once every full moon when there's an R in the month.

Elvis eats chocolate faster than I do. I make a return visit to the fridge for another bar, then unable to face the sight of two synchronised bottoms wobbling in time to naff music, slump down at the kitchen table and flick through the latest issue of *Cosmo*, Elvis drooling on my bare feet.

Minutes later, Nicky staggers past me, eyeing my second Kit-Kat covetously, and pulling a bottle of Evian from the fridge, guzzles it greedily.

'Hi, babe,' she finally says when she's got enough breath back to speak. 'I don't know why this is called Keep Fit, I feel like I've just been run over by a bus.'

'Where's Pol Pot Belly Pig, the desperate dictator, gone to?'

'Shhh!' Nicky giggles. 'She'll hear you.'

'Good, I might get the sack then.'

'She's changing.'

'Well, that *was* the whole idea. Hopefully into a better person . . .'

'She's changing,' Nicky repeats, giving in to her

lack of will-power and snatching my last finger of Kit Kat, which I've been waving in front of her teasingly, 'into something less sweaty.'

In the sitting room, Amanda has emerged from Nicky's shower and is perched on the sofa, pulling on her Gucci boots. Hearing her name, but fortunately not the other comments, she looks up. I wait for the usual onslaught of questions.

She smiles.

I smile back in surprise.

She looks back down at her boots.

'Leaving already?' I ask, mainly as a prompt.

'I've got to go, my course starts in half an hour.'

'Course?' I query, curious.

'I've booked up for some lessons in Cordon Bleu cookery,' she says without looking up. 'I thought perhaps I should do something useful with my life.'

I can think of things that are far more use to everyday life than Cordon Bleu cookery, but if it keeps Amanda happy, and out of my hair . . .

'Brilliant idea!' I enthuse.

Nicky raises her eyebrows at me in amazement.

'Besides Eddie likes good food,' Amanda adds, shrugging on her fake fur jacket.

Ah, so that's the real reason. I knew the silence on that particular subject was too good to be true, it's all part of the big transformation into Eddie Farrar's ideal woman. What's she going to do at this launch party? Kick the chef out of the kitchen and whip him up a personal meal for two, complete with Champagne, candles and herself, stretched across a large plate with a fresh strawberry in her navel for dessert, screaming, 'Cream me, Eddie, cream me!'

In an attempt to become our vision of Eddie's ideal woman, Amanda has not only enrolled on a Prue Leith Cordon Bleu Cookery course but a wine appreciation course as well, and on learning the state of Eddie's house, has decided the next trip to the local Poly will be for an intensive study of Interior Design and perhaps a little Feng Shui for added harmony.

I should be eternally grateful to adult education. The more time Amanda spends 'improving herself', the less time she has to badger me about Eddie, usually demanding a full run down of his entire day to include how many times he sneezed, scratched, or went to the loo.

Amanda is scheming, manipulative, and I think slightly insane, but as much as I love to hate her, I can't help liking her in a strange sort of way. It's like there are two Amandas, and I occasionally get to glimpse one that's not far off being a decent human being. Despite being incredibly bossy with her, there's an underlying kindness and even a genuine affection in her treatment of Nicky, and although I really worry sometimes, when Nicky's dragged off on yet another one of Amanda's mad self-improvement schemes, I can see her beginning to get back some of her old self-assurance. Nicky's always been very competent but not particularly confident, unless stuck in a court of law where she suddenly becomes a cross between Kavanagh QC, Quincy, and Ally McBeal without so many hang ups. Amanda has enough confidence for eight people and some of it's beginning to rub off.

So far as Amanda and I are concerned, we're kind of wary of each other, like two wrestlers eyeing each other from distant roped corners, with Nicky in the middle as referee. We know that in order for us to put on a good show for the crowd, we need to work together in a cooperative manner, but in the end one of us is going to have to submit, and neither of us wants to be the one on the floor in the other's stranglehold.

You know when a girl says that she needs new clothes, there's normally a huge discrepancy in her actual definition of need.

Well, I *literally* have no clothes.

In my wardrobe, I have the following items:

one pair of deck shoes, complete with holes;
one pair of Cats, semi-decent;
one pair of Levis previously Nicky's;
one skinny rib T-shirt, and one chunky sweater, ditto;
several sun-bleached items that used to be clothes, and now look like dusters;
three black polo shirts kindly donated by Lazy Daisy's with, appropriately enough, little smiling daisies embroidered just above my left boob, which are fine for work but not exactly going out or day wear material;
two pairs of black jeans, as above, but thankfully

no daisies, smiling or otherwise;
one pink dress – no further description needed
   here.

For the first time in the past couple of years, I actually have a bit of money to go shopping, and head off before my lunchtime shift to reacquaint myself with the delights of Oxford Street.

I still can't afford the lure of couture, but plenty of bargain bucket shops have sprung up between the bona fide boutiques. Trash fash. My favourite. My theory is if you can't afford the good stuff, and trust me I'd love to be able to, then you should immediately shoot to the opposite end of the scale, the fashion equivalent of junk food.

I do have a quick moment of self-indulgence first by having a delightful rummage through the Kookai sale then wander awe-struck around the ground floor of Selfridge's, through the handbags, and into make up.

I always feel totally in awe of the perfectly made up sales assistants. I would desperately love to book in for a make over but feel far too intimidated, especially by the ultra-trendy über-babes with the perfect poker faces at the Mac counter, who ignore me with confidence-bashing finesse.

Instead I sod off to the places where the plastic bags don't have logos, and I don't have an inferiority complex, and wade happily through the sale rails and bargain bins until I happen to glance at my watch and realise I should have been at work ten minutes ago.

I head off down to Daisy's at stampede pace,

hurling myself bodily in front of passing taxis in the vain hope of actually getting one to stop, and finally burst through the heavy front doors like a bag lady on speed, forty minutes late, only to come to a screeching halt as I spot a familiar pair of figures ensconced cosily at one of the restaurant tables.

Simon and my mother.

What the hell are they doing in here?

They're side by side in one of the corner booths, talking conspiratorially. Plotting, no doubt. They must have got wind that I work here and have set an ambush. I can just see it now – the faked surprise when they *just happen* to spot me behind the bar.

Fortunately they're head to head, and didn't spot my somewhat dramatic entrance. Digging in my plastic bags, I rapidly don my new fake Raybans, the Deputy Dawg hat I bought with the lovely fur ear flaps to keep me warm on cold night watches, and slash the bargain bucket fuschia lipstick I bought on a mad impulse across my mouth. I've seen my mother once in over two years. Before that I spent three years swearing that universities didn't let their students have holidays. She's always protesting that she sees me so infrequently she barely recognises me when we do meet, is it too much to hope that an impromptu disguise will fool her? Probably, but anything's worth a try.

'Not the look for you, Belle,' Dot says sarcastically as I slide in alongside her behind the bar, apologising breathlessly for being late. 'The hat and the lipstick could be a fashion statement . . . I suppose . . . but the sunglasses? *Inside*?'

'It's the new paintwork,' I tell her, 'it's so bright it's giving me a headache.'

'It's not the paintwork that's too bright, it's your lipstick. Oh, well, at least we'll be able to spot you if we have another power cut. One of the builder's bum brigade drilled through a mains cable earlier.'

'You're joking! Is he okay?'

'Well, let's just say it was a good job one of the other incompetents had started a flood or he wouldn't have been wearing his rubber wellies. As it was, he escaped with minor burns and a rather punkish hair style. Perhaps you should lend him your hat to cover the damage,' she muses. 'Then again, I think he'd probably stick with the hair as a less embarrassing option.'

Just to complete the picture of sophistication that I am not, I stick my tongue out at Dot.

'I know I asked for suggestions about new work gear . . .'

I turn round in mortified embarrassment at the sound of a familiar laughing voice, and come face to pink lip-sticked, sun-glasses, stupid-hatted, tongue-hanging-out face with Eddie.

'Annabelle?' He lifts up my sunglasses and peers underneath. 'It is you!'

'Of course it's me,' I mutter grumpily, embarrassment making me defensive.

'The look's very . . . different,' he states tactfully.

'She's making a statement,' Dot sniggers.

'Yeah, stating loud and clear that she's got no sense of style whatsoever,' yells Sylvia from the other end of the bar.

'I don't know,' Eddie murmurs, looking pointedly at my ear flaps, 'I've always admired people who've never felt the need to be a slave to fashion.'

He's taking the piss.

His mouth isn't laughing but his eyes are.

Strike that. His mouth *is* laughing, it's just fighting the visible evidence of laughter, wobbling at the edges, a minor earthquake of giggles causing tremors in the muscles.

' "Where did you get that hat, where did you get that hat!" ' chorus Dot and Sylv, arms around each other's shoulders, swaying side by side like old time musical entertainers.

Yet again my efforts to remain inconspicuous are drawing more attention than if I just acted normally.

'I'm hiding,' I hiss at them pointedly.

'From what?' asks Eddie.

'It's not a what, it's a who.'

'Okay, from whom?'

'Him.'

I surreptitiously point out Simon who is now at the other end of the bar, alone. I don't know where my mother is, probably on another legendary loo trip. Either that, or she's turned back into a bat and flown out of the window.

'Who is he?'

'A mistake.'

'Oh, right, yes. Had some of those myself. Want me to get rid of him?'

'Could you?'

'Definitely, if it makes you take off that stupid hat.'

Eddie comes behind the bar and heads over to Simon, who's currently waving a tenner at Sylv in the vain hope he'll stop chatting up a gorgeous young biker and serve him. A few minutes later I watch in thankful disbelief as Simon heads out of the door without so much as a backward glance.

'Thank you so much.' I smile at Eddie, taking off my hat and running a hand through my flattened hair. 'I was starting to cook!'

'No problem.' He shrugs.

'But how on earth did you manage to get him to leave so quickly and so quietly?'

'Easy.' Eddie smiles disarmingly at me. 'I told him you were desperately in love with him, but far too shy to admit it, and that the old-fashioned, subtle approach would be a better way of luring you out of your shell and into his waiting arms.'

Eddie's smile turns into laughter as I stare at him in open-mouthed horror.

'I think he's gone off to catch Tiffany's before they close,' he says, eyes dancing merrily. 'I hear they've got a rather fetching new line in engagement rings.'

My shift ends at seven and afterwards I drag myself back to Nicky's, brain flickering like a light bulb about to expire. I stagger bleary-eyed out of the lift, shoes in one hand, brain slumped knackered and comatosed against my cranium, to see Amanda flitting in and out of Lucy's old apartment, lugging boxes from the corridor.

I'm hallucinating.

I've had a hard day, and I'm seeing things.

'Hi, Belle!'

Okay, now I'm hearing things too.

'Amanda?'

'Yes.'

'What are you doing?'

'Moving in.'

Dear god, please, no. Not this, anything but this. I slump against Nicky's door.

'I've taken over Lucy's lease, now that she and Gordon have got the divorce settlement sorted,' she calls happily over her shoulder. 'Isn't it just perfect? I can pop round for breakfast tomorrow morning and we can discuss our plan of action.'

Just perfect. The psycho across the corridor. What was that film? *Single White Female*. She's moved in on my life, and now she's moved into the apartment opposite.

How am I going to break it to Nicky?

Nix is in the bedroom, attacking her hair with a hot brush, getting ready for dinner at Mezzo with an antiques dealer who has actually somehow managed to make the rare leap from one night stand-in to second date.

Why do most hair appliances look like lethal weapons? Maybe it's because they're part of a girl's arsenal for tracking and attacking members of the opposite sex. I wonder whether I should wait until she's unplugged before I hit her with the good news?

She hears me enter the room and, looking up, smiles at me in the mirror. A rare, rather nice smile.

Shame I'm just about to be the one to kill it off.

'Er, Nix . . .' I venture hesitantly, 'you know I said you shouldn't give back the wedding presents? Well, I've changed my mind . . . starting with the flat.'

Nicky rolls home at four in the morning.

The door bell goes at eight.

Amanda's at the front door still in her robe and fluffy mules.

'Talk about bringing your work home with you!' Nicky mutters crossly, as she's dragged out of her pit, eyes hollow, hungover to her green gills.

She perks up a little at the bag of freshly baked croissants Amanda's brought with her, and with the ravenous hunger of the newly woken drunk devours three in a row whilst Amanda makes herself at home and starts to perk a pot of coffee.

This is ridiculous. It seems that nowadays I can't even breathe without Amanda being there. Next thing I know she'll be knocking her own personal door through from her place to Nicky's, so that she can pop in and out at will.

I'll be sitting in the bath and she'll suddenly snorkel up from the suds at the other end, demanding an Eddie update!

She's adopted us, we're her newfound best friends, she seeks our opinion on everything from clothes to cuisine, and then ignores absolutely everything we say to go her own merry way as usual.

That said, there is something infectious about her – when she's not on a manic-depressive kick – but then again, the same could be said of bubonic plague.

The door buzzer sounds. Now I know it's not Amanda because she's already here, so who else surfaces this early?

As the other two are stuffing their faces, I'm the one expected to go and answer it. Rolling my eyes and muttering about slavery, I pointedly thump my coffee cup on the table between them and head for the front door.

It's the local Interflora delivery boy, who's been to the flat so many times since Nicky suddenly became single we're on first name and cards at Christmas terms.

'Flowers!' I yell at Nix, chucking them on the coffee table.

'Who from?' she yells back from the kitchen, where she's just tucking into her fourth croissant, a little more slowly than the first three.

'Oh, probably yet another poor misguided soul who feels that a few wilting blooms will win them a place in your heart. Or if not a place in your heart, then at least a return ticket to your knickers.'

Nicky comes out of the kitchen, pokes her tongue out at me, and stuffs the remaining half of her croissant in my mouth to shut me up.

'Ooh, pretty!' she exclaims. 'Whoever it is must be keen, there are at least three dozen stems here!'

She eagerly pulls out the little white card attached to the cellophane, and reads the message.

'Er, Belle . . . they're not actually for me. They're for you.'

'For me?'

She nods.

'From Simon.'

'Simon?' I repeat dumbly.

Thank you so much, Eddie Farrar, for your kind intervention!

Nicky holds the card out to me.

I automatically reach out to take it from her, but rather than reading it, simply look dumbly at her and the huge bunch of red roses she's still clutching on to.

'He wants to take you out to dinner.'

'Why?'

'I don't know, why do men usually want to take a woman out to dinner?'

'Sex, probably,' Amanda calls from the kitchen, breaking her second croissant in half and spreading a thick layer of butter over the warm pastry.

I'd almost forgotten she was in there.

A temporary state of bliss.

'Well, he's gonna have to want,' I snap. 'It would take more than a few flowers to tempt me back into Simon's Y-fronts!'

'Ferrari?' offers Amanda.

'More like frontal lobotomy. You keep them.' I chuck them back at Nicky. 'Add them to the Interflora hot house you're cultivating in your bedroom – that's if you have room. There are so many flowers in there, Kew Gardens have started to re-route visitors. You couldn't do me a favour and take Simon too? Add him to your harem. You've got so many men, you wouldn't notice another one . . .'

'You're right,' Nicky mocks herself, 'I'm just like a double decker bus – always room for one more on top!'

Nicky's wild social life may be cause for amusement, but it's also the cause of our first row since I made Jamie's Action Man break off a long-term affair with Nicky's Sindy, to go out with my new Barbie.

Not that Nicky and I really row, it's just sometimes when you feel someone is doing something that isn't particularly good for them, you feel duty bound to step in. After all, friendship is nothing without honesty.

What Nicky does with her sex life is her business, but the morning I wake up to find yet another prat wandering round the kitchen in Nicky's dressing gown, is the morning I decide that if I'm a true friend I should voice the concern I'm feeling in buckets about the number of prats that have been seen wandering round the kitchen in her dressing gown recently.

I wait until this morning's prat has trashed Nicky's bathroom, used the last of the milk on the last of the Cornflakes, and sworn at Elvis twice before finally leaving, before tackling her about the fact that she's turning from prim to promiscuous at an alarming rate.

She's in complete and utter denial about this fact.

'It's just sex, Belle,' she laughs, grimacing as she sips on a black coffee.

'It's dangerous.'

'Only when you do it hanging off the balcony without a safety harness,' she quips.

'It's not funny, Nix.'

Her smile fades.

'I'm not a silly school girl, Belle. Haven't you ever heard of condoms?'

'Haven't you ever heard of self-restraint?' I retort without thinking.

Nicky's face falls.

'Look, I'm sorry, Nix, that was uncalled for. What you do is up to you. But I don't think what you're doing is making you particularly happy. Come on, be honest, *is* it making you happy?'

'Oh, totally orgasmic!' she snaps mockingly. 'I'm going to take the dog out!'

She storms from the room, Elvis hugging her heels. Two minutes later I hear the front door slam.

Ladies and gentlemen, Elvis has now left the building. Repeat, Elvis has now left the building.

How great can life get?

My best friend's turned into Cassie Nova.

My mother's turned into Cilla Black.

Amanda the Mad is breathing only inches from this spot, permanently.

Simon's out booking the vicar.

I am a living lie.

And to cap it all, Elvis has eaten my only handbag.

I'm going back to bed!

An hour later there's a knock on my bedroom door. It opens a touch, and a hand waving a pair of white lace knickers slips through, closely followed by Nicky's head.

'I didn't have a white handkerchief.' She smiles uncertainly at me. 'Truce?' She withdraws the knickers, and comes through the door herself.

'I'm sorry, Belle.'

'No,' I emerge from under the duvet, 'I'm sorry. It's your life.'

'No, you were right.' She flops down on the end of my bed, and sighs heavily. 'I think I've just been trying to prove to myself that men still find me attractive.'

'That's what Jamie said.'

'Oh, he did, did he?'

I nod. 'Not just a pretty face, that boy.'

'No, he's got a pretty everything else as well.' Nicky grins.

She gets under the duvet at the other end of the bed, sliding two slabs of ice on to my shins.

'Jeez, your feet are freezing!'

'This is what I miss,' she sighs, ignoring my shriek of complaint, 'having someone to warm my feet on in bed. It may sound totally un PC but I don't think we were made to be single. Well, I certainly wasn't anyway. I know things are different nowadays, it's not automatically expected that you'll meet a man, get married, have kids . . .'

'Wish someone would tell my mother that,' I moan.

'But I must admit, it's what I always expected I'd do. Now look at me!'

'Well, you've always got your mates, babe.'

'I know,' she smiles warmly at me, 'and I'm bloody lucky and wouldn't change you for the world. But it's not that, Belle, it's having somebody to cuddle in bed at night, to talk across the pillow to. You know, a warm bum in your stomach . . .'

'There's always Elvis.'

'Yeah, but he farts more than Richard used to.'

She laughs softly.

'I don't know, Belle, call me old-fashioned, but that's what I want.'

'Call you old-fashioned? Not after the last few weeks I wouldn't, babe, anything but!'

Nicky smiles wryly.

'I suppose I have gone a bit mad, haven't I?'

'Just a bit.'

'Call it making up for lost time,' she suggests. 'We agreed I should snog a few frogs.'

'Yeah, but that didn't include playing major league leap frog with them as well.'

'Perhaps, joking apart, I was hoping one of the frogs I snogged might actually turn into something wonderful . . . something meaningful . . .'

'You'll meet someone else, babe, maybe not today . . .'

'Maybe not tomorrow,' Nicky mocks, yawning widely.

'No, I'm being serious. Richard may not have realised how lucky he was but he missed out big time with you. You've got a hell of a lot to offer someone, Nix. You're funny, warm – well, apart from your bloody feet – you're bright, beautiful. You'll find your prince, babe, I'm sure you will.'

I tail off as the soft sound of snoring alerts me to the fact that Nicky has quietly slipped away into the Land of Nod.

I watch her for a moment, lips parted softly, eyelashes fluttering like moths against a window as she falls gently into a dream.

Has Nicky got the right idea?

Should I be out there trying to find myself a mate for life?

Is that really what life's all about?

Love.

It seems to me that to love is to leave yourself open. Open to getting your heart turned inside out, and your feelings trampled into the dirt. You are basically turning the welfare of your emotional being over to another person, and since when could that be considered safe and wise?

Besides, do I really want to join the ranks of coupledom? To have to answer to someone else for my every move? I had enough of that when I was living at home with my mother.

I do sometimes feel a stab of envy when I watch Nicky getting ready for one of her many nights out. It might be quite nice to get dressed up and be taken out for dinner. To be wined, dined and romanced.

But what happens when the romance is over and everyday life kicks in? Does ecstatic anticipation, dinner for two, walks in the moonlight, fun and laughter, actually transcend into happy ever after? Or does that deliciously delightful duet descend into daylight drudgery?

No, love is madness. My life is strange enough as it is without adding any more insanity.

Besides, the only person I've met in the last decade who I find even remotely fanciable is Eddie Farrar (not that I'd ever admit this to Jamie), and to get involved with him would definitely be madness.

Amanda would probably fillet me with one of her new kitchen knives.

Oh, well, at least I'd be gutted by an expert.

Thursday night, half an hour to closing.

Dot's being chatted up by the only two customers left in the bar, both vying to see who can get the best view down her cleavage; Sylv is in the kitchen making a mega-sandwich to assuage the boredom rather than any real hunger pangs, piling every single filling in the fridge between two halves of a whole baguette; I'm absentmindedly washing the same ashtray five times over, as I dream of a hot date I've got with my duvet, a late movie, and a bargain bucket I'm not sharing with Elvis no matter if he literally drowns me in drool.

I look at my watch. Twenty minutes to go now. Ben'll be here any minute to lock up, and I am outta here! Slob City, here I come.

Instead of Ben, though, we are honoured with yet another visit from Eddie, who heads through the door looking ultra casual in Levis and a pale green Ralph Lauren polo shirt.

'Where's Ben?' I hiss to Dot, as Eddie winks at us and heads over to empty the tills.

'Skiving. Think he finally got himself a date.'

'Really? Doesn't have much luck with women, does he? Don't know why, he's lovely.'

'He's too bloody nice. Us women are weird like that. More attracted to the bastards. Well, at least I always seem to be.' Dot sighs heavily. 'Not that I've done much dating recently. The last time I went out to dinner with a fella, it was fish and chips out of newspaper with Sylv, bless him. Suppose I can collect him from the kitchen now the boss is here. Tonight,' she states dramatically, 'we're going upmarket and stopping for a pizza on the way home. There's living for you!'

She reaches beneath the counter and pulls her handbag from under a pile of tea towels in one of the drawers.

'We're off now, Eddie, okay?'

'Sure thing.'

Dot heads towards the kitchens to extricate Sylv from the fridge, and Eddie turns to me.

'Staying for a drink?'

'I'm not talking to you,' I reply, turning away.

'Women!' He rolls his eyes. 'What have I done?'

'Apart from pretending to be a chauvinist? Simon.'

'Simon? Oh, yeah, the one with the crush. What about him?'

'He sent me flowers!'

'Oh my god, he sent you flowers! I don't believe it! The audacity of the man!' He throws his hands into the air in mock disbelief. 'I can't work you out, Annabelle Lewis, women normally complain when men *don't* send them flowers, not when they do.'

'It depends who it is that's doing the sending.'

'So flowers from Simon the Suck aren't appreciated?'

'You guessed it.'

He looks at me for a moment, and then smiles.

'So are you staying for that drink or what?'

'Not. I've got a hot date.' Kentucky Fried Chicken here I come.

His eyes narrow.

'Well, I haven't got time to hang around tonight anyway.'

'Oh?' My cool melts a little.

'Maybe I've got a hot date too.'

'Well, I hope yours is a little more exciting than a bargain bucket and an old movie.'

The smile returns.

'A Chinese take-away and a re-run of *Bladerunner*,' he offers.

I sit down on one of the bar stools.

'Well, that's sad enough to warrant some company. Make mind a Bud.'

I spend most of the following day in bed.

I eventually emerge from my pit with just enough time to shower, eat and run for my next shift, and stagger bleary-eyed into the kitchen in search of food and fruit juice. There's a note from Nicky pinned to the fridge.

She and Amanda have gone out to paint the town bright scarlet. No doubt they are at this very minute Eddie hunting, trawling through the assorted bars of Soho and Oxford Square, before heading down to Lazy Daisy's to wobble drunkenly round the dance floor in the hope that he might show.

It's not fair!

I don't get to have any fun any more.

I was up half of last night after my shift ended, lurking in a bush at the end of Eddie's drive, to make sure he didn't have any nocturnal visitors. I spent all of this morning chasing – and losing – his madly speeding Porsche around the M25, and now I've got to get changed at lightning speed, and go and serve sweaty, demanding clubbers drinks until the early hours.

I don't think so.

I'm going to give myself a break.

I've got to, nobody else will.

I phone in sick, hacking desperately like a TB patient down the phone to Ben, who sympathetically advises lots of bed rest; then gleefully, but slightly guiltily, curl up on one of the sofas in my dressing gown, with a large bar of chocolate, a grab bag of smokey pig crisps, my duvet, a bottle of cheap red wine, an old slushy movie, and a large pepperoni, spicy beef and mushroom pizza hurtling towards me on the back of a Piaggio.

I've just got to the bit in *Ghost* where a white and shimmering Patrick (rubber hips) Swayze is kissing a tearful Demi goodbye forever, tears streaming down my face like Niagara in full flood, when the door bell rings.

Pizza!

Pulling my ratty old dressing gown around me, and scrubbing the back of my hand across my soggy eyeballs, I trudge to the door and yank it open, rootling in my purse for a stray twenty-pound note I know is lurking in there somewhere.

'Annabelle?'

I stop rootling and look up in horror at the sound of a familiar voice.

Eddie!

I swallow a horrified shriek, and the mouthful of crisps I was still chewing get lodged in my throat, making me choke.

'Er . . . I just wanted to make sure you were okay. Ben said you sounded like you were at death's door.'

Perhaps I should have been an actress after all. All that sham coughing and spluttering I did down the phone to poor old Ben when I called in earlier was obviously convincing enough to make him think I'd at the very least got the plague or something. I'm not acting now, though. I've got the sharp edge of a hastily swallowed Walker's lodged in the soft flesh of my oesophagus. I know I've fantasised about having a gorgeous man's strong arms wrapped around me, but I never thought the first close encounter would be the Heimlich Manoeuvre!

The choking subsides to an oxygen-starved splutter, as the crisp begins to lose the sharp edges and go soggy with an overdose of saliva.

'He was right.' His face a picture of concern, Eddie takes me gently by the elbow and guides me back to the sofa. 'You sound terrible . . . you look terrible . . .'

I do? Oh, god! I don't want him to think I look terrible, I want him to think I look gorgeous at the least.

I've always thought Wurzel Gummidge had the right idea: an assortment of heads for differing occasions. No need to spend an hour staring bleakly into your dressing-table mirror whilst trying – and failing – to recreate the latest look on the front cover of this month's *Vogue*. Just whip into the cupboard, pull out the appropriate head, attach and look instantly gorgeous. Either that or somebody should invent make-up transfer stickers, like temporary tattoos. Just place over your face, rub gently on the back with a ten-pence piece, and – hey presto, instant perfect make up!

'Look, can I get you something? A glass of water maybe.' He looks about, assessing the layout of the flat. 'Or have you got any cough mixture anywhere?'

Oh, pooh! I can't have him poking about the flat looking for cough remedies. What if he goes in my room and spots his own underpants hanging jauntily from my bed head! This thought produces a fresh fit of coughing.

Fortunately he stops in his hunt for the bathroom and a non-existent medicine cabinet and, turning, searches for something instant to offer me.

His eyes light on my half-finished bottle of Ernest & Julio Turning Leaf.

'Medicinal,' I offer hopefully, thankfully managing to gain control of my choking fit, 'seems to be the only thing to soothe my cough.' I reach for my glass and take a huge swig of red and then smile inanely.

His eyes sweep over the food debris also cluttering the surface of the table. The screwed up purple-blue wrapper from my half pound of Dairy Milk, the half-empty Grab Bag of Smokey Bacon, the box of barely touched Thornton's I found stuffed away in the kitchen drawer whilst looking for the corkscrew, given to Nix by an admirer, then put out of sight, hopefully out of mind in honour of her latest diet.

'Er . . . feed a cold.'

He must think I'm a complete hog.

Actually he thinks I'm mad.

I can see it in his face.

She *is* ill. Mentally ill. Now how can I get out of here without being killed, slowly and painfully?

I think I'm wrong, though.

Instead of heading for the nearest exit, he's smiling at me.

Making no further references to my so-called illness or my own personal favourite cures, he sits down on the other sofa at right angles to me whilst I frantically try to check my face in the metallic handle of the table spoon that's sticking out of my half-eaten tub of Ben & Jerry's Cherry Garcia.

'Nice place.'

'Belongs to a friend.'

'Oh.' The smile disappears. 'And he's gone out and left you to fend for yourself . . . very nice.'

'*She* had a date. Besides, I've got Elvis to look out for me.'

Elvis, who was asleep half under the table, opens one eye at the mention of his name, slowly thumps his stubby tail, then promptly goes back to sleep again.

'Some guard dog you are,' I chide him, poking his fat backside with my toe.

Elvis manages to wake up enough to inspect the new arrival. He sniffs in friendly fashion first at Eddie's feet, stubby tail beginning to rotate madly, then clambering uninvited on to Eddie's lap, sticks his velvet brown nose into his pockets then finally, with a happy sigh, buries his velvet soft head in Eddie's crotch and falls asleep again.

I feel absurdly jealous, even more so when Eddie begins absentmindedly to stroke the snoozing puppy's head.

'I think he likes you.' I smile inanely. 'Then again, he likes everybody.'

'Thanks!'

I'm just about to offer Eddie a glass of wine, when the door bell goes. Oh, hell, that'll be the pizza. How do I explain this one? Wrong address? Prank call?

However, I open the door not to find something hot and cheesy and strewn with mushrooms and pepperoni, but Nicky, drunk, swaying and tearful.

'Can't find my bloody keys,' she sniffs. 'Can't bloody see.' Nicky rubs the back of her hand over her face, smearing mascara everywhere, and totters into the room on her pulling Pradas. 'Can't bloody

do anything right . . . oh, bollocks!' The last expletive is borne of the fact that she's just tripped over
the rug.

Eddie stands up, gently and apologetically tipping a
grumbling Elvis off his lap.

'I think I'd better go and leave you to it.'

I smile my thanks.

'I'll see you at work tomorrow.'

'Oh, you'll be in, will you?' There's just the slightest trace of sarcasm in his voice, but it's tinged with
good humour.

'I feel better,' I mumble as he smiles knowingly at
me.

'Who was that?' Nicky sniffs, as he closes the door
quietly behind him.

'Eddie,' I reply, suddenly realising that if Nicky's
back, then so is Amanda. Shit! I hope he manages to
escape the building without bumping into her. I'd
have a hell of a lot of explaining I couldn't do if they
met in the lift or something. That's if he ever got out
alive. She'd probably slam on the emergency stop,
imprison him for days and insist on eating him for
breakfast, lunch, tea and dinner.

'*The* Eddie?'

I nod. 'I chucked a sicky. He just came to see if I
was okay. You know, checking up on errant employees . . .'

She's far too drunk and absorbed in her own
misery to take the questioning any further, merely
collapses on one of the sofas, one shoe held aloft in
each hand, tears pouring unchecked down her face.

I sit down in the space Eddie's just vacated. It's still warm.

'What happened, babe?'

Her response is a fresh shower of tears.

I hazard a guess.

'Is it Richard?'

She nods.

'We went into Shakers – you know, that club down in Soho near the Thai restaurant we used to go to when we first moved back to London after uni?'

'Yeah, I know it.'

'Well, Amanda and I walk in and there he is, on the dance floor, wrapped around this gorgeous brunette. You know the sort of thing: squeezing her bum like he's testing melons, practically eating her face off with his gob like a bad plastic alien out of a badly made B-movie . . .'

She stops and breathes in deeply, shuddering with suppressed emotion.

'It was just such a shock, seeing him again, and seeing him with someone else.'

'You wished it was you?'

She shrugs. 'You know, that's the oddest part, I don't think I do. Although I'm not over the hurt and humiliation, I think I'm over him.'

'So why the tears?'

'I don't know,' she wails, perversely crying harder. 'Yes . . . yes, I do know, actually. It's because I feel such an idiot!'

'But why? You weren't to know things would turn out the way they did.'

'I feel like an idiot,' she looks up at me with big, wet eyes, 'because that was the man who only a few months ago I was prepared to swear to spend the rest of my life with. And now I see him tonight, tackily tongue-probing the tonsils of another woman, and feel almost nothing! Do I know myself so badly?'

'I must admit, I don't know what made you get involved with someone like him in the first place. I didn't think the ultimate smoothie would be your type.'

'You know,' she replies thoughtfully, tucking a stray strand of hair behind her ear, and then scrubbing her hand across her eyes to dry them a little, 'if you'd have been here I probably wouldn't have done. You'd have seen through him in a matter of minutes.'

'Maybe, but you probably wouldn't have listened to me.'

'Then again,' she muses sadly, 'if you'd have been here I'd never have stood a chance in the first place. He'd have fallen madly and passionately in love with you instead.'

I decide this one doesn't merit an answer and wallop her with a cushion instead, which fortunately makes her giggle.

'Did he see you?' I ask her, offering her one of the remaining squares of Cadbury's.

'Oh, yes. But you'd have been so proud of me, though, Belle.' She smiles wryly, smoothing her ruffled hair. 'I played it *so* cool. I didn't get upset, I didn't make a scene, I didn't even *speak* to him. I just sort of *acknowledged* him. You know, a little inclination of the head. Like the Queen.' She devours the square, and reaches for the rest of the bar.

'Like the Queen?'

'Laike the Queeeeeen.' She does her interpretation of a royal accent. 'Kind of regal and refained . . .' She starts to giggle again.

'And then what?'

'And then I grabbed the nearest gorgeous guy and stuck *my* tongue down *his* throat in full view of Rat Face Richard, before grabbing my bag and Amanda respectively and leaving.'

'Oh, god, who the hell's that now!' she wails as the door bell rings. 'If it's Amanda, tell her in case she's forgotten she actually lives *next door*.'

'Don't worry, it's probably the pizza. Finally. It's only about an hour late.'

'Oooh, junk food.' She stops sniffing and beams broadly. 'Sod diamonds, Belle, you're truly a girl's best friend.'

'I thought junk food itself was a girl's best friend?'

'Yeah, that and spot concealer.'

'And don't forget chocolate.'

'Doesn't that class as junk food?'

'Nah. It's in a league of its own. Like alcohol.'

'So a girl's best friends are diamonds, junk food, spot concealer and chocolate?'

'Which just goes to show, doesn't it? A girl can never have too many friends.'

The encounter with Richard seems to be a turning point in Nicky's life.

To put it bluntly, it's like she has laid a ghost and therefore no longer feels the need to lay the living. Not that she slept with *all* of the men she dated. That would have been one for the *Guinness Book of Records*.

Nicky's Ideal Man

Thoughtful, kind and honest, with a good sense of humour, and a nice arse

Well, that says more about Nicky than the sort of man she's after, doesn't it? It shows me that she's finally getting over the 'meet it, greet it, date it, mate it' section of her life, brought on by being Richarded in such an overwhelming fashion.

At least, I hope she is. There's nothing worse when you're basically celibate than the sound of someone in the next room coming to a noisy ecstatic climax. Even if it is your best friend. No, strike that, *especially* when it's your best friend.

Chapter Nine

Another night in a bush.

This time I'm perched in an evergreen outside a rather nice restaurant in Epping Forest, on a tip off from Dot that Eddie's taking someone out to dinner.

After forcing a protesting Arnold on the farthest journey he's been in the past two years, Eddie's hot restaurant date turns out to be a small blonde lady in her fifties, who upon further consultation from memory of the *Guinness Book of Eddie* could quite possibly be his mother.

I'm currently parked in my usual camouflage – a bush – in the gardens of an old stone rectory that's been converted into a rather exclusive French restaurant.

I'm lucky, Eddie sits at a window table in clear view of my bush.

Ten minutes later he's joined by a beaming woman who looks a little like a smaller version of a very jolly Judith Chalmers. She grabs both of his hands and kisses him gleefully on each cheek.

Nicky's mobile phone, which has really become

more my mobile phone in recent weeks, starts to play a muted version of 'The Nutcracker Suite', heralding an incoming call, making me jump as far as is possible in the confines of the undergrowth.

I'm sure it's a common sight, bushes ringing.

With some difficulty, space being a little confined stuffed inside a conifer, like pimento stuffed inside an olive, I pull the phone from the inside pocket of my jacket and look at the caller display.

Surprise, surprise, it's Amanda.

My finger hovers over the Divert button, before I give in and accept the call.

'Annabelle?' Her hushed harsh tones are eerily clear. She could be standing behind me rather than hissing at me down a telephone line.

'Well, it's not Talking Pages . . . although I could put you on to some numbers for good French restaurants.'

'For god's sake, Annabelle, will you cut the crap and tell me what's going on!'

'He's having dinner with his *mother*, Amanda.'

'Are you sure it's his mother?'

'Well, unless he's into much older women. Which I suppose shouldn't be ruled out . . .' I tease, the damp and cramp making me cruel. 'Don't worry, she fits the description to a T – she even looks like him. It couldn't be anyone else but his mother. Unless of course he is Narcissus after all, and finds older women who remind him of himself attractive . . . or would that made him Oedipus? I never was very good on Classics.'

Amanda sighs tetchily.

'Well, you'd better stay on, just in case,' she orders.

Just in case what? Unless his mother's been taking tips from mine and is suddenly going to produce an eligible bachelorette from her handbag, there's really not a lot of point my hanging around like a spare prat.

I enviously watch them inside the cosy lamp-lit cavern of William Morris wallpaper and Beardsley prints, eating, drinking and laughing. They laugh a lot together. In fact, although I obviously can't hear what's actually being said, by the body language and the obvious camaraderie, they appear to get on really well.

I wish I was inside with them.

Apart from the fact that I haven't eaten since breakfast, and my stomach is rumbling like there's a herd of stampeding elephants trampling through my gut, they look like they're having such a good time!

I'd probably get along much better with Eddie's mother than I do with my own. I bet she doesn't try and run his life with a rod of motherly iron. She looks fun, regularly bursting into peals of delicious laughter that even I can hear through two layers of double glazing as they giggle their way through four courses of wonderful-looking food.

And here I am, stuck outside in yet another bloody bush.

I should have parked in the car park, instead of in a lay by just down the road, and watched from the relative comfort of Arnold. Then again, he'd have

SARAH HARVEY

been really discreet amidst the assorted Mercedes, BMWs and others of that ilk that are currently gracing the restaurant car park.

What I really should have is a van. A nice van with a mattress in the back, a mattress with pillows, and a duvet, and a kettle, and maybe a microwave for when I'm starving, and a TV for the boring bits.

Failing that, perhaps I could adapt one of those bins on wheels, cut some little holes in the bottom of it for my feet so I could wheel up and down the road like Charles Hawtrey on a Carry On mission. It'd be better than standing in a bloody bush. At least it would keep out the draft.

Oh, sod it, I'm going home.

Abigail and I are doing the Sunday lunchtime shift together, one down as Sylv and David have jetted off on a last-minute to Ibiza, to get burnt, get down, get loved up, and get totally spaced out in Space, before staggering back to Britain a week later, more in need of a holiday than before they went.

As usual Abi is moaning about Bloody Jerry, whom I have yet to meet, much to my disappointment. (Do you detect the sarcasm in that last?)

'Bloody Jerry,' she sighs heavily, raking a pale long-fingered hand through her thick auburn tresses, in exasperation. 'I'm sure he's messing me about. The problem with working shifts here is that I never know what he's up to, or where he is.'

'Well, if you never know where he is anyway, what makes you think he's out on the pull?'

'The usual,' she sighs, knocking the top off an orange juice bottle. 'New aftershave, new underwear, shaves a lot, showers more than twice a week, and the clincher, after four years of me nagging him not to do it, has suddenly, overnight, stopped biting his toenails in bed.'

'Yuk! This is a man you're worried about losing?'

'He has other more redeeming qualities.'

'Such as?'

'Well, he can do other things in bed besides biting his toe nails.'

'I agree you would have to be pretty flexible in the pelvis area to be able to get your toe nails between your teeth!'

I really have to stop myself from offering to find out for Abi whether Bloody Jerry is being a jerk. It would be a bit difficult explaining to her what my other job is. She's a lovely girl, with a mouth on a motor. The next thing I'd know, my insalubrious sideline would be all round the club, questions would be asked, and my real reason for being at Daisy's might just come out.

'Well, if you really wanted, I could find out for you.'

So much for not letting on. You know, sometimes I'm convinced my mouth isn't connected to my brain. Oh, well, I don't have to go into how well qualified I actually am to check up on Jerry for her, I can just offer to help out as a friend, can't I?

'You what?'

'I can find out if Jerry's messing you about or not.'

Abi stops viciously slicing a lemon as though the

knife is slicing into Jerry rather than rind, and frowns at me.

'And how do you propose to do that then?'

'Ask him out.'

'No . . . you're not serious, are you?'

I shrug.

'It's up to you. If you think he's ripe to be plucked by another woman, then why don't we get in first?'

'And what if he says yes?' She bites her bottom lip in concern.

'There's always the possibility that he'll say no.'

'And I suppose if he does say yes, then at least I'll *know*, rather than just guessing . . .'

'Exactly.'

'And you'd do that?'

'Wouldn't have offered if I didn't mean it.'

Abi stops for a moment and looks at me, head on side, her bright eyes slightly narrowed in disbelief.

'So what are you going to do?'

'Well, you tell me where I can find him, then leave it to me.'

'As simple as that?'

'I don't know about simple, but that's where we start . . . if you want to?'

Abi leans back against the bar and looks at her hands for a moment, then looks back at me, her face breaking into a slow smile.

'What the hell! Go for it. Why not? I've got nothing to lose, have I?'

She nudges me in the ribs, as I squeeze past her with a rack tray of glasses.

'Talking about men, I think you've got a fan.'

'You what?'

'You're being watched.' She tilts her head in the direction of Eddie, who is seated at one of the restaurant tables with Ben and the tasty Italian I first saw in Black Betty's who turned out to be his accountant.

'Don't be daft!' I tell her, pushing past and starting to load the glass washer.

'Come on, Belle, don't say you haven't noticed the way he looks at you?'

'He does it to all of the girls, he's a big fat flirt.'

'Well, he never does it to me. Would that he did.' Abigail pushes a lock of strawberry red hair out of her eyes and narrows them lasciviously at Eddie, who despite her protestations has turned to talk to Ben.

'Would you just look at that broad back?' She exhales a long lustful breath. 'Imagine scraping your finger nails down that! Okay, keep your hair on.' She reluctantly turns to serve an impatient customer who is frantically waving a folded twenty like a traffic cop at a roadside speed trap, flagging down a speeding motorist.

Having served the customer, however, she's straight back at my side, and straight back on the same subject.

'Ooh, you are such a lucky girl, Annabelle.'

'I am?' I ask distractedly, stacking the rapidly emptying lager fridge with fresh bottles of Bud.

'He's looking over again.'

'Abi, what are you on!'

'If you don't believe me, look for yourself!'

'He's not looking at me. And if he is, he's probably just making sure I'm doing my job properly.'

I slide a sideways glance in his direction only to find that Abi's right and he's staring. Straight at me. He catches me looking and smiles, that quirky sideways twist of his lips that is teasingly sexy.

'See,' she gloats triumphantly, 'told you so. Stop playing coy, babe, you must have noticed?'

Okay, so maybe I had noticed that he's pretty friendly, and it's not just the after work drinking sessions which are becoming a bit of a bad habit.

We get on well.

Too well.

I've seen him in action. He's an expert flirt. But there's definitely something more between us than the light-hearted banter he shares with the other girls. I can feel it. Unfortunately I'm not the only one who's noticed this.

I meet Jamie for a coffee after work in a waterfront café just around the corner that serves the most incredible hot chocolate fudge cake.

Jamie and I, on the pretext that we've both had a hard day at work, order double portions each, and head for a table in the window that overlooks the Thames. The day is bright but as usual in what has been a pretty dismal British summer so far, it's too cold to sit outside. A westerly wind is tickling the surface of the river, sending grey murky ripples undulating toward the boats moored on the far side.

'So how's the job going?' Jamie asks, getting stuck

into his first piece of fudge cake with frightening speed.

'Fine.'

'And how are you coping, working so closely with Eddie?'

'I can cope with him, it's Amanda that's the problem.'

Two more bites, and Jamie will have completely demolished one huge slice of cake. I've never seen anyone eat as quickly as him, except perhaps Elvis. There's a moment's silence whilst he sets to work on the other slice, and then starts talking again.

'I've seen you watching him, Belle.'

'Well, that might have something to do with the fact that watching him is what Amanda pays me for.' I cross my eyes at him, and suck some stubborn fudge off the end of my fork.

'Sure, but the only time I've ever seen that expression on your face before is when you had your first ever Walnut Whip.'

'You remember that? I don't. But you know what it's like being a junkie,' I joke, shovelling more cake into my mouth, 'it never seems like there was life before the addiction.'

'Exactly,' Jamie states, somewhat smugly.

'What do you mean, *exactly*?'

'You said it yourself. Addiction.' He finishes the last of his chocolate cake and starts to look hopefully at mine, a little like Elvis at dinnertime.

Here we go again. The dreaded diagnosis from Dr Lurve.

'I do not fancy Eddie, Jamie.'

'Oh, dear, she's still in denial,' he says dryly.

'I'm not in denial!'

'Denying the denial,' he groans. 'This is worse than I thought.'

'I do not fancy Eddie,' I repeat through gritted teeth.

'Then why are you still doing this crappy, crazy, DIY detective thing? I know you, Belle. You hate it when someone tries to tell you what to do, but here you are, letting Amanda boss you round like she owns you.'

'I need the money.'

'You could get another job.'

'Not that pays as well as this.'

'Rubbish! You're not letting Amanda pay you for the time you're working in the bar. And don't deny that one as well. Nicky told me, so I know it's true.'

'Well, it didn't seem right,' I mumble, 'him paying me to be there, when I'm only there because she's paying me to be there to watch him. If you follow that.'

'Yeah, I follow it. Perfectly. Look, Belle, I agree that you're working at Daisy's to keep an eye on Eddie, to get to know him, to find out what he's all about . . .'

'You do?'

'Yeah, but I just don't agree that you're doing it for Amanda . . . Think about it, Annabelle. Please. You say you hate dishonesty. Well, isn't it about time you started being honest with yourself?'

It's really annoying to have a step-brother who's almost perfect. Bright, beautiful, and always right.

Okay, so I admit it, I like the guy.

All right, I more than like him, I fancy the pale blue pants off the man.

Don't ask me what it is. Yes, there's the usual: the physical attraction, the mental attraction, the sexual chemistry, the fact that we share the same rather warped sense of humour. But there's more, something else, something indefinable.

I can't get this man out of my head. I find myself thinking about him at the most unexpected times, in the most unexpected places – often in the most unexpected positions – but, hey, I haven't had sex for nearly two years so I think I can be forgiven a little fantasising.

Bloody Jerry.

Twenty-nine. Irish. Black hair, blue eyes, wicked smile, and the smarmy, cheeky charm of the original rogue.

I can certainly see what Abigail sees in him despite the terrible reviews I've had so far about him being a bigger flirt than Casanova let loose in a nunnery with a directive to corrupt the converted.

It's lunchtime. We're in a bar. What's new? I seem to spend half my life in bars at the moment. Bars, bushes and bed. Such a dizzy social whirl.

Nicky's in the loo, I'm standing at one end of the bar waiting to be served, whilst the bar maid is standing at the other being chatted up by Bloody Jerry. I can hear his lilting Irish brogue float across the murmur of a relatively subdued Sunday lunchtime crowd, as the most outrageous flattery tumbles from his tongue like hot strawberry sauce poured over ice cream. The bar maid being the ice cream, of course. I can see her melting from here.

Eventually, though, she has to scrape herself off the floor to serve the ever-growing queue of customers, fortunately starting with me. I order four large vodka and Cokes, two each for me and Nix, partly for Dutch courage, and partly because I have a feeling it might take a while to get served again.

The bar maid wouldn't last long at Daisy's, I think to myself disdainfully. We actually work hard for a living. We have standards she couldn't reach if she stood on a tall bar stool.

Wow! Pride in my job. That's a new emotion.

Taking my drinks, I head for a recently vacated table in one corner of the room, where I can sit and see without really being seen myself.

Nicky returns from the loos, fresh slash of Paloma Red across her lips, cleavage rearranged to best advantage in her V-neck Kookai top, her hair teased into a tousled 'I've just had rough sex and loved it' kind of look.

She looks good.

She looks like the Nicky I used to hit the town with before I went away, the Nicky who could pull at sixty paces with just one long lingering look under endless eyelashes. She's still about seven pounds over what she used to weigh, but the extra curves suit her really well.

She feels good, too, you can see it in her air and

attitude. Attractive with a capital A. A confidence that turns heads.

As she sashays past Bloody Jerry, he quits holding the bar maid's gaze long enough to do a double take that lasts the length of her walk over to the table.

Nicky's noticed.

'What's up?' she whispers, looking worried. 'Did I tuck my skirt in my knickers or something?'

'No, but I think you just removed all your clothes . . . only mentally,' I add, as the worried expression changes to one of confusion. 'Bloody Jerry just burned them off with his eyeballs.'

'Well, thank goodness for that,' Nicky jokes, 'I was beginning to think I was the only woman in this room he didn't find attractive. I could have been *very* insulted.'

We sit and watch Jerry for half an hour.

Although his eyes are dancing round the room like an over-sexed drunk at a party where the women outnumber the men by ten to one, so far the body hasn't actually attempted to follow.

After an hour, another two vodkas each, and some monumental flirting but little else from Jerry, I decide it's time to move into action.

I turn to Nicky, and smile briefly.

'Oh, well, here goes.'

Her mouth twists into a wry smile.

'Should I wish you luck?'

'I don't know.' I shrug. 'I'm not very hot on etiquette in social situations at the best of times.'

'How about break a leg? I suppose that could be

more appropriate, seeing as you're putting on a pretty major act.'

'Well, let's just hope it's a good enough act to fool Jerry.' I smile briefly at Nicky. 'Although I don't want it to be that good,' I sigh, thinking of Abigail. 'I hope he says no, Nix.'

'I suppose that depends on what you're going to offer him.'

'How about a night of no-strings raw sex?'

'That should do it,' she laughs.

Once at the bar, I order yet another drink and slide a sideways look at the target. He's looking at me. Well, he's looking at my legs to be more precise, but eventually the gaze slides upwards.

I smile.

He smiles.

Thirty seconds later I repeat the same sequence.

Look. Smile. Get smiled back at.

When the smile is returned on the third occasion, I take the bull-shitter by the horns and throw him my best 'come hither' glance.

He doesn't come, and he doesn't hither. In fact, he gets up from his seat and heads for the door marked Gents, leaving me standing at the bar leering inanely at an empty bar stool, and feeling decidedly stupid.

This is absurd. He rejected me, which is great, but I feel insulted! What's wrong with me?

No, I don't mean why do I feel this way? I mean, *literally* what's wrong with me?

'Am I a dog?' I whisper to Nix, having crawled back to our table with a red face.

She bursts out laughing, which isn't a good idea when trying to swallow a large glass of white wine.

'Don't be ridiculous!' she snorts. 'You're probably just not his type. You don't fancy every man you meet, do you?'

'Of course not!'

'There you go then.'

'Yeah, but he apparently chats up every woman he meets.'

'That's only what you've heard, could be a gross exaggeration.'

'Maybe, but I've seen him in action today, haven't I? He hasn't exactly been hiding in a corner.'

Nicky chews thoughtfully on the bottom corner of her lip for a moment.

'Why don't you let me try?' she says slowly.

'You?'

'Don't look so shocked, Belle, I could take it as an insult.'

'You know that's not what I meant . . . I just didn't think that it'd be the sort of thing you'd *want* to do.'

'Well, I've had enough practice flirting over the past few months.'

'I suppose he did stare rather hard when you came out of the loo,' I muse.

'Did he?' she says, pretending to be coy.

'You know he did. His eyeballs weren't just popping, they were exploding!'

Nicky smiles to herself.

'Maybe you should have a go,' I say, warming to the idea. 'It'll be quite nice to just sit back and relax and let someone else go and make a tit of themselves instead of me.'

'Cheers, Belle! Thought you were supposed to be my friend?'

Nicky stands up, smooths down her skirt, shrugs her escaping bra straps back on to her shoulders, and casts a quick glance at her reflection in the window.

'How do I look?'

'Knock out.'

'Any tips?'

'Picking up a man is like trying to pick up a turd without a pooper scoop. If you pick one that's too slimy, you'll end up getting shit under your fingernails,' I tell her, trying not to laugh.

'Ugh, Belle! You can be so gross sometimes. Well, here goes nothing.' Winking at me, she affects a walk that's more undulation than perambulation and rolls over to the bar, standing a few feet down from Jerry so as not to be overly obvious.

She doesn't need to be overly obvious. Jerry noticed her the minute she stood up and started walking. Whereas I was obviously not Jerry's type, Nicky is his type *and* some.

She smiles at the bar maid, who reluctantly heads over to serve her some more drinks.

She takes her Gucci wallet from her Jane Shilton bag, to pay for them, and promptly drops it on the floor, loose change spilling out and rolling in every direction. Jerry is instantly off his seat, enthusiastically gathering money like a child claiming eggs in an Easter hunt.

He hands Nicky her escaped change, she thanks him profusely, adds a pint of Caffrey's to the round she's buying and stays at the bar chatting for ten minutes, whilst I watch them intently.

Clever girl. A modern update on chucking your hankie under a fella's size nines. Jerry eventually returns to his seat, and Nicky to our table, smiling broadly to herself.

'Well?' I sound like Amanda thirsting for info.

She parks her arse and hands me my drink.

'He's actually a really nice guy.'

'What did he say to you?'

'No.'

'You what?'

'I asked him out, and he said no.' Nicky smiles. 'You know, I was kind of disappointed, I could quite fancy him . . .' She looks over to where Jerry has returned to his bar stool and smiles briefly. 'However, whilst he thanked me for the offer, he informed me that he was practically a married man, then proceeded to spend the next five minutes telling me how wonderful his girlfriend was.'

'You're joking, aren't you?'

'I'm being perfectly serious. He's totally infatuated.'

'But he doesn't behave like he's totally infatuated.'

'Trust me, Belle, he's all mouth, but definitely not no trousers. They were kept well and truly in place. In fact, I got the impression you'd need a crow bar to get him out of them.'

'But he's such a flirt!'

'Yeah, but I don't think he follows through. Sometimes it's nice just to flirt . . . it doesn't have to mean anything, or lead to anything for that matter. I think with Jerry it's purely recreational.'

'You mean, he flirts for a hobby?'

'Something like that, yeah. It's just a bit of harmless fun.'

'But what about the new image, the new clothes, the new aftershave?'

'Hasn't Abigail ever considered that could be for her? If she's moaning to you, then it's quite possible he's picking up vibes that she's not happy and has smartened himself up in an effort to impress her.'

'I suppose that could be a possibility . . . Did he say that?'

'Not in so many words. But the impression I got is that he's well and truly hooked, I think he must have said "Abigail" about forty times in our conversation.'

'Unless his other woman's got the same name?'

'Come off it, Belle!' Nicky shakes her head. 'Stop looking for problems, the guy's straight.'

'I suppose so. I just want to be really sure before I tell Abigail.'

'Hey,' she jokes, crossing her legs and pouting her red lips at me, 'he turned down the opportunity of a date with me, what further proof do you want?'

Eddie turns up at the end of my next shift, with dark shadows under tired eyes, heads behind the bar and helps himself to a large brandy.

'I've had a really shitty day. I'm going to work my way along the optics until I pass out, then hope my hangover's so bad the headaches of today pale in comparison.' He turns round and smiles weakly at me. 'But you know what they say about drinking alone.'

'Sure.' I smile wryly, picking up my coat. 'I know what they say, but it never stops me.'

'Are you going to join me or do I have to beg?'

'A bit of begging wouldn't go amiss. That's where most men belong, down on their knees.'

'Yeah, and that's where most women drive them,' he retaliates, pouring me a brandy, handing it to me, and taking my coat away.

'So I don't get any choice? I'm staying.'

'Correct and correct,' he replies, sitting down on a bar stool. 'You wouldn't let me get drunk on my own?'

'And miss out on all the fun?' I say sarcastically, sitting down next to him. 'Like the late night, the nausea, the hangover . . . Cheers.'

We touch glasses and he downs his double in one go. I follow suit and he heads behind the bar again, returning with the bottle.

'Saves getting up and down all the time.'

'After we've drunk most of that, we won't be able to,' I agree. 'We're just missing one vitally important thing.'

'We are?'

'Food.'

'Food?'

'You know, the stuff you put in your mouth and chew. Vital to life and personal pleasure . . .'

He heads into the kitchen and returns five minutes later with a plate of sandwiches that he plonks down on the bar in front of me with a mild flourish.

'Happy now?'

'Well, it's not exactly Cordon Bleu but at least you're vaguely more domesticated than I thought you were.'

'Well, how about this then?' He pulls a bar of Cadbury's from his back pocket and hands it to me.

'Eat your heart out, Raymond Blanc.' I stroke the familiar purple wrapper lovingly. 'Come to me, my pretty.'

Half an hour later the chocolate's gone, the sandwich plate is still nearly full, and the half-full bottle is almost empty. We've had a heated argument about sexual equality which somehow, as our alcohol levels rose, degenerated into a discussion of the merits of chocolate versus dry roast peanuts.

'Think we need another one?' Eddie dribbles the last few millimetres of brandy into my glass.

'Absolutely . . . my turn, though.'

I attempt to get up from my stool but my legs aren't quite connecting with my brain and even if they were, my brain isn't functioning enough to co-ordinate itself, let alone other body parts. I reach out to grab the brass rail that runs around the bar to steady myself, and accidentally knock the bottle with my elbow so that it falls on to the wet wooden surface of the bar and spins towards me.

'Truth or Dare?' Eddie instantly announces through a mouthful of chicken sandwich.

'You what?'

'Well, if we're playing spin the bottle,' he grins, 'then it's Truth or Dare.'

'I didn't know we *were* playing spin the bottle . . .'

'But you set it spinning.'

'That was an accident . . . oh, okay. Truth.'

He looks at me consideringly for a moment, a wicked gleam in his eyes.

'Okay, what's your favourite sexual position?'

'Well, I'm not answering that one!'

'If you don't answer, you have to forfeit.'

'What's the forfeit?'

He thinks for a moment, then getting up from his stool, heads behind the bar and returns with a bottle of tequila.

He pours a double measure straight into my half-full brandy glass.

'Drink.'

'What?'

'It's your forfeit.'

'You're joking?'

'Unless you want to answer my question.'

'You know, this doesn't seem a very fair game,' I grumble.

'Well, it works both ways.'

Of course it does. Truth or Dare. The opportunities are boundless! I wonder if I could make the dares so outrageous that he'll ask for truth every time. I can find out everything I need to know in one evening, and the best bit is he'll probably be too hungover to remember my Spanish inquisition in the morning.

'Okay. Fair enough.'

Picking up the glass, I look him straight in the eye and knock back the double shot in one go, managing to suppress an involuntary gasp as the tequila brandy mix burns a liquid trail down my throat.

'Okay, your turn. Truth or Dare?' I rasp.

'It might not be my turn, we haven't spun yet.'

'Well, hurry up and spin then!'

He takes hold of the centre of the bottle, and with a twist of the wrist sends it spinning across the wet bar, until the momentum begins to wane and it slows to an agonising pace, finally ending up pointing straight at a grinning Eddie.

'Ha!' I shout triumphantly. 'Your turn! Truth or Dare?'

'Truth.'

'Okay . . . Tell me the five qualities you most admire in a woman.' Clever one there, Belle.

'Do women have that many qualities?'

'It's a good job I know you're joking or I wouldn't be spinning the bottle, I'd be braining you with it.'

'Balls.'

'I bloody would! I'm not scared of you, you know!'

'No! I meant, I like a woman who's got balls.'

'What, like lady boys? Met a few of those in Thailand, I can tell you!'

'Belle!' He shakes his head. 'Okay, let me rephrase that, I like a woman with guts.'

'What, fat and Rubens-esque . . . okay, okay, only joking. Well, that's number one,' I prompt.

'Brains.'

'Good one. Next?'

'Beauty.'

'Cliché!'

'Yeah, but I'd be lying if I didn't add it, and I do know there's more to beauty than just looks.'

'Okay, you've redeemed yourself a little. Next?'

'Sense of humour.'

'Very important,' I agree.

He nods.

'She'd need one to put up with you.'

'Oi!' he cries indignantly.

'Sense of humour,' I remind him pointedly. 'Very important.'

'Nice arse. Oh, come on!' he cries as I put on my disapproving face. 'That's top of the list for most women, so why can't I have it on mine?'

Okay, so his ideal woman is a brainless beauty with a nice arse and funny balls . . . Hang on, have I got that the right way round?

I shake my head, hoping to clear the heavy alcoholic fug that's settled around me like a rain cloud lovingly hugging a rain god.

I can normally drink most people under the table. I know it's not a claim I should be particularly proud of, the fact that I can stomach so much alcohol without passing out, throwing up, or generally acting like my brain's been removed, but I am.

This is the first man I've met who matches me stage for stage.

We're alcoholically compatible.

Isn't that terrible?

SARAH HARVEY

No, it's not actually, it's bloody fun.

We both move on to the 'wouldn't it be great to do stupid things?' stage at exactly the same time.

It's always difficult when one of you is in the right drunken mood to dance on tables, and the other one's either two steps behind and watching in embarrassed thin-lipped disapproval, or two steps in front and passed out cold on the floor.

Not that we actually get up and dance on the table. Why do that when we have a whole night club to ourselves?

Staggering precariously downstairs into the cellar, me treading on his heels as I lurch down behind him in the dark, Eddie switches on all of the lights. The club is nearly finished. An abandoned bucket in one corner and a set of step ladders the only evidence that the rogues from Reading have been here today.

Eddie heads over to the DJ station.

'Okay, let's see if this thing works properly . . .'

'You know how to drive it?'

'You know my philosophy, Belle.'

'I know – if you need it, you need to know how to work it.'

Eddie switches on enough power points to work Blackpool lights, presses a few buttons, and inserting one of the pre-recorded tapes that Damon the dreadlocked demon DJ from Black Betty's has mixed up, sends music suddenly pounding out of the huge speakers I'm standing next to, making me almost jump out of my size fives.

For some unknown reason, we seem to have a

336

Christmas selection. A pumped up garage version of 'Jingle Bell Rock' begins to blare out at high decibels, and a rather drunk Eddie throws himself enthusiastically on to the dance floor.

Everybody has a flaw, even the most perfect of people.

I've just discovered Eddie's.

He can't dance.

I expected him to be great, like he's so good at everything else, but although there's a basic sense of rhythm, that's all it is – basic.

He doesn't care, though, he's completely oblivious, so unselfconscious he just throws himself on to the dance floor and into the music and thoroughly enjoys every moment until George Michael's honeyed voice oozes meltingly out of the speakers, as 'Last Christmas' slides into gear.

Moving closer, we begin to dance with each other, falling comfortably together, moving in easy harmony.

I was wrong, he can dance, just not the frenetic garage and house music the spaced out DJ normally plays. I bet he could dance a perfect tango.

Either that or our bodies just fit so well together there's no way anything could be unharmonious.

Stop it, Annabelle.

You are not enjoying this.

This is purely research on behalf of Amanda.

A pretty enthusiastic attempt at lambada follows, legs flailing, until we're both almost collapsing on the floor in a fit of hot and hysterical laughter. Fortunately, the music changes just in time to stop us doing any permanent joint damage.

It's four o'clock in the morning, and we're doing a very short, very undignified, but very enthusiastic conga around the large empty dance floor, his hands on my waist, his head resting on my shoulder, so that I look like Zaphod out of *Hitchhiker's Guide*. That is until we take a corner too fast and I lose my number two.

I dance on for a few moments, until I realise my waist is now handless, and the second head has gone, and turn to see Eddie, somebody usually so cool and so in control, slumped in a giggle-infested drunken heap on the floor.

I like this Eddie. This mad, sad, funny, drunken giggle monster.

I like the other Eddie, too. They complement each other. The human dynamo is a human being after all.

I've got this urge to give him a huge hug, but offer him my hand instead, and attempt to haul him upright.

Unfortunately, the fact that he weighs over three stone more than me, and that my own equilibrium has been somewhat unbalanced by the amount of alcohol I've sunk in the past hour, means that my leverage isn't quite up to the job, and having managed to pull him only about four inches into the air, we both topple backwards on to the dance floor.

I'm lucky. Whilst he hits the ground at full force, his body cushions my fall. We end up with Eddie flat on his back, and me somewhat compromisingly on top of him, his arms instinctively flung about me, to protect me from the impact as we hit the ground.

I hear a somewhat sickening thump as the back of his head hits the floor.

'Are you okay?' I whisper after a moment's silence.

He nods, eyes damp with laughter and probably a bit of pain as well.

'You?'

'I think so. At least I had a soft landing.'

'I'm not surprised. I've had so much booze, it must feel like you're lying on a water bed.'

We both begin to roar with laughter again, then suddenly fall silent, eyes locked, mouths only millimetres apart, so close I can feel his warm breath mingling with mine, so close I can almost feel the touch of his lips against mine.

I suddenly feel very sober.

'Er . . . I think it's time I went home.'

He nods his agreement, but his arms remain wrapped around my waist.

'Which means we have to get up off the floor,' he suggests.

Still neither of us attempts to move.

I can feel the beat of his heart against my breast. It's pounding methodically in time to the music. Far too fast for a normal heart rate.

And then we're kissing.

I don't quite know who started it.

I'm the one who stops it, though.

Bloody reluctantly.

Pulling my mouth away from his is like forcing two magnets apart. There's an invisible drag that's just pulling me back into another free-falling kiss, our eyes open and locked the whole time, tongues tasting, lips sliding sensuously.

Somehow I manage to pull away again and, lips and face burning like they're on fire, stagger to my feet and sprint out of Daisy's as fast as my alcohol jelly legs will take me. Like Cinderella, only I get to keep both shoes. The problem is, she got her man in the end, didn't she? I have a feeling the ending of this fairy tale is going to be a bit Grimm.

Well, I've done it again.

Oh my journey through life I've come across several paths that have been quite clearly signposted 'route to disaster'. Anybody would think I'm dyslexic the way I just ignore the big bold black warning letters, and trot off merrily down into the hazard-filled precipice.

There's nothing else I can do.

I've got to back off.

I could quit the job, but try explaining that to Amanda and Nicky.

Besides, I don't want to leave.

If I wasn't spending all of my spare time running round like James Bond on speed, then I could really like working here. I could be glad of this job in a few months' time. It's not as if I'm going to carry on with my other *career* forever.

The pay's good, the hours are flexible, I like my colleagues, Ben's great, Dot and Abi are fellow inmates, and the others are a great bunch. And as for the boss . . . whoah! Down, girl.

I'm just going to have to pretend I feel nothing, to him, but most of all to myself. Denial with a capital D for Don't.

I could start by putting bromide in my Pepsi Max, or having hormone suppression therapy.

He walks past, I breathe in the air like I've just strolled into the bakery section at Sainsbury's. Either that or I scuttle out of his way like a crab heading for the nearest rock.

I don't know what's wrong with me.

The only sudden desperate passions I've experienced recently have been for coffee-flavoured Walnut Whips, and they're far easier to appease than this one. It's a new and rather frightening experience. A whole deluge of emotions that have simply drenched me like a well-aimed water bomb.

I want this man.

I want this man more than anything I've ever wanted before in my life.

More than I want chocolate.

More than I wanted a horse when I was eleven.

More than I wanted Simon Le Bon when I was thirteen.

More than I wanted a car when I ripped up my L plates and landed my driving licence.

Okay, so I haven't done well on the denial front.

I try avoidance.

He walks in one door, I shoot out of another one; anytime a barrel needs changing I'm the first to volunteer, so that I can skulk in the cellar; anytime a works night out is organised, I volunteer to hold the fort back at Daisy's, in charge of the agency staff with my whip.

When he appears to lock up, I'm sliding surreptitiously out of the door like a convict escaping open prison, rather than staying on for what had become a bit of a regular drinking session.

I've even contemplated taking up smoking so that I've got a good excuse to sidle outside into the alley every half an hour to hide behind a dustbin.

Dot runs into the Ladies for a loo break to find me yet again perched on the edge of a hand basin, chewing the last piece of cuticle on my left thumbnail.

'You're either got a severe bladder problem or you're hiding out from a certain someone again,' she chides me from her cubicle.

'Is it that obvious?'

Dot emerges from the loo, washes her hands, and props her arse next to mine on the cold white ceramic.

'You're the only girl I know who actually runs away from Eddie Farrar instead of throwing yourself at him.' She pulls a crumpled cigarette packet from her pocket and lights up. 'Why on earth do you keep avoiding him, Annabelle? It's obvious you two have the raging hots for each other.'

'That's exactly why I'm avoiding him,' I mumble, starting on the other hand. That and a certain blonde-haired maniac named Amanda the Mad.

'Oh?' Dot raises her eyebrows and looks knowingly at me. 'Look, I know his reputation precedes him, but trust me, Belle, he hasn't really earned it. A lot of the rumours just started out as wishful thinking. Trust me, I've known Eddie since he was a kid. He's a lovely guy.'

Two 'trust mes' in one very short speech, automatic anathema to my instantly suspicious nature.

'Since when did you turn into Cilla?'

'I like you, Belle, you're different, you'd be good for him.'

'I would?'

She nods.

'Yep. Unless he sacks you first for skiving so much.'

Dropping her unfinished cigarette down the plug hole of the sink she's perched on, she stands up and heads for the door.

'Well, back to the old grindstone. One of us has to do some pint-pulling this evening.' She winks at me. 'Don't stay in here too long, Belle, it's not healthy, oh . . . and think about what I said, okay?'

Think about it? If I think about it any more my head will explode. Eddie's all I've had on my mind for the past few weeks.

Is Dot right? Would I be good for him?

Would he be good for me?

Certainly wouldn't be good for my health.

If the stress doesn't kill me, Amanda will.

Chapter Ten

Guilt and worry affect different people in different ways.

Some stop eating, some can't sleep, some bite their nails to the quick, some get snappy and irritable, others get extremely drunk in a bid to blot it all out.

Personally, I stop eating, stop sleeping, have far too much to drink, and generally feel like I should cut off my own feet to make amends to whoever it is I'm feeling worried or guilty over.

I phone Ben, claim a personal problem (Amanda, Eddie, my nerves), book a few days' annual leave, and lounge around Nicky's flat looking morose, eating chocolate, trying and failing to avoid Amanda, and replaying that kiss over and over in my head, like a favourite song on rewind.

It doesn't help that an overexcited Amanda is in and out constantly, parading a variety of different outfits, hairstyles, war paint, shoes – she even whips across with an assortment of outrageous underwear – expecting me to help her choose the most appropriate for D Day. Or should I call it E Day? As if I really want to help choose the knickers she's hoping Eddie will be peeling off with his teeth!

Nicky's noticed that I'm not my usual self, and has diagnosed overwork as the cause. She is now fussing round me as I lie prostrate on the sofa, offering me chocolate biscuits and endless cups of sugar-filled tea in the hope that the two will help to sweeten me up.

I think she's feeling guilty about all the time she's spent out of the flat gallivanting with Amanda or in general party animal mode, but she's my friend not my wife so she's entitled to a social life. Although I must admit I've been a little peeved that the wildly exciting social life she seems to have found herself these days doesn't include me because I'm always out 'working'.

Her latest suggestion for 'cheering up Annabelle' is a night out on the razz.

Although I really don't feel like razzing at the moment, I decide that a night out on the right side of the bar for a change might actually do me some good, and allow Nicky to talk me round with some gentle persuasion.

'Look, take a night off and we'll go out. Just kick back and relax, go wild, get drunk and party. Like we used to at uni.'

'I don't know, do you think we've got the stamina, now that we're old ladies?' I summon up enough energy to tease her.

'Well, if you stay on the sofa any longer, it's going to have the outline of your bottom permanently imprinted in the fabric . . . wouldn't you rather be parking your bum on a bar stool, large V & C in one hand, gorgeous man in the other?'

'I don't know about the gorgeous man part, but the large V & C sounds good.'

'Is that a yes then?'

'Although I could have the large V & C right here . . .'

'Well, if you want to stop in on your own like a sad git and watch repeats all night, while I go out and party till I drop . . .'

'Okay.' I grin, heaving myself off the sofa. 'You sold me.'

'Great!' Nicky beams. 'Although I did promise Amanda that we'd do something together tonight . . .'

I can see she's just itching to ask me.

Guilt makes me put on my martyred face and decide to put her out of her misery.

'Why don't we ask Amanda to come along too?' I sigh, with extremely bad grace.

I feel even more guilty when Nicky the big softie hugs me and thanks me for being so thoughtful and selfless.

'I know you're not keen on Amanda, but underneath it all she's really quite sweet.'

'Must be very deep.' I grimace.

I think back to the laughing girl in the photograph in the office at Daisy's. Perhaps Nicky's right. Maybe I should get to know Amanda a little bit better before I judge her.

It's got nothing to do with the fact that if we take her out she might meet someone else, and hopefully

SARAH HARVEY

get over this total fixation on Eddie.

If she did, I'd be doing her a favour really, wouldn't I? After all, he's not interested and it's completely unhealthy to be so totally obsessed with somebody who doesn't want you.

My sudden burst of altruism has got nothing whatsoever to do with the fact that this love thing is definitely viral, because I've caught a rather unhealthy dose of interest in the man myself.

I surprise myself by taking a lot of time and trouble over getting ready. I'd forgotten what fun it is to get ready for a night out with Nix, sharing clothes, make up, good-natured insults, and a bottle of wine, as the stereo blasts out Pete Tong to get us in the mood to boogy.

Amanda arrives half an hour early, her curvy bits squeezed into a Moschino dress that is at least a size too small, boobs spilling over the top of the clinging hot pink Lycra sheath like melting ice cream. Her hair is piled high on top of her head, completing the Knickerbocker Glory look. All she needs now is a cherry on top and a brave man ready with a big spoon.

She looks fabulous. Completely edible.

It's pretty obvious why she's made such a monumental effort.

She's hoping that we're going to spot a certain person.

Personally, I'm hoping we're not.

Yes, I'm still avoiding him like he's from the council and I owe back tax, but it's not just that. What if he saw us together? Amanda and me. Would he twig, put two and two together and make a perfect four? Is it plausible that I could be friendly enough with Amanda to be out clubbing with her, but not know her connection to him?

I don't believe Amanda's even thought about the possible consequences of Eddie's seeing us together. Either that, or as the launch party for Daisy's draws nearer, and my information relays become increasingly infrequent, she's decided my 'anonymity' doesn't really matter any more.

I don't know who's more jittery: her in case we don't see him, or me in case we do.

Amanda stares round each wine bar that we stagger into en route to whichever night club is being graced with our presence this evening with a haunted expression, hoping against hope that one particular person is going to walk through the door, and absolutely deflating with disappointment every moment that he doesn't, like a party balloon slowly losing air until it's sad and shrivelled.

There are obviously no bushes in bars – the odd plant, or perfectly shaped bay in a terracotta pot in the posher offerings, but no bushes – so I spend my time hiding behind Nicky and my hair. I don't have a fringe, so I muss my hair over my face and stand in dark corners like Cousin It at an Addams Family party, only I'm having much less fun than that particular party animal.

I suddenly mind very much that I've been lying to Eddie, and I suddenly need very much to tell him the truth before he finds it out for himself and hates me for it. Then again, how on earth could I explain everything *without* him hating me for it? I've spied, lied, delved through his drawers, dirty laundry and private affairs, and generally insinuated my way into his life, like a verruca eating its way into flesh.

What would he think?

Scrub that question.

I know what he'd think.

He'd think I'm a toad.

A stinky, smelly, slimy, warty toad at that.

I may feel a sudden desperate need to tell him everything, but how on earth can I actually do that? I think I should have stayed at home on the sofa.

It's sod's law, really, isn't it?

There are three reasons why I don't want to bump into Eddie:

(1) I'm with you know who and that would be rather difficult to explain;

(2) I snogged his face off last week, and that one would be rather difficult to explain to rather a lot of people;

(3) I'm incredibly embarrassed about both of the above and don't want to *have* to explain anything to anybody, thank you very much.

This is why we actually *do* bump into Eddie.

If I wanted to see him, I wouldn't be able to find him to save my life.

I know that choosing Black Betty's as our venue

to boogy away the end of the night somewhat increases the odds on our actually bumping into him, but I was outvoted two to one and dragged down there, not actually kicking and screaming but grumbling majorly.

It's not long before I spot him. About the length of time it takes to swallow yet another large vodka and Coke or two.

Usual routine. Through the door, pause for three seconds in order to be noticed, pause for a further three seconds to have a quick room scout ourselves, then head for the bar. Madly wave a twenty around for at least fifteen minutes until we get served. Knock that one back, decide that we should have got a couple while we were up there, head back to the bar, madly wave another twenty.

It's on the second foray for alcohol that I see him.

He's leaning on one end of the bar, wearing a pale blue-green Paul Smith shirt that's a slightly lighter colour than his eyes, and laughing with Mitch the head bar man. I should have brought my hat and sunglasses, I'd mingle with the crowd, but unfortunately nobody is brave enough to stand too close to Amanda, whose Eddie radar must have been dulled by the amount of white wine she's consumed because she has yet to get him in her sights.

He spots her first, leaning back against the bar, elbows behind her on the brass rail that circumnavigates the curvaceous wooden edge, the position thrusting her mega-boobs forward like twin headlights on an advancing car. Then he spots me, cowering in the shadow they're casting.

Unfortunately, whilst I'm still thinking that I can get away with the fact that I could just happen to be standing next to her, and don't know her from Adam, Amanda turns and speaks to me.

I decide it's an opportune moment to make a dash for the loos.

He's too quick for me.

Just as I'm reaching for the swing door into the Ladies, a hand grabs my arm and spins me round. For a moment he looks pissed off, and then he breaks into one of those delicious grins.

'Annabelle, where the hell have you been for the past few days?'

'I took some time off . . . I cleared it with Ben first,' I stutter, aware that I sound like a school girl excusing truancy.

'Why did you run off the other night?'

'The other night? Did I? Can't remember much, was *really* pissed,' I chirp stupidly.

He gives me a strange look, but fortunately doesn't pursue the matter any further. Very unfortunately he moves on to another subject I don't particularly wish to discuss.

'Is she a friend of yours?'

He indicates with his head over to Amanda, whose Eddie radar has unfortunately just been kick started on to level ten and who is now staring straight at us, a strange expression on her face.

I don't think a pretence at ignorance is going to work twice. I'm going to have to do what I tend to do practically every day of my life at the moment: lie. And quickly.

'Well, I wouldn't exactly call her a friend. She lives in the flat opposite. Nicky and Amanda have got quite friendly, we go out sometimes.'

That wasn't too bad, almost the truth really.

'So did we.' Eddie looks over at her again nervously, but fortunately she's turned to speak to Nicky and doesn't notice.

'Sorry?'

'Go out sometimes. We used to go out sometimes.'

'You did?' I try to sound surprised.

'Yeah, a group of us used to hang out together. We went out just the two of us once. She needed a partner for some charity thing. To be honest, after that she got a bit . . . you know . . . well, I think she wanted more than just friendship.'

'And you didn't?'

He shakes his head.

Well, this is a far cry from Amanda's version of till death us do part.

'Don't get me wrong,' he continues, 'she's a nice enough kid . . . sorry, that sounds so patronising, doesn't it? I don't mean to, but she's just a bit . . . a bit . . .'

'Flaky?' I offer.

'You think so too?'

I nod vigorously, feeling strangely disloyal.

'For want of a better word, yeah.'

I feel a bit guilty. I suppose I should be building Amanda up. Telling Eddie how wonderful she is.

Getting in a few hints about the Cordon Bleu cookery, her nose for a good bottle of plonk, and flair for interior design.

'I suppose she's okay, really,' is about all I manage. Yeah, Annabelle, great build up. I try again.

'She can be quite a laugh sometimes.'

He's looking at me like he doesn't believe that *I* believe a word I'm saying. This is why I never became an actress. I'm brilliant on my own. In the safety of my solitary, audience-less company, I'm good enough to play opposite the Greats, but when it comes to having an audience I need to convince, I go completely to pot.

To my surprise, though, he starts nodding like he agrees with me.

'Yeah, she can be good fun.'

She can?

'But she can be a bit . . . er . . . I think obsessive might be a bit strong, but . . .'

I don't. Bang on, more like. Oh, dear, what have I got myself into?

'It's my own fault.' He shrugs. 'I should have been straight with her from the start, but I didn't realise how she felt to begin with, and when I had an inkling that she might fancy me, I didn't want to say anything in case I was wrong, because that would have made me look too arrogant. After that I didn't know what to say because I didn't want to hurt her feelings. In the end, I just started avoiding her. Cowardly, but effective, I'm afraid.'

I blink at him in surprise.

Fly-Fishing

It may just be my bad luck, but I don't think I've ever met a man before who takes responsibility for his own actions.

I used to see a guy who felt that everything that went wrong in his life was always someone else's fault. If something went wrong, it wasn't down to him, it was life, the universe and everybody in it, doing their best to balls it up for him.

I'm impressed.

I'm also confused.

According to Amanda there was a damn sight more to an admittedly short relationship than just a few duty dates.

I suppose as much as she's played it up, he could be playing it down.

'Are you sure you weren't actually an item?'

'You think I'd forget something like that?' He half laughs. 'She's not my type, Belle.'

Well, we'd all already sussed that one out.

'She might have changed since you last saw her?' I offer half-heartedly.

'She has.'

'Yeah?'

He nods vigorously.

'She must have put on about two stone!'

'Why are men so shallow? I meant her personality!'

'Come on, Belle. Of course I'm going to notice her outward appearance. Admit it, it's the first thing *anybody* spots about someone else, and if anyone tells you different, then they're lying to impress. I bet you walked into this bar and wrote off half the guys

355

before you'd even spoken to them because they didn't look right.'

It's a good job it's dark or he might just see me blush.

'Make that all of them and you're pretty much spot on,' I admit, smiling shame-facedly.

'Besides,' he continues, 'I haven't even spoken to her yet, so I can't judge the personality.'

I think this one will soon be remedied.

She's on a course set for us.

'Hopefully, she's balanced the weight. You know, gain a few pounds but lose a few hang ups.'

He's not being horrible. In fact it's a far politer way of describing Amanda than I would have used. At the moment I'd describe her as a heat-seeking missile, burning a course through the crowd set for impact – or destruction.

My destruction probably. We haven't had a chance to get our stories straight! What if she tells him we've been bosom buddies for ages or something?

I'm surprised at how cool she actually plays it, though. Having breezed through to us like A-man-da on a Mission, she suddenly does yet another amazing Amanda U-Turn and almost completely ignores Eddie. She simply smiles at him briefly in acknow-ledgement, then asks me if I'm ready to leave as there's a taxi waiting.

I'm actually quite glad to get out of there myself.

I couldn't face any more questions from Eddie on Amanda as at the moment I haven't had the time to think up any plausible answers. I also have a feeling that our change of subject from the night in question, me lud, was only a temporary reprieve. My giddy excuse that I was too drunk to remember much would only work on a man with the same brain cell count as an amoeba, and that's definitely not Eddie who's brighter than the North Star.

. What makes things worse is that I've never seen Amanda so animated, even singing in the taxi on the way back to Limehouse, much to the disgust of the taxi driver, who I can tell is concerned that if she's drunk enough to be singing *Turandot* in the back of a black cab then the next thing that comes out of her mouth might be a regurgitation of the stuff that got her in this state in the first place, rather than another aria.

What he doesn't realise that Amanda isn't euphoric on alcohol. She's played her first set, and played it to perfection. Kept her cool, and breezed through. Her eyes are shining brighter than the dusting of stars settled above the upside-down fondue set that is the Millennium Dome. Mad Manda has had her Eddie fix, and she's now on a major happy hormone high.

What's even worse is that she keeps breaking off the tribute to Maria Callas to grin inanely at me, like I'm suddenly her bestest friend in the whole wide world.

I feel like dirt.

When she hugs me at the end of the evening and, biting her bottom lip to stop it wobbling, thanks me profusely for the evening, and for absolutely everything, then I feel even worse.

I'm not dirt.

Dirt's too clean.

I am scum.

What's more, I am the scum that forms in toilet bowls that haven't been cleaned properly for a couple of years.

My brief period of self-induced purdah now broken, I return to work at Daisy's. I'm greeted by the girls like the returning prodigal, which should make me feel great but actually serves to make me feel like an even bigger heel.

What makes my life even more wonderful is that now that Eddie's aware of our 'friendship', Amanda no longer feels the need to sit at home waiting for me to return with news of him and becomes almost a permanent fixture at Lazy Daisy's, perched at the end of the long wooden bar, like a figure head bolted firmly to the prow of a ship.

Two words spring to mind, like Blatant and Obvious. (Also Bugger and Off, but I can't really say that to her, now can I?)

She's also working incredibly hard to get Ben on side, and has decided that the best way to do this is by flirting outrageously with him.

I keep telling her that chatting up Ben isn't exactly going to help her cause with Eddie, but she's got it into her head that if she can get Ben constantly chuntering on about how gorgeous she is to the actual object of her affections, then he's going to start thinking that just maybe he's missing out on something wonderful.

Fortunately, Eddie doesn't come in very much at the moment, which is a severe disappointment to Amanda but a huge relief to me.

I still have my stolen snog complex in a big way, and it really doesn't help that my lips are just begging for a return match.

The cellar club opens unofficially on the Saturday two weeks before the big official opening of Lazy Daisy's, for a test run. To make sure the huge DJ desks are working properly, that the wiring isn't as faulty as the builder's invoice, and the plumbing is actually connected to the water supply rather than a beer barrel.

It's Saturday night chaos even before we more than double our capacity. So it's all hands on deck . . . including the boss's.

How can I avoid Eddie when we're confined within a five by thirty space, where if you don't suck in every inch, your bodies are bound to brush as you rush past each other? He hasn't tried to talk to me again. I think this might have something to do with the fact that every time he comes near me, I find some excuse to sprint off in the opposite direction.

My heart sinks even lower into my beer-stained Cats when, bang on half-past eight, the Wicked Witch of the North Circular flies through the door on her broomstick. Well, staggers through on three-inch Pradas to be more precise, swinging her school girl-style cookery basket like the Wolf disguised as Little Red Riding Hood wearing her mother's clothes.

She's brought cake.

She's been to a cookery lesson in a Gucci dress and Prada shoes, and has now come in to hand out her handiwork, like a mad Easter Bunny without the ears, buck teeth or fluffy tail.

The only person who doesn't think this odd behaviour is Ben, who's on his fourth chocolate brownie already.

She's obviously hoping to impress Eddie with her culinary skills. Perhaps I should have told her he hasn't really got a sweet tooth, but for some strange reason that's never actually come up in conversation. Can you pick up the sarcasm here? Or should I be more obvious?

'Well, yes, Amanda, he likes good food, fine wines, travel, music, nice cars and decent conversation, but do you know something? He doesn't eat cake. Yes, I was quite shocked about that myself too . . .'

Just to make my evening even more special, I head back out to the bar after a brief coffee break I cravenly took in the bottle store, to find Simon parked on a bar stool, eyes roaming eagerly around the place like a German spotlight attempting to pick out escaping Britons . . . namely me.

This is turning into the evening from hell.

All I need now is for my mother to appear in a whoosh of smoke and a swirl of cape like Count Dracula out for my blood, and my night is complete!

Simon spots me cowering behind the largest of the neon brewery signs, and starts madly signalling to me like a course bookie doing tic-tac.

He's obsessed. I have my own personal Glenn Close

in the form of a fat, balding, lovesick merchant wanker.

I don't understand it. I'm hardly the prize of the century. We didn't have the love affair of the century either. It was a misjudged, mismatched moment of madness that lasted for five months too long. So why does he still want me?

Amanda is also flagging me down for some reason from her end of the bar. Would it be appropriate to scream? I wonder. Perhaps I could hurl myself backwards down the steep cellar steps and get whisked out of the war zone by some pleasant paramedics.

'Sorry, can't talk, totally manic!' I yell at each, then grab Dot in desperation. 'Dot, babe, help me, I'm being stalked by two lunatics.' I surreptitiously point them both out. 'Do me a favour. If they want serving at any time, will you or one of the other girls do it, please? Pretty pleeease.'

'Great!' Dot pulls a face at me. 'The bint with the brownies and the lovesick bloodhound. Pass on the nutters, why don't you? Now if it was a tasty man then I might just help you out, but that's not what I'd classify as a tasty man . . .'

'Pleease, Dot,' I grovel, 'I just can't face either of them tonight.'

'I suppose so,' she pretends to sigh, 'but you owe me one.'

'I'll do anything . . .'

'Talk to Eddie.'

'. . . *except* talk to Eddie.'

I've now got Amanda at one end of the bar, mooning over Eddie, and Simon at the other end, mooning over me. Maybe I should get them together and let them moon over each other. It could be a match made in heaven. They're both big, blond and bolshie so they might get on like a house on fire. Not to mention the fact that it would literally kill two birds with one stone for me. The only problem is that to introduce them, I actually have to speak to them, and for someone who's stubbornly refusing to acknowledge the existence of either party this would be pretty difficult.

To top it all, whilst Amanda's mission to win Eddie isn't really going according to plan, her sub-mission to get Ben to submit to her ample charms has succeeded beyond her wildest expectations.

She's chatting to him now, leaning forward, elbows pressed together so that her cleavage turns from merely enormous into mega-gorge proportions.

Ben, ever the gentleman, is valiantly struggling to maintain eye contact only as she guzzles glass after glass of red wine and gasses on in a loud voice about how much she loves a good bottle of Shiraz or Sauvignon every time Eddie gets within earshot.

It doesn't take him long to disappear upstairs to 'do some paperwork'. Ben's a different story completely, though. He's totally smitten. He'd already confessed to a stunned Dot of a long-distance crush still lingering from when he met her first the previous year, and keeps sidling up to me, opening his mouth as if to say something, then rushing off again.

He finally corners me in the beer cellar whilst I'm

struggling to change a barrel of Carlsberg.

'You're a friend of Amanda's, aren't you?' he asks, taking over without being asked to.

'Well, I know her, yes,' I hedge, inspecting one squashed finger and a broken finger nail.

'Do you know if . . . I mean, is she . . .'

'Single?' I put him out of his misery.

'Yeah.' He grins shyly. 'Well, is she?' he demands as I hunt out a crate of tonics to take back up with me.

'Sort of.'

'What do you mean, sort of?'

How the hell do I answer this one?

'Well, I think she's keen on somebody.'

'Oh.'

His face falls.

'Damn.' I don't know if this expletive is because he just dropped the barrel on the end of his scuffed left Cat or because of what I've just said.

'But I don't think it's reciprocated,' I add quickly, surprised at exactly how disappointed he seems to be.

'Really? You see, I was thinking about asking her out for dinner or something – what do you think? Do you think I should ask her out?'

'I can't say that, can I? Only you can decide.' Very diplomatic, Belle. I turn round and continue my hunt for tonic bottles, but he's still hovering behind me.

'You wouldn't ask her for me, Belle? Well, not ask her exactly – that's a bit playground really, isn't it? But sound her out, so I don't make a total tit of myself if she's not interested.'

Well, I could tell him now that she's not interested.

Not unless he suddenly has a major person and income transplant. In fact, a mind transfer with Eddie would really be his only hope at the moment.

Then again, why is it such a mad idea?

He's totally smitten with her. It's odd, but it's completely genuine. And Ben's lovely, a solid rock, a cosy old knitted jumper that you throw on in winter. I know that doesn't sound very flattering, but I think he's exactly what Amanda needs. A calm to her storm. A secure wing for a mental patient. No, don't be cruel, Annabelle, I chide myself at this point.

Or would the cruelty lie in foisting Amanda on to Ben just to cure myself of a guilty conscience? Then again, Eddie doesn't want Amanda, no matter how many shared interests she pretends to have or whether she dyes her hair that shade of golden-brown he admired on someone last week. There'd be nothing wrong with a bit of match making if it ended up making both Ben and Amanda happy.

As a friend, though, I feel obliged to warn him a little first . . .

'You do know she's as nutty as a fruitcake?'

'Yep.' He nods.

'And you do know she's got a bit of a crush on Eddie, don't you?'

His eyes drop to the floor.

'I'd kind of guessed, yes.'

'And you're still interested?'

The beam returns.

'Absolutely. She's great. I've never met anyone like her before.'

'Count yourself lucky . . . oh, okay.' I smile at him as he pokes his tongue out at me in good-natured reproof. 'Leave it with me, I'll see what I can do.'

I choose the next morning, Sunday, when the waft of Nicky cooking bacon and eggs mid-morning lures Amanda yet again across the corridor to join us, bringing brioches and Buck's Fizz as her contribution.

I wait until we're on the balcony, enjoying a rare day of sunshine in what has so far been a pretty dismal spring to summer weather-wise, and then casually throw into the conversation the fact that she appears to have made a bit of a conquest.

I should have been more specific.

Eddie's is the name to spring immediately to her one-track mind, and therefore when I tell her it's Ben she's disappointed, which is not a good start.

I'm just trying to think of a way to get her to warm to the idea when she has another one of her sudden changes of heart and starts to look incredibly pleased, this huge smile slowly spreading across her face like the sun emerging from behind a cloud that dared to obliterate its welcome rays.

You see, Amanda has a cunning plan.

I know exactly what she wants to do.

Mainly because she proceeds to tell me her entire cunning plan in minute detail, but also because it really should have been so bloody blatantly obvious from the outset that she'd use Ben in some way to further her cause.

The immediate fantasy to spring to her manipulative mind is a double date where the evening ends in a good old-fashioned partner swap, but the reality of Eddie actually having to have a female date to be able to go on this soon sinks in and scuppers that one.

I do try to point out that it's not fair to use someone as lovely as Ben, but she simply falls back on the old 'all's fair in love and war' line that's her favourite justification for absolutely everything at the moment.

I wish I'd kept my mouth shut.

Strike that, I wish I'd never agreed to this whole bloody thing in the first place. If I'd known how difficult it was going to be to do this . . .

So near and yet so far.

To want something you can't have.

And I'm not talking about Amanda here. I keep telling myself that it's just a silly crush, an infatuation. It's probably because I know I can't have Eddie that I want him. We women are supposed to be like that, aren't we? That must-have dress that is so much more desirable because it's out of your price range. The disgustingly gorgeous cake that suddenly becomes twice as disgustingly gorgeous as it usually is because you're supposed to be on a celery stick and carrot juice only diet.

If somebody took Eddie, stripped him naked and plonked him in front of me tied in pink ribbon and with a label saying 'ALL YOURS', then I probably wouldn't even want to get my scissors out and unwrap . . .

Who am I trying to kid? I'd sod the scissors and use my teeth.

★ ★ ★

I never thought I'd actually end up going to Mother's country weekend, let alone end up looking forward to it, but I really need the break. Apart from feeling so frazzled, I want to put some distance between me and London, Amanda, Lazy Daisy's, and most of all a certain man who shouldn't be so bloody attractive.

An added incentive is that my mother has, quite out of character, extended her invitation to Nicky, stating that she could probably do with the break after all she's endured. I think the invitation has less to do with altruism than my mother's reckoning I will be more likely to show if Nicky's also on the guest list. I'm hoping that Simon will have something far better to do than drive all the way down to Cornwall for a weekend where he'll know precisely two people, one of whom will be doing their best to avoid him at all costs.

We all pile into Jamie's cluttered Golf for the journey down. Not very subtly manoeuvred by my step-brother, I end up in the back seat fighting for room amongst the medical journals, text books, and freshly muddy rugby kit, with Elvis dribbling on my hair from the hatchback behind me.

Jamie's car is a mobile junk store. The only good thing about it is you can always guarantee to find some chocolate lying around somewhere. Well, you can if Elvis doesn't sniff it out first. He has a first-class addiction to chocolate. They say babies take after their mothers and Elvis is Nicky's baby.

I manage to beat him to a half-eaten bar of Bourneville, then curl up under Jamie's slightly smelly Goretex to catch up on some much-needed sleep.

It's dark by the time we get there.

Trent House is an old farm set into the sloping side of a bay that overlooks the English Channel. On a clear day you can look across the sea to Alderney and Guernsey. At the moment, we can just about make out the tumbling edge of the sea as it breaks against the sands below us.

Lights are blazing from nearly every window. Instead of the family gathering I was expecting, there appears to be a pretty riotous party going on.

As we squeeze in between the cars parked along the narrow driveway, Mother staggers out of the front door, dressed for the country in an immaculate red Chanel suit and two-inch black patent heels.

'Darlings, at last! You're finally here! I was beginning to think you weren't going to make it!'

I was expecting a tirade for being late, but instead my mother's acting like she's actually pleased to see us no matter what the hour. She staggers over and practically pulls me out of the car and into an unexpected embrace.

My mother's being affectionate, that can only mean one thing. I sniff the air. Yes, a definite aroma of gin. She's drunk. I think I prefer her when she's drunk, not least because she's always pleased to see me when half cut on a lot of Gordon's with ice, a slice, and as little tonic as she can get away with.

She even manages to hug Nicky.

Her face falls at the sight of Elvis, though.

'What on earth is that?' she demands, as Elvis falls thankfully out of the boot and begins to carry out a prolonged watering of a nearby bush.

'It's a puppy,' I reply dryly, brushing hairs off my duffel bag which Elvis has been using as a sleeping bag.

'Well, I can see that, thank you, Annabelle, but where did it come from?'

'Well, sometimes, when a male dog meets a female dog . . .'

'You know, I'd forgotten how great this place is.' Jamie steps in, puts an arm around my mother, and begins to shepherd her inside, throwing me a 'Don't start' glance back over his shoulder.

'Well, that was a world record,' Nicky giggles nervously, still not quite recovered from the shock of being hugged by my mother. 'You normally manage at least two civil sentences before the fighting starts.'

'What do you expect when the first thing I see when I get here is that!' I indicate the large silver Saab parked next to my mother's Mercedes.

'Simon's?'

I nod morosely.

'But you knew he'd been invited.'

'Yeah, but I'd kind of hoped he wouldn't actually come. I came down here to get away from the stress factors in my life, not be forced to socialise with them.'

'Well, it looks like there's a bit of a crowd, you might be able to avoid him. Somehow I don't think you'll be able to avoid your mother, though . . .'

'Annabelle!'

My mother's calling us to follow them in.

'Annabelle, are you coming in? I've got a surprise for you.'

'Yeah, it's six foot, balding and desperate to get into your knickers!' Nicky sniggers.

'They wouldn't fit and they wouldn't suit him,' I mutter grumpily.

'Oh, I don't know.' Nicky grabs her overnight bag and whistles for Elvis, who's head first in a bush. 'He might look quite good in pink lace and bows.'

'Perish the thought! Ooh, I think I feel sick . . .'

The minute I step into the hall, Mother grabs my arm and tugs me along behind her, heels clattering on the terracotta floor tiles, to the back of the house.

'Look, we've only just got here. Can't we even dump our bags in our room before we start socialising?' I complain.

'No time,' she explains briskly. 'He's got to go in half an hour.'

Ooh, good, Simon can't stay. I suppose I can just about manage thirty minutes of the man. I stop struggling like a kid being led into school on its very first day.

'After all, as they say, time and tide wait for no man,' Mother continues cryptically.

Nix was right on one count and one count only. The surprise is definitely bald, but the surprise is definitely *not* Simon. Standing out on the patio overlooking the black undulation that is the ocean, separated from the partying, dancing throng not only by a brick wall but also by a layer of calm indifference, is my father.

A sighting of my dad is almost as rare as an elusive comet which explodes into the atmosphere, blazing brightly, every few years or so.

I haven't seen him for nearly three years. I kept expecting to bump into him whilst overseas, propping up the bar in some oriental beachfront gin palace somewhere. In fact, every time I saw a pair of deck shoes topped by a pair of bandy yet sturdy legs and a bald head, my heart skipped a beat in case it was him.

It never was.

He still smokes Café Crèmes, held between thumb and forefinger so that the main body of the cigar is hidden in the palm of his hand.

He used to stand in the garden and smoke them like that, trying to hide the fact from my mother, blowing the smoke out of the side of his mouth so that you didn't swallow a lung full when he talked to you.

He has a plaster on practically every finger of his right hand, and a large red inflamed lump he claims to be a jellyfish bite on the ball of his left thumb. When he spots me, his weathered face breaks into the broadest, most creased of grins, his whiter than white teeth baring in a genuinely ecstatic smile, emphasising the wealth of laughter lines around the corners of his mouth and eyes.

I think that's probably where I got my urge to travel from. Every time I see him he's always so relaxed and happy, but I think I've realised it's more to do with his philosophy of life than his position on the planet. He's so laid back, he's horizontal. Everything just skids over the top of his bald head like it's greased against emotional weather. Probably all the sun tan lotion he's been slapping on since the seventies. Yet get shampoo build up, don't you? He's probably got a permanent layer of lotion a couple of millimetres thick all over his skin, guaranteed to deflect the sun's harmful rays and anything else stressful that life might have to throw at you. An addiction to good brandy might also help. Purely medicinal, of course, although to him it seems to be a cure all for everything from a headache, to mosquito bites, to a raging hangover.

'Dad!' I yell so loudly everybody around me jumps.

I'm enveloped in a bear hug of monster proportions.

'When did you get back?' I mumble into the thick wool of an old Aran jumper that smells of tobacco and sea salt.

'This morning, although I'm not exactly back. We're on a stopover – repairs, restocking, that sort of thing.'

'We?'

'Me and a boat full of other old codgers who refuse to grow up or die easy.' He grins, finally releasing me. 'We're heading off tonight, but I couldn't go without seeing my baby girl first. I was worried you weren't going to get here before I went.'

'You're leaving already?' I wail, deflating with disappointment. 'But I've only just got here!'

'I'm afraid we're on a tight schedule.'

'Can't you untighten it and stay around for a bit?' I complain. 'I haven't seen you for three years!'

'I'm know I'm just a selfish git, but you don't need an old codger like your dad hanging around and interfering. You've got your own life now, Belle. If I stayed in Britain, I'd be stuck in my rocking chair in some home for old reprobates somewhere, slowly rotting away, and you'd probably pop round once a month on a Sunday for a duty visit, then wheel me out and back in again on birthdays, at Christmas, and for special occasions.'

'Not true!' I protest.

He raises his eyebrows at me.

'No?'

'No.' I stop pouting and grin at him. 'I'd visit on Father's Day too.'

Dad beams broadly, and looks at the huge watch on his left wrist.

'So, you've got – oooh – at least ten minutes to tell me about your life. Anything special going on? Any-*one* special?'

I'm silent.

'Well, that's different from the usual resounding no.'

'I suppose there is someone.' My god, I've finally admitted it.

'You don't sound very happy about it?'

'It's complicated. And that's putting it mildly.'

'It's not him, is it?'

Dad jerks his head surreptitiously towards Simon.

'No!' I deny vigorously.

'Well, thank god for that. Your mother was hinting that there was something meaningful going on there.'

'Hatred's meaningful.'

Dad's smile quirks back into life. He's so weathered that when he smiles his whole face creases.

'Glad to hear you've grown out of that one.'

'Yeah, I just wish he'd grown out of me too. It's like trying to shake off a bloodhound.'

Simon's sitting somewhat precariously on the low stone wall that borders the terrace, swaying slightly on his fifth can of Caffrey's plus the wine that would have been flowing freely with dinner.

Behind him is the seriously sloping lawn tumbling down towards a small copse that is the only boundary between the end of the garden and the cliff edge, which is extremely dangerous when you're drunk. One false move and you're on a non-stop gravity-induced run, the weight of your legs pulling you ever nearer a tree or, worse, a free fall on to the rocks below.

Like a wheelchair pushed down a flight of stairs. One swift yet sneaky push and the weight would make him fall like a rolling snowball.

One problem solved.

I suppress a laugh that would have graced Boris Karloff.

Dad draws on his cigar, the end glowing in the soft gloom of dusk.

'I know your mother wouldn't hold me up as a shining example to our only child, but if you can follow in my footsteps in just one respect then I'd be pretty pleased. You've only got one life to live, Belle. For God's sake, make sure you don't waste it. It's too bloody short. Sometimes you just have to sod guilt and live for yourself.'

'Like you, eh? Live life to the full?'

'Of course! Looks like my lift's arrived . . .'

I haven't heard any cars pull up, but when I follow Dad's gaze he's looking out to sea, to where a large yacht is just mooring off shore.

'Wow, that's so romantic!' Nicky murmurs into my ear as Dad starts his goodbyes. 'Think your dad would fancy a younger woman?'

'Sure he would, but you'd only get to see him about twice a year.'

'The perfect man!' She grins.

After more hugs, a few tears, and a very long goodbye, we watch Dad head down the steep cliff steps at the end of the garden, then climb into a dinghy that's been despatched to the beach to pick him up.

There he goes again. Not exactly heading off into the sunset, it's too bloody dark, but certainly making his own happy ending.

For a while we watch the yacht motor out to sea, lights swinging in front like car headlights, then reclaiming our bags from where I unceremoniously dumped them in a doorway, follow a still frighteningly convivial Mother up to the room I always used to have as a child, on the first floor, at the back of the house overlooking the sea.

It used to be pure Laura Ashley, with chintz curtains and a patchwork bedspread I always loathed. Now it's pure undiluted white – the walls, the ceiling, the bedclothes – the only hint of colour being the light dusting of yellow pollen on the phallus of the heavy scented lilies littered like discarded items of clothing about the room.

It's very sacrificial virgin, and very pretentious.

I kind of like the new look.

'I'll share with Nix, I was expecting to anyway,' I squeak, reaching out to grab Nicky's wrist as my mother, instead of ushering her through the door after me, begins to nudge her in the direction of the next flight of stairs.

'Don't worry, darling, I've put Nicola in one of the attic rooms . . .'

Nix shoots me a frightened look as though she's about to be locked in a bare cobweb-strewn room and left to rot, instead of shown into a rather cosy peach offering with gables and a magnificent view of the darkened coastline.

The house is heaving with people who'll all need somewhere to crash, and Mother puts me in a room on my own?

Her apparent generosity is explained by the appearance of a burly form from the room next door.

'Hi, Annabelle, it seems we're neighbours.'

Simon lounges again the frame Noël Coward-style, practically filling the doorway.

Great. That's why Nicky's a flower in the attic. It leaves the coast clear for Simon to slide into my room in the middle of the night and attempt to seduce me with his magnetic personality.

What woman could resist him?

Me, that's who!

'I've put Simon next door . . . he's such good company!' Mother calls back, her laughter affected and far from the melodious tinkle she was aiming for.

I throw them both a murderous glance and scuttle quickly into my room, before Simon can foist his company on me by offering to help unpack my knickers or something.

I can only loiter in my room for so long. Fortunately I'm rescued by Nicky and Elvis, who slide into my room without knocking.

'He's gone,' she whispers, depositing a wriggling dog on the floor boards. Elvis starts to chew on a lily, sneezing as his black nose is covered in heavy yellow pollen.

'Yeah, but for how long?'

'Not long judging by the amount of time he waited outside for you. I nearly sent Elvis down to pee on him or something, I thought he was going to lurk there forever!'

'Brilliant! Why on earth did I come?'

'Well, I did wonder about that one myself . . . I know you said you needed a break but I thought that was *from* your mother, not with her.'

I fight the urge to confess all to Nix. I feel mean keeping secrets from her but to tell her everything would only put her in an awkward situation. Nicky in the middle. Besides Amanda would probably do her Gestapo bit and torture her with aerobics sessions until she confessed all.

'Although you did get to see your dad.'

'Yeah, for about twenty seconds!'

Simon reappears at my side when we go back downstairs, with a bottle of Moët and two glasses.

'Thought you might like a drink after your journey.'

He hands me the glasses to hold whilst he pours the frothing liquid into each. I wait till he's finished, then taking a large swig from the first, hand the second glass to Nix.

'Cheers, Si, that was really thoughtful of you. We're totally parched after that long drive down.'

I feel mean for a moment, but it's only a brief moment.

Seeing as how we've missed dinner, which I'm relieved about because I'd no doubt have been plonked next to Simon, or worse still opposite so that he could play footsie at will, Jamie and I, followed by a reluctant and school-girl shy Nicky, head for the kitchen and raid the huge fridge, annexing some smoked salmon that was probably earmarked, along with a mega bag of crumpets and scrambled eggs, for breakfast.

'Do you think she's invited all of her exes?' Jamie looks around, fearful of spotting his father and new wife Priscilla, whose strong-arm tactics have earned her the nickname Priscilla the Gorilla.

'Don't worry, there are only ten bedrooms, she hasn't got room for all of her exes.'

'How many are there exactly?' asks Nicky, feeding half a buttered crumpet to a drooling Elvis.

'Four husbands, about five or six fiancés, and lots of uncles who used to visit for the odd weekend.'

'And wear the spare robe,' laughs Jamie, buttering Nicky another crumpet which she immediately passes on to Elvis.

'Ah, yes, the legendary spare robe,' she laughs, licking melting butter from her fingers. 'I've heard all about that.'

'It's probably hanging in her en-suite right now in case she pulls tonight,' I laugh bitterly. 'You know, it's really weird when your mother has a healthier sex life than you.'

'You haven't got a sex life,' Nicky points out bluntly.

'Exactly,' I moan, nicking the next crumpet before Jamie can give it to Nicky and Nicky can give it to Elvis.

'Well, there's always Simon.'

'Exactly, there's *always* Simon. Everywhere I turn there's Simon . . .'

I try my best to put him off. Every time I catch him looking over, I take a deep breath, hope that nobody else is watching me, and thrust a finger up my nose or in my ear. I even scratch myself in antisocial places until I spot a rather good-looking young local eyeing me in total disgust and turn flame red with embarrassment. I toy with the idea of projectile vomiting over his chinos, but in the end decide I'm far too knackered from all the dork dodging, and pissed from all the booze Simon, Jamie and Nicky (who sloped off to bed at the first opportunity) have been tipping down my neck. I slope off to bed myself, putting a chair against my door handle to stop unlawful entry, and drunkenly shoving the chest of drawers in front of the interconnecting door in a bid to protect my chastity.

My head spinning from the effort of furniture removal whilst drunk, I throw open the sash window and breathe in the clear sea air in the hope that its purity may have a cleansing effect on my toxicity.

The clouds have cleared and the sky is brilliant with stars. The sea is a dark, tumbling, hypnotic, whispering mass of water. It's almost as though it's calling my name.

'Annabelle . . . Annabelle . . .'

Hang on a mo. The sea sounds remarkably like Simon.

I turn to look at the door, where the whispering is actually coming from.

Oh my god, he's followed me up!

The door handle, thankfully jammed by my well-placed chair, rattles as he tries to turn it.

I squeak in fear, step into the window frame, pull the curtains behind me, like a stage curtain screening an actor from the audience, then slip out on to the window ledge, legs dangling, bum perched on the lintel, scrunched up into a corner so that if he does manage to get in, he hopefully won't see me.

'Evening, all.'

A voice to my left makes me jump so I nearly fall off my perch.

Jamie's perched on the window ledge of the bedroom next door.

'What are you doing out here?' I hiss.

'Smoking. You?'

'Hiding.'

'From?'

'Take a guess.'

'Er . . . could it be Simon, by any chance?'

'Got it in one. Bloody Mother only went and put him in the room on my other side. He's been rattling at my door!'

'You don't fancy a re-run there then?' Jamie leans out precariously from his own ledge and passes me the bottle of wine he's been swigging from.

'Are you kidding!' I reply, taking a grateful pull and then handing it back. 'Been there, done that, and wouldn't bloody do it again!'

'I thought you wanted something to take your mind off you-know-who?'

'Who?'

'Come on, Belle, don't play ignorant with me. Eddie the Entrepreneur, the man who makes you drool like a lovesick fool.'

'Oh, okay, you're right,' I finally admit with bad grace. 'I do like Eddie, rather too much actually, but Simon . . . I'd rather buy a vibrator.'

'Annabelle, I'm shocked!' says Jamie, clearly not in the least.

'Yeah, well, I'm an adult now, aren't I? Well, officially, anyway. I can have sex with whatever consenting inanimate object I choose.'

'As long as the consenting inanimate object isn't Simon?'

'Got it in one.'

Jamie draws deeply on the cigarette in his other hand then exhales a lung full of smoke, sending it curling ghost-like into the dark curtain of the sky. He must be really pissed, he only ever lights up when steaming.

'Do you remember when we were kids, we used to think that twenty was positively middle-aged?' he asks, laughing lightly.

'I know, now look at us both.'

'Yeah, heading towards our dotage at the grand old age of twenty-five.'

'Only just, thank you very much. Don't forget you're a few months older than me.'

'We both thought we'd be married with kids by now.'

'Count ourselves lucky we're not.'

'Too true.' I see the end of Jamie's cigarette glow in the darkness as he inhales again. 'Relationships are far too bloody complicated.'

'I agree, we're much better off single.'

'Don't want to go through all the crap other people put themselves through in the so-called name of love.'

'Far better to be on your own.'

'Absolutely.'

Silence for a few moments.

'So when are you going to ask Nicky out then?'

'The next time I've had enough drink not to care if she says no,' he admits frankly. 'And what about you? When are you going to sort out the mess you've got yourself into?'

I don't know. I shrug, the shoulder action causing me to wobble precariously on my ledge. 'It's sod's law, isn't it? I've finally found something I want with a burning passion.'

'And you can't have it?'

'Exactly.'

'Well, all I can say is, it's better to regret something you have done, than to regret something you haven't.'

'You know, I think that's what my dad was trying to tell me.'

'Sometimes you have to listen to your parents.'

'We do? But that goes against everything we learnt in childhood!' I exclaim mockingly.

'I know.' Jamie sighs, taking another swig. 'It's a galling moment, when you finally realise that your parents were usually right after all.'

'I take it my mother's not included in that one?'

'God, no! There's an exception to every rule.'

'And I certainly take exception to my mother.'

'Do you want me to check if Mr Persistent has taken a hike?'

'Would you?'

''Course . . . hang on a mo.'

Jamie's back in two minutes.

'Gone back downstairs.'

'Are you sure?'

'Went down to check. He's slumped in a corner being consoled by your mother.'

'But what if he comes back?'

'Well, there's an easy solution to that one . . . swap

rooms with me. That way, if he attempts to slide into your bed in the middle of the night, he's in for a hell of a lot more than he bargained for.'

'He is?'

'Oh, I'd say about eight inches more . . .'

'Don't boast, Jamie.'

Just when I thought things couldn't get any more complicated, they do. Fate steps in, or rather Cupid steps out of line and fires an incredibly wonky arrow, in a mind-bendingly odd direction.

I wake up the next morning to a beautiful day, sun shining through the gauzy curtains, sending Jamie's yellow room as bright as a Dulux ad, Dad's words running through my head. Get up full of optimism then stagger downstairs in jeans and a t-shirt, hair unbrushed and the only concession to make up a hastily slapped on layer of mascara, and some eye-liner round my tired slitty eyes, to find Mother and Simon at the kitchen table eating breakfast together.

This shouldn't be odd, but Simon is spreading melting butter on warm croissants, firmly ensconced in the 'spare robe', thick hairy knees poking out of the front of the wrap, and looking bloody smug.

Come to think of it, they both looked bloody smug. Identical smug smiles, on identical smug faces.

I could have screamed. In fact, I think it's quite possible that I did. Just a small one, immediately suppressed by my hand which stayed over my mouth for a further few minutes, glued there by shock and the fact that I've suddenly lost all muscle control.

My mother is sleeping with Simon, the respectable ex. This is repeated several times, very slowly, and it still won't sink in.

Severe Shock with two capital S's.

Does this follow Mother's theory of waste not, want not?

She's expended so much effort, energy and time on him she just had to get a result of some sort?

The worst of it was they didn't seem in the least embarrassed that I found them together. They were acting like it was the most natural thing in the world to be seated across the table from each other, Mother's right foot resting slightly, but very obviously, against Simon's hairy left ankle. I'd forgotten how hairy his legs were. It must be like playing footsie with a Brillo pad.

The shock horror is soon replaced by a total sense of disbelief, like if I stood there and blinked often enough, for long enough, I'd finally open my eyes and he'd be gone.

But he didn't disappear in a puff of my indignation. He remained there, his solid bulk as horribly real and evident as ever.

Like a nightmare in still life.

It's not the age difference. That's their choice. My mum's a young at heart fifty something, Simon's an old thirty something. They kind of meet in the middle in mental years. It's just the thought that . . . well, it's a frightening thought that somebody you once got naked with (albeit very misguidedly, to be looked back upon with severe regret and much cringing) has just got naked with your own mother.

SARAH HARVEY

Did he compare us whilst he was actually, you know . . . at it? Is my mother's body better than mine despite the fact that she's twenty-six years older than me? Has all the gin she drinks preserved her body the way it was when she hit the legal age limit for pouring all that booze down her throat?

This is the stuff psychiatrists' dreams are made of. I decide the only therapy I need right now is a large bottle of something alcoholic, I don't really care what – Windolene would be a blissful escape right now.

They look so horribly pleased with themselves.

What's worse is Simon's attitude.

He's changed roles with frightening rapidity from former lover to potential father in one swift sex session.

Sex.

My mother doesn't have sex.

She's my mother.

When he started to call her 'Honey', feeding her pieces of his croissant, licking his fingers slowly and suggestively after shoving yet another buttery morsel into her open mouth, I decided it was time to leave. It had been time to leave from the very first moment I walked into the room and found them there together, but it's like anything that isn't good for you, it held a certain awful fascination.

I travelled back to London in the back of Jamie's Golf, with Elvis chewing my hair for the majority of the journey, and didn't tell him to bog off once.

When I break the news to Nicky back in the flat, she says nothing, simply raises her eyebrows in disbelief then fetches two glasses from the cupboard and a bottle of chilled white from the fridge.

It's only when we're halfway down the first glass that she looks at her watch to check that it's not April the first, opens her mouth, manages only to exhale a little air, then lapses back into disbelieving silence.

She assumed my instant desire to escape from Trent House was just my usual reaction to having to spend too much time in the same place as my mother, and having been quite keen not to hang around for long herself, was happy to be bundled back into Jamie's car and carted straight back to London.

Now she's as gob smacked as I was the moment I stepped into the kitchen and found them together with that unmistakable intimacy of the just had sex.

'It won't last,' Nicky finally says.

I shake my head in agreement.

'Simon's a control freak, my mother's a control freak, in reality how long could it last? They'll be like two despots from neighbouring countries in a temporary alliance: comfortable in bed together for a while until they actually have to decide who's going to be number one boss of the outfit.'

'And then it'll be an end to a rather strange *entente cordiale*?'

'You do realise this is all your fault?' I announce, my bottom lip protruding sulkily.

'It is?' Nicky's eyes widen in disbelief.

'You introduced me to him.'

'You said you'd forgiven me for that!'

'I had when he was over ten thousand miles away. Now I'm not so sure.'

'Well, you don't have to sleep with everyone I introduce you to!'

'Somebody had better tell my mother that!'

'It does solve the problem of getting him off your back.'

'Don't even go there, Nix!'

She pats my hand rather ineffectually.

'It might not be so bad, Belle. I mean, what's the worst that could happen?'

'Oh my god.' I suddenly have a horrible thought. 'What if they actually get married?'

'They wouldn't?' Nicky asks incredulously.

'Why not?'

'Well, it would be her fifth time for starters!' Nicky exclaims, like Mother's greedily going up for far too many helpings of pudding.

'Exactly. She obviously likes getting married, so what's stopping her from doing it again? Five weddings and my funeral!' I sigh.

'You could be a bridesmaid.'

Is that the smallest hint of a smile I see playing about my best mate's lips?

'I mean, you missed out on your first opportunity this year, didn't you? And tell your mother if she wants a dress,' the smile erupts into full-blown mirth as Nicky snorts hysterically and collapses face first into her wine glass, 'I know of one going spare . . .'

★ ★ ★

I'm not rostered on at work again until Friday. I spend the next few days hiding out in my room, refusing to see Amanda who's hovering round the flat like a large trapped bluebottle, no doubt hoping I'll be persuaded to go out Eddie hunting for her, and forcing myself to face up to the facts.

Not my mother. I'm pushing that one way to the back of my mind, it's far too weird to handle at the moment. My main concern is my own libido, not hers. You see, I've fallen for Eddie. Big time.

My mind keeps wandering back to that kiss. Well, two kisses to be precise. Would that I could make it three . . . and I'm not specifying where my lips are going to fall for the third.

I give myself a quick mental cold shower by thinking of my mother's foot rubbing Simon's hairy ankle.

Ugh!

Jamie's right, I've got to sort this mess out once and for all.

I've got to tell Eddie the truth.

Goodness knows what I'm going to do about Amanda, but I do know that, like my father said, it's time I started living my life for myself instead of someone else. I'm going to come clean, tell Eddie everything, and hope that he can forgive me for the deception. And if he can't . . . well, I'll deal with that one when it comes to it.

Friday finally arrives and I head for work with trembling knees – well, trembling everything to be precise, especially my resolve.

Wish I could serve myself a few vodkas, could do

with a bit of Dutch courage.

I've decided that I'll wait for a quiet moment and ask for a word in private. Either that or hope that if I actually act a bit more approachable this evening, he'll ask me to stop on for one of our after work drinking sessions.

I've been psyching myself up to tell him everything all day.

I'm scared, petrified even, but the sense of relief is just as strong as the sense of fear. I'm also amazed at how anxious I am to see him, after only a few days away. I'm like Elvis waiting for the tin opener to be pulled out of the drawer.

But, as usual, whenever I want to see Eddie, I don't.

By ten there's still no sign of him. The clock crawls round to eleven and nothing. At twenty past, Dot taps me on the shoulder.

'I see our lord and master's decided to put in an appearance.' She indicates with a nod of her head towards the door.

My stomach lurches up into my lungs for a moment.

He's here!

Here goes.

I take a deep breath and turn round, only to see Dot staring over at Eddie in disbelief. He's here all right, but he's not alone.

Just behind him, hand slipped quietly and confidently into the crook of his arm, is a girl.

She's blonde, slim, and beautiful.

I hate her already.

They don't even acknowledge us, no usual wave, wink, joke or insult, just head for the restaurant and, choosing a table in full view of the bar, sit down close together and fall deep into conversation.

As Angus, one of the waiters, pours them both a glass of Champagne, she leans in and whispers something in Eddie's ear, putting her hand on his knee as she draws closer. He bursts into peals of laughter and looks down at her, smiling that gorgeous lop-sided smile of his.

I feel like I've been punched in the guts.

Ripping off my apron, I hurl it somewhere in the direction of the bin and grab my bag from under the bar.

'Belle, what on earth are you doing?' Dot squeaks in concern.

'I'm sorry, Dot, I've got to go.'

'But, Belle . . .'

'I'm sorry!' I yell, and sprint for the door.

I get back to Nicky's place to find Amanda and Nicky reclining, one on each sofa, cucumber on eyes, slathered in matching pale green face packs, fingers resting in bowls filled with olive oil.

No lights are on, the room is illuminated by the glow of hundreds of little night light candles nestled upon every surface, flickering haphazardly like skittish fire flies in a gentle wind.

A strange low-pitched wailing, like the sound of a drunken cat being swung round at high speed by its tail, is pulsing from the speakers of the expensive hi-fi system.

'What on earth is that racket?'

'It's the song of the whale, it's supposed to be very relaxing,' Nix mutters, trying not to crack her face pack.

'Well, it's giving me a bloody headache.' I slump down on the floor next to her feet.

'Ooh, aren't we a Miss Grouchy Pants tonight?' she teases. Nonetheless, she pulls one hand from its oily bath and, reaching for the remote, turns the stereo off.

On the television, in complete contrast to the manufactured air of mystical calm and harmony, Christopher Lee is currently, and silently due to the fact that the sound's turned off, sinking his fake fangs into the neck of a fake virgin with obvious relish.

Show me a bar of chocolate right now, and I'd get that very same expression. I need some comfort food with a capital C, for calories and cholesterol.

Unfortunately, there is absolutely nothing tempting to eat in the flat. The other two have gone on some strange diet where you can only eat things that are green, like lettuce and mange tout. The most exotic thing we have is a bowl of cold pasta verde with pesto and green olives, or a rather sad-looking bowl of guacamole, both of which look pretty rank. I've racked my brains to try and think of a biscuit or a cake or a chocolate bar that's green and failed dismally, and my attempt to introduce salt and vinegar crisps was greeted with such horror you'd think I was trying to poison them both.

392

Amanda, as usual totally oblivious to anyone's emotions but her own, wants an instant Eddie update.

'There was no sign of him all evening,' I mutter.

'No sign?' she repeats.

'No sign. Not until last orders when he saunters in with some blonde bimbo hanging off his arm,' I growl.

Amanda sits bolt upright, spilling olive oil on to Nicky's scatter cushions, her cucumber slices sliding down her face like huge green tears to disappear into her copious cleavage, like coins being dropped into a slot machine.

'You're joking!' Her face creases into a major frown, causing her face pack to crumble like concrete being hit with a sledgehammer. 'Son of a bitch!'

'Offspring of a hell hound,' I drawl sarcastically. 'Couldn't have put it better myself.'

'How could he!'

'With all the slippery ease of a slimeball.'

'I don't believe it.'

'Bastard.'

Nicky looks from Amanda to me, and back again, like a spectator watching a verbal tennis match with insults being batted back and forth over an imaginary net.

'I think we need a drink,' she mutters, and scuttles into the kitchen.

She reappears a few minutes later with a bottle of Champagne and three glasses, her face scrubbed clean apart from a few green crusty bits stuck around her hairline.

'I was saving this for a special occasion,' she waves the Champagne in my direction, 'but I have a feeling we need it more now than when we're ecstatically happy about something.'

Oh, well, the bottle's green, so perhaps it's allowed.

'There's probably a perfectly reasonable explanation.' Nicky grins at us hopefully, deftly twisting wires and popping the cork.

'Yeah, like he's on a *date*,' I growl.

'It could be his sister or something?'

'He hasn't got a sister.' Ignoring the two pieces of cucumber still nestling between her boobs, Amanda makes a grab for the glass Nix has just poured and knocks it back in one go.

'A friend?'

'A close and personal one,' I drawl sarcastically.

'Belle, you're not helping!'

'You've got to go down and find out!' Amanda snaps.

'Yeah, you're right.' I take a brief slug of Champagne, then thumping my glass on the table, get back on my feet.

Nicky's still looking at me oddly.

I attempt to sidle into my bedroom like a crab shooting under a rock, but she's too quick for me. She follows me in and shuts the door behind us.

'What's going on, Annabelle?'

'I'm just going to grab a jacket before I go, it's gone a bit cooler out.'

'That's not what I'm on about and you know it!' she whispers tartly.

'I don't know what you mean,' I mutter.

'Well, that wasn't just sympathy anger for Amanda's sake, now was it? Is there something you want to tell me, Belle?'

'Nope.'

Well, that's not a lie, is it? I *don't* want to tell Nicky I want Eddie more than I want a non-repayable limitless charge card for Harvey Nicks.

'Then why are *you* so pissed off that Eddie might actually have somebody?' Nicky persists. 'You were more upset about it than Amanda.'

Why am I so pissed off?

I can't give Nicky an answer. You see, I'm pissed off because I'm jealous. I'm so jealous I'm greener than Hyde Park in spring. And I'll tell you something else: Amanda's not the only one who won't be able to sleep tonight unless I find out that a certain someone else is sleeping alone.

I get back to Daisy's just before one.

Dot doesn't even need to ask why.

'They left about ten minutes after you shot off . . .'

'They did? Do you know where they went?'

'Haven't got a clue, sorry. Belle, Ben wants to see you . . .'

'It'll have to wait, I've got to go.'

'He said it was important!'

'So is this, Dot. You're the one who keeps telling me I should talk to Eddie!'

'I know, but you really pick your moments, don't you?'

Dot looks at my crumpled face, and gives me a quick hug.

'Go on, you get out of here, I'll fend off Ben for you.'

It's gone two in the morning. There are no lights on in the house. Eddie's either already home and in bed, or he's in another club somewhere, settled in a dark corner with a bottle of good red and a bad bottle blonde!

I'm stuck in a bush watching his house. I've been here for the past twenty minutes. I look like a commando in my work outfit of black jeans and black T-shirt, over which I pulled Nicky's black suede jacket to keep out the cool night air.

I hardly thought when I threw on my clothes that morning: Hmm, better wear black today so I can blend into a bush later.

The problem is the bush is pretty sparse. It's okay in darkness, but if somebody comes down the road with their headlights on, which considering it's the middle of the night and pitch black is a pretty strong possibility, I'm going to be lit up like an elephant hiding in a Christmas tree.

This is ridiculous.

It's cold, it's late, and I'm standing in a bush with my feet sticking out of the bottom.

I don't know whether to laugh or cry.

I think I should go home.

Unfortunately, there's something that's keeping me rooted firmly where I am. It's not the fact that a stray twig has stuck quite stubbornly through a belt loop in the back of my jeans, or that a major hank of my hair is similarly pinioned.

And I'm not going to lie to myself that I'm here for Amanda either.

I'm here for me.

For purely selfish reasons.

Because I've finally admitted to myself how much I want Eddie, and it's sod's law that when I do that, someone else steps on to the scene!

It's also sod's law that the exact moment I decide to move position to somewhere a bit less conspicuous, is the moment Eddie arrives home.

I've just extricated myself from the bush, and am gazing like a totally sad git back at his house before trotting off down the road and attempting to access his garden from the back.

The distinctive throaty growl of a Porsche engine is the first warning sound, but as usual he's driving far too bloody fast for me to be able to make a swift getaway. His car rounds the corner, headlights spotlighting the road like mega-watt halogens sweeping the crowd at a rock concert.

I'm lucky in a way. My decision to take that last backward look means that I don't get caught in the open road, but as it is I have to dive to the floor and crouch behind a car which leaves my arse in full view. Oh, well, it's big, it's black, it hopefully blends into the night . . .

I stick my head as close as I possibly can to the front bumper of the Range Rover I've dived behind, convinced that I can be seen. I've finally discovered the reason people have Range Rovers in Central London. So that idiots like me can hide behind them in the middle of the night!

As soon as the car's slowed and I can hear the electronic gates swinging open, I head off down the road at full pelt, my footsteps echoing loudly on the tarmac.

Well, if he didn't know I was there before, he probably does now!

This theory is backed up by the sound of the same car coming back down the road at great speed in reverse.

Oh, shit! What on earth do I do now? I'm frozen to the spot for a moment, eyes searching frantically for an escape route.

There is absolutely nothing else I can do. I hurl myself through the gate of the nearest house, a very ungraceful swan dive into their shrub border, and lie in the undergrowth until I think the coast is clear. Then, eyes sweeping frantically from side to side, hurtle back across the road and round the corner to where I left my car.

I'm shaking, but the strange thing is I'm laughing my head off too.

Adrenaline is coursing through my veins, pumping round my blood stream like brandy-laced Champagne.

What if they've got security cameras or something?

My mother and Simon will probably turn on the TV, post-coitally cosy, side by side on the sofa, and there I'll be, grinning out at them from the *Crime Watch* 'do you recognise this mad person?' section.

And the shitty thing is, I still didn't get to see if he went home alone. There could quite easily have been a bottle blonde reclining in the passenger seat next to him, long legs crossed temptingly, cleavage flaunted like a flesh-coloured Venus fly trap.

I fumble in my pocket for my car keys, agitation making me clumsy, then attempt to insert them in the lock.

I ignore the sound of a car driving towards me.

I ignore the fact that it pulls up beside me, engine growling like a big cat spotting the prey for today.

I revert to the childish theory of if I can't see him, he can't see me, and determinedly remain facing my car door.

I hear the sound of an electric window sliding down as I finally manage to insert the key in the door lock.

'Annabelle.'

Oh, dear. I'm suddenly and acutely deaf.

'Annabelle!'

It's no good. I turn slowly, a stupid goofy grin on my face for want of a better expression.

'Er, hi there.'

His face is pained, frowning. I suddenly wish I was back in the bush.

'Annabelle? I thought it was you. What on earth are you doing here?'

Good question, but not one I can answer. What *am* I doing here? I don't think I could get away with 'Smile, you're on Candid Camera.' I find the only way I can answer is with the truth. The question is, should it be the truth, not quite the whole truth, or nothing like the truth?

'Er . . . I came to see you.'

That's not lying, is it?

'So why did you do a disappearing act when I drove past?'

'I changed my mind.' I shrug. Thank god it's too dark for him to see how much I'm blushing. 'I . . . er . . . I suddenly realised how late it was.'

'Get in the car, Annabelle.'

I stare silently at him.

'Get in the car,' he repeats, enunciating each syllable like a teacher with a slow child. I get in the car.

He drives in silence the hundred or so feet back to his house and presses a button in the car, at which point the iron gates swing open as if by magic, then swing shut behind us after he's driven through. A far easier entrance than my last exit from this house.

He doesn't say anything, simply gets out of the car and, expecting me to follow, lets himself into the house through a side door which leads into a utility room, then through to the kitchen.

'Do you want a cup of coffee or would you prefer something a bit stronger?'

He's just found me lurking outside his house, I've got mud on the sleeve of Nicky's jacket and leaves and various other bits of garden debris in my hair, and he's talking to me like I've just dropped round for a social visit.

When I don't answer he opens the fridge and takes out a bottle of chilled wine, then reaches into a cupboard for two glasses and leads me through the hallway and into the lounge, actually apologising for the decor as we go.

'Sorry about the state of the place, I haven't even got round to decorating yet and I've been here for nearly a year.'

'It's not that bad,' I manage to stutter.

'You haven't seen upstairs.' He grins and grimaces at the same time. 'There are water nymphs in the bathroom, and you wouldn't believe what there is in the main bedroom.'

'Mirrored ceiling.' I nod my agreement, without thinking.

'How did you know?'

'Er . . . educated guess?' I offer, mentally kicking myself for being so careless. 'Goes with the flock wallpaper and water nymphs.'

This explains the drastic contrast of high taste and bad taste. Eddie's lovely things sitting awkwardly in somebody else's idea of decor. He gestures for me to take a seat, then kicking off his shoes, sits down next to me and proceeds to pull the cork from the wine.

'I bought the house from the guy I bought Daisy's from. He sold up everything and buggered off to Marbella for one hell of a retirement party. Apparently he was supposed to be a bit of a stud in the seventies. You should have seen the place with all of his stuff in – it was like walking into a time warp. I think he was hanging on to old memories from his heyday in the form of this decor. I can just see it now: leopard skin sofa with zebra stripe cushion covers, lava lamp bubbling away in the corner. Very tasteful.'

He pours us both a very large glass of white, and handing me a bowl full, finally asks the question I've been dreading.

'So, why did you want to see me?'

Here we go, I knew this part couldn't be avoided forever.

'I'm just curious,' he adds dryly, 'seeing as you've been avoiding me like the plague recently.'

'You'd noticed,' I murmur, hiding my face in my drink, knocking back half of it in one go.

'A bit hard not to, really. Even thought about changing my deodorant for a while.'

'You smell fine.' I'm lying, he smells wonderful. Not just of aftershave, but a mixture of soft scents that go to make up his own unique aroma, as potent as any aphrodisiac. He looks at me sideways through what I've just noticed are surprisingly long eyelashes.

'I thought you were trying to give me a big, not very subtle hint that you weren't interested? I've done it before myself, remember.'

He refills my glass without asking if I want any more, then taking a large strawberry from the bowl of fruit on the coffee table, offers me first bite and pops the rest into his mouth.

It's not a calculated move, not a scene played for seduction, but the casual intimacy of the act has my stomach turning somersaults with lust.

Oh, Belle. NO, Belle. Not again.

'That I wasn't interested in what?' I try to sound casual.

'Annabelle!' He raises his eyes to the ceiling. 'Can we stop playing games, please?'

'Okay, if we're being up front, who was the blonde?'

He bursts out laughing.

'Bait.'

'You mean, jail bait,' I huff.

'I mean Annabelle bait. I needed to see if it both-ered you.'

'But that's cruel.'

'Yes, but it was also effective.'

'I meant cruel to her.'

'Contrary to popular myth, not every woman I meet finds me completely irresistible.'

'Well, she was certainly putting on a good act then.'

'Is that a hint of jealousy.'

'Don't flatter yourself.'

He suddenly looks concerned.

'That's the thing, Belle – am I flattering myself or do you feel the same way as I do?'

'I don't know,' I whisper, staring down at my feet.

'Oh.' He sounds disappointed.

'I don't know,' I continue, forcing myself to meet his gaze, 'because I'm not sure that I know how you feel.'

'How can you say that?' He laughs in disbelief. 'It's so bloody obvious. Everybody else knows and I haven't had to say a word to them, but you! You want it in writing and signed in blood!'

Yeah, my blood when Amanda catches up with me.

I've got to tell him.

'Eddie, there's something I've got to tell you . . .'

Shaking his head, he leans across and gently pulls a dead leaf out of my hair. 'Don't say another word,' he whispers slowly, then leaning in, kisses me softly on the lips.

He pulls back for a moment, watching my face, judging my reaction, then when I don't throw up on the carpet or wallop him, leans in again and kisses me for longer.

I was really drunk last time we did this and it felt good then. Now I feel drunk, but drunk on lust and longing. There's just one small thing spoiling it all. He doesn't know the truth, hence he doesn't really know me.

It's not fair.

But then again, as Amanda so frequently says, all's fair in love and war . . . I mean, why feel bad just because he doesn't know everything about me? There are loads of things I don't know about him yet. Admittedly they're along the lines of what he likes for breakfast, or what side of the bed he likes to sleep on, although I have a feeling I may not be ignorant on that count for very much longer . . .

I know I shouldn't be leaping into bed with Eddie – well, snogging on the sofa to be precise – but I will be leaping into bed with him. I know it. He knows it. And do you know something? I don't care. I don't care about morals, I don't care about Amanda, I don't care about consequences, in fact I don't care about anything – I only know that I have never wanted anybody this much in my entire life.

I also know that at some point in the not too distant future, I probably will care, very much. That the guilt will come flooding back like water released from behind a makeshift dam. But at the moment the only thing I can think about is the feel of his mouth against mine, and hell, if this is so damned wrong, then why does it feel like the most *right* thing I've ever done in my entire life?

Holding on to my hands, he stands up, pulling me with him.

This time he doesn't need to spell it out.

He leads me upstairs into the bedroom.

I remember the last time I saw those underpants, and feel a momentary pang of guilt before this is totally squashed along with all of the other pangs of guilt by the overpowering feeling of desire that's hurtling through my body and mind with indecent haste.

It's odd, the pants don't look so hilarious with him actually in them. In fact, they look pretty damn' sexy. I do, however, have this overwhelming desire to get him out of them rather quickly.

Strange, he seems to have the same urge to help me out of mine too. Thank goodness I finally threw out my old grey three-year-old faithfuls, and got some new ones.

Falling back on to the cool white linen, we simply lie and hold each other for some time, breathing each other in, eyes locked. Silent. Totally blown away by the sheer pleasure of touch. Until first our hands, then our lips, begin gently to explore . . .

★ ★ ★

I wake the next morning to see my own reflection, ruffled and glowing, grinning down at me.

Never again will I make fun of mirrored ceilings.

The space in the bed beside me is warm but empty. I roll over and bury my face in the crumpled linen, breathing in the heady smell of Eddie and sex.

What have I done?

Well, no, I know exactly what I've done . . .

But what have I done!

On the bedside table next to me is a tray with more strawberries, orange juice, cold coffee, and a wilting rose hastily plucked from the garden.

Propped against the glass is a note.

'Belle, had an early meeting but you looked so peaceful I couldn't bring myself to wake you. Will see you tonight, save me the first dance. Love, Eddie. P.S. Key enclosed, keep it. You'll need it.'

I hold the small metal object that fell from the folded note tight in the palm of my hand, and my heart that was as buoyant as a helium-filled balloon sinks lower than my toes.

You see, I already have one of these.

The one Amanda gave me.

The door bell goes, waking me from a heavy sleep.

I can hear the sound of Nicky's shower going next door, which means that I'm going to have to be the one to go and open it. I drag my weary body out of bed and shuffle into the sitting room.

It's Jamie.

'Hi, wicked step-sister.'

'What are you doing here?' I yawn, pushing my hair out of my face.

'I'm Elvis sitting.'

He waves two greasy paper bags at me, and grins broadly.

'Fish and chips for me, and sausage and chips for Elvis. Got any sauce?'

Plenty.

'In the kitchen . . . what's the time?'

'Seven. I would have thought you'd be getting glammed up for tonight, not still staggering round in your dressing gown looking like death.'

'Seven! Oh, shit!'

This is what you get for staying up all night, making up for over two years of celibacy, then staggering home bandy-legged to slide back into your own bed to sleep off your excesses.

You see, whilst last night was *the* night so far as my love life's concerned, tonight's going to be *the* night for Amanda.

The grand opening of the new improved Lazy Daisy's, and the official launch of the new improved Amanda, where Eddie gets the full on effect of her new improved personality.

'Why didn't you wake me up?' I wail to Nicky as she totters out of the bedroom on her pulling Pradas.

'I didn't know you were still asleep.'

Jamie's tongue's hanging out more than Elvis's at the sight of Nicky in a new knock out dress from Joseph. A little bias-cut black number that flows over her curves like hot black treacle poured slowly and sensuously.

'Thought you'd already got your cement mixer chundering, ready to pile on the slap . . .'

'That was probably just Belle snoring,' cuts in Jamie, grinning evilly.

'I was talking metaphorically!'

'Is that like talking dirty?'

I leave the other two trading banter and stagger groggily into my shower, to try and blast away the confusion that's settled over my brain like mist hugging the coastline.

Half of me wants to break into the hugest, stupidest, smuggest grin my face has ever sported, and the other half just wants to burst into tears.

What a mess!

By the time I'm out of the shower Amanda has arrived.

I shuffle out of my room wrapped in two towels in time to see her prance into the room like a race horse turned out for Ascot, hooves oiled, coat gleaming, teeth bared in excitement.

She looks like a sparkling silver barrage balloon, her boobs floating above the neckline of the dress like they're full of helium and fighting to escape.

I have to admit it's an impressive cleavage.

I quite like my boobs. They could be a bit bigger but they're pretty symmetrical, quite a nice shape, a decent offering really. But the only time I've come near a cleavage is when I forcibly pull in the centre panel of my Wonderbra, and staple it so that the cups are touching.

Fly-Fishing

Amanda looks kind of majestic. Splendid and voluptuous. The *Queen Mary*, freshly painted and full steam ahead. I resist the urge to chuck streamers at her as she sails regally into the middle of the room, treading delicately across the deep pile of the cream carpet on a pair of gorgeous strappy silver Miu Miu sandals.

She's had her roots done, and the silver highlights shot through the long, now completely blonde thatch, match the rest of her outfit.

Nix, who's currently in diet mode again and was nibbling despondently on a Ryvita to stave off the hunger pangs, drops it on the table, and stares at Amanda in open-mouthed admiration.

I can almost read Nicky's thoughts. If Amanda can look this sensational at well over a stone heavier, then Nix is going to sod the torture of abstinence from all of her favourite foods and get stuck into the calories with relish.

It's not only Amanda's appearance that's different, but her attitude. For the first time in ages she feels drop dead gorgeous, you can see it in her. A rebirth of sexual confidence.

At least we've made her feel better about herself, which in turn makes me feel a bit better about myself. Not a lot better, I can tell you, but just a teeny tiny bit.

Jamie wanders out of the kitchen, chip paper in hand, seemingly unaware of the fact that Elvis's teeth are firmly attached to the hem of his chinos.

He stops dead upon catching sight of Amanda; the

piece of tomato sauce-covered fish that was travelling from paper to mouth hovers in mid-air, the mouth that was opening in anticipation of food dropping wider at the sight of this silver vision.

'Do I look okay?' Amanda's staring down into her own cleavage as she re-arranges her boobs in the strapless bodice of her Space Age dress.

I pop a finger under Jamie's chin and lever his mouth shut.

'Great,' I reply, not really able to trust myself to speak.

'Just great?' Amanda looks up in disappointment.

What does she want from me? The woman looks fabulous. I feel a strange sense of pleasure, mixed with the desire to try and send her out in one of my grandmother's bri-nylon curtain cast offs.

'Emphasis of the grrrrr.' Nicky smiles kindly. 'You look totally wow! Unlike Belle.' She looks pointedly at my towel turban and toga. 'Is that a new Moschino, babe?'

I look down at my own dishevelled self, lack of dress temporarily forgotten by the appearance of the walking glitter ball.

'Er . . . yeah. I'm running a bit late, aren't I?'

'Well, you'd better get a move on, the cab will be here in a few minutes.' Amanda's obviously anxious to get to Daisy's and start the big seduction.

I think I'm getting a headache.

'It's going to take me longer than that.' Say about three weeks and several counselling sessions. 'I'll have to meet you down there.'

Nicky and Amanda are ready to party, and I'm ready to confess all.

Peering out of the kitchen window, whilst raiding the fridge for comfort food to line my stomach against all the alcohol I'm going to consume later, I watch them pile, laughing, into a taxi, then head back to my room to stuff cake, then see if I can stuff myself into the slinky little dress I've borrowed from Nicky.

In typical Eddie style, he's shipped in a load of agency staff to man the bars, so that the regular crew can enjoy the evening as well.

This means my usual uniform of jeans and polo shirt can be abandoned in favour of something a little more flattering in the form of a lime green Karen Millen that sets off the last vestiges of my tan and some two-inch Miu Mius that are more strap than shoe.

I half-heartedly show off my new look to Jamie, who's settled in on the sofa, Bud in one hand, remote in the other.

'How do I look?'

He glances up at me and his eyes widen.

'Blimey! You look gorgeous.'

'Don't sound so bloody surprised,' I growl, slumping down on the sofa. 'Maybe I should just stay here.'

Jamie pushes me straight back off again.

'Not!' he states firmly as I wander over to the doors leading on to the balcony and rest my hot forehead against the cool glass.

'What's up, Belle?'

I gaze out of the window. The sun is beginning to

sink below the skyline, casting an orange glow over the city.

'I'm going to tell him.'

'Eddie? You're going to tell him how you feel? About bloody time too!'

'Not how I feel.' I slide a sideways look at Jamie, and smile weakly. 'I think it's gone beyond that.'

'You haven't . . .'

'I have.' Despite the butterflies, I can't help the smile turning into a grin.

'Lucky you. The last time I had sex we were under a different government.'

'Really? The last time I had sex we were under a duvet.'

'Ha bloody ha . . . so now what? Are you going to tell Eddie about you and Amanda, and see if she kills you? Or are you going to tell Amanda about you and Eddie and see if he does it first?'

'Cheers, J, I knew I could count on you to cheer me up. Look, why don't you come with me? I'm sure Elvis won't vandalise the entire flat whilst we're gone.'

'No, just the parts he can reach.' Jamie strokes Elvis's silken head.

'I could do with the moral support.'

'I could do with the free booze!'

'So why are you here then? I got you an invite, didn't I?'

'Well, it's either the fact that I'd feel a touch responsible if Elvis ate all of the furniture, the fact that once I'm alone I can try on all of Nicky's underwear, or a pathetic attempt to earn brownie points in the hope that she might pay me for baby-sitting in kind.'

'Cite all of the above, and I think we've just about hit on the answer. I would have thought you'd want to come along, though, make sure she didn't get back into major pulling mode?'

'Ah, you see, I'm cleverer than that. If she does pull, then Elvis and I are right here to scupper any action when she gets back. Two of the biggest, fattest, hairiest gooseberries out, eh, Elv?'

'What if she goes back to their place, Jamie?'

He sits bolt upright, almost tipping Elvis off his lap.

'Shit! I hadn't thought of that.'

'I'm only teasing. Nix has gone past that now. Besides, I'll keep an eye on her for you.'

'Great! You'll keep an eye on Nicky, but who on earth's going to keep an eye on you?'

The first thing I spot when I finally make it down to Daisy's is Amanda, rotating in the centre of the crowd like a giant silver disco glitter ball.

She's having a total blast, attracting a lot of attention, men gazing longingly down that Cheddar Gorge cleavage, totally awe-struck by the silver vision that is bumping and grinding her fulsome funky stuff on the dance floor.

The builders are also strutting about on the dance floor, scrubbed up and out of their usual uniform of checked shirts, ripped denims and cracked leather boots. Somebody should tell them the funky chicken's not particularly funky any more.

They wave madly when they spot me, gesturing for me to fight my way through the throng and join them in a wild session of elbow flapping.

Fortunately I'm saved by the appearance of a jubilant Abigail, her wild red hair clashing gloriously with the hot pink dress clinging to her slender frame.

'Annabelle, you finally made it! I thought you weren't going to show up for a while, and I really wanted to say thank you. You're Wonder Woman, you really are!'

She grabs my hand and plants a massive pink-lipped kiss on both my cheeks.

'Jerry?'

She nods enthusiastically.

'You're not going to believe it, he's actually . . .'

'What?' I demand.

She takes a deep breath, eyes gleaming with excitement. 'We're moving in together!'

'Moving in? Honestly, Abi, I thought for a moment you were going to tell me you were getting married.'

'You're joking, aren't you? For Jerry, this is the ultimate commitment.'

'But he practically lives with you already.'

'Sure he does, but now his toothbrush, his clothes, and his wide-screen TV are moving in too.' The grin broadens. 'I'm getting a wide-screen TV! Yippee! No, seriously, thanks for what you did. I still can't quite believe we had the audacity . . . but it bloody worked, didn't it? Thanks for your help, Belle. Catch you later, huge drink owing!' She hugs me tight again then bounces off to impart the good news to

Ben who's wading through the crowd towards us waving frantically.

I immediately start wading in the opposite direction.

I feel mean, but Nicky imparted the news yesterday that he and Amanda went out for a drink whilst we were in Cornwall and I really can't face the 'does she/doesn't she' analysis that he no doubt wants to go through. The 'what did she say's, and 'do you think she likes me's, that I really don't have a sensible, or truthful, answer for. This is probably why he wanted to see me last night, to run through the in-depth analysis of what chance he stands.

Fat chance or no chance.

Poor Ben.

The sooner I get this whole bloody mess sorted out the better.

I've decided to take it in stages.

I push my way through the throng in search of Nicky, who's not with Amanda on the dance floor. I'll make sure that she's okay as promised to Jamie, then find Eddie. Then, assuming I'm still in one piece physically and emotionally, I'll speak to Amanda and insist that she comes clean with Ben, or at least lets him down as gently as possible.

As usual, though, Eddie has his own sense of timing that is completely uncoordinated with mine.

I head back upstairs to the main bar area, but just as I reach the top step a pair of strong arms slide around my waist and warm gentle lips brush lightly against the back of my neck, making me shiver deliciously.

Even after only one night together I'd recognise the smell and the feel of him anywhere.

I turn around, unable to stop a broad smile from spreading across my face as Eddie pulls me into a darkened recess at the top of the stairs and kisses the last breath out of me.

'Hello,' he whispers finally, pulling away.

In the dim light, I can see him smile softly at me. 'I've missed you today, isn't that strange?'

I take a deep breath, needed due to the fact that I have no oxygen left in my lungs, and also to steady my nerves, and attempt to plunge straight in.

'Eddie, there's something I need to tell you . . .'

He cuts me short by kissing me again.

Oh, sod it. I don't want to tell him. I want him to stay in totally blissful ignorance forever. And boy, is this ignorance blissful.

Eddie finally pulls away and runs a finger down the curve of my cheek.

'Sorry, Belle. Can't talk now, I'm playing congenial host to a bunch of people who loaned me a lot of money. Come with me, if you like? You can charm the pants off them for me.'

'Do you think I can get them out of theirs as easily as I got you out of yours?' I tease him.

'Are you calling me easy?' He fakes outrage.

'Well, if I offered you a full action re-play in your office in . . . say . . . twenty minutes, would you be there?'

'It's a date.'

I head for the loos to replenish the lipstick Eddie

kissed off. I've just got time to hunt out Nix, have a swift double as a bracer then meet Eddie in his office, not for a re-run of last night . . . would that that were the only reason, I've always had this fantasy about office desks . . .

I shake my head and force my mind back to the subject in question. The truth. Or rather the lack of it in the past few months.

Getting Eddie to meet me in his office is the perfect way of getting him on his own.

'Annabelle!' a familiar voice echoes around the tiled room. 'I've been looking for you all night. Might have guessed I'd find you hiding out in here. It's getting to be a bit of a regular haunt for you, isn't it?'

Dot swings through the door, glass of Champagne in hand, mega-cleavage polished up and ready to party in a tight red dress with a very plunging neck line.

'I don't need to ask what happened last night. Eddie's been grinning to himself all evening.'

'That could have been because of the blonde,' I tease her.

'Not when she's Mitch's girlfriend.'

'Really?'

'According to Ben, yeah. Borrowed especially for the occasion. He certainly went to a lot of trouble to get you out in the open, Belle.'

'What do you mean.' I look up sharply.

'You've been hiding your feelings, haven't you?' she teases, then spots the tears that are suddenly pricking hotly at the corners of my eyes.

'Belle?' She stops grinning, and looks at me in concern. 'What's the matter, darlin'?'

'Oh, Dot. I don't know what I'm going to do! My feelings aren't the only bloody thing I've been hiding.'

I look up at her from under damp eyelashes.

'Want to tell me about it?'

I shrug feebly.

'I'm a good listener . . . and you ought to know by now that I don't shock easy.' She laughs lightly but her face is tinged with concern.

The relief of finally telling Dot the truth is marred by the fear that I might just lose someone who has become a bloody good friend over the past few months. But to my surprise, when I finally finish the whole sordid story, she heads over and throws her arms around me, pulling me into a tight, affectionate hug.

'Good on you, love,' she mumbles into my hair.

'You don't hate me?' I pull back and blink at her in surprise.

'For what? Men have always called the bloody shots, it's about time someone tried to even things up. I'll tell you what, darling, if you ever need any new recruits for this business of yours, then you know where to find me.'

I laugh weakly.

'So what do I do now, Dot?'

She shakes her head.

'If I've said it once, I've said it a thousand times . . . go and talk to him, Belle.'

'But he's going to hate me!'

'No, he won't. I know Eddie. He'll hate the lies, but he couldn't hate you, Belle . . . he cares about you a lot, you know. He'll get over it. But I think it's best that he hears it from you.'

'Do you know where he is at the moment?'

She shakes her head.

'Last seen trying to be pleasant to a bunch of arseholes with more money than manners, but he won't have gone far, this is a big night for him, Belle.'

'Yeah, and I don't want to be the one who ruins it. Maybe I should leave it and talk to him tomorrow?'

'Over breakfast?' Dot says playfully.

'What, soften him up with rampant sex first? Do you think that would make things better or worse?'

'For you or for Eddie?'

'Oh, it would definitely make things better for me. If I tell him tonight I might never get another chance to take him to bed,' I joke.

Dot looks at her watch.

'Well, your twenty minutes is almost up, what's it going to be?'

'Truth,' I reply, more firmly than I feel. 'It's got to be, hasn't it? I owe it to him, and I owe it to myself.'

Dot walks with me through the crowded bar, to the door marked Private which leads through to the bottle stores, the staff loos, the back entrance to the restaurant kitchens and the stairs leading up to the first-floor offices.

She catches my hand as I reach out to push my way through and squeezes it reassuringly, saying nothing.

I head towards the stairs. I haven't got butterflies, but several elephants are doing backstroke in the bile that's building up in my stomach.

I'm so nervous, I almost don't spot the couple entwined in a passionate embrace at the end of the corridor. It's dark, but that silver arse is unmistakable.

There's only one person Mad Manda could be snogging with that much passion and enthusiasm.

It has to be Eddie.

But it can't be . . . Unless . . .

Maybe he is a major rat after all. Instead of being right up there shining away at the top of the man scale, that rare thing of beauty, the honest, gorgeous, genuine guy, he's down there with the rest of them, right at the bottom of the snake's tail.

'A woman a day keeps frustration at bay.'

However, when they finally pull apart, laughing and breathless, hands still touching faces like they don't actually want to stop, it's not Eddie but a big blond beaming bear of a man instead.

Ben.

Amanda was snogging Ben.

Rephrase that. Amanda was devouring Ben like he was a truffle, and she was a pig with a sensitive snout.

This is major league leading on. I didn't agree with the Ben plan in the first place. This isn't just a mild flirtation to make Eddie jealous (some hope), this is a full on, faked up affair that's going to leave Ben totally devastated when it inevitably ends.

That's it! This farce has got to come to an end, once and for all.

I wait till Ben tiptoes off, smiling like the Cheshire cat, then head after Amanda, growling like a pit bull, and back her into one of the ground-floor store rooms.

'What the hell are you playing at!'

Amanda blushes.

I didn't know she could do that.

'Oh, hi, Belle.'

'Don't you "hi, Belle" me, I saw what you just did.'

'Oh. Right. Well, it just sort of crept up on me, and then it stopped creeping and hit me straight between the eyes.'

'What are you on about?'

'Ben and me. We went out for dinner when you were down in Cornwall. I was sort of hoping that we'd bump into Eddie and he'd realise that he was insanely jealous, then I saw Ben hugging that red-haired girl tonight and suddenly *I* felt jealous,' she laughs. 'Would you believe that!'

'But they're just friends,' I state dumbly.

'Well, I know that now, don't I? It was just that we had a really good evening together. He was so sweet and so funny, and so . . . well . . . so real. I've been living with this fantasy for so long. You know, I think I was more in love with the idea of who I thought Eddie was. It took Ben to make me realise that I never really knew him at all. I mean, Ben was happy to chat about Eddie, which at first I thought was really great, but then I realised he was talking about someone I didn't even know.'

'But I thought . . . I mean . . . I thought you really liked Eddie?'

'So did I. But he was my Rudolph Valentino.'

'What do you mean?'

'The heart throb on the big screen, projecting this image. I fell in love with an image. Well, you could hardly call it love, now could you? It was a silly crush, a stupid obsession that went way too far . . .'

'But what about last night? You were really pissed off when I said he was with someone . . .'

'Last vestiges of the foolish obsession?' She shrugs.

'And tonight, getting all tarted up . . .'

'For me,' she states simply. 'For my own self-esteem. And for Ben.'

'Why didn't you tell me?'

'Well, I didn't really know for definite until tonight, when I saw Ben and that red head . . . Besides, I've been trying to talk to you for days, Belle, you've been avoiding me like the plague. And I don't suppose I blame you, really. God, I've been a self-obsessed cow, haven't I? It's a wonder you ever put up with me. Never mind, I'll be out of your hair from now on.'

'Why? What happens now?'

'Now I've finally started being honest. With myself and with everyone else.'

'What do you mean?' I ask in alarm. 'You mean, you've told Eddie about . . . did you tell him about me? You know, what's been going on?'

She nods happily. 'I finally told him everything.'

'But why?'

'Ben said I should get it all out in the open.'

'Ben knows?'

This gets worse.

'Well, we went back to the flat after dinner, and he found the photos – you know, the ones I had of Eddie – and he's such an easy guy to talk to. We'd been chatting away all evening, I felt like I'd known him forever after just one date. He's so sweet, he sent me a dozen red roses the very next day . . .'

'The photos, Amanda!'

'Yeah, well, he saw the photos on the coffee table, and it just all came out. Ben's such a good listener. He didn't judge me at all, but then he could see how bad I felt about it all, especially sending you round to hunt through Eddie's house.' She grimaces. 'So he said, why didn't I just explain to Eddie and apologise? You know, ask for absolution. It's true what they say about confession being good for the soul. So, you see, it's all sorted out now . . .'

'When did you tell him?' I ask numbly.

'Just now. I was going to leave it until after tonight, you know, get the opening out of the way, but I just bumped into him in the corridor, and he seemed in such a good mood, I thought I'd take advantage of it . . . catch him whilst he's smiling.'

'And how did he take it?' I stutter.

'Oh, he was a bit shocked, I think, but he was pretty decent about it. But after all, that's what he is, isn't he? A pretty decent kind of guy.'

She surprises me again by hugging me enthusiastically.

'Thank you for everything, Belle.'

Thank you for everything.

At least one person's happy.

'You can stop working here now.' She beams. 'Isn't that great? You know, you've been looking really frazzled recently . . . anyway, I've promised my new man a slow dance so I'll catch you later, Belle, okay?'

And with that she's gone.

Skipping off down the corridor to join Ben on the dance floor, like the last few months never really happened.

Would that they hadn't – with the exception of last night, of course.

I slump down on a crate of orange juice. It's not exactly comfortable, but my legs are suddenly feeling a bit wobbly.

Word spreads around this place faster than fire through the desert bush. Soon they'll all know what's been going on.

They're all going to hate me!

And Eddie . . .

Oh, god.

Then again, what did I expect . . . a happy ever after ending after such a crappy undercover beginning?

'Belle!' A voice shrieks my name and I jump a mile.

Thank god it's Nicky.

She's swinging round the door frame, Bud bottle in hand, big grin on slightly drunken face.

'What a fantastic party! I've been propositioned more times than an Amsterdam tourist . . . What's the matter, babe? You look like you've just discovered the man of your dreams, only for him to confess that Jamie's more his type than you are.'

'I just caught Amanda snogging Ben.'

'You what!'

'You heard me.'

'Well, she's hardly going to make Eddie jealous, snogging Ben out here where no one can see them, is she?'

'She wasn't doing it to make Eddie jealous. She was doing it because she's fallen in love with Ben. At least, that what she says . . .'

Nicky makes the mistake of letting go of the door frame she's swinging off, and hurtles forward into the room.

'Seriously?'

I nod slowly, sighing so heavily I blow my carefully blow dried hair out of place.

'But I don't understand it. She was so excited about the party . . .' Nicky pauses for a moment, blowing her fringe out of her face. 'But then, I suppose that could have been because she knew Ben would be here,' she muses.

'Did you have any idea about this?'

'Well, she has been spending a lot of time talking to him, and I suppose if I think about it she has started to mention him more than Eddie recently.'

I don't believe this.

I've been killing myself staying away from Eddie.

I've been beating myself up because of the guilt of not managing to stay away from him the night before last when we . . . well, you know.

And now what will he think of me?

'What's the matter, Annabelle?' Nicky peers into my

face. 'It may not be the result we were expecting, but that doesn't matter, does it? Amanda's really happy.'

She grins at me. I don't respond.

'Your nightmare is over.'

I still don't respond.

Nicky sits down on the crate next to me.

'It's Eddie, isn't it?'

I blink at her in surprise.

'You know?'

'Well, I kind of had my suspicions. Come on, how long have I known you for? Well, that's one good thing. At least the coast's now clear for you to take a shot yourself.'

'And you think he's going to want me?'

'Why not?'

'He knows, Nix, Amanda told him everything.'

'Oh.'

'Exactly.' I lean my head despondently on her shoulder. 'I mean, I was going to tell him everything myself anyway. I tried last night, but . . .'

'Last night?' Nix queries, turning to look at me so abruptly my head slips off her clavicle.

I can't help this stupid, loopy, après-amazing sex grin from sliding on to my face, despite the dire situation.

'You didn't?' she breathes incredulously.

My grin gets broader.

'What was it like . . . what was *he* like?'

'Wonderful . . . gorgeous. Oh, Nix, what am I going to do?'

'You've got to speak to him, Belle.'

'And say what? How on earth can I explain it to him now that Amanda's stuck her size sixes straight in? I can't begin to imagine what he's thinking.'

'At least let him know it isn't *all* a set up. Let him know that your feelings for him are real and not part of the charade.'

'That's what I've been telling her.' Dot's in the doorway. 'He's upstairs, Belle.'

The room's in darkness, the only light the dim golden glow of the street lights outside, and the eerie luminescent blue of the neon sign on the building opposite.

He's standing with his back to the door, staring out of the window, shoulders set in a taut, tight line.

I slide silently into the room, leaning back against the door so that it closes behind me. The slight click as the latch slides home alerts Eddie to the fact that he is no longer alone, and he turns to face me.

'Hi,' I whisper nervously.

'Annabelle.' He exhales slowly, and is momentarily silent before raising one eyebrow and asking me sarcastically, 'That is your real name, isn't it?'

'Of course it is!' I bluster in embarrassment.

'There's no "of course" about anything any more, is there?'

I'm too late. He thinks that everything I've ever said and done has been some elaborate fabrication for my own sordid purposes. I can just imagine how tactfully Amanda broke it to him.

Another awkward silence whilst I pick at the spot

of peeling paint on the door frame, and he just stares at me disconcertingly.

He finally speaks.

'So you were paid to be with me then?'

His bluntness makes me reel a little.

'Well, I wouldn't put it exactly like that. It sounds so like . . . like . . .'

'Prostitution?' he replies coldly.

'What! God, no! You think I was paid to . . . no . . . that's not what you think, is it? I mean, that bit definitely wasn't in the agreement!'

'So you just did that for self-gratification, did you?'

'That's not fair!'

'And that's what you've been is it? Fair?'

'But . . .'

'But what!'

But I think I'm in love with you.

Why would he believe anything I tell him? He'd probably just laugh in my face; and by the look on his at this precise moment in time the only emotion he could feel towards me would be complete and utter contempt.

'But . . .' I falter again, unable to meet his angry, accusing gaze. 'I think I'd better go.'

'Yeah, I think you'd better do that too.'

I open the door then hesitate and turn back. He's turned away again, once more facing out of the window, staring into the night.

'Look, Eddie . . . I'm sorry.'

Sorry. Such an inadequate word.

He's silent for a moment. His voice when he finally

speaks is little more than a whisper.

'Yeah, so am I, Belle. So am I.'

Why is it that a life that was a life before is suddenly a life no more?

I wasn't unhappy before I met him. I still have all of the same things in my life as I did then, but why are they suddenly not enough?

Well, I still have all of the same things apart from my job, my self-esteem, and a major portion of a heart that I previously didn't think gave a damn about all that love stuff. I went away to try and 'find myself', pardon the cliché. Now I feel more lost than ever.

Perhaps in the two final months of my travels that I never got, I might have found what I was looking for.

Me.

I could see myself in Eddie. That may sound narcissistic but I think everybody is searching for somebody who totally understands them, with whom they can feel completely at ease, who won't judge . . . even when given cause to.

It doesn't help that Amanda and Ben have spent the rest of the weekend having a major love-in across the corridor, the yelps, shrieks and laughter, even the sound of popping corks, assailing my ear drums with nerve-grating regularity as they frolic round the flat like two overweight, oversexed lovebirds.

Monday morning, after another sleepless night where my head's spinning like the washing machine on the final spin cycle, where sleep comes in snatched, two-minute, headache-making moments, and where I finally drop off due to exhaustion at 7 a.m. only to be woken by the sound of the animals across the corridor waking up to yet another noisy, steamy, shag and slush session, I finally reach a decision.

Pulling on my clothes, I slip quietly out of the flat and head for town.

'What are you doing?'

I momentarily stop hurling the contents of my underwear drawer into my duffel bag, and turn abruptly, and somewhat guiltily, at Nicky's indignant shriek.

She's standing in the doorway, arms crossed, green eyes verging between upset and accusing as she registers first the backpack, and then the heaps of clothes I'm struggling to squeeze into it.

'Well, I've finally found something to spend my hard-earned pennies on.' I attempt a grin, but Nicky's still staring at me in outrage.

'I've got a ticket back to Sydney, I'm leaving in the morning.'

'You what!' Nix shrieks in horrified disbelief.

I drop the pair of socks I was squeezing into a front pocket, and sit down on the bed.

'I've got to go, Nix. I'm sorry, but I can't stay here. Not now. I know, I'm running away again, aren't I . . .' I tail off at the sight of her stricken face.

'But you can't! I need you. I've only just got you back, you can't go.' She comes and slumps down next to me in dejection. 'I know you're upset at the moment, Belle, but it'll blow over. Trust me, I've been there myself. Give it a few months and you'll look back and laugh . . .' It's Nicky's turn to tail off. 'Who am I trying to kid? I don't bloody believe that so why on earth should you?' She takes my hand and squeezes it hard. 'I've never seen you like this over someone before, Belle. You really liked him, didn't you?'

I nod slowly.

'Yep. Which is why I can't hang around, knowing that he hates my guts, the only contact with him gossip from madam over the corridor. I can just imagine it now. 'Ooh, well, he was with a new one last night – I think this is the fifth blonde this month, although there was that brunette from the brewery, and the little red head he danced with in Betty's the other night . . .'

Nicky bites her bottom lip, but nods in empathy.

'You'll be okay, Nicky. You've got Elvis. And, besides, you don't need me here playing gooseberry.'

'Gooseberry?'

'Blimey, Nick, for somebody so bright, you can be really thick sometimes.'

'What are you on about, Belle?' The green eyes cross in confusion.

'Jamie.'

'Jamie?'

'Yes, Jamie. Open your eyes, Nix, he's madly in love with you.'

'He is?'

'Yes!' I practically scream at her.

She stares at me open-mouthed for a few moments before I see the corners of her lips begin to twitch into the biggest, broadest, most beaming Nicky smile I've ever seen.

'Well, I'll be darned!' she drawls in a fake American accent before a fresh onslaught of disbelief causes the smile to fade.

'Are you sure? I mean, it's like Prince Charming suddenly saying, "Sod Cindy, I want one of the Ugly Sisters".'

'Don't you dare run yourself down, Nicola Chase,' I admonish her. 'He thinks you're wonderful. In fact, he's so besotted it's kind of sad, really.'

'Well, he did offer to be my last fling before the wedding that wasn't. I thought he was only joking.'

'Many a true word is spoken in jest . . . especially when it's by Jamie. Put him out of his misery, Nick.'

'How?'

'Well, you can either shoot him or shag him, which option do you prefer?'

Jamie gives me a lift down to Heathrow the following morning, with Nicky in the back seat of the Golf, clinging on to my rucksack with one hand and Elvis with the other, alternating between smiles as she looks gooey-eyed at Jamie, and then tears as she looks at me.

When we get to the airport, I practically have to wrestle my backpack out of her grasp before I can leave it at the check in desk.

'Are you sure you're doing the right thing, Belle?'

Jamie looks sorrowfully at me as I hand over my bag to the desk clerk. 'I mean, look at the state of Nicky. Couldn't you stay for her, if for no other reason?'

'I would have thought you'd be pleased I'd made her cry, it means you get to mop up the tears,' I joke half-heartedly. 'It's not as if it's forever, I'm just going to finish the last two months of my trip that I cut short before.' I turn to Nicky. 'I need to finish what I started, babe. You understand, don't you? I promise I'll keep in touch, and I'll be back before you know it.

Nicky nods morosely, using Elvis as a large hairy makeshift handkerchief. A security guard spots the dog grumbling as Nicky wipes her face across his silky back, and taps her on the shoulder.

'Er . . . excuse me, miss, you're not really supposed to bring dogs in here.'

'He's a guide dog,' Nicky snarls. 'He'll hopefully guide me back home after I've got stinking blind drunk 'cause my best mate's buggering off over the other side of the world again, without a thought for those of us back here who love her!'

The security guard, with three daughters and two ex-wives who all suffer from PMT, beats a hasty retreat.

Nicky turns to me and grabs hold of my wrist. Her hand's cold and her bottom lip is wobbling treacherously again.

'Do you really have to do this, Belle?'

'You said you understood, Nix.'

'I did? Was that just after you told me about Jamie?' she whispers. ''cause if so that was some serious side tracking on your part, and it doesn't count.'

She has reinforcements waiting by the entrance to the departure lounge. Dot, Sylv, Abigail, and even Ben are sitting on the floor next to the passport desk, drinking coffee and looking decidedly fed up.

'We figured we could make an impromptu picket line across the boarding gate so that you couldn't leave,' Sylv tells me when I'm in earshot.

'You're not really going, are you, babe?' Abigail, in a pink fake fur coat that clashes gloriously with her wild red hair, struggles to her feet and hugs me tight, kicking over Sylv's half-drunk coffee without noticing.

Ben gets up out of the mess, and when Abigail finally lets me go, pulls me into a bear hug.

'Thanks for coming to wave me off, Ben,' I mumble, finding it hard to look him in the face. 'I was worried you might have fallen out with me.'

He lets go and shakes his head vigorously.

'You're still my mate, Belle. You never really lied to us, did you? Besides, if it wasn't for you, I wouldn't have Amanda. She wanted to come, by the way, but she's got a hair appointment.'

I raise my eyebrows at him.

'She couldn't cancel, the waiting list's three months . . .'

I raise my eyebrows higher.

'Shallow can be good,' he offers weakly.

'So long as you're happy.'

'She makes great brownies.'

'The key to a wonderful life together,' I reply, then hug him again. 'Just kidding. I really hope it works out for you. A word of advice, though – keep her well away from aerobics tapes.'

Dot's next in line for a hug, big pale eyes already ominously red. We hang on to each other for a few minutes, me fighting back the tears that are threatening, Dot sniffling into the shoulder of my jacket.

She finally steps away and rubs the back of her hand across her face, streaking mascara and lipstick across her usually immaculately made up face.

'I'm sorry, but I'm going to say it again. You shouldn't just run away – you've got to talk to him, Belle.'

I shrug.

'Already tried that, Dot.'

'You call that talking!'

'He's told you the gist of the conversation then?'

'More or less. He just needs time to cool down, Belle. It was a shock.'

'Well then, he's got at least two months, hasn't he?'

'So that's it, you're definitely going?'

'No, I'm just standing in an airport with my backpack and a plane ticket, because I thought it would make a change from standing behind the bar,' I quip half-heartedly.

A rugby scrum of a group hug follows from which I have to hook my duffel bag out like a pro and escape up the wing, Nicky practically hanging on to my ankles. If I didn't know better I'd think they were trying to hold me down so I missed the flight altogether. As it is they're calling for the last few remaining boarders when I finally make it through the gate.

There's a bit of light relief when I look back and see that Jamie and Nicky are holding hands. I wouldn't be surprised if I got called back from Australia for another wedding soon. They've wasted so much time getting together, now they've actually taken the first tentative steps into a proper relationship it will probably travel at a faster pace than my aeroplane.

I've worked so hard over the past twenty-four hours convincing Nicky and Jamie that this is a good idea, it's only when I'm on my own in my plane seat that it actually strikes me it might not be.

I suddenly feel very alone, and there's only a hundred-yard stretch of tarmac and a building between me and my friends. What's it going to be like when I'm on the other side of the world?

It didn't feel like this the last time I set off with my backpack. That was the beginning of my big adventure. For some reason this feels more like an end.

I can't help a huge hot tear from spilling out and rolling slowly down my face, and turn away in embarrassment as an even later arrival sits down in the vacant seat next to me, scrabbling in my hold-all for the tissues I know Nicky shoved in there earlier.

'Fancy joining the mile-high club?' pants an out-of-breath voice.

'I beg your pardon?' The sniff turns into a surprised splutter as I look up from the depths of a man-size.

'We've got a lot of hours to kill, it's a hell of a long flight.'

I'm hallucinating. I fully intended to lose a lot of brain cells once the hostesses had wheeled out the booze trolleys, numb the hurt I'm feeling with at least four double vodka and Cokes, but this isn't an alcohol-induced dream, this is the real thing. Five foot nine, broad-shouldered, blue-eyed, sexy-mouthed reality.

'Eddie!' I squeak. 'What on earth are you doing here?'

'Well, I'm really pleased to see you too, Belle.'

'But we're moving . . .'

He leans past me to look out of the window, the tarmac rolling slowly below us as we begin to taxi towards take off, and nods in agreement.

'Well, that's what planes normally do when they're trying to take off.'

I look at him incredulously. 'You mean . . .?'

'I'm coming with you.'

'You what!'

'You heard.'

'But . . .'

'Well, I did tell you I've always wanted to travel.' He fastens his belt and, leaning over, slots mine into place, carefully tightening it to fit.

'But . . . what about work?' I mutter numbly, to the back of his head as he bends over my lap. 'You said you had too many commitments . . .'

Sod too many commitments. What about the angry, hurt man I left in Daisy's the other night? He's doing it again. He's caught me out, and now he's acting like nothing's happened.

'Someone I know told me it was never too late to follow a dream.' He smiles, straightening up.

'But I'm going to be away for at least two months . . .'

'Two months! Dot told me you were going for two weeks! Oh, no! Somebody stop the plane!'

The horrified expression that I'm just starting to emulate dissolves into a huge grin.

'Just kidding. Do you think twenty pairs of underpants will be enough? I did have twenty-one, but I seem to be missing a pair.'

'But . . .'

'So many buts, anybody would think you don't want me to come with you?'

'You're totally serious, aren't you?'

'Well, we've just hit the runway so I'd bloody well better be.' He smiles briefly. 'But if I get withdrawal symptoms we're coming straight back.'

'We?'

'Yeah. We, as in you and me. No arguments.'

'But I thought . . .' I shake my head, trying hard to take in the fact that Eddie is now securely parked in the plane seat next to me, smiling, instead of as imagined frequently over the past thirty-six hours cursing the day he ever met such a deceitful, duplicitous, lying . . .

'I thought there wasn't a you and me,' I whisper hoarsely.

'I was pretty angry.' He nods. 'No, strike that, I was

REALLY angry. You lied to me, Belle. You made me feel such a fool . . .'

'And now?'

'You've got a lot of friends, some of whom fortunately are also very good friends of mine. In other words, Dot and Abi went for the frontal assault, whilst Ben snuck up behind and kicked my blinkers off. Metaphorically speaking, of course. Can you imagine Ben being able to sneak anywhere in size eleven Docksiders?'

'Blinkers?'

'Yep. I couldn't see past my own hurt pride, my sense of what's right and what's wrong, my own moral standards . . .' He looks at me slyly through narrowed eyes, and adds in an undertone, 'And your lack of them.'

I colour up until I realise that he's still smiling, and still talking.

'And you know how I like a woman with loose morals.'

He pauses for a moment, the smile replaced by a more serious expression.

'But when I thought past all of that, all I could see was how much I'd miss you if you weren't around, and since the advance party weren't able to persuade you to stay . . .' he shrugs '. . . here I am.'

'*You* sent them?'

'They somehow managed to persuade me that you might just have a bit of a thing about me, that perhaps everything that happened wasn't in your job description . . . I mean, some of the stuff you did was definitely beyond the call of duty.'

'But . . .'

He places a finger firmly across my lips to silence me.

'No more buts. I want to be with you, Belle.'

'As simple as that?'

'Well, you've got to say yes first.'

'To what? Your coming to Australia with me? Because whether I say yes or not, this plane's going to take off in about twenty seconds.'

'True,' he replies, 'so that only leaves my first question without an answer.'

'Your first question?'

That sexy, quirky smile slides on to his face as he leans towards me and slowly and deliberately brushes the lightest of kisses across my mouth.

'Like I said, it's a long flight.'

Smiles must be as viral as love. I can feel one spreading across my own face right now, a heart-stoppingly delirious smile that I have a feeling might stay with me for some time to come.

'So we have a choice of the in-flight movie double bill or full-on membership of the mile-high club?' I sigh and shake my head in mock deliberation. 'Difficult decision.'

'Well, that depends on whether you believe in sex before marriage.' He reaches out and pushes my hair out of my face, fingertips tracing the line of my cheek bone.

'Before, during and after,' I reply, catching his hand with my own and pressing a kiss into the palm.

Fly-Fishing

Eddie cups my face in his hands, eyes bright and laughing as he leans in to kiss me again, this time long and lingering, broken only by the slight jolt of the plane as the wheels lift from the ground and fold into its undercarriage.

'Well, I really don't know what the vicar would say about during . . .'